VALLEY OF BONES

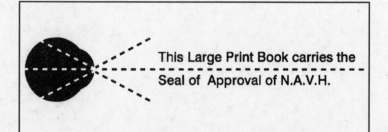

A BYRNES FAMILY RANCH NOVEL

VALLEY OF BONES

DUSTY RICHARDS

THORNDIKE PRESS
A part of Gale, a Cengage Company

Farmington Hills, Mich • San Francisco • New York • Waterville, Maine
Meriden, Conn • Mason, Ohio • Chicago

LIBRARY OF CONGRESS CATALOGING-IN-PUBLICATION DATA

Names: Richards, Dusty, author.
Title: Valley of bones / by Dusty Richards.
Description: Large print edition. | Waterville, Maine : Thorndike Press, 2017. |
   Series: A Byrnes family ranch novel | Series: Thorndike Press large print western
Identifiers: LCCN 2017016993| ISBN 9781432839376 (hardcover) | ISBN 1432839373
   (hardcover)
Subjects: LCSH: Large type books. | GSAFD: Western stories.
Classification: LCC PS3568.I31523 V35 2017 | DDC 813/.54—dc23
LC record available at https://lccn.loc.gov/2017016993

Published in 2017 by arrangement with Pinnacle Books, an imprint of
Kensington Publishing Corp.

Printed in the United States of America
1 2 3 4 5 6 7 21 20 19 18 17

VALLEY OF BONES

PROLOGUE

The evening sunset painted blazing colors off some towering cloud formation that hung on for a long time into twilight. Way west of him, the formation made a red firestorm going down over the distant Colorado River and California. Chet Byrnes studied the day's end from his camp for the night in the juniper/pinion country west of Center Point.

The four-man team was headed for his Hackberry Ranch up on the rim, run by Shawn McElroy and his wife Lucy. Chet was checking to make sure their large cattle operation had all they needed and things were going smoothly. In camp with him was Jesus Martinez, a young man in his early twenties, married to Anita, who was the former maid of Chet's wife, Liz. Jesus and Anita owned a small ranch of their own near the Prescott Valley main ranch.

Also there was Miguel Costa, who had

married Lisa Foster, now Liz's head of the house, where she had replaced the late Monica. Miguel would someday take top place as Valley Ranch foreman when Raphael decided to retire. The fourth one in camp was Fred Taylor, an orphan teenager, who had been scraping a bare living in Prescott's alleyways before Chet hired him.

Liz didn't accompany them this trip because she and Lisa had six students they were coaching in English so they could attend the nearby one-room Cherry School House. They were successful so far, with over nine ranch kids already there doing great on their grades.

Chet's work as a U.S. Marshal had been quiet for the past six weeks. His superiors knew how busy his ranching enterprises kept him and only asked for help when they really needed him. What Jesus called the real tough cases.

The Northern Arizona Stage line was making two stagecoach runs a week from Gallup to the ferry on the Colorado at Hardeeville, plus two additional runs using buckboards each week over that route carrying mail like the stages did. Most Wells Fargo shipments went by stage. And the shiny steel wire that tracked the route was sending lots of telegrams across the territory. Chet's partner on the wire and stage setup, Hannagen, was busy in D.C. trying to get Congress to okay payment to build a line from the existing one down to Prescott. That would connect Arizona from top to bottom. Well, almost. The Grand Canyon cut off a part of the territory, leaving the strip north of there with little development and little communications.

In the south, on the border, a former Texas schoolhouse classmate of Chet ran the newly acquired BBP Ranch below Tombstone. Jerry and Twilia Boyd, now with children, ran the ranch with a great crew. Chet purchased it from a great old pioneer, John Davidson, who wanted the ranch to remain an active cattle operation and not some absentee rich man's toy. Jerry's wife, Twilia, had received a large inheritance and they asked if they could buy the ranch from Chet. All but the paperwork was done.

Chet had no doubt they would meet John Davidson's restrictions, even though Chet now owned the ranch. Jerry would continue it as a family ranch. He finally had word that Davidson's attorneys approved the deal. A good family, after moving all over, now had a great ranch of their own.

Chet had left Texas over five years earlier

to get his family out of a very bloody feud. He never expected to have so many ranches, a stage line, a contract to furnish beef to the Navajo reservation, a telegraph company, two sons, and a wife as sweet as Elizabeth.

He watched the last of the sunset and hoped for the development of the railroad to come one day. It would shut down his stages, yes, but it would be a big step for more commerce to come to the northern half of Arizona. It would certainly make a better future business environment for his two young sons, Rocky and Adam. Ready to turn in while night draped the earth, he knew that the rails would, someday, bring statehood to this land as well.

CHAPTER 1

Having risen early, the group rode out for the Hackberry Ranch.

Lucy McElroy came out on her porch holding her baby boy in in her arms. A small pretty blond daughter, barely walking, was hidden in the lower part of her dress.

"Well, boss, and you guys, welcome to Hackberry Ranch. You know that it belongs to some great guy named Chester Byrnes who lives in Prescott Valley."

Chet laughed at her greeting. "Lucy, anyone been around asking that blond-headed daughter of yours for a date?"

"No sir. I'd shoot them." Then she laughed. "Chet, I dread those days."

"Don't. They will come. You know every-one with me but Fred Taylor, our horse wrangler. Liz sends her love and well wishes. She and Lisa have several ranch children they are teaching English to, so they can enroll in the Cherry School."

"Wow, she is busy. Come on into the house. My sister Hannah is making coffee and doughnuts right now."

Fred and a ranch youth took the horses.

"Fred, when you get them put up, come to the house," Chet told him.

"I'm coming, Chet. Thanks, ma'am," he said to Lucy.

Starting for the house, Lucy continued with her information. "Shawn is out with his right-hand man Spud. They calved lots of first calf heifers this spring and hardly lost any calves or momma cows. Those two are a real tough pair of working cowboys."

"Spud's wife Shirley doing all right?"

"Yes. They have a good spring and a windmill setup that waters the land. The men made her an irrigation system. Once a week most of the crew go up there and hoe the weeds to help her. She has almost two acres of garden. It will mean lots more canning, but we will help her. She is really proud, and we and all the men and ranch families will be eating real well this winter.

"How are things going for you?" she asked Chet as he scooped up her daughter, carrying her inside.

"Not many problems."

"You said Liz is all right. How is Susie?"

"Fine. We were there a short while ago, before Sarge started for Gallup with the monthly herd."

"I thought maybe she'd be having another baby since Irwin is walking."

Chet laughed. "She is getting behind you. Her and Liz, huh?"

"Yes."

"I have no news. Liz and her first husband had no children. I know it bothers her, but I guess it is all up to God. Hi, Hannah," he said to Lucy's sister, the shorter, dark-eyed youngest one, busy making doughnuts in hot grease on the range.

"We figured you'd be coming after Lucy read me that last letter."

"Oh we're just making sure everyone is getting along and doesn't need anything. You aren't engaged?"

"No. Who'd have me? The boys around here aren't much to choose from."

"I bet several would."

"Oh, no." She busied herself with making the doughnuts.

They all sat down at the table.

"I saw the invoice on my desk. Did you get that new mower?"

"Yes, and our blacksmith Deacon repaired the others for this season. Shawn has most of those homesteads with mowable acres fenced for haying. He planted twenty acres of alfalfa close by. Hampt, via May's letters, sent him directions. It is up and doing great."

"Victor has a new place at Camp Verde, he's planting this spring. He's another Hampt student."

"You really have spread out. How are Bonny and JD getting along?"

"Great. They will have grapes and citrus this fall."

"I knew Miguel took Cole's job. Where is Spencer?"

"Back finishing up the new home place headquarters at Oracle. He's the one that rolled out the telegraph wire across the territory in such record time."

"I knew that. Liz wrote me that the railroad has renamed Center Point as Flagstaff?"

"Guess they have precedence over me."

They were laughing as Hannah delivered the doughnuts and poured coffee to all the cowboys. The ooh's and aah's about her treat made her smile.

When Shawn and Spud returned, Lucy's daughter ran to Shawn talking a hundred miles an hour and then she went and sat on Spud's lap as the two men joined the party at the table. There were more laughs and compliments to the cook on the doughnuts. Lucy explained who married who, in the Byrnes community, to her sister. Hannah had met most of the women on her visits to Prescott Valley for weddings and such, so she was able to assure the married men she was not flirting with them and that she had met their wives.

Shawn and Chet had left the table and gone into the living room to talk business. Shawn assured him he had enough help, including enough boys who needed work, around to put up the hay when it was ripe.

"I have already put up tons of hay and we will have even more if we have rain. I think we can find enough water at some of these places, but we could use a steam engine to pump water enough for irrigation in the dry years."

"I hear you. I will have Liz search for the pump companies and learn what they know."

"There might be some in California. A guy who worked here, but went back to live with a woman who asked him to return, made me think we needed one for the dry years. He mentioned California. Victor can use the Verde River water but there are no rivers like that on the top up here. The Colorado River is too far down to suck water from."

"We can sure find out. When we started our telegraph company everyone said no one needed it. But we are already doing big business on it. And the use will increase, plus it saves Cole lots of unnecessary trips when he has problems. Four hundred miles is a lot of road to cover east to west. Spencer headed up building that telegraph operation just like Cole did with the stage line, and my partner had no doubts that it would succeed. He knew that I had to have a man, somewhere in our fold, who could build it in record time.

"Jesus insisted I had to have Spencer on that job. I worried some, not that I doubted his ability, but none of us had ever stretched slick wire that far. Well, he took hold and it worked."

"You guys did a helluva job putting it up. We are doing good with the cattle so far. We are still rounding up maverick cattle. I will pass five hundred head of mother cows by this fall. Spud and some of the other men are super at rounding them up without it costing too much."

"Are the local people still mad at us for rounding them up?" Chet recalled the complaints they had gotten a year or so back.

"I don't listen. They could have caught them. They're loose and out there. Maverick cattle are free to capture, brand, and own. There are still lots out there that have escaped the hot iron. Lucy's dad told me the ranchers around here were too lazy to even try. He's been up here for years. That's how he got his herd when he first came here. In those days there was no market at all, but the mines down on the Williams River have changed that."

"I have had some requests from them, but they won't pay what the government will pay for them at Gallup. I talked to two different beef suppliers over there. They told me I was too high, so I'll bet they, for the price they want to pay, are cull killers. I know what Sarge sends over on the Navajo contract. He does not ship cutter cows or thin cull cows to them."

Shawn agreed.

Chet said, "If you need more help, if those ranchers come around and bother you again, hire what you need. I want no one hurt, but we won't be pushed around, either. I won't complain at any costs. You are in charge up here."

Shawn nodded and thanked him. "Between you and me, I'm damn lucky to have Lucy. I know some folks think I only wanted this ranch job. But I took her because she is such a special person. You know I've heard you talk about her. She's tied down with two kids right now but she wants so bad to ride with us and round up maverick cattle. And she will. I love her and never could have imagined her accepting me."

"Good. Her daughter accepted you right off."

"I love that, too. They are my kids. They won't know the difference. When they're grown and ask me, I will tell them, and I won't run their father down."

"Shawn, I believe you are a mature enough person to handle it like that."

"Thanks. What's next?"

"I will tell you, but you can't say anything about it. There are coal deposits on the Navajo Reservation. A Navajo lady I met coming here five years ago has been at our setup at Center Point. She wants me to help her people get a contract with the railroad, when it comes, for the Navajo to supply the coal for the trains."

"Can you do that?"

"I hope so."

"It would make jobs for her people, wouldn't it?"

"Yes. But there are greedy people in Washington, D.C., who would try to steal it. I am going to make my best effort to make sure that doesn't happen."

"I am glad you handle all that kind of business. All I want to build is a great cow herd."

Chet laughed. "So, you won't put on a suit and go back there and talk to them?"

"Chet Byrnes, I'd do just about anything you asked of me. You gave me chance to join the Force when I had no experience at law enforcement. But please, Chet, don't ask me to do that."

"I think you'd make a sterling supporter to help me there."

"Chet, I am not a scholar or a professor or a lawyer."

"No. But you have a great sense of how to handle things that few men have. You must have been born with it. I saw it when you went to work on the Force. Later no one else besides you could have convinced Lucy that she needed you. And she did need you. Indeed she did. You handled it in the way that it needed to be handled. Whether you know it or not you have some powerful skills. All I ask is continue to use them wisely."

"I was not aware of having any such skills. Now I know I will do as you say — use them wisely. But I'd rather not have to go back to

Washington." He shook his head hard.

"I share that same feeling, but I will have to go." He rose and went to watch the flames of sunset through the clean window-panes. Anthills turned into mountains sometimes, and he feared that this might be one of those times. In six weeks he would have to be in Washington, D.C., talking to officials about allowing Native American people to run a coal mine operation supplying the railroad with fuel.

These Navajo people with their hogans and colorful woolen blankets would rather be left alone with their own gods in this land. They'd suffered harsh imprisonment and, when released, a long death walk back to get *home.* Now the iron rails were coming. That steam power must have coal and water to cross their land. Their ground yielded that power.

If the tribe had this new business, in time they could be more self-sufficient and provide better for their people, who had so few skills they could use in a white man's world.

How would he ever start to convince those people in Washington of all that? God help him.

And he hoped Liz was all right back at home.

CHAPTER 2

The trip from Arizona Territory to Washington, D.C., proved to be a complicated one. Liz, Spencer Horne, and Chet took a stage to Tucson and then to Lordsburg, where the railroad tracks ended. Chet had no doubts about his choice of men. Spencer could cover his back, and he understood the Navajo people since so many worked for him on his telegraph line building. He'd rather have Spencer than any lawyer outside of his Tucson lawyer, Russell Craft, who was too busy in Tucson court to leave the territory.

Spencer's wife Lucinda and her two children were moved to the Prescott Ranch and two ranch girls were hired to help her. She cried at the parting but told him to go help Chet and thanked Chet for selecting him. The onetime widow of a Diablo Ranch hand killed during roundup made his man Spencer a good wife. Liz promised him Lisa would educate Lucinda while her man was gone. Spencer had sung Lucinda's praises in helping him get the wire up in record time.

The three took the train from southwestern New Mexico to Fort Worth. With passenger trains restrained to 20 mph because of the danger of wrecking, the trip proved lengthy. They rested a day and a night in a Fort Worth hotel and then climbed the passenger car steps to continue the clacking, rocking way of trains to finally descend at the busy central train depot in Washington, D.C.

A man from the U.S. Marshals office met them at the impressive depot building.

"Nice to have you here sir. My name is Harry Nelson. I am your guide here. Chief Marshal Kenneth Samuels send his best regards and said to tell you he appreciates all your work to bring down crime in the territory."

"Things are slowing out there, I think," Chet assured him.

They went to the hotel and their rooms proved to be as hot as the rest of D.C. Hot and humid as hell. Chet felt the humidity made it worse than any desert oven heat. There was some ice tea and water served to them in the fancy restaurant where the cost

22

for a meal would have fed a family for two weeks or longer in Arizona.

They attended meetings in high-ceilinged rooms with important members of Congress, along with the law agency representing the Navajo tribe, Jacobs, Sorrels, and Rhodes. Congress members were anxious to get out of the D.C. heat, and wanted all put off until the fall session. Chet saw no chance of them allowing the Navajos to handle the coal business. Spencer learned that the Tucson Ring also had a man, or more, spreading rumors to any official who would listen that the Navajo would only buy guns and bullets if they had the money from the mine business. They pushed on how well white business members would handle the coal business and better serve the railroad than a band of Indians who would mess around and cause delays that could hurt many of the businesses using the railroad.

The main man who was heading the others in the dissidence was a man by the name of Archie Thrasher. Spencer pointed him out in the hotel lobby, and Chet cornered him.

"You Archie Thrasher?"

The big man turned to study him as if Chet was less than dirt. "Well, you must be Marshal Byrnes. How are your blanket-assed Indians doing?"

"The Navajos are not blanket-assed Indians. They would do a lot better if you and your crooked schemers stayed out of messing with them."

"It is obvious to anyone with a lick of sense that those uneducated Indians could not work any mining operation nor deliver coal to the tracks on time for the trains. It would then make big problems for shippers, especially those with food products that would spoil while waiting for the coal to be delivered."

The man behind the bushy graying mustache needed a fist in his face, but Chet held his temper. "I suppose the people who have controlled all the crooked business in southern Arizona think they can do it better and plan to steal the coal from the Navajo."

"You need to prove that statement."

"No. More congressmen need to read the nonrefundable beef contract that your outfit has with the reservations and you'd be out of business."

"Listen, your shoddy outfit is not going to continue delivering beef right to the Navajos."

"I beg your pardon." Chet was opening and closing his fists at his side.

"Thrasher, I recommend you apologize to

Chet," Spencer said. "Everyone knows the bony cattle your operation delivers. The beef we deliver is always in good condition."

"Well, you won't be doing it much longer. I can inform you of that. We intend to win the next bid on the Navajo beef account."

"Thrasher, your reputation at that will not sway anyone to accept your bid. You have tried it before and failed miserably."

"You wait and see. Your days as a supplier of their beef will be over shortly."

Thrasher gave them a snort and stalked out of the lobby.

"I may just shoot that bastard," Chet said. "When we get home I want him and all his kind put in that prison they are planning for Yuma."

"I have seen you angry before, but I believe that man made you real mad."

"Spencer, he did. For years, Old Man Clanton's sorry beef supplying has grated on me as crooked business that goes on unchecked. But I think we had better cover our butts and look into what they are planning to do to get the contract from us."

"You are to meet the Navajo lawyers and the chief tomorrow?"

Chet nodded. He still felt his heart beating hard in his chest as he tried to calm down. Before he was through he hoped and planned to uncover enough corruption being done by the Tucson Ring to shut them down forever.

Liz knew he was still upset when they met upstairs in the hotel room. "What went wrong?"

"Spencer and I just got off meeting a man, Thrasher, who told us he would have the Navajo beef contract shortly."

"Can he do that?"

"He belongs to the Tucson Ring, and that bunch might try anything. They get by with wholesale corruption down in the South now."

"What can you do?"

"I will talk to the people at the Indian Bureau and see what they know."

She threw her arms around him and hugged him. "I know when you are mad, and I read that like a clock when you walked in that door." Really, anyone could tell Chet's mood immediately, by the look on his face. "You will meet with Chief Manuelito tomorrow?"

"Yes, he and the lawyers. Sarge has met him several times taking cattle over there. He says the chief is a really smart man."

"That is why we are here, right?" Liz asked.

"Yes. Blue Bell asked us to come help him

set up the mining deal so the Navajos could move into our world as businessmen."

Liz looked away and shook her head. Chet knew she thought he and the tall Navajo woman had had an affair, but it never happened. Not that the woman was not attractive. He had met Blue Bell on his wagon trip over the Marcey Road from Texas when her horse had died while she was traveling home. He gave her another horse, and before she rode off, they had long talks about her concern and efforts for her people. This was what guided her. She would not be associated with a white man. He heard that her people were starving. He sent them beef and other foods, and continued to feed them. Now all he wanted was to help her and her people find a place in the world. They respected one another.

Even Jesus once asked him confidentially if the two of them ever had an affair. Chet had told him no and that the reason was she was too involved in her people for that to happen.

The next day's meeting with the chief in his hotel room was a warm one. Manuelito, a tall Navajo in great physical shape, wearing his blanket, was seated in a large chair. He rose and greeted Chet with a handshake.

Chet introduced Spencer and he shook

his hand. Two chairs were delivered, facing the chief, for them to sit on.

"Do you miss the cool winds of Prescott?" the chief asked.

Chet chuckled. "Yes. Very badly. Like you do the winds of Heaven in the Sky."

Manuelito's eyelids closed some and he nodded, his mouth tight, before he said, "This is a very poor place to live."

"I agree. What do your lawyers think about the coal mining chances?"

"There are many people who are afraid the Navajos might make a success of the business. They do not want this."

"There could be money made selling coal."

The chief held up his index finger. "Money rules all here, doesn't it?"

"I am sure it does. Have you heard of a man named Thrasher?"

"Yes. He lives in Tucson."

"He says they will take my beef contract away from me."

The chief shook his head. "Money, huh?"

"They didn't deliver in the first place, which was why I got that contract."

"The Indian agent said he never wanted them back. Your handling of it is the smoothest thing that happens for him."

"Please keep an ear to it. If things change,

I would like to know. And I will keep talking to as many as I can to let you have the coal business."

"You deliver good beef on time. You have helped one of my people get a stage stop and have hired my people to string the wire. Now you help with this. We are amigos, Chet Byrnes."

"I have a few more meetings to talk to people about your Navajo coal business. I have a feeling someone made a deal under the table, but we won't know what until things start to happen."

"We have several white men squatting on the reservation. They say it is federal land and they can homestead it. It is not federal land. The great white chief gave us that land in our treaty. I think they are waiting for something to happen, then they will do something. I know not what, yet."

"Won't the army make them leave?"

"Sometimes. But they come back."

"You need me, send a telegram. I know about this now."

Manuelito smiled. "Thanks once more. Again, you are proving you are a friend to us."

"Nice to meet you, sir," Spencer said.

"You ride with a good man. You two be careful. That Thrasher may have a plan to

29

kill you."

"He better not try unless he has his funeral suit on," Chet said as they left.

They took a taxi to the Indian Bureau and met with the head of the bureau, Henry Hampton, and his staff.

"Thanks for this meeting," Chet said. "This is my man Spencer. Since we came here we have been threatened with loss of our cattle contract to a Tucson consortium. Is that true?"

"No," Hampton said and laughed. "We have to deal with that same outfit in southern Arizona, but no one at the agency in Gallup wants any part of their underhanded ways. Your reputation and what you get done down there is the best in the business. In fact we'd like another supplier down there."

"My ranch on the border would be glad to fill any other beef contracts you need filled."

Hampton asked one of his deputies when the contract would be available.

"Two years. That Tucson bunch has a Texas congressman who orders us to deal with them."

"I understand but, if for any reason that breaks earlier, I will have enough numbers to fill your needs."

"Good to know."

"We have talked to congressmen and other committees. I am afraid, so far, I have done little good for the Navajos and their coal mine operation. I can't stay any longer. I have several ranches to operate and plan to go back to Arizona quickly."

"I understand you serve as a U.S. Marshal also?"

"We handle their rough cases. Arizona needs to improve to ever become a state. Crime gets lots of coverage across the U.S., and we get our share of newspaper articles on those that happen in our region. People think we have some kind of a climate that spawns it. We don't, but yes, there is lots of law enforcement work being done."

"Good luck on statehood. And keep up the good work of supplying us your good beef."

"Thanks. Ranchers in northern Arizona appreciate the beef contract. It isn't only our ranches, but many individuals sell us cattle to fill that contract."

Chet and Spencer shook hands around the room and left.

"Boss man, it does not sound like they want Thrasher back again at Gallup."

"You are right. But money talks. We need to listen close."

Spencer nodded.

There were so damn many things to keep up to date and informed on. He felt disappointed with their results but hoped he was doing well enough to have some success, somewhere along the line. The people in D.C. never bothered to go out west to check on anything. It was always up to him to go to them, if he wanted something done. Congress was going home that Friday. Laws, to be repealed or passed, would wait until cooler days on the Potomac. Chet was ready for the creosote desert and cool turpentine smell of the high country. This busy place with tailored suits and top hats was not where he belonged, for damn sure.

CHAPTER 3

There must have been some kind of a bug in the air. Many people in the passenger cars were vomiting on the train ride across east Texas. The nauseating stench and the rocking motion only brought more people upchucking from the open windows, or onto the aisle floor heading for the rest rooms.

Even standing on the porch over the hitch between cars, the sour smell saturated the air and burned Chet's nose. Liz had a short spell of it. Spencer looked as upset as Chet felt. He wondered if he'd throw up any minute. What made them so sick and why so many? Probably never be an answer. The conductor was as white as a ghost and the two black porters gave up mopping to join the bunch on the steps throwing up on the tracks.

Totally exhausted, they departed the train at Fort Worth and found a good hotel. They had baths drawn and their clothes sent out to be laundered while they settled down. After putting on clean clothing from their bags, they ate supper at a fine restaurant. Liz said, "I think I can still smell that train ride."

"I was on a boat one time in the Gulf and I got seasick, but this was worse than that," Spencer said.

"I have to say it was different. I think it was a chain reaction. Someone got sick and more were added until all of us were sick," Chet said.

The others agreed.

"That whole Washington, D.C., deal bothers me. I never was in a fight where I felt so helpless. And no one I found wanted to help us. That really was a disappointment. Like they knew it all. Wouldn't listen or didn't want to listen to our side of the Navajo deal. You'd think people would agree that anything to make the Navajo self-sufficient would be a good deal."

"We did strike out," Spencer said.

"Blown out was more like it."

"What next?"

"Go home. Tend to our businesses and forget about it."

"You think Thrasher has enough pull to get the Navajo beef contract from you?"

"I don't doubt anything that Tucson Ring

can do, but we now have a good record of the way we are handling it, and we were told Gallup does not want any changes."

"I want to tell you, you two are not heroes in D.C. and, unfortunately, we did not help anything," Liz said.

"Well, business as usual in the territory."

"I certainly hope so."

"We better get back on the train tomorrow and move on to San Antonio." She laughed. "And hope we don't get on a sick one again."

Both men agreed.

They arrived in San Antonio, with no issues, and took the westbound railroad for New Mexico. West Texas floated by over the clack of the rail joints and still no sickness. Four days later they were rocking in the stage for Tucson passing the towering Chirichua Mountains, headed for the next stage stop that side of Benson.

Both men wore their guns, as uncomfortable as they were, seated in the bench seats. The hot summer sun was baking them in the dusty interior when they rode through the boulder-strewn Texas Canyon.

A shot was fired and the driver, alone on the box, halted the double team with a loud "Whoa."

Both men had their guns out.

"Get flat on the floor," Chet told his wife.
"Give me a gun."

Spencer, already on his knees, handed her a small .30 caliber pistol from his vest.

"How many on your side?" Chet asked.

About then one of the holdup men demanded they come out with their hands high.

Wrong request.

Both men came out shooting. Chet took the right side, and shot who he thought was the leader in the chest. The man's rifle went off harmlessly in the air and his horse crashed into the other holdup man. Spencer was firing away on his side of the coach and horses screamed. The driver fought the two teams to hold them from running away.

Chet shot a fleeing robber's horse, and he went nose over in a flip, sending his rider into the dust, his own horse trampling him. Another man, trying to escape on foot, was ducking uphill through tall boulders, but Chet's last bullet took him square in the back. He screamed and went facedown.

"You all right, Spencer?" he shouted.

The driver holding up the reins spat over the side. "He's fine. They ain't. I never seen such shooting in all my life."

Liz stuck her head out of the coach door. "Those banditos never saw the likes of U.S.

Marshal Byrnes and his deputy Spencer, either, before they died."

"The two over here are bleeding to death," Spencer said.

"These two aren't moving. Liz, give me your gun. The one up in the rocks may only be wounded."

He helped her down and left, with Liz telling him to be careful.

As he started up the hill, he heard the driver ask Spencer what they should do with the bodies.

"Stack them up like cordwood for the buzzards."

Good enough. Chet went on through the maze of tall, straight-sided boulders, the small gun ready in his hand. He spotted the groaning man lying on his face and carefully approached him. It might be a trick. Standing over him, the gun cocked, he reached down and rolled him over with one hand. The man had his pistol ready, but Chet shot him in the face before he could even pull the trigger.

He slumped back in death.

"Chet, you all right?" Spencer shouted.

"Yes. This one ain't."

He shoved the revolver into his waistband and knelt to check him for any ID. A many-times-handled letter came from his vest pocket.

Dear Charles,
   I hope you found some honest work in Arizona. Things in Texas are hot and dry. Your sister had her second child, a boy she named Roy Dean. Her husband and your dad hope it rains to save the cotton they have planted. Write me when you find time.

Stella Andrews
Granite Corner's, Texas

"What did you find?" Liz asked, having joined him.

"He's from Texas. Never heard of the place, but there are lots of places I don't know about. His mom hoped he went straight. She sent him the letter general delivery to Tombstone. Name was Charles Andrews."

"He doesn't look very prosperous to me."

"He was a hired hand."

He put his arm around her shoulder as they walked back down to the others. The other robbers were laid out beside the road. Spencer stood over the body of the man they thought was the leader. He had unmasked him and handed Chet a telegram he found.

BYRNES WILL BE ON THE STAGE FROM LORDSBURG JULY 24TH OR 25TH. STOP HIM. BK.

It was addressed to Skip Nelson, Bowie, Arizona Territory.

Chet gazed down at the dead leader, gray beard and all. He sure didn't know the man. He didn't know any BK, either, and it was obvious he was the one that wanted Chet stopped. Someone must have spotted the three of them at Lordsburg or farther back in crossing New Mexico to have gotten that message to them. No telling. The younger dead man had a letter from a girl in Casa Grande who must have been a dove and wanted him to take her away from her job like he promised. His name was Dick Hardy. The last two had nothing that told their names, were in their twenties, and were in worn-out clothing and had not had a bath in some time.

The total amount of money in their pockets came to eighteen dollars and three two-dollar whorehouse tokens from the Wild Peacock House of Ill Repute in Tombstone.

"Take off the boss man's boots. He doesn't have a money belt," Chet told Spencer, who had bent over to see if he had any money on him.

The left boot produced several loose twenties and some single dollar bills. The two men nodded. The right one held over two hundred in twenties.

"Give the driver forty. Spend the rest on your wife and kids," Chet said to his man.

The driver protested, "Why Mister Byrnes, you don't owe me a thing."

"Shove it down in your pants. Spencer is sharing it. They damn sure don't need it."

Pete took off his hat and thanked the three of them.

They found nothing but some tattered *Police Gazette* copies in their saddlebags. Chet didn't consider the horses or their saddles worth much. They did collect their firearms and stowed them in the luggage rack on the back of the coach.

Those weapons loaded on board, Chet said, "You haven't seen them before, have you?"

"No sirree." Pete shook his head.

"Fine. Let's go. The law can have their bodies." He helped Liz back into the coach. Pete climbed up and took the reins. Spencer sat and with the door shut he hollered for Pete to go on.

They had one more stage stop, then they

would pull into Benson. When they came off the grade Pete hurried the team downhill. At the stopover Pete drew a crowd as he told them that five stage robbers were dead back up in the Texas Pass thanks to Marshal Byrnes and his deputy. Horses were swapped for fresh ones, and after a short break they left the excited people there talking about the robbery and the tough lawmen.

It wasn't long before they rolled up to the Benson stage office. Before he got down, Pete told a barefoot boy they'd been robbed and for the deputy sheriff to come quick. The youth jumped to his feet and tore out. A bunch more people nearby heard him and ran over full of questions. They were all talking at once.

"Who did it?"

"Why, U.S. Marshal Chet Byrnes and his man of course. They are stacked up there like cordwood waiting for the funeral wagon."

Chet stopped at the coach door and read off his list of names. "Skip Nelson, Charles Andrews, Dick Hardy, and two unknown guys. Also, anyone ever heard of a guy called BK?"

No one had.

The deputy took down all Chet knew and

shook his head. "I never heard of them. I will send the funeral wagon to get them. That BK guy might just be a fake name. I don't know anyone by those initials, but he might be in Tombstone."

Chet agreed.

"What are your plans?" the deputy asked.

"I'll go to Tombstone tomorrow. Those men came to kill me, my wife, and Spencer, and I want the ones behind that plot."

"Yes sir. But if the word is out, there could be twelve thousand more just like them down there who may try the same thing."

"We will see. Excuse me, I'm going to telegraph Prescott and get some of my men down here to help."

"Yes sir."

He and Liz headed for the telegraph office across the dirt street to wire Jesus Martinez and Miguel Costa. The telegrams read:

BOTH OF YOU GRAB SOME CLOTHES, BEDROLLS, SADDLES, YOURS AND OURS, AND COME. FIVE MEN TRIED TO AMBUSH US IN TEXAS PASS. NO ONE ON OUR SIDE WAS HURT. WE WILL BE IN TOMBSTONE WHEN YOU ARRIVE. BE CAREFUL THIS AMBUSH BUSINESS MAY BE CONTAGIOUS. GIVE OUR LOVE TO EVERYONE. CHET

Chet had lots to do. The two wouldn't be down there in less than two days, but, in the meantime, he and Spencer could look around. Someone had to know what BK stood for. He'd need to know that to find him. Something would turn up sooner or later. Those things always did. But, sometimes, it took longer than he liked.

Strange that the telegram to the outlaws had been sent to Bowie from Tombstone. He'd check with the key operator when they got to Tombstone. Many times they knew the senders. That might work. He damn sure intended to find out who wanted him and Spencer dead.

CHAPTER 4

Tombstone was not Prescott in the summertime. The heat and dust from the busy wagon traffic and horses was bad. Virgil Earp was a town marshal Chet trusted, and Chet found him the next day in the city police office.

He rose and shook Chet's hand. A big smile shone behind the full mustache. He said in his deep drawl, "Good to see you again. Word's out, Chet. You and your man are hard on stage robbers these days."

Chet handed him the list of names. "You know any of them?"

"I saw their names in the paper this morning. I don't know any one of them. If they were around here they weren't on any police blotter. What else?"

"BK signed the telegram telling them we were coming. It was sent from here to the robbers in Bowie. No one in Bowie knew any of them, but someone thought they saw the leader, Skip Nelson, or someone that looked like him, riding around town."

"He might not have been using his real name in town."

"The telegram was sent to the name on this letter I found."

"I'll keep my ear to the ground. I learn anything, you be around?"

"Alhambra Hotel."

"Wish I could help you more. Watch your back. They only failed to get you once that we know about."

Chet agreed.

"Your lovely wife along?"

"Yes, we've been to Washington, D.C., on business."

"How did you like that?"

"I didn't. Prescott is a better place to be in the summer than here or there."

"Amen. We stopped up there on the way here. We decided down here there was more to do. But it is nice up there in the pines. I'll put some feelers out. Someone knows this BK, or I learn anything, I'll send word."

"Two more of my men are on the way. They will be here in another day."

"Jesus is the tracker's name?"

"Yes. He's been with me a long time. Has a ranch of his own and a wife now, too."

"He really grew up, didn't he?"

"Yes. Saved my life several times, and he knows how the law works. He can read and write, and has good judgment."

"The tall blond fellow that worked for you?"

"Cole Emerson. He's running the Northern Arizona Stage Line for me and my partners."

"You strung wire across the territory up there?"

"From Gallup to the California. Cole oversees that, too."

"My heavens, Chet, with ranches all over, how do you do it?"

"Hire good men."

"You sure know how to do that."

"I am going to need some saddle horses."

"I bet Texas John Slaughter has some you can borrow. He's a big cattle rancher and a trader who moved here. All these liveries have are plugs and are too high priced. I'll get John word."

"Thanks." Chet shook his hand and left to meet Spencer and Liz at Nellie Cashman's restaurant for lunch.

Spencer had not found anyone who knew the men on the list. Liz said she had talked to several women in dress shops and they knew nothing about them, either. After lunch Chet offered to send her on to Prescott to cool off. She refused and went back to their room.

The two men went by the telegraph office and learned nothing about BK. Then they went to the Alhambra Saloon to hang out and listen. Tombstone had lots of bean spillers who, for money, could find out anything. None came by. Late afternoon, a short, freckle-faced cowboy in chaps parted the swinging doors.

"Is Marshal Byrnes in here?"

"I'm him."

"Could you come outside, sir?"

He and Spencer frowned at each other, but rose and, with care, walked out the swinging doors into the too bright sunshine.

"My name's Herman Limerick, and I work for Mister Slaughter. He sent you six good ranch horses to ride while you look for those outlaws."

"Why? He doesn't even know me."

"He knows you do lots of good for folks. Marshal Earp said you needed four good horses. My boss told me to bring two extra."

Spencer shook his head after looking them over. "Did you bring all his good ones?"

"No sir. Mister Slaughter don't keep any sorry ones on the place."

"How much do I owe him?"

"Nothing. Send word when you are through with them and I'll come get them. Good luck in catching those criminals."

"Well, Herman, thank him. We can put them in the livery."

"No sir. I'll help you."

They boarded them at the O.K. Corral, and invited Herman to stay for supper. He declined, saying he needed to get back.

At the hotel, Liz could hardly believe their good fortune when told about the quality of the horses.

"I just knew we'd have to rent some plugs to ride," Spencer said. "Them two guys won't believe us, either, when they get here."

"I hope they bring saddles, but we can fix that if they don't," Chet said.

"Where will you ride to first?" she asked.

"Fort Bowie, where they got the telegram. They must have stayed with someone or had a hideout near there."

"Waiting for Jesus and Miguel?"

"Yes."

"Good." She gathered them both by the arms. "I am cooking supper for you both at Nellie Cushman's."

Supper went fine, and on the way back a poorly dressed man with a shaggy beard stopped them.

"You want to know who BK is?"

48

"Yes."

"Ten bucks." He held out his grimy palm.

"You know for sure?"

"Damn right or I'd never stopped you." His gray eyes were shifting around like he feared detection.

Chet got out the bill. "Now who is it?"

"Bracken Kilton."

"What's he do?"

"Runs a whorehouse and does anything you want done for enough money."

"Where?"

"Anyone can tell you."

"If you're lying to me I'll drown you in a horse tank."

"I ain't lying."

Chet handed him the money.

He had a name. He'd been lied to before, so he wasn't satisfied that meant anything but maybe it was a lead. Virgil would know. Sounded like a well-known guy.

In the morning he'd ask Earp.

"That make you feel better, the name?" Liz asked.

"I don't know if it will help or not. We can check it out in the morning."

"Our two will be here sometime. Until then, there are usually willing mouths that might say something that would help."

"We well may have met him."

"You two go on upstairs. I'll check around some more."

"Spencer, you be damn careful. They'll kill you in a minute knowing you are working for me."

Spencer nodded that he knew, and left them.

"Chet, this is not very pleasant for you, I know," she said climbing the stairs.

"I am more concerned about you being here than I am worried about myself."

"I am fine."

"We've been through so many things together, including that lost herd we drove to Nebraska. I know you're strong but I don't want one hair on your head hurt or disturbed."

She laughed and hugged him. "It won't be, big man. I love you."

"Good thing. I wouldn't know what to do without you."

"I understand. Ever since you dried my feet coming out from wading, I've been your woman and I feel the same way."

"We will catch the ones that set up the ambush. People talk. Things get out. We won't quit until we do."

"What about the Force?"

"I thought about them. They are still doing border duty. Roamer and the brothers are working real hard to end the border bandits. I hate to call them off that effort."

"What about Buster Weeks down there below the border? He's tried to get you."

"Those five stage robbers were hired by someone to end my life. I doubt that Weeks has that much money, but he could be in on it, if a bunch got together. Hiring a murderer usually costs big money unless the hired ones are desperate. Those five were not rich, but they wouldn't have done it for nothing. If Buster sent them, they'd have probably been Hispanics. These weren't."

"Lots of people hate you for ending their criminal activity. Old man Clanton does not love you nor does that Thrasher in D.C."

"That could mean the Tucson Ring. I wouldn't doubt anything they'd do to keep their control on things." The two swept into their room.

"You will find them," she smiled and nodded. "I know you that well."

"Wish I was that damn sure right now."

"Trust me. You will before it is over."

They went to bed. He held her despite the heat and wondered about it all.

The next morning, Spencer met them for breakfast in the hotel restaurant.

51

"You two sleep well?"

"Yes," she said.

"That guy, Bracken Kilton, I found out, has a house of ill repute over at Gleason. It's a tent city. He deals in human traffic, drugs, stolen goods, and illegal whiskey."

"Nice news. But, it seems to me, he has to have been hired by someone. A guy like that wouldn't simply want to kill us. He'd be too busy trying to make money. Someone hired him to do it and he hired those five. It has to go beyond him."

"That may be harder to prove, huh?"

"Exactly, but we can start watching him when our men get here."

"Your ten bucks may not have been wasted."

"I feel a damn sight better about spending it now."

"I told him he'd solve this," Liz said.

Spencer quickly agreed. "I knew that, too. Chet will solve this business."

"Not without all of our heads," Chet said between bites of his breakfast.

Jesus and Miguel arrived that evening and took a room in the hotel. They met them the next morning. Both men still looked road weary as Chet explained the stage holdup and five dead road agents in the

Texas Pass.

"No one knew them?" Jesus asked.

Chet shook his head after giving the food order. "Kind of strange. But they were not from around Benson. Someone telegraphed them, at Bowie from Tombstone, that we were coming by stage sometime in the next two days. They were poorly dressed drifters, led by a guy no one recognized. We did get word that someone named Bracken Kilton was behind it. The snitch wouldn't say much more. Kilton operates a whorehouse, and other deeds over at a tent city in Gleason."

Jesus nodded. "He don't know me. I can ride over there and check him out."

"You have some old clothes?"

"Yeah."

"Take Miguel along. Rent some worn horses at the livery. A rancher named John Slaughter loaned us six good horses to use, but he might recognize Slaughter's horses, they are real sharp. And be careful. This Kilton sounds like a real killer type."

Jesus smiled and shook his head. "We get the junk to ride, Miguel."

"Guess 'cause we're Mexicans." He grinned at his words.

They all laughed.

"How are things at home?"

"Quiet. Everyone is fine. My wife says we will have a baby next winter."

"Jesus, how wonderful."

"Yes, Liz, we are pleased."

Chet said, "More mouths to feed. Good for you two."

"Oh," Miguel spoke up. "Lisa said to tell you, Liz, all five of those last children are at the Cherry School House already and doing good."

"They really learned fast. Wonderful news."

"How did Washington, D.C., go?" Jesus asked.

"Spencer and I could have stayed home." Chet shook his head. "There is something afoot for white interests to take over the Navajo coal business, but no one would give us any answers."

"Tell him about Thrasher," Spencer said.

"Who's he?" Jesus asked.

"Tucson Ring man. He threatened to take our Navajo beef contract away from us."

"How?"

"Don't know and can't say he won't, but they tried it before and failed. The Navajo agent assured us he wouldn't get it, but who knows? We went to lots of meetings that were a pure waste of our time. I even talked to Chief Manuelito, and he said money was what talked up there."

"You said he appreciated our efforts for his people," Liz spoke up.

"Yes. But neither he, his lawyers, nor us did one ounce of good in D.C."

"That was a shame."

"Jesus, it really was. I never felt so damn worthless in my life."

"I understand. Miguel and I will change our clothing, check out this guy at Gleason, and see you three later."

"Be damn careful. You both have my authority to arrest any criminals breaking federal law."

"Good. We may need to do that."

"Do you have money?" Chet asked.

Jesus nodded. "Enough. See you later."

When the pair left them, Spencer asked what came next.

"I think if there is anything at Gleason, those two will find it. In the meantime, we can check out some other places nearby. We might learn something up at Saint David and then ride over to Bowie. I know some people up there."

Liz agreed. "I will stay here. It's hot out there and while it isn't cool here, I can read in the shade."

"Fine. We should be back by supper time."

She laughed and clapped Chet on the

arm. "I know you two too well. You will get busy and will forget to come home. So don't worry, I know how to order food."

"We will be back, unless we learn something."

"I trust you."

They parted and Chet went to the O.K. Corral Livery. His men had brought their saddles, so they saddled two of Slaughter's horses, made sure their rifles were in their scabbards, and rode out of Tombstone taking the road north through the tall saguaros and a carpet of short grass, to St. David. The red-colored Dragoon Mountains rose on their right and traffic was plentiful on the road. Riders, buggies, buckboards, freighters, and even a few riding donkeys passed by as they hurried northward. To the west the Whetstone Peaks rose purple in the brilliant sunshine and its rising heat.

Chet figured by then his other men would be in Gleason. Maybe they'd learn something.

Spencer followed Chet as he reined in at the farm of a man he knew. They found Marcus Thornberry hard at work repairing his horse-drawn sickle bar mower.

Busy riveting new sections on the mower bar, Marcus looked up and hollered at them from where he was working. He put down his hammer and shed his gloves. "Marshal Byrnes. What brings you down here?"

They dismounted and shook hands, and Chet introduced Spencer.

"Business as usual. Five men, two days ago, attempted to hold up the westbound Lordsburg Stage at Texas Pass."

"I heard that failed with deadly results."

"Exactly. You know any of those men on the list?"

"No. But there have been many strangers coming into the area. Most of them are worthless. Sorry I can't help you more."

"We are riding on to Bowie. They received a telegram there from Tombstone saying that we were coming."

"Now isn't that something. Using a telegram to ambush someone."

Chet agreed. "No one in the telegraph office down there remembered a thing about the sender."

"They have lots of business, I bet."

"Yes, they do. We better ride. All things quiet around here?"

"We have to fend off chicken thieves mostly. Oh, and watermelon thieves can get bad, too."

"Tell the missus hi. We're gone."

"I will. Stop by anytime."

As they rode off, Spencer looked back at

the white house under the big cottonwood trees. "He have more than one wife?"

"No. Not every Mormon has more than one wife."

Spencer nodded like he wasn't sure and they rode on.

It was mid-afternoon before they reached the small village of Bowie. At the Alright Saloon, they had lunch at the free sandwich bar, and Spencer drank a cool beer. Chet had a sarsaparilla. The bartender, not busy, was friendly and said he didn't know any of the bandits from the holdup.

One of the older men in the place, sipping beer, said he heard those men were staying at Calhoun Springs.

"Where is that at?" Chet asked.

"Up the wagon tracks, go north three, four miles."

"What's up there?" Spencer asked.

"Some hell-raising woman and a bunch of worthless tramps."

It sounded, more than likely, that that was where they were staying. Chet paid for his drink and their beers. Then they went to find the telegraph office.

The operator at the Bowie telegraph office recalled Skip Nelson coming by asking if he had a telegram. "He'd come by, stick his head in the door, and ask, "Anything for

Nelson?" Then he'd be gone, did that for near a week. I never knew where he lived or what it was all about."

"Never saw him ride out after that?"

"No. He took it, thanked me, and left. I saw his name in that news story and decided that was what it was about."

"Thanks."

Outside the telegraph office, Chet decided it was too late in the day to go find those Springs and they better get back to Tombstone. It would be way up in the night before they got back anyhow. He and Spencer pushed the good borrowed horses and close to ten p.m. put them in the livery and walked the three blocks to the Alhambra.

Liz, Miguel, and Jesus were seated on a bench on the porch. A quiet weeknight in town and not many of the miners, who worked one of three shifts a day, were out on the boardwalks.

"Learn anything?" Liz asked, rising and straightening her skirt.

"Yes. It's a damn long ways from Bowie to back here. How about you two?"

"BK runs a pretty sorry ship," Jesus said. "His employees all need a bath. He has pigs loose and they smell. I asked if he knew where I could find Skip Nelson. He said he had not heard from Skip in some time. He might not have heard he was dead. He asked why I needed him. I said I owed him ten dollars. He said he'd give it to him for me. I acted like I didn't trust him. Then he made some half-naked teen girl come out of his tent and offered her services to us. We shook our heads. He said he had more. We left."

"He might be the man, but, me, I don't believe he is smart enough to hire men to murder you," Miguel said.

"You think that teen girl that came out was a slave?"

Both men nodded their heads.

"The one he offered to us didn't say anything," Jesus said.

"If he is dealing in sex slaves we need to stop him when we get this holdup business settled."

"Well, we will have to hold our noses going anywhere near there."

Liz laughed. "I bet you two are hungry," she said. "You can get food over across the street in that bar diner."

Chet nodded and they all crossed, Chet and Spencer to eat some chili and beans while the other two and Liz sipped on coffee. There had to be a link to someone besides Kilton who planned, hired, and had the funds to pay for them to get killed. Chet couldn't connect all the parts yet. Someone who wanted him and Spencer dead.

Aside from riding up to those springs mentioned as a base, they'd about used up all the things they could to find the planner. Someone came into the bar and asked Jesus to step out onto the dark boardwalk. Chet frowned, and his hand closed down on the pistol grip in his holster. Jesus waved him back, motioning that he could handle it.

They sat in silence, ready for something to happen at any minute, looking at each other with little patience, waiting on Jesus. If a mouse had farted they'd instantly have had their guns out. Then they heard Jesus said to the unseen party, *"Gracias."* And he came back in.

He sat on the stool and nodded that he had something.

"The man behind the plot to murder you is Jason Fulbright. He's the ranch foreman at the CYR Ranch. That guy just now was a snitch I have used before in our work down here. Those guys you killed had a meeting with Fulbright at the ranch two weeks, or maybe longer ago. Then they rode clear around the Chirichuas over to Bowie not to be noticed, but they stopped on the way at some bar and drank too much, which made them loose-tongued. Nelson told a dove over there he was going to be the man who shot that damn Marshal Byrnes causing all the trouble for the Tucson businessmen in D.C."

Still whispering, Chet asked if the snitch knew who Fulbright worked for.

"A man named Thrasher and his partner, Louis Benfield."

"That's the mouthy bastard we met up there in D.C.," Spencer swore.

"Exactly," Liz said.

"I'm sorry," Spencer said to apologize for his language.

"No apology necessary. That sums him up. Feel better now, Chet Byrnes?"

"A whole lot better. How did this guy know all that?"

"That dove told our man's cousin what the robber said to her about killing you. That guy was on his way over here when he stopped by that place, visited with her, and she told him. That guy knew his cousin worked for some of us and he thought he could use the information for some money."

"Without her testimony, how do we hang the crime on this ranch foreman?"

"Spencer, I am thinking on how to do that. Let's get out of here and go to our hotel room. There could be too many ears."

Chet put some money down for the waitress and they left for the hotel. It had cooled some and in their room they discussed all they knew and who was in on it and what they could use for credible evidence.

Chet felt lots better after what Jesus learned. The information cost thirty dollars, Jesus said. Ten of it was for the informant's cousin. That was fine. Chet knew that Thrasher and his men would have the best lawyers in the West to defend any of them if they were arrested. He needed something bigger than that for them to ever serve time behind federal prison bars.

"While we figure this out, let's get Fred to come down here to check out that Kilton guy and his white slave business," Jesus said. "Fred's tough enough to do that and they wouldn't suspect him."

"I'd hate to put him in a tight spot. Tough as he is, he is still in his teens and he lived through some of that already."

"He's a survivor. He'll manage. One of us could meet him at your friend's house in Saint David with a horse and bring him down here the back way. Let him investigate that outfit."

"Liz, can you please write a letter to Lisa and have her set Fred up to get off the stage at Saint David? He should bring his old clothes, in a sack, so he can wear them going to Kilton. But I want it clear. We get

63

him the hell out of up there if things cave in on him."

"I can do that in the morning. And I will have her send a telegram when he leaves that the new baby is born."

That made everyone laugh and agree.

"Good. We have that working," Chet said. "Meanwhile I want this Fulbright checked out. I wonder why he never came under our looking glass when we were down here running the Force. He may be new on the scene. We also did not know all the components of the Tucson Ring back then because it was all very secret. It still is, so I wonder how we can find out more details about them."

"I can go to Tucson and get my relatives to help me find out more about them," Jesus said. "I bet they know lots. We just never looked very closely at them before."

"Liz, tell Lisa that Miguel will meet Fred."

"Yes."

"And Jesus, you please remember that that bunch hires killers. I don't want your widow on my hands."

Jesus laughed. "Me, either."

"Spencer and I will check on Fulbright. Now, that's enough for tonight. It's cooled off enough to maybe sleep. Thanks, everyone."

In bed, Liz told him, "I knew you'd crack this one."

"Thanks for the confidence. I still see a long road ahead of us."

"Your ranches run. Your cattle sales continue. Sleep easy, my love. You always figure these things out."

"I love you. Good night."

Dawn brought more ticking of the slow clock. After breakfast, he mailed Liz's letter to Lisa at Prescott. Jesus and Miguel went to check out Fulbright. He and Spencer found Virgil Earp playing pool in the nearly empty barroom.

Virgil broke the deal on the opening shot. He rose up to appraise his break. "What brings the mayor of Prescott out so early?"

"More questions."

"Ask." Virg tossed his head at the other man. "That's Joe Penny. He'll seal his lips."

Joe, a man in his forties who was wearing cowboy garb, smiled, nodded, and shook their hands at Chet's introductions.

"Jason Fulbright?"

Virg stood back for Joe to shoot. "Ranch foreman. Runs the CYR. A big tough Texan. Has a bad temper and gets into brawls easy. We have put some knots on his head on several occasions. Always has a big lawyer to represent him like he has never done anything wrong. But he knows we will arrest him and pound on him if he resists and has taken his drinking business down on the border in those cantinas where he can reign over them whenever he wants to."

"We could better observe him down there then?"

"Yes. Oh, and he works for two Tucson businessmen who own the ranch."

"I have some pretty good information that Fulbright hired those men who tried to kill us."

Virgil set the cue stick butt down on the table rim. "I am not surprised. But prove it, huh?"

"Yes, that's the hard part."

Virgil bent over to make his shot and pocketed the three ball. "It will be harder than that."

Chet agreed as Virg walked around the table to make another shot. "There might be some wanted hands down there who'd share some information on him to avoid being arrested and jailed to be held for the Texas authorities."

"Any names you know?"

"Curly Bob out of — damn I forget that town. Randy Walker, he may use another name. Curly comes from Sequin, Texas."

"Thanks."

Virgil looked up and smiled. "Those two stay out of Tombstone. They know me, too. You get the chance, you tell them, I told them to talk to you."

"Thanks. Nice to meet you, Joe."

"My pleasure. I met your nephew in Tucson a while back. JD?"

"He's working hard south of there."

"Boy, he's a go-getter. He was selling cattle that day and driving a hard bargain. He really works at it."

"He's going to have a great ranch operation. It is his to run."

"I was impressed."

"Thanks. I appreciate that."

Virgil caught his arm. "Remember what I said about Fulbright. He's tough."

"Thanks. Both of you."

Spencer said the same and they left the bar.

"Blackmail wanted men?" he asked Chet.

"Virgil's been in this law business all over. You have to use what you have to work with."

"Fulbright sounds tough."

"Hell, Spencer, they're all tough in a corner."

"I am not afraid of him. I mean we have our work cut out for us."

"We have had that all over. Now we need the goods on Fulbright."

"Any more ideas?"

"No. I think we are doing all we can. Things will have to work out as we gain more information."

"We always had pursuit before and we got them. These we have to wait until they screw up."

"Exactly. Let's go check out those cantinas down on the border."

"Sure, you going to tell her we are going?"

"Yep. I'll get Miguel, too."

"I'll bring the good horses for the three of us to ride today." Spencer laughed.

"Great idea."

He told Liz where they were going, gathered Miguel, and the three men rode to the border, talking about their options along the way. Miguel told them he'd been down there in that area a few years earlier when he was coming north.

There were three such cantinas on the border, each a few miles apart. The Rooster Club was the first place they stopped at and drank some Mexican beer. Miguel talked to the bartender in Spanish about who was coming and going there. The man said that no such a man ever came there.

They rode onto the next place a short ways from the first. They called it Border Town in Spanish. A rather chubby young woman named Becca sat with them at their table as if expecting some business.

"Tell us who comes here," Chet said and scattered some silver dollars on the table.

"Cowboys."

"Name one for a dollar."

"One name for one dollar?" She raised her dark eyebrows.

"Go ahead."

"Curly Bob Larsen."

"Take two dollars for him."

She laughed, picking up the coins very carefully with her long fingernails.

"Texas Jack Holt."

"Does he work for the same outfit?"

She pulled up the low-cut dress with both hands. "*Sí,* he works there, and so does Rip Billings."

"Take two more dollars."

She smiled and added them to the ones in her left hand. Chet knew this was a lot easier than her earning them. "You know what they are wanted for in Texas?"

She looked around to be sure no one was around. "Only two told me."

"Which ones?"

"Bob shot his father-in-law for trying to

take his wife away from him."

"He say why?"

"He said she was fourteen and she wanted to go with him."

"Had he married her?"

She shrugged. "He told me he shot him for trying to stop him from taking the girl."

"The girl go along?"

"No. That made him mad, too."

"What about the other wanted man? Rip?"

"He held up a Texas bank with some guys. He got thirty dollars for doing that. Said the rest ran off with all the other money and left him afoot in New Mexico."

"Why did they come down here?"

"They knew the boss, Fulbright, from Texas."

"What did they do for him in Texas?"

She shrugged her shoulders and had to put the coins down to haul up her dress again.

They downed their beer, thanked her, and started for their horses.

As they left she thanked them and told them to come back anytime.

Los Olivios had one huge olive tree that towered over the rusty tin roofs of the smattering of buildings. One man was playing a guitar and another beat a tall drum with his hands. A drunken ranch hand was trying to dance with a scantily dressed woman in the dust. It was quite a show as Chet and his men slipped up to the bar, ordered a beer, and stood watching the action.

The dancer started to sing as she danced. She had an operatic voice that made chills run up Chet's sweaty back under his shirt. Such a voice out there in a wilderness of catclaw, creosote brush, and alkali dust all shaded by an enormous olive tree. What a crazy place.

Nothing more to help them find out the plans to kill him and Spencer. It was way past midnight when they rode back under the stars, fell out of the saddle at the O.K. Corral livery, and walked the three blocks back to the hotel, leaving the night man to rub down and grain their weary horses.

Liz sat up in bed as he unlocked the door. "You made it back?"

"And I don't know much more. I am tempted to leave all this to my men and go home."

"You would be nervous as a cat in room full of rockers at home. You will get a break soon but obviously today was not the day."

"One of the men that works for Fulbright is wanted in Texas for shooting a girl's father that he was eloping with. Then she didn't come away with him. The other robbed a bank and his fellow robbers left him afoot in New Mexico with none of the money."

Liz was laughing. "More winners, huh? You eat anything?"

"I am going to sleep. I can eat tomorrow. Oh, and there was a woman at Los Olivos, a border cantina, who sang opera as good as anyone I ever heard. She made chills run up my spine."

"Why is she down there?"

"Damned if I know," he said as he undressed and crawled into bed.

She hugged and kissed him. "Sleep tight. You are tired."

"I am that. . . ."

Morning came and he could hardly get up; his eyes were gritty from dust and sun made them feel burned to the core. He washed his face and then shook his head, drying his face. "This job is endless."

"They all are that way at first. You just don't have enough evidence. Rest easy. I imagine Jesus will be back tomorrow and have the information on the ring, and I'll bet Fred is coming to help you get what you need on the white slaver. Sit back and take it easy for today."

Things started to happen, finally. First

Jesus returned and had a vague outline of the men involved in the Tucson Ring.

"Thrasher and his ranch partner Louis Benfield are part of the ring. There is a grain dealer named Collier, a big store man named Horace Algood. He owns the Southern Arizona Mercantile. A man named Goldman belongs, and two brothers, Alfredo and Carman Renaldo. There are more, but I could not pry anything more out of anyone. They have big lawyers and a member or two on the statehouse committees. Probably more than that, but this is what I found out for starters."

"These are the men that want you dead?" Liz asked Chet.

"Yes. You heard, that whore heard that I was getting in their way in D.C."

"I think JD does business with some of them," Liz said. "When we get home I'll look for their names on invoices."

"We damn sure don't need to support them."

"We got some hardware up at the Oracle project from the Southern Arizona guy," Spencer said. "We can find it elsewhere."

"Yes."

The "baby" telegram came and they rode to St. David to meet Fred at Marcus Thornberry's house. Miguel was going to take him by the back road, to Kilton's place, to spy on him.

"Hey, thanks for asking for me. Everyone at the Prescott Ranch said tell you hi. They miss every one of you but understand how important this is. What can I do?"

"Fred, this is a dangerous assignment. There is a man over in Gleason named Bracken Kilton, they call him BK. Originally we thought he was in on the stage holdup where they tried to kill us, but he probably wasn't. However, we think he's involved in white slavery. We know you understand this kind of thing. He has a real tough sleazy outfit. We want to nail his hide in court. That means we need witnesses in court to testify. They have to be credible. He does not know you, we feel sure, so we want you to get in there and see what you can find out. He will kill you if he thinks you are going to expose him. In any case if things looks too tough for you, you get the hell out. One of us will be at the Alhambra Hotel. Maybe it will only be Liz, but the rest will be checking in."

"I can try. How do I go in?"

"We have a sorry horse that can be spared. We will draw you a map to get there. Just be damn careful."

"When do you want a report?"

74

Chet spoke up, "Take your time. As long as a week. I figure in a few days you will know the story. But you coming out unscathed is my first request."

"Man, I am sure glad you asked me to do this. And have faith in me."

"We have that. Just be careful."

"What else are you doing?"

"We have been watching a guy who supposedly hired those men that tried to kill us. He works on a ranch south of here owned by some of the Tucson Ring players."

With that all said, the boy was on his way.

Chet knew, from the Marshal service report wired to him, that Fulbright had been born in Texas. He had some scraps there growing up and served in the Army during the war. He married a woman after he was discharged and got into two shootings. After the second he abandoned his wife and two kids and fled Texas before the trial.

Authorities in New Mexico wanted to interview him about some rustling, a shooting, and a double hanging at a small ranch. That was what they had on him. No brush with the Arizona law except drunk and disorderly charges by the Tombstone municipal police.

Thrasher had no past charges nor did his

partner Benfield. Chet felt they were hiring out all the bad deeds they needed done.

There was no word from Fred. Jesus and Miguel watched him through field glasses each day and reported that he looked like he fitted in with the outfit.

Then on Thursday night Fred slipped into town and met with Chet and his crew.

"Two men brought two white girls in today and sold them to him. They had them doped. Bracken wants me to take them down to the CYR ranch tomorrow night. He says no one knows me and he figures I can get down there with them all doped up and Fulbright will pay me the money for them, then I am to come back up there and give him the money."

"How did this all happen?" Chet asked him.

"I am guessing. From what little I know, Fulbright has contacts in Mexico to sell them or has some coyotes to take them to Mexico City for him. That makes Bracken mad because he says that Fulbright gets lots of money for them and he takes all the risk and only gets a pittance."

"We need his Mexican connection, too."

The others agreed.

"Whoever expected that?" Miguel asked shaking his head.

"I had no idea. Fred, after you deliver them, get the hell out of there. We will be close by but don't linger there."

"I understand. I'd never imagined anything this big until those guys showed up with those two girls in their wagon yesterday. It must be a regular thing."

"Where did they come from?"

"I am not real sure but I could identify the kidnappers if we can find them."

"Give Jesus a description of them and their horses and wagon."

"I will. They're real tough guys, too."

"Which way did they go?"

"Back north. One guy had a beard. Wore overalls, and a dust-coated floppy black hat. He wore brogans. The other guy was thirty maybe. He had not shaved and wore a gray felt hat. Looked more like a cowboy. Talked with a lisp. They had some good mules pulling a green wagon."

"That might catch them."

"Don't you wonder where they kidnapped the girls from?" Liz asked.

"That bothers me and we will find out, but first I want both Bracken and Fulbright arrested. I'd love to arrest their Mexican connection. If I could involve Thrasher in this arrest I'd be more pleased. But we now have the proof, and we will save those two girls, whoever they are."

"You can't risk either their lives or Fred's."

"Of course."

"Can you go back safely, Fred?"

"Sure."

"Remain on your toes. We will be close by if you need us."

"I know that. I'll be fine."

"You've done a great job for justice. Thanks."

"I'm ready to shed these rags and help you."

"It won't be long. We'll bring them along to the ranch tomorrow."

Fred was gone. Chet's group nodded their heads.

"This forces us to arrest both Kilton and Fulbright. We need a buckboard to take the arrested ones to Tucson."

"Miguel can rent it and drive it. Spencer can guard it to Tucson. The three of us will protect the girls and Fred can help us."

"He never said anything about the other females in the camp at Gleason."

"We will have to sort that out. They may be the same thing. Get some rest. We'll need it in the days ahead."

In bed, not sleeping, he lay awake thinking. If Fulbright was involved with the white slavery and the hiring of men to kill Chet, he hoped he would be able to prove that, too.

All he could do was hope it all went well.

CHAPTER 5

Night came slow. Miguel had rented a good team and rig to use to deliver the arrested to Tucson. Chet and Jesus planned to leave town mid-afternoon, like they were going somewhere. Chet wished he had a guard for his wife, but she told him she had a gun and could use it. He hoped she did not need to. He kissed her good-bye, and told her to lock the hotel room door and that he'd be back as soon as he could.

Virgil had recommended a place close to the ranch where they could watch the exchange take place. He and Jesus rode like they were going west, then turned on dim wagon tracks that led south. They stopped in an isolated spot. Jesus went back and checked. He was certain they had no one tailing them, and they made their way closer to the ranch.

Under the shade of a few cottonwoods, their horses stood hipshot in the canyon.

Before he went home Chet decided he would go by and see John Slaughter and thank him for supplying those fine horses.

Jesus slipped up on the ranch carefully. He came back and said Fulbright had no guards posted but that he did see the shadows of six men in the bunkhouse.

From their location they would know when Fred went by in the wagon to deliver the girls. There would be a good moon shining, so no trouble seeing from a distance when he drove up to the ranch.

Fulbright had no idea he would soon be arrested. Then they would go back and arrest Bracken Kilton.

"What will you do about Thrasher?"

"When we get to Tucson I'll get a search warrant for his house and business and in getting all the records I hope to find enough evidence to rope him in."

"What will you do after that?"

"Ask the federal judge for all the records of the five others."

"Five others?"

"Those five other men that we know are in the ring."

Jesus shook his head and squatted on his boot heels. "Wow. I never thought of that."

"I have been thinking about it. It could prove interesting."

"Can they stop you?"

"They may. They'll have some good lawyers who will ask why we are questioning them, that they are simply honest businessmen."

Jesus was on his feet and using his field glasses. "You better look. These guys coming may be going there for the exchange tonight."

By the time Chet had the glasses focused, the two riders were out of sight. Then they reappeared on higher ground. "Well, bless my soul, I don't know the other rider with him, but that damn sure is Thrasher."

What will happen next?

He began to pace back and forth. With Fred involved this could be a real shootout. He couldn't let anything happen to that boy like they did taking his nephew Heck. He vividly recalled carrying Heck's limp, bloody body down the road, meeting the posse sent, too late, to help him. *Oh, Lord, don't put me through that again.*

"You all right, Chet?"

"Yes. Just some bad memories of what happened to Heck when I started home from here years ago."

"That was the Heck you told me about?"

"Yes, that was him. Thrasher must be in on this slave-selling deal."

82

"I have no doubt."

"I won't hesitate to arrest him or his partner."

Jesus nodded. "I'm with you. It's still hours away but it's getting more complicated by the minute, huh?"

"Yes. I'd have brought more backup if I'd suspected this was going to happen."

"Too late now."

"Yes. It is up to us, Jesus."

"We've had some close calls. We can handle them."

"I agree."

"I don't know if it will happen, Jesus, but I sure hope future people appreciate what all we've done for this territory."

"They will. We are going to leave this world a better place in fifty years."

Chet laughed. "I sure hope so."

Darkness took forever. They got their horses and checked their cinches, all their weapons, and the handcuffs and leg irons in their saddlebags. Then they waited as the moon rose. Finally, they heard the sounds of a wagon harness jingling and hooves plodding on the road into the ranch. They made sure it was Fred's hat. He was delivering the two girls. Chet and Jesus rode to the side, easing their way through the bunchgrass and low brush. They heard Fred holler *whoa* and then he pushed closer to the dark buildings. There were voices. He and Jesus dismounted and knew the horses would ground tie. He pointed for Jesus to go west and he headed for the other side of the house.

The ranch bunch were holding lanterns, inspecting the two girls in the wagon.

When he felt certain Jesus was ready, he yelled, "Hands in the air or die. U.S. Marshals. We have you surrounded."

Fred dove off the wagon and scurried to the side, away from the bunch of men. There was mass confusion, and one man broke for his gun. Chet shot him. The others held up their hands.

Someone dropped a lantern, and the fuel caught fire and illuminated the scene.

Jesus shot a man that was on his belly, under the wagon, ready to shoot them.

"Hold that lantern high. Fred, disarm them."

Jesus ran to help him.

"One ran off, Chet," Fred shouted.

"We'll get him." To his right, a man busted out the front door armed with a shotgun.

Chet downed him with his pistol, and the gun went off into the porch floor. Fred ran up and jerked the weapon away from his hands. "We've got a bunch of them."

"Is Fulbright here?"

Jesus said, "Damn right. So is Thrasher." He had them on the ground and was cuffing them. "This must be his partner."

"You can't arrest me," the man protested.

"Unless you're the king of England, you're going to jail and stand trial."

"You can't make anything stick. I did nothing wrong."

"There are two girls doped up in that wagon that you intended for delivery."

"I just was checking on my ranch."

Chet heard the buckboard coming. *Thank God.* "What do we have, men?" he asked.

"Four men in cuffs. Two men wounded."

"And one ran off," Fred said.

"Was he one of your hands, Fulbright?"

"Go to hell, you son of a bitch."

"I almost did, thanks to you. Up in Texas Canyon. But instead I shot those bums you sent. And I stayed to catch you selling those white slaves so I could jail you and your bosses. You should know not to send dumb boys to do a man's job. Better off if you do it yourself."

"We missed all the action, Miguel," Spencer said, getting off the buckboard. "You did great, Fred."

"The one on the porch is dead."

"He won't be missed. Hey, you even have

the two ranchers, don't you? I recognize old Thrasher from D.C. Nice job."

"How are the girls?" Chet asked.

"Sleeping."

"Spencer, search the house. We need all the papers and files in there in boxes to take with us."

"You have no warrant to do that," Thrasher shouted.

"Oh yes. We are on a crime scene. We can search without a warrant to get all the information for the crime report and who was involved."

Spencer and Miguel took on the house, returning in no time with lots of records. They loaded the boxes into Fred's wagon and covered them, being careful not to disturb the two girls.

"Make one more search. I want anything that will send them all to federal prison."

In the house Fred stood on the dry sink and brought down a large pottery jar and handed it to Jesus while he climbed down. Jesus turned it to the candlelight, took one look, and called out to Chet.

"Get over here, Chet."

"What is it?"

"Pictures of naked girls. Lots of them. These must be the ones they've sold?"

After looking at one Chet sighed. "I think

they were made to use to sell the girls they enslaved, and they kept the pictures."

"It is illegal to take such pictures," Jesus said.

"Who enforces it? Put them in the wagon. It might add ten years to their sentences. Two of you need to ride to Gleason and arrest Kilton."

"Jesus and I can," Miguel said.

"Take Virgil Earp with you. He can interview the girls over there and maybe we can prove they were slaves, too. Have him hire some guards to protect those girls until we can get back, and be sure they have food and medical aid. I can pay for it out of the marshal fund."

"Take Liz along?"

"If you don't get her killed."

"I'll get Virgil to drive her over after we have Kilton in chains."

"Handle it. If we have all this solved, I will send you a telegram and you two can bring Liz and the prisoner to Tucson."

"We can handle that," Spencer said. "What are your plans?"

"Chet, let them take those passed-out girls to a doctor in Tombstone. They are going there to get Virgil. We will have a wagon full including the wounded ones," Jesus said. "Fred can bring the girls to Tucson when they are well enough to give their testimony."

"Better plan. It's getting late. We have the live ones and the dead in this wagon. You have the women in yours. Fred, please get our two horses from out back and let's roll," Chet said after the wagon switching was finished.

"I'll get them. Be careful."

"We will."

The night dragged on during the lengthy journey. Finally they were at the top of the grade heading down through the thick saguaros that populated the last long slope to Tucson. The moaning wounded hurt his ears. The cussing of Jason Fulbright and Thrasher had been shut off with threats to bust them with a rifle butt if they didn't close their mouths. Benfield had kept quiet.

Someone had wired the sheriff, Ben Reyes, in Tucson. He was there, along with bondsmen and lawyers, who had heard about the wire, and were trying to crowd past the deputies holding them back.

Ben told them all to get back. The prisoners had to be booked and then they would see about bond and any releases. A big man in an expensive suit stepped past them and told Sheriff Reyes that both Thrasher and Benfield were honest citizens and had no business being treated as common criminals and herded into the jail with felons.

"Larry Christian, your clients are going to be processed right along with the others as prisoners and charged by Marshal Byrnes as real felons are done."

"I'm sorry, but if you want to wear that badge much longer you better get them out of that jail right now."

"That a threat? You want a cell beside them?"

"You would not dare."

Ben tapped him on the chest. "I certainly will do that, so don't say one more word."

"You have not —"

"Deputy?"

"I'm leaving —"

Chet leaned over and tried not to smile. "He have a hearing problem?"

Ben's face in the early morning light showed his anger. He nodded sharply.

They had the last wounded one on a stretcher and took him inside.

"It is all over, folks. Disperse now."

"Have some men put that wagon under lock and key. I have lots of evidence in those crates. The two girls they doped are at the doctor in Tombstone. Fred will bring them when they can travel. One more guy is being arrested in Tombstone to join them tomorrow."

"Hell of a roundup."

One by one the prisoners were stripped, given prison clothes, and registered.

"Name?" the clerk asked

"I won't be in here long. You don't need it," Thrasher said.

"You are going to be charged with white slavery, mister. Tell me your name."

"Archibald Thrasher."

"Your address?"

"Post office box 36, Tucson, Arizona Territory."

"Step over there and put on prison clothes."

"I will be bailed out shortly."

"Wearing those prison clothes or naked. What will it be?" the deputy asked.

"I'll do it."

"Name?"

"Louis Benfield. I was just checking on my ranch."

"Address?"

"510 San Marcus. Tucson."

"Step over there and put on those clothes."

"I am not going to be here long."

The clerk was a big man, and his patience looked close to exploding. He rose up. "You have hearing problems?"

"No sir." And he did as told.

"Jason Fulbright, Tombstone."

The next prisoner was a bowlegged cowboy. "Jennings Carter — Tombstone."

"Alfred Crown. Tombstone."

"Red Combs — Tombstone."

"Jerry Brown — Tombstone"

"What are the wounded ones' names?" the clerk asked.

"Pete Hale," Chet said. "The one worse off is Jim something."

"Manning," Red said.

"Thank you."

"Add Bracken Kilton. They are bringing him in today."

"I have it."

"Thanks."

"What now?" Ben asked.

"I need warrants to search both Thrasher's and Benfield's town houses and business for more records. I have a jar of some thirty or more naked girls' pictures I feel they sold in the past. While we don't know where they are, the grieving parents that lost them need to see their faces."

"How much did they sell them for?" Ben asked.

"I never heard, but I think some brought high prices. I hope I have some of that information in the records in that wagon."

"My men stabled those horses. They were worn out."

"I knew that it was a long drive over here last night."

"Get your man. My cook is bringing all of you breakfast in my office."

"Thanks."

"You are getting to be a regular customer of mine," Ben laughed, taking him upstairs. "My clerk is making you a list."

"We arrested them after dark under some coal oil lamps. It got pretty tough. There is a dead man on the porch that I suppose we need to send for. We had no room. He was resisting arrest. Came out with a shotgun in the middle of it all."

"I will send a local funeral home down to get him and have the body brought here."

"The federals will pay the bill."

"They will feed them, too," Ben said with a smile.

"The ring is going to be on you. There are two of them in jail."

"I saw who you arrested. I am a lawman, not an appeaser. The federal government is charging them for high crimes. I have no say-so about that or their release."

"Thanks for breakfast. I see Jesus found his."

His partner looked up and smiled. "Pretty

damn good, too."

"Hell, anything would be good."

Chet sat down like he'd shed a large load, bowed his head, and silently prayed thanks. It had been a really long night that finally worked out. "I need to apply for those search warrants."

"I can go explain your situation to Judge Allan Cantor. He's sitting in. But he's a tough, law-minded man."

"I'll be —"

"Just eat. I can talk to him and speed the process." Ben left them.

"Long night, partner."

"I could lay on the floor and sleep for a week."

"Jesus, we did it."

"We usually do."

"Counting Fred, it takes five of us now."

"More outlaws."

Chet never did more after that but nod and eat. He was right.

CHAPTER 6

The headlines read WHITE SLAVERS
CAUGHT AGAIN.

U. S. Marshal Chet Byrnes and his men
swung a wide loop and have the Pima
County jail brim full of suspects in a
roundup of the white slave sellers. Last
night he and an associate brought these
men to the jail. Here is the list of the men
to be arraigned today.

Archibald Thrasher
Louis Benfield
Jason Fulbright
Bob Larson
Rip Billings
Texas Jack Holt
Red Combs
Pete Hale (wounded) Curly
Jim Manning (wounded)

According to our information there is one more prisoner being transported over here to be tried along with them. His name is Bracken Kilton.

When the federal marshals arrested the above men they had two doped-up teenage girls that they intended to sell. The females' names will not be released. Sheriff Ben Reyes hopes these arrests will end the "white slave trade" in the region. The punishment for those found guilty of such a crime is ten to twenty years of hard labor in a federal prison.

U. S. Marshal Chet Byrnes of Prescott has been on a relentless chase to round up the slavers and other lawbreakers in our territory. Byrnes, who asks for little credit for his efforts, has been a strong force on the border for several years stopping crimes committed on residents, especially the enslavement of individuals and their children. His prosecution record is one hundred percent so far. All are currently serving federal prison sentences. Hats off to our defender.

Didn't take them long to get that copy out.

Ben came back into the room. "Judge signed the warrants. I am sending two deputies to both residences to guard everything. No one will get to anything, until you come and take it all. And no bond hearings today."

"Spencer, Fred, and Miguel will be here sometime. Maybe my wife Liz. Jesus and I will be sleeping at the hotel."

"We can handle it."

Two hours later, Liz joined him in bed. They both slept until late in the evening. When he woke up she was brushing her hair.

"You get Kilton?" she asked.

"Yes," he answered.

Liz sighed. "I could hardly leave those poor girls once they woke up. They both live near Thatcher and gave the authorities the names of those who brought them down to Kilton. It was so sad, but at least they aren't in Mexico in slavery. Their parents are coming for them. The doctor said he thought they'd be okay. Those three girls Kilton kept in his camp are not sane. No one knows them. Virgil Earp says he has a church group who will care for them until the state can move them to a care place."

"That was how Miguel and Spencer found them," Chet said.

"Kilton should be hung for what he did to them. The doctor said that the doping and the fear drove them mad," Liz answered.

"I am not the judge."

"I recall you telling me about chasing some killers and rapists across the Verde wilderness and that you hung them. I want them hung after I found those poor girls in that state."

"We have better law enforcement now," Chet said.

"No!" she cried. "He needs hanging."

He held her tight as her tears soaked into the shirt he had on. "He and the others will get what they deserve here in court."

"Oh, Chet. This deal has me so upset. Those men had only one purpose — to sell and get rich."

"They're in jail and their fancy lawyers can't get them out on bond to skip away."

"I know. I know. But it is such a bad crime. Killing them would not have been as mean."

"I need to go see the sheriff. He is helping us. And I have two houses to search for evidence."

"I can help, but we had better eat first."

"Yes."

He woke the others and they all got up and dressed. Not one of them was completely rested but they stumbled downstairs and ate in the restaurant. It was seven p.m.

"How did it go?" he asked them.

"Kilton was no problem to arrest. Liz and a woman that Virgil recommended interviewed the women. They decided none of the three were in their right mind and a church will protect them until Arizona can find a place for them. No way they can testify in court," Spencer said as their food was served.

Miguel added, "The other two girls are fine. A doctor is tending to them. They will testify and we have the names of the kidnappers who brought them to Kilton."

"The sheriff has all the men under lock and key. So next we search Benfield's and Thrasher's houses and businesses for more evidence. I have no idea what we will find, but we will look." Chet held up his fork. "The wagon and the contents from the ranch are under lock and key at the jailhouse."

"Were their lawyers still at the jail door?" Jesus asked.

"Some of the young ones," Spencer said.

"The sheriff cut off their big lawyer last night. He threatened to remove Ben from office if he didn't bend and Ben told him what to do — go home."

"I bet we haven't heard the last of him," Spencer said.

"This will be a larger fight than our last

one. We have a new judge sitting, but so far he's held their feet to the fire. Liz, Fred, and I will take Archibald Thrasher's house then his business. You three do the same for Benfield's place."

They parted after supper.

Late in the night, Liz, who sat under a lamp on the dining room table of Thrasher's house, found large amounts deposited in Thrasher's account. They were listed as cattle sales.

Liz called to him. "Chet, come here. Can you tell me how he sells cattle year-round to get such large amounts?"

"I have no idea."

"In January he made two cattle sales — one for five thousand and another for three."

"Does it continue?"

"One month he made three sales, one for as much as seven thousand dollars."

Chet looked over her shoulder at the details. "Some of those checks were from Diego Obregon in Nogales. See there. I bet he isn't buying beef."

"I bet he's the Mexican connection."

"I agree. We will get him, too. Take damn good care of that ledger."

"Wait. Jefferson Carlisle paid him seven thousand dollars for more cattle a month ago. He lives at Silver City, New Mexico."

"At this rate we may not get home for a while. Any more hits in the U.S.?"

"Yes. Two different buyers paid three thousand apiece for more cattle."

"What else?"

"Over here are more. One buyer lives in Colorado. One in California. The deputies who were here when we came said Thrasher's wife and children went to live with their friends here in town."

"He didn't get her to burn all of this before we got here, so I bet she had no idea what he was doing."

"You want more evidence?" she asked him.

"If you find it."

"I am ready to sleep some more."

"Back at the hotel?"

"Yes, this place makes me feel creepy." She stood and hugged her arms.

He took the ledger with them and told the deputies on guard they needed more time to search but both needed some sleep.

The two said the house would be protected until they told them the search was over.

Chet thanked them and they left for the hotel.

At seven a.m., the entire crew was in the

restaurant.

"Did you find anything at Benfield's house?" Chet asked.

"We didn't read all of them. But he had correspondence with some potential buyers in his desk. Notes on buyers too," Spencer said.

"Good. He will do time."

A waiter brought him a note from Ben. The judge wanted to go over plans at ten a.m. He had already been getting pressure from D.C.

"I can go back and finish the search of Thrasher's house."

"Jesus will go with you."

Jesus nodded agreement.

"Wire Virgil at Tombstone to be sure those two girls are under armed guard when they are transported to Tucson for the trial. No telling what the ring will do to get their men off."

"I can do that," Spencer said. "We never thought about that."

"Everyone go armed and find Fred a badge so he can be armed. The ring will do anything, including kill all of us. Always go two or more. I am going to meet with the judge. Pressure from Washington means they're upset. We have a strong case, and they want it swept under the rug before headlines expose their members committing criminal activities for profit."

Spencer shook his head. "This isn't like catching rustlers with cattle in their hands without their brand, is it?"

"Much more complicated."

"That's for damn sure."

Chet and Miguel headed for the justice building. Spencer and Fred would send the wire to Virgil and then search Benfield's house for more evidence. Liz and Jesus were going to finish the Thrasher search.

Ben took Chet and Miguel to Judge Allan Cantor's office.

"Judge Cantor, this is the lawman who brought that gang in. Miguel Costa is one of his men."

"You have sure caused a big fire, but I must commend you. Arresting that bunch took courage. I understand you have two victims to testify."

"Two girls. They were seriously drugged, but they are being brought here."

"You have some parties arrested with them who, their lawyers say, were swept up in the arrests but were innocent of any crimes, merely checking on their interests at the ranch."

"Your Honor, we have uncovered a lot of damning evidence on both those men, tying them to their involvement in the slavery trade."

"Marshal Byrnes, this is an incredible number of arrests and evidence you and your men have uncovered. I have no plans to cut those two out of the case set up by the staff of prosecutors. Thanks for informing me."

Two other men in suits were hustled in.

"Marshal Byrnes, these men are your prosecutors. Richard Murray and Carl Burton."

"This is my man Miguel Costa. Nice to meet you." They shook hands.

Chet realized they were certainly not ranch folks — both, obviously by dress and speech, were from the Midwest or east of that.

"We were held up by some concerned citizens on the street, sir, or we would have been here sooner."

"Held up?"

"Some businessmen who feel Mr. Thrasher and Mr. Benfield are being held under false charges."

The judge said, "Marshal Byrnes, you might explain."

"They are not innocent. I have enough evidence to send them to jail for twenty years."

"Excellent. We made them no promises except we would present our case."

"No one can pressure a court to forgo the prosecution of anyone arrested by authorities and charged with crimes."

"Yes sir. But why are these businessmen so adamant about their innocence?"

"You two have not been here long. There is a ring of unscrupulous businessmen who manage the economy around here undercover. Those two accused belong to that secret society."

"Thank you, Marshal. Sir, we intend to prosecute the entire lot of them after we see the entire evidence. The sheriff asked we not consider bond for them since they could be security risks."

"I agree, but you understand you must charge them in my court and they can plead if they want to."

"How soon?"

"No later than two days from now."

"Marshal."

"We have enough witnesses. I am having the two underage girls they had doped being brought here."

"They will not have to testify in court, will they?" Burton asked.

"No. Their testimony can be taken and read in the court and hearings."

"Good."

"Let's set up prisoner interviews to begin this afternoon," Chet said.

The pair agreed to meet Chet and Miguel at one-thirty at the jail.

Chet thanked them and excused himself and his man.

"What did you think about our prosecutors?" Miguel asked.

"They are damn sure not as tough acting as my last team in a similar situation, but this is who we drew. I hope they will surprise me."

The first prisoner they interviewed was Thrasher.

Chet led the interview. Thrasher demanded his lawyer be there.

"We want to know what you would like to tell us about why you were at the CYR Ranch on the evening you were arrested."

"I have nothing to say."

"I have evidence that you participated in several cases of white slavery."

"You have no such evidence."

"A U.S. Marshal will shortly be at the residence of a man in California. He paid you for a female slave last March."

"You —"

Chet got in his face. "These charges are

only a sliver of what we have on you unless you confess and testify against the rest. This could be your last chance. The rest of them will testify against you to save their butts. I don't intend to waste my time. You ready to confess or not?"

"I want my lawyer."

"You need to tell me and these men what you know or I am going to ensure you spend the full twenty years in prison. We have more names of buyers. You don't believe they won't testify who they bought them from? You won't get out of prison until the full term is satisfied. Or we can try you one case at a time, add it all together, and you will never get out of jail."

"I want my lawyer."

"Prosecution can lock you up for your life and you will never breathe outside air again in your lifetime. What is your choice?"

He put his head down and cried.

"You made your bed, now sleep in it. I am going to send you back to your cell and you will not get another chance to testify after you refuse my offer. I guarantee you if you won't testify you will have a cell in federal prison working at hard labor until the day you die."

"I won't do that —"

Chet opened the door and told the deputy

to put him back in his single cell.

The next one was his partner Benfield. He was trembling when he was seated. "Where are my lawyers?"

"We only want to make an offer to you. If you will testify against everyone, we will ask the judge for some easing of the sentence you face as a white slaver. The full term for just one crime is twenty years of hard labor. We can sentence you for several, and it will end up being life"

"I want my lawyer."

"You are not listening to me. If your cohorts accept my offer to testify, then you will rot in prison."

"What in the hell do I have to tell you to get out of here?"

"Not get out of here but receive a lesser sentence."

"How do I know you are telling me the truth?"

"These two men will tell you how it will go if you plead guilty and put yourself on the mercy of the court."

"No. No. They'd kill me."

"No. They're going to prison."

Benfield shook his head in defeat. "They tell me my wife and children are gone. I have no reason to live."

"If you testify you will shorten your time

in prison."

"I don't care."

"If the others testify you will get the maximum sentence. This is your chance to save prison time."

"Shoot me."

"There is no easy way out." Chet called for the deputy to take him back.

"Were those our best bets to get a confession from?" Murray asked.

Chet shook his head.

They brought Fulbright in. He took on an arrogant attitude and asked what the hell they wanted to know.

"Will New Mexico prosecute you for murder?"

"Huh?"

"I have a wanted sheet for you from there."

"What are you talking about?"

"You might plead guilty to the white slavery charges, testify against the others, and spend ten years in a federal prison?"

"What are you saying?"

"That by telling us all you know, you might beat facing a murder charge in New Mexico."

Fulbright blinked. "How do I know that would work?"

"Take the chance."

"No deal. Two-year sentence and go home free is what I want."

"There are others that will take my offer and you will serve the full term of twenty years, Fulbright."

He shook his head.

"Last chance?"

"No."

The ranch hands were unresponsive to any offer to plead guilty.

Late in the afternoon Richard Murray and Carl Burton sent word to the judge they would charge all the men in his court at ten a.m. the next morning. Murray spoke to the press about the charges. The girls arrived under the security Virgil set up. The mother of one of them accompanied the girls.

Chet and Liz met them and assured them all they had to do was testify to a clerk and they would not be named or have to appear in court.

Jane Olson was the mother of Glena Olson, a blond fifteen-year-old, and she was very protective of both girls. Mary Rupert was also fifteen, a brunette and a friend of Glena. Her mother was bedfast at home and Jane said she promised to protect her.

Liz visited with Jane and the two girls, who were very subdued. They were farm girls and probably Mormons, as such church members formed that community. They had a guarded house to stay in, and Liz asked if they needed anything. Jane thanked them and asked Chet privately if the two men named as their original kidnappers were being sought. He promised her they would be arrested and punished. She thanked him.

"What's next?" Liz asked leaving the courthouse.

"Lawyers and more," he said disappointed that there were no confessions.

"Will it be a long one?"

"Depends," he said as they walked toward the restaurant.

"On what?"

"How the judge wants to handle it. It may be one at a time. Lawyers would like that, choosing a new jury for each defendant and hoping to find a sympathetic one out of the lot."

"That could take months."

"Did you get off letters to the U.S. Marshals across the country on those customers he sold to?"

"We can do that tomorrow."

"Nothing else at Thrasher's house?"

"Nothing we could find. The ledger is the best thing we have. It was almost like he wanted to brag about it."

"He was so overbearing in D.C. I could have killed him there for threatening to take away the Navajo beef contract. I am satisfied he was just blowing off hot air."

"I think you will get them put away."

"There are so many things to get done."

"You are just one man."

"That is it. One man." He reached over hugged her shoulders and kissed her cheek, then they went inside to join the crew at the table reserved for them.

"Ten a.m. tomorrow?" Jesus asked him.

"Yes."

"We won't be called to testify?"

"No. They will be asked how they plead to our charges."

"Lawyers will want bond set. The judge will refuse them on grounds they are all at risk to run."

"We have the names of those two men who originally kidnapped the girls?"

"Jasper Whiles and Conroy Taylor. Small ranchers living close to Thatcher."

"When we get the trial dates set, I want us to go find them."

"I think they have been Kilton's source, getting him girls to feed to Thrasher and his bunch."

"These girls had to have come from a

rural area. Where else have they taken them from?"

"Teenage girls run off a lot with boys who turn them over to guys like Kilton. People look for them a while and give up, thinking they ran off and married some guy."

"Really, Fred?" Liz asked.

"I bet they got a half dozen teen girls like that in Prescott while I was on my own those two years."

"Didn't anyone look for them?" Liz asked.

"Lots of girls get discarded like I did and have to survive on their own. These guys take them away."

"Were those two girls they took to Thatcher like that?"

"I don't think so. But one girl's mother was bedridden. I bet that Mary was on her own or close to it and she looked like just the kind to kidnap."

"You must have had pure hell in those years you were on your own."

"Liz, I lived minute to minute. Surviving came first, food next. There are lots of threats to get you to subjugate and serve another homeless stronger than you. Girls hung onto guys for that reason, and they simply sold them to slavers for what they could get when they got tired of them."

"Imagine an underground of them in

Tucson or Tombstone?" Chet said shaking his head. He'd never realized such societies existed.

"Fred, and now? It must be nice to be a marshal?" Liz said to him.

He showed his chest and badge. "Liz, it's wonderful."

They all congratulated him.

After the meal the bunch went back to their rooms and to bed. Liz ordered a bath for Chet while he shaved.

Later he studied the dark ceiling and wondered how the rest of his business was doing. This whole thing needed to be over, but he saw no soon end to it. Finally he fell into a restless sleep.

CHAPTER 7

The judge, after their arraignment, asked if any one of the defendants wanted to plead his guilt or innocence. No one offered a plea. He said the accused had two weeks to get prepared for trial. There would be no bond in their cases. Then he refused several objections to that ruling, telling them that the matter was settled, and closed the hearing.

Chet checked with the two prosecutors. He wanted to find those first kidnappers of the girls. His estimation of the time needed was that it would require a week unless they had problems. Both lawyers agreed they should be found, arrested, and brought to the trial. They told him they'd handle things on that end.

They drew straws. Jesus was to take Liz back to Prescott. Chet hated parting with Liz, but she wanted to go check on things, do some banking, and make sure the ranches were still there. Miguel, Spencer, and Fred would ride with Chet and look for the pair. Jesus would then come back. They'd leave him directions where they went. But if he couldn't find them he was to wait in town for them to return.

With two packhorses, they left in the early morning for the Thrasher area. They made good time, and checked in with local law, who told him the pair left headed north.

Miguel talked to a man who said they probably went up into the White Mountains. Conroy Taylor had an Apache woman who he lived with part of the time. They might find him around Fort Apache.

They rode for three days before reaching the high country.

"She lives on the Black Fork," an Apache man from the fort told them. These were the good Apaches. Geronimo and the bad ones were hiding down in the Sierra Madres.

He scratched a map in the dirt and pointed eastward into the towering pine-clad mountains, showing Miguel how to find her. Fred held the horses and Chet bought a sack of hard candy in the store. Spencer was repairing a girth. Ready to ride, sucking on a lemon candy, Chet looked hard at the vast mountains. Such a scene would have challenged him five years earlier. In the cool mountain breeze he was grateful for all the lower temperatures and hoped they found Strawberry Sami, the reported love in Conroy's life.

The pungent flavor of turpentine filled his nose. He decided he was going to buy this good horse from John Slaughter. No, not just this one, all of them. They'd wear them to the nub during this wild chase through the reservation. Not fair to give them back to Slaughter in that condition.

The clear water in the stream beside him looked so inviting swelling over the rocks, hiding fat Gila trout, the Apache giving directions had said. He would eat one in camp that evening if they had a way to catch them. He booted his horse across the stream and splashed out onto the other side. He twisted in the saddle and asked Miguel what he'd said to him.

"I said a few trout would be good to eat but he told me to be on our toes. We're almost to her place."

"I vote for trout after we catch him."

"I vote for them if he ain't here."

"Fred," Spencer said. "We're having trout for supper."

Back down the line with the packhorses, Fred said, "Hurrah. No jerky and beans."

Miguel drew up beside Chet. "See the painted horses grazing down in the bottom meadow? This must be Strawberry's hangout."

"I smelled the smoke when we crossed the creek," Chet said.

"You expect trouble?"

"They may recognize Fred if they are here."

"You don't expect them to be here?"

Chet turned his palms up in the expression of not knowing.

A small Apache woman wrapped in a blanket came out of a wickiup and asked them what they wanted

Chet stepped down. "Strawberry, is Conroy and his friend here?"

She shook her head.

"Have they been here?"

She nodded. "Just Conroy."

"Where did he go?"

She shrugged.

"Can we catch some trout?"

She shrugged.

Miguel said, "You find out where he went and we'll catch the trout. Fred knows how."

She showed him a place to sit on a worn red Navajo blanket spread on the ground. "I knew this morning you were coming to see me."

She took a place a distance from him and sat cross-legged facing him.

"Is that good or bad?"

"Good."

"What good could I do for you here?" he asked.

"I am stealing your strength." A small smile formed in the edges of her dark lips.

"I can't feel it."

She nodded satisfied. "You have a strong woman. She lives on a mountain."

"Yes. I love her. Is she okay?"

She nodded. "Two-three days you will find him." Her head toss was eastward.

"Thanks."

"Strawberry, if I can ever help you, contact me." He got up and thanked her again.

The fish were breaded and sizzling in two skillets by the time he walked over to their camp setup.

Fred was smiling as he knelt over them. "What did she say?"

"She said that in two or three days we'd find him."

Fred frowned. "She a fortune-teller?"

"A *bruja* is what they'd call her. I never felt one before. No, that is not right. I felt one before and dried her feet."

"Huh?" Fred asked.

Chet smiled and shrugged. He had one of

his own and never realized it. He drew in a large breath of mountain air. *I'll be home soon.* "Him and his buddy will be down by Socorro."

The fish tasted wonderful. He left Sami some Arbuckle coffee, and they rode off as the sun peeked over New Mexico. Their trip was steep off the east side. They only had trails to use. By the third day they rode into juniper country and entered the edge of Socorro.

They put the horses up and had them grained to recover some of the weight they'd lost going over the mountains. Miguel took off to talk to locals and returned shortly to the café where the others were relaxing.

"Both our wanted men are staying with a woman in the barrio."

"I knew you could get this information," Chet said.

"We going to go arrest them?" Miguel asked, looking a little impatiently at them.

Chet stood up. "Come on, guys. Miguel wants to go home."

"Damn right." Miguel nodded his head.

They laughed.

Neither of the men put up any resistance. Chet had them temporarily housed in the county jail. He recalled it from the days they held JD there on some drummed-up charges. None of those lawmen were there, and the new ones were very respectful to the U.S. Marshals.

The next day, Chet checked with several of his cattle sellers. They told him there would be lots of beef cows for sale in the fall. Satisfied, he told them he'd be back and buy some. Miguel and Fred were set to take the horses back to Tucson. He and Spencer would transport their prisoners on the new railroad tracks to El Paso and then by train to Lordsburg and a stage to Tucson. It looked like a three-day trip while the riders would be over a week getting back.

With their prisoners in cuffs they met the passenger train and rode the shiny tracks to El Paso. They put the prisoners in the city jail overnight, took baths, and slept through the desert night in a hot hotel room. Next, they were on a westbound train that took twenty hours to Lordsburg, then another dusty, long, rocking stage ride to Tucson. The city baked in the midsummer heat with no way to escape it. He had three letters from Liz to open. All was good.

Jesus met them the next morning. "All is well at the jail, though no one has taken your offer."

"Glad you didn't try to find us. We went

all over hell to find an Indian woman called Strawberry. Those White Mountains are some pretty places."

"Cool?" Jesus asked laughing.

"Damn right," Spencer said.

"I sent a wire last night for Liz to tell all the wives we were fine, that Miguel and Fred were bringing home the horses from Socorro, and we still had all the prisoners in the hoosegow."

"What about the buyers we have information on?"

"I sent letters and the information to those state offices of the U.S. Marshal services to investigate. There is no mail on any arrests so far."

"Can they arrest them?" Jesus asked.

"If they can prove they bought a girl."

"They are as guilty as this bunch."

"You would have to find one sold and get her to testify."

"That would be hard."

"There is a buyer down at Nogales I'd like to arrest. Diego Obregon."

"What do we have to do to get him?" Spencer asked.

"Testimony that he bought one or more."

"How can we get that?"

"Someone comes forward and says they know he bought girls."

"That would be tough to find." Jesus shook his head.

Chet agreed. "If we could find one of those sold girls, and we could get her to testify, that would be great."

"We could protect them?"

"Yes, we would protect them."

"Let Fred and I go to the border and learn about this guy. He goes back and forth across the border. Living there he has no idea we want him. Somewhere there is a *puta* who will testify she was sold by him."

"Be damn careful. He would cut your throat in a minute if he knew what you were up to."

Jesus nodded.

"First trial is in two weeks. I have no idea who is first, but Murray warned me it would be long and drug out. Either of you two need to go home?"

"I went home already and spent a day with my wife. Send Spencer."

"Thanks. I would like to go," Spencer said.

"Get on the first stage north. Be back in a week."

"Thanks, guys. I am gone," Spencer said while already on the move. "See you in a week."

When he went out the door, Jesus said, "I

bet Liz will think you should have gone with him."

"She understands my responsibility," Chet said.

Jesus shook his head. "She is still is a wife and woman."

"I know. But she understands these things."

He wired Liz that Spencer was coming home for a visit while they waited for the trial.

Back at the prosecutor's office he heard the two lawyers' ideas on prosecution. When they had their case scripted, they asked for his input.

"The last time I had several men that wanted to turn state evidence. That made it a damn sight easier to convict them. Here we have stonewalling on all their parts. I believe ten years is better than twenty and someone will break and testify."

"Who?" asked Richard Murray.

"I want to try something on Fulbright. Can we get someone to pose as a New Mexico officer to come and interrogate Fulbright about the murder charges against him over there?"

"I know a man in the territorial police and if he has time he would do it," Richard said.

"Wire him. Tell him who we have and we

need to move him into pleading guilty. And to come as quickly as he can."

Three days later, Herrera Angeles, a New Mexico territorial policeman, arrived.

Chet and Richard Murray met him at the stage office and they went to Murray's house. The conversation went quickly. The man listened and agreed with them that they needed Fulbright to testify. New Mexico really was not pressing to try him. Witnesses were gone or deceased. Fulbright didn't know that. Besides, the ones they hung and shot were rustlers anyway.

"I can get it closed if he goes along with testifying against the others in this case. How's that?"

"Good. Can we also get the judge to give him a much lesser sentence?" Chet asked the two prosecutors.

"I'd say damn right, but I want to ask him first." Carl put on his coat and rushed off.

Murray's lovely Hispanic wife served them sweet rolls and coffee while they waited.

"I am sorry you never met my wife, Liz, while she was here."

"Oh, you two will be back down here again, and I am sure I will meet her then. I have heard so much about the both of you."

"We've been so busy. It was not an oversight. I promise you."

"Your courting her is almost folklore around here. She came looking to buy a famous horse you have at your camp below Tubac and you two fell in love?"

"She can tell it to you. It was a whirlwind day we spent together, and she wrote me asking if she could come back to the border and meet me again. I never let her go back."

"I have seen her, she is a lovely lady."

"Close up she is much more than that."

"I imagine so. My husband told me she found most of the evidence you got from Thrasher's house. You know I heard his wife went back to Texas with their children, they say to file divorce papers."

"He will pay for his crimes."

Later that day, Chet and Murray met up with Angeles and Jesus. They took Fulbright into a secure place, uncuffed him, and told him to sit down at the small table.

"We have a plan you may like."

"I doubt it, but I will listen." If his dark eyes could have cut them down, Chet figured they'd all four be dead by the hard looks he sent Angeles, Jesus, Murray, and Chet.

Chet introduced Herrera Angeles as the head of the New Mexico Territorial Police. A little lie would not hurt. They were not

125

testifying in court.

"Captain Angeles is here to help you if you will help us."

"How's that?"

"He knows how important your testimony against the others would be if you gave it in court."

"I am not a stool pigeon."

"Listen," Chet said. "Captain Angeles says he will drop the charges against you over in New Mexico in trade for your testimony here."

"If I don't?"

"Then, when you are released in twenty years, he or one of his policemen will be at the gate to arrest you and bring you back to New Mexico to stand trial for a double murder there."

"What else are you giving me?"

"A four- to five-year sentence instead of twenty."

"Two years."

"No. That is my best offer. Take it or leave it."

"I have to testify all I know at each trial?"

"That is the deal."

"I need time to think about it. You'd have to protect me."

"I can guarantee we can do that."

"Son of a bitch. This is bad. Twenty years

or five and no prosecution in New Mexico?"

"I am asking you first. I'll ask Benfield next."

"That cowardly bastard would scream to tell it in a minute. All right, what comes next?"

"We will have a court clerk take down all your testimony. We need the story from the beginning, all you know, and then you will sign it. Two of us will be in here to guide you and if we think you did not tell us all of it or you are lying, we will challenge."

"What if I forgot something? Can I add it later?"

"Yes." Everyone in the room but Fulbright looked relieved. Head down, he shook his head like he could not believe he had agreed to do that.

They took a break. Chet went to find the men's toilet, then stuck his head into Sheriff Ben Reyes's office.

"You're smiling."

"Yes. He's going to testify against them."

"That is the best news I ever heard."

"Amen. We must make sure he is adequately protected."

"No worries. We will get that done right now."

"Thanks. And I need to send my wife a wire."

CHAPTER 8

The day turned out long as Fulbright was telling a very complete story, from the beginning, about the white slave trade with Thrasher and Benfield. He listed two more Tucson businessmen who had big parts in the sales.

Spencer and Jesus were there listening to every word that spilled out of their witness's mouth.

Two clerks took turns writing down his exact words. The room was very hot, but they knew of no more secret place to do this and be as secure.

Jesus came out and talked to Chet. "He started at the beginning. I am impressed. He has a very sharp memory. We have only had to correct him twice about a relationship he had that we didn't agree with. He even apologized for his mistakes. His testimony should put them all in prison."

"That is what we needed."

Sheriff Ben Reyes sent deputies to arrest Aaron Coulter and Talman Brooks who arrived two hours later, along with their screaming lawyers standing to the side while their clients were put in prison clothes and cells.

Murray and his partner were busy filing papers for their hearing before the judge. The two and Chet also had a private session with the judge, telling him about the cooperation of Fulbright and that they were having his testimony written down and when done, Fulbright was going to sign it.

"You three know we have to share that confession with his defense lawyers?"

"Yes sir. From that we found two more men to charge tomorrow. We already have them in cells waiting for their arraignment," Murray said.

The judge nodded.

Ben came down the hall. "I don't have as secure walls as I thought. Perhaps they figured out, since we arrested Coulter and Brooks, that someone is testifying, but the lawyers are downstairs screaming, wanting to know what is going on in here."

"Murray can handle it. Have him send them home. They can read the testimony when we get finished and have it signed."

"Is he still giving testimony?"

"Yes, and we will be taking down more tomorrow."

Ben shook his head. "You picked a winner. I paid Angeles's expenses out of my treasury. He went back and I thanked him for all he did for us."

"The Marshals will reimburse you."

"Thanks. I am so proud we are rounding up so many of these criminals."

"You bet."

At six p.m., they fed Fulbright supper and told him they'd be back at eight in the morning to continue. Chet took both clerks and his crew to a fancy supper. Both young men were impressed with the day, and the meal, and promised to be there in the morning on time to start back up.

Chet and his men took a taxi back to the hotel. Fred was seated on the bench in front and jumped up.

"You had supper?" Chet asked him.

"In the hotel restaurant. I figured I would starve if I waited for you. How did it go?"

"Fulbright caved. We are taking down the story about the entire operation. Ben arrested two more men from town who were involved, and they will be charged in court in the morning."

"Wow, we are winning, huh?"

"Damn right we are. Breakfast at seven.

Jail at eight. Get some rest."

"Oh, I checked on the horses at the livery. They are doing great since we got back," Fred said.

"I need to go meet Slaughter and thank him."

Jesus agreed. "We will have some time now that we have this deal nearly sewed up."

They all went off to bed.

What will happen next? Chet looked at the light, reflected on his ceiling from below, for a long time.

In the morning over breakfast they talked about the day ahead. Chet assigned Spencer and Jesus to continue to make sure Fulbright was on track in his confession. Then he told Fred he could join them but let them handle it while he just listened.

Fred agreed, excited to be included.

Liz sent him a wire telling him that Miguel was there, that Lisa said thanks, and she wanted to know when it was his turn.

He sent one back telling her the trial started in ten days and told her to come back with Miguel when he came.

He checked into the secret room. Jesus was reading the statement back to Fulbright.

Fulbright was nodding.

"When will it be finished?" he quietly asked Spencer.

"An hour."

"Good."

"He even testified that the guy, Diego, in Nogales was involved and that they had made several sales down there."

"We need him on this side of the border and brought here. Anyone else?"

"Someone in Juárez they use also."

"What about those private sales that show in Thrasher's books?"

"When we get through on this read-back we can ask him."

Chet nodded.

The reading finished, Chet asked him, "Some of these girls bring big prices?"

Fulbright shrugged. "The real pretty ones do. One of those girls they brought in the other night might have brought eight thousand dollars. The other one twenty-five hundred, maybe three."

"Before the war broke out slaves were sold that way, weren't they?" Chet asked, trying to recall what he could remember of the slave market.

Fulbright nodded. "I saw big, powerful slaves, when I was a teen, bring ten thousand dollars at auction in Texas. Yellow women, good-looking, seven-eight thousand dollars. Thrasher had a book with a list of contacts who buy the high-priced ones."

"Any idea where he kept that book? They could be traced down and watched."

"It is a small black book. I bet he had it on him when you arrested us."

"Spencer, go ask Ben if he has that in the possessions they confiscated."

Spencer was gone and came back shortly, waving a small, leather-covered book.

Chet thanked Fulbright and sat down to look at the pages of addresses. They were from all over and they had notes. Like "likes freckled one" or "goes for blue eyes."

"What does it say?" Jesus asked.

"There's a helluva lot of buyers around this country, Mexico, and Canada. Some from overseas, too."

"We have the tip of an iceberg in this book. We thought, when we trapped those guys in Tombstone back a few months ago and had them sent up, that was the end of this deal. It damn sure is more widespread than anyone imagined."

"I am going to have a list made of each of these names and addresses and the list sent to D.C. The national office needs to check on this."

Fulbright signed the testimony and they witnessed it.

"We have to make printed copies now for the prosecution and the defense," the head clerk said. "That will take two days."

"On Friday we can meet with the defense attorneys, and they will have a week to figure out a new defense before the first trial starts. Now, this Diego guy in Nogales? What are you going to do about him?" Burton asked.

Chet looked at Jesus.

"Miguel will be back soon?" Jesus asked.

"I imagine my wife has him packed already."

They laughed.

"I think Fred and I should get on the stage, go down there, and see if we can arrest this guy and bring him back," Jesus said.

"You can get on the stage but no wild deals. If you can make it work, then fine. Make the arrest but no big shoot-out. We can get him short of that."

"I want to get him rounded up with the rest."

"I do, too, Jesus. Just don't get too furious."

Jesus smiled. "We won't, will we, Fred?"

"Hell no."

"Go."

Chet shook his head. "Diego Obregon — we will make sure there is room for him in that crowded jail."

Jesus and Fred were taking the four p.m. stage to Nogales. Chet and Spencer had their heads together with Murray and Burton going over all Fulbright had said in his confession.

"He's pretty complete about Thrasher's and Benfield's involvement, but some of the ranch hands were simply onlookers," Murray said.

"They don't know we know that," Chet said. "We could offer them amnesty before they find out and get their testimony. Anything we get will be more evidence against the main ones."

"Chet, you don't miss a thing, do you?"

"Try not to, Carl. Really try not to."

"You ready to go through this all over again?"

Chet nodded. "One by one and separate them."

That afternoon one by one they interrogated the individuals.

The ranch hands were tired of jailhouse food and the quarters. Some admitted they knew about the business but saw none of the profit and kept their mouths shut to keep a precious ranch job. Their testimony didn't look worth the time to write up for the prosecutors or Chet.

After speaking to the judge and explaining the situation, with his approval, Chet told the hands that they had a week to get out of Arizona and not come back. Looking powerfully relieved, they agreed to leave after dark and be gone. He gave each man twenty dollars and said the wounded men could go, too, since both were near healed. Come dark, all were gone.

Now they had five defendants. Six counting Jason Fulbright.

The big lawyer asked where the ranch hands were.

When Chet told him they were released and gone for good, the lawyers raised hell about everyone there being prejudiced toward their clients. Their complaints fell on deaf ears. By this time Chet realized that they would raise hell about anything so as to get attention and perhaps have someone slip up on something and give them something they could use for their clients. Who knew?

Day two since Jesus and Fred left for Nogales. Then Chet got a wire.

D. O. IS ARRESTED WE WILL ARRIVE AT 2 PM TODAY. F AND J

He handed it to Spencer, who laughed.

"Guess after lunch we can help escort the prisoner to jail."

The newspaper had the headline ARRESTED ONE SQUEALS ON THE REST.

The federal court today informed the defendants that one of the defendants, Jason Fulbright, the accused ranch foreman, will testify against all those arrested in the white slavery case that goes to trial next week. It was just confirmed to the defense attorneys that he would be the prosecution's star witness. A copy of Fulbright's confession, which is very long and extensive, will be printed in tomorrow's paper in its entirety. It looks like there are severe accusations against several local businessmen now being held without bond in the Pima County Jail. A number of what the prosecution calls simple ranch hands have been released and were told not to be in Arizona after seven days. That they were personas non grata.

News from Nogales Regarding More About This Case

A Mexican National citizen, Diego Obregon, was arrested yesterday while doing business on this side of the border. Actually U.S. Marshal Jesus Martinez arrested Obregon in a house of ill repute and in a statement by the U.S. Marshal said he will be also included in the charges of the white slave trials that are starting next week in the federal court. Mr. Obregon will be charged for his involvement in the transporting and the sale of white girls as slaves from the U.S.

"No mention of Fred."

Spencer read it and laughed. "Hope they didn't embarrass Fred by leaving him out."

Chet shook his head. "That boy has seen more and done more than most of us to survive in this world."

"He don't talk much about it. But he really has seen it all."

"You know, I wondered once why you picked him. I don't anymore. What you saw that in that raggedy-dressed alley rat I sure didn't know. Undercover he's better than any of us and has been since the start."

"And now he wears a badge."

"No doubt he will be good at his job."

"We better get down there and welcome them. I am sure the newspaper will be there, too."

Chet was amused when Jesus stepped out of the coach, waving to them over the gathering that heard they were coming. Their prisoner came off in cuffs next, and then Fred in the stagecoach doorway waved at everyone and they got a round of applause.

Chet hailed a taxi, loaded both men and Obregon in it, and sent them to the jail. He and Spencer left in the next one to join them.

Pushed into the jailhouse, the accused said, "You sonsabitches. My ambassador is going to sue you. You can't arrest me. I am not a citizen of this country."

"No, but you are in its court system, and it may be twenty years before you see Mexico again."

Fred joined the conversation, smiling. "Sue me. I haven't got any money."

Jesus shook his head. "I am about to stick a sock in his mouth. I am so sick of listening to him."

"He will soon be smothered in the jail."

"Thank God."

"You two did great. Thanks a bunch."

Chet got word that his horse supplier was coming to Tucson and wanted to have lunch with him. He sent a telegraph asking where and when to meet. John sent one back saying he'd be there Thursday and to meet him at the Bankers Club, a private one used by the more successful businesspeople, lawyers, and the élite. He fired one back that he would be there noon on Thursday.

Slaughter was a tall man with a mustache, and when Chet approached, he smiled. "I have seen you before. Great to finally meet the famous law-and-order rancher."

"Hey, we enjoyed riding your horses. They are fabulous. We rode them clear over to Socorro and brought back more white slavers."

"Anytime you are down here without mounts holler. I've got a shit pot load more of them out at the ranch."

"How are things going?"

"My wife was bringing my children out here from Texas and she died. We didn't know exactly why. She'd never been seriously sick, and just like that I lost her. It sure shattered my plans, but I didn't come here to cry on your shoulder."

"My first wife was killed in a horse jumping accident and it was something she did all her life and never had a problem. Then my second wife died. I have two boys. So I know how you feel. We have to move on."

"I am. I am working on a big deal. Do you know anyone who needs some good cows and calves? Say about three hundred and fifty of them?"

"How much apiece?

"Quick cash deal. They are sound and I'd help deliver them. There's no loan against them."

"How much?"

"Tell me where you need them?"

"Behind Mount Lemon."

"I heard about that deal. You stole that place. Twelve thousand dollars for the herd. They all have calves. We could lose some along the way, but the calves are old enough to drive that far. The cows are half British or better. None over five years old."

"You must have a hot deal cooking."

"I do, and when it is over I'll tell you about it, but I need the cash in my hand. Fast."

"My banker in Prescott will send it down in forty-eight hours."

They shook hands. "The cows and calves are in that country south of Tombstone. My vaqueros will get them up. We'll get a water contractor to set up some overnight stops and they will be on your ranch in two weeks."

"That's done. Now I want to buy those horses we used."

"You just did."

"No, that was a cow deal. You know I own

a Barbarousa stallion and my nephew is handling his colts —"

"How in hell's name did you get him? Chet, I come from Texas, too. I know that strain and they never let a stallion get out of Mexico."

"Long story, but the short of it is, that a young man took his mare down there and made a deal. He said that if his mare beat their horses in a race, he wanted her bred to the senior stallion. If he lost they owned the mare. This mare could run and the family couldn't say no. The mare ran against three of their best and she won. The mare had a golden stallion and the boy came to me and told me he was too poor to own such a colt. I paid a good price for him and now have some sons. Actually my current wife came by my camp below Tubac looking to buy one and got me instead."

"You don't owe me a colt like that."

"Yes, I do. In the next six months we will deliver him to your house."

Slaughter collapsed back in his chair. "Call me any time you ever need horses to ride. That is unbelievable. When I get him I will have photographs made and send them to all my old buddies in Texas and say, 'See what I found in Arizona?'"

Chet felt he'd known John all his life, it

was all so natural. "I still have to go to Socorro this fall, and I will need another herd for a new place up on Crooks Road."

"Wire Joseph Chavez in Socorro, and when you are ready tell him what you want and he will gather them, help you get them home, and you won't have to camp over there gathering them yourself. Most honest man in New Mexico I know, and he will work."

"Obviously you're a cow trader."

"But I don't have a beef contract like you have with the Navajos, and I know how well you service that contract, rain or shine."

"I have an Army sergeant who got out of the service to become a cowboy. No one would hire him. I saw potential in the man. He rides like he has a pole for a backbone, but he can work men and he eats details for breakfast."

"Those cav soldiers all ride like that. Straight in the saddle. You can see them coming a mile away."

"He also married my sister."

"You are damn sure doing things right. All kinds of people brag on it."

They finally ordered lunch and laughed the rest of their time.

"What about these businessmen you have in jail?"

"The two girls they were going to sell were innocent farm girls. They were planning to sell them for big money into a horrific life. Those girls did nothing to deserve that. Three more lost their minds being doped and handled. The judge can't give those greedy bastards enough time in prison for what they did."

Slaughter nodded. "I knew you did lots of law work. Found lost people and put the sorry ones behind bars. And built an empire. That impressed me. They said you came to Arizona to get away from a Texas feud?"

"Men killed my brother in Kansas and scattered the herd. His twelve-year-old rode back to get me. They aren't walking on the face of this earth anymore — but it was either get out or die."

"I can savvy that. They shot you once making an arrest, too?"

"That taught me I was not indestructible."

Slaughter smiled. "I like that. We aren't, are we? Lost wives, lost money on deals and made some, too. It hasn't been all sunshine, but you know what, no one would ever believe it if you told them that it is with God's help things happened the way they do. I'll be back here in two days with a paper transferring the mother cows to you for the money."

"Good. My man, Miguel, will be here shortly to help us."

After lunch he told Spencer to get word to Toby that his cattle were coming and wire Miguel to come as they had a herd to move.

That evening as they left the restaurant in the golden fire of sundown's last moments, a sharp-faced woman in her twenties caught his shirtsleeve.

"Hold up here. You are the son of a bitch that has ruined my life and those of both my small children. I just want to tell how you destroyed my life. What for? Two dumb farm girls who will never amount to a pile of shit, and your glory will be magnified as the great lawman."

"Are you Thrasher's wife?"

"Damn right. I am Joann Thrasher. Broke, in debt, and desperate."

"Why did you never stop him? You had to know his big money wasn't coming from a real business or ranch. There is nothing that makes that kind of money. I say those and many more girls he sold into slavery deserved a lot better than what he put them through. Crime should never provide a way of life. You lived it and never stopped him. Someone had to stop him. Your little girl there could have been sold by him."

"You won't ever understand. You've completely ruined my life and the lives of my children."

"Good night. He broke the law, not me."

"Where did she come from?" Fred asked.

Chet shook his head. "I suppose from her gold mine to a housekeeping job. What a bitch."

Liz wrote that she and Miguel were on their way. The trial was scheduled to begin Monday. The next morning, the crew rode to look at Slaughter's cows and calves. They saw most of them and told Chet he made a very good buy. The cattle were great. Chet and Jesus took the late stage back from Tombstone. Fred and Spencer took a room, stabled the horses, and were to join them Saturday night in Tucson.

"What is all this rush on those cows and calves?" Liz asked when she arrived.

"Slaughter couldn't tell me, but he needed money for something and he needed it now. He'll tell me the details when it's over. The cows have no money borrowed on them. We saved lots of money and have calves now, too. The cattle we will buy at Socorro will calf next year."

"We are not broke but —"

"The price was right."

"Oh, I agree. You are the trader. That

ranch will start paying for itself a year sooner than the high place."

The trials began. Fulbright did his part testifying for the prosecution. How he was drifting around when Thrasher found him in Mexico. Said he had a ranch and needed a tough foreman for it. That some cattlemen up there were pushing his man around. So he took the job. He had not been there long when Thrasher told him how they could make big money selling white girls. He didn't like it, should've quit, but jobs were hard to find and the one he had spoiled him. What ranch foreman got a hundred-dollar bonus almost every month? He had no idea that his bosses were making thousands off their sales.

It was good testimony, and cross-examination by the defense didn't sway his story nor dissuade any jury member as far as Chet could see. The judge might even give him less time for the crime in light of his testimony against Thrasher and Benfield.

The jury was out an hour and found all three guilty of white slavery. Now it was up to the judge to sentence them. He could do it as one charge, or sentence for each case making it multiple crimes.

Members of Benfield's family fainted. A

gray-headed woman hysterically tried to get by the bailiffs. "Your Honor. Your Honor. My son is a family man, not a criminal."

Under his breath Spencer said to Chet, "Benfield's wife and children have already left for Texas. She must have expected the outcome."

Chet agreed and they left the courtroom.

"I have reservations at that good place to eat," Liz said as she squeezed his arm.

"Sounds wonderful."

The crew walked by them, up the street.

"Chet," Jesus said sharply.

He at once saw that Jesus referred to three armed men approaching them from across the dirt street. Spencer drew his gun and shielded Liz on one side, and Chet shielded her on the other. Without waiting, Fred shot the man who had raised his pistol, spinning him around. Number two was a shorter man. His bullet plowed into the dust hard as Jesus's shot struck him in his chest. The third one ran, and Spencer dropped him in his tracks with two bullets into his back.

They were all dressed in dirty peasant clothing; one wore a sombrero, and they all wore sandals.

Police came running from everywhere. Three out-of-breath deputies came with guns in hand.

"You guys all right?" the lead man asked.

"We don't have gunfights in our streets," the Hispanic policeman in charge said sharply to Chet.

"Sanchez, these men are all U.S. Marshals."

"Why in the hell did they want to shoot at U.S. Marshals?"

"The court just found those slavers guilty, and I guess these men didn't like that."

"Oh, señor, excuse me. These men were dummies to try, no?"

Chet nodded. "I am glad no one was hurt by a stray bullet. Sanchez, this is my wife, Elizabeth Byrnes."

"So glad to meet you. You go. We can have them buried."

"Who do they work for?" Chet asked.

"I am not certain, but he will be in irons at the jail in the morning to talk to you. I promise."

"*Gracias.* I will be waiting. We have supper plans. Good day."

"They simply wanted to shoot us?" Fred asked.

"Not everyone appreciates what we do, Fred," Jesus explained.

Fred reset his big-brim felt hat on his head. "I am learning, Jesus. I really am

149

learning."

The meal went fine and with even more watchful eyes they walked to the hotel in the dying sundown. *Lots more careful,* Chet decided.

In the room, Liz held and kissed him. "I recalled lots of things tonight in those few minutes on the street. The raid on my hacienda. Hearing boots and noisy spurs coming on the stairs. I had only seconds to secure a loaded pistol, cock it, go out the bedroom door when I saw them. I shot the one on the right. The other guy fell back, and I shot him when he landed.

"I heard the last one repeatedly shouting for them from outside that he was coming to back them. I could hear him running forward. I had crossed the great room and was close to the two steps up to the entranceway when he appeared in the lighted front door way. Out of his breath, he never regained it. I shot him until the gun struck empty. He lay still, spread across my already deceased husband's body."

"I am so sorry tonight made you remember." Chet wondered who sent those three gunman, and that they thought they could shoot them down and get off scot free. They had that look on their faces — we will kill them like dogs.

"It wasn't your fault, Chet, or you'd have prevented it from happening. I simply can't imagine what made those three men think they could gun us down."

"Me either. Fred sure never hesitated."

She quickly agreed. "He's real. You can tell he's had to make decisions to save himself. The others are experienced with facing death. This was a hard one."

At breakfast the next morning they learned that a minister from the border had brought in two women that Diego Obregon had sold. The two were to testify against him at his trial. The team found them hotel rooms, meals, and guards. The prosecutors took down their testimony.

Murray came by and smiled at them. "Good news. This last one you arrested has confessed. I think his lawyers feared he'd be charged for twice the cases and that could make it impossible for him to ever get out of jail."

"Have you spoken with the judge?"

"Fulbright will serve three years."

"I agree. His testimony was what we needed. The rest?"

"Ten years if good behavior. Do you expect any more efforts by the ring to get them pardoned?"

"They will try."

"Maybe we could question them about the ring?"

"You could do that."

"I think from what we know their families will be supported by the ring while they are in prison for their silence, so they may not talk."

"Thrasher's wife said you ruined her life and her children's lives as well," Spencer reminded him.

"We will see. Thanks, Murray. If you don't need us anymore, we're going home."

"Yeah," came the cheer.

"I hope we can work together again. Both of us thank you," Murray said and left them.

"May I wire Lisa to have a party ready Saturday night?"

"You sure may do that. We have our receipts to turn in to get paid for our work and expenses. Go buy us some stagecoach tickets. Wait. Fred, take the Slaughter horses to our camp below Tubac so they will be there when we need them."

"One of my cousins will do that," Jesus said.

"Better. There are two stages going north to the ferry a day. It will take both of them to haul us. Find seats and maybe pay someone to wait a day."

Spencer went to handle that. Jesus and Fred went to ready the horses.

"We can go pack our bags," he said to his wife.

"Oh, you will be a big help at that."

He hugged her shoulder. "I bet I can do it."

They laughed and left the prosecutors' offices. Out in the street he was aware of every place a shooter could get off a shot at him. Once in the hotel lobby he stopped Liz, told her to wait, and went back to see if they'd been followed. Nothing was out of place. The usual traffic passing, by wagon and on foot. It would be a damn relief to be back at Prescott Valley, where it would be safe and much cooler at the same time.

"Find anything?"

"No. Just traffic. I don't think they are through, but for now we can probably breathe easier."

"Good."

They went upstairs to their hot room.

"Chet, all my life I lived in Mexico and it was hot, but you spoiled me at Prescott so badly I may never want to go back home."

"I've never known such a hot place, either. I will really be glad to be back home."

"And you have no pending problems?"

He smiled at her. He really didn't know of

anything pressing enough to get him off his cowhide couch at home.

Chet, Liz, and Spencer took the first stage available. The rest would follow eight hours later. Slaughter's horses would be stabled at the Tubac headquarters. That meant in three days the whole bunch would be home.

Chet teased Spencer about his wife. "Will Lucinda know you?"

"I don't worry about that. She is the best thing that ever happened to me, and her children are the frosting. She is so happy at Prescott, but she said she'd go anywhere we need to go. It was so great to have her along building the telegraph line. I knew I really had a keeper during the hustle and bustle we had stretching that steel in the sky. It was so nice to have her every night rocking me to sleep. No place was bad and nothing amounted to a problem for her. I really am grateful I found her. She is learning to read and write and is excited about it."

"I know," Liz said, leaning forward. "Lucinda is a fine lady. You did very well."

"Thanks, Liz."

The hot wind swept the coach, rocking and spurring up dust from sixteen hooves. Winding through the saguaro-studded desert they rocked toward Papago Wells, where the road split — one went west to

Yuma and later California, the other north by northwest to Hayden's Ferry and the capital to be called Phoenix, then, eventually up the Black Canyon route to Prescott.

The stretch to the Wells from Picaho Pass was short, but Chet was grateful to get out and flex while fresh horses were attached to the coach. Still more desert carpeted the area, with many Indian villages eking livings out of patches of irrigated ground. The Gila River was so low they dispensed with use of the ferry, and the animals must have enjoyed splashing through the shallow flow, then digging in to haul the stage back up onto the flat.

Their driver, Hailey McBrown, halted the team and told folks that they had a few minutes to stretch before they continued. He tied off the reins and scrambled down while Chet helped Liz down.

McBrown took one horse at a time, down the line, checking each harness.

Chet, curious, left Liz with Spencer and walked over to ask the man if anything was wrong.

"Ever have a feeling you need to do something like this?" McBrown shoved his stained felt hat back and shook his head.

"I have lots of those days."

"They look fine. The workers keep the

harness well-oiled and ready. I just hate a wreck. Let's load. All is well."

"What did he think was wrong?" she asked, taking her seat.

"He was concerned but found nothing."

"Good."

They rode on and finally made Hayden's Ferry long after dark. The next stage left at noon the following day. He found them a room and wired ahead they'd be there the next night at midnight. They slept, and next morning were up to eat breakfast. It was windy and it swept some dead cottonwood leaves and dirt around the buildings and then northward on the wings of its hot breath.

He'd damn sure be pleased to be home a hundred miles north and way up in the sky. They went in the door of the stage station where the clerk smiled.

"Howdy, Mr. Byrnes. Good to see you and missus again."

"Me, too, we finally are going home."

"If there ever is an opening up there, put my name in." Then the clerk laughed.

Chet agreed to do it. They waited with Spencer. At last on board for the final leg of the journey they rocked on to the Salt River Ferry crossing and then headed north. It would be late night before getting home but they were bound in that direction. When they reached the altitude where ghostly forms of juniper brush shone in the moonlight and cooler air sought them, he smiled — *home at last.*

CHAPTER 9

Bare-footed, Chet went downstairs into the cool early morning air. The mourning doves were all he heard outside as the house waited for the rest of the ranch to awake. The vaqueros were already eating breakfast at the dining hall, and soon the children would be awake and would follow their mothers, who ate after the men left to check on cattle or whatever else needed their attention.

The pungent aroma of ponderosa pine mixed with some cooking fire smoke filled the cool house. Lisa had lamps on in the kitchen. Her husband, Miguel, and Spencer looked hollow-eyed as they raised their cups of coffee at him. "Welcome home."

"Welcome to you. They ran a second stage for you guys?"

Spencer nodded. "Yes. I was grateful, too."

Lisa swept by with a cup for Chet. "It's good to have you all back here."

"You have any plans for us today?" Spencer asked.

"Yes. You catching up on sleep. If we plan anything for tomorrow, we will send word."

Spencer smiled. "I don't want to miss out on anything."

"We won't count you out."

He rose wearily. "I'll go to sleep for two days then."

"I will line up moving those cows and calves I bought from Slaughter up to the Oracle Ranch. That will give that place a good start. The Socorro cows will go to Toby at the Rustler's Ranch. I should hear back from Joe Chavez by next week. Slaughter says he's the most honest seller over there."

When Spencer was gone, Miguel asked if everything in Tucson went the way he wanted.

"Yes, they're in prison."

"Fred told us men in Tucson tried to kill you?" Lisa asked.

"They never had a chance. Very stupid play in my book."

"We are glad you and Liz are safe."

"Lisa, so am I. And now we are back here for your great cooking. Anyone been around asking for us?"

"No."

"Better."

Miguel laughed. "You are worn out?"

"Tucson isn't bad except in June, July, and August. I told Liz that."

Lisa shook her head "You didn't need to get up so early."

"It's habit."

Raphael made his report on the ranch operation, and later Chet took a nap. There were stirrings about the big party coming up at the end of the week. The biggest things in store for them. All was good.

The next day Colonel Hardy Sullivan drove out to the ranch to discuss the upcoming auction of the Three V's Ranch. Sullivan had two partners, Tom Shay and Bernie Wilkerson. Their firm handled most of the large ranch and pure-breed sales in the territory. Chet considered them a very high-class set of businessmen who knew how to handle purebred livestock auctions.

Sullivan, a tall man in his forties, took his hat off when Liz invited him in and took it from him. Then she went to the living room door to tell Chet that Sullivan was there.

The two men met and shook hands in the center of the living room. Chet showed him to the leather chairs Liz had bought especially for such meetings.

"I guess you are staying up here what with that large auction date growing closer," Chet said when they took seats.

"Yes. That is typically how we handle setting them up. I wanted to talk with you and hope you would share any intentions you have about the ranch's sale, since you are the largest ranch owner in the territory that I know."

"Hardy, if I may call you that, I have been in Tucson helping prosecute some white slavers who kidnapped two young farm girls to sell in Mexico for a horrible life of prostitution. That is settled, and they won't be out of jail for years, so all I know is that Mitchel Van Roy, who died a year ago, left his widow Alice that ranch and they had no close heirs."

"Exactly. I fear her husband let his laborers only do small details, so they did not know how to run that large ranch. He ran the ranch until he died."

"My brother-in-law, Hampt Tate, who married my brother's widow May, told me all about that when we attended Mitch's funeral. Hampt knew Mitchel well. They were almost neighbors. As for my plans regarding the sale of the ranch, as of today I have no plans to be involved."

"I am disappointed to hear that, Chet. To

buy that ranch will require a person with the finances who understands ranching in this region. That ranch, in the wrong hands, or under weak management, might end up being a big problem for your operations. I am not here to force you to participate, but rather I am here to talk to you face-to-face and warn you about the possibility of this spilling over and harming your operations."

"Hardy, my men are some of the greatest ranch managers in the United States. If you think the Three V's might affect my holdings, I will gather and have them inspect the ranch's total operation. They then will tell me what they think I should do about the ranch. Thank you for your concern."

"Anything that they need, me or my partners will be glad to show them. Nothing is hidden."

"Thank you. I know you're seriously selling almost a kingdom for a poor lady."

Chet sent Fred down to the Verde Ranch to get Tom and Victor and to explain his needs from them. Then he appointed Spencer to go get Hampt.

Chet said, "You two can inspect this ranch together after we have a meeting here. Miguel, you go get Toby. Maybe he needs to bring Talley here while he helps you with

162

the inspection.

"I want every damn weakness and strength in that ranch and what you'd do if you ran it or if you had the money to buy it — or not. Simply tell him we need him for a few days on a secret project. You and Toby can appraise the ranch like the others."

Liz was laughing when they rode off in all directions, like something was on fire. "What about the party we planned?"

"Liz, I completely forgot about those plans. After the conference at the house we can make a decision about the party, but I am certain we can have it. This ranch is not a life-or-death situation, but we do need to know what we should do. I am sorry. I am counting on these leaders of mine to give me the advice I need to know to decide about whether we need the ranch or not."

"Chet Byrnes, come here. I love you." She hugged him. "Have you ever thought you have enough?"

"No. I have two sons who, someday, might want to ranch."

"Or play piano and sing?"

"They don't look like they're headed that way, but if they don't want to, they won't have to ranch." He rocked her in his arms. "This territory is fast becoming a very wanted place. If there were rail tracks up where the stage line is running that ranch would be worth four times the price it will bring in three weeks."

"You're certain of that? The train is coming, we know that. It is just a matter of when. If the value of that ranch will increase like you say, then you need to buy it."

He kissed her forehead. "I was thinking that way this morning. You and I need to look at the expenditures we will have to make on it first."

"Who would run it?" She hugged him possessively again.

"It depends on what it needs."

"I understand."

"You know what? We are having the party."

"Hey, you decided. We don't need the conference first? The party is on?"

"Damn right."

Fred, Tom, and Victor, another ranch worker, arrived at the Valley ranch first around midday. Spencer and Hampt were seconds behind them. Miguel and Toby would take more time. Lisa served coffee and rolls in the living room and everyone bragged on them.

While they drank and ate, Chet filled them in. "Miguel has gone for Toby and I sent a boy for Jesus, so he will be here shortly. The auctioneer for the Three V's Ranch, Colonel Sullivan, was here earlier. He'd like us to be bidders. I called you all in to go look and tear it apart. What all it needs. What we'd have to spend money on. Who would be the best man to run the place? I know we are all partners in these ranches, and I rely on you men a lot," Chet finished.

"While we were in Tucson, a cattle buyer named John Slaughter furnished us with some great horses to use down there. He also sold us three hundred and fifty mother cows and calves — all half British breeds or greater — as a very good deal because he needed the money immediately. He is a very nice guy and a sharp businessman. We will stock the Oracle Ranch with those cattle. That will be under way shortly."

"Fred told us about him on the way up here. That saves you a big headache and a year better start on cattle to sell," Tom said.

"Exactly. We still have to stock Rustler's Ranch, but John also gave me the name of a seller over at Socorro who sounds like the person who needs to get that ranch stocked, too."

"Chet," Hampt spoke up next. "Mitchel Van Roy's ranch has lots of old cows he should have culled. I knew him well before he died and we visited a lot. He also has some ancient mossy-horned cows he wouldn't part with."

"Tell us about his hay operation, Hampt?"

"He hated having to grow, mow, or do anything like that, so his haying operation could have been better, but there are some artesian wells up there."

"Then I will count on you figuring what we have to do, since you are the hay expert."

Everyone around the living room nodded in agreement about that.

Hampt shook his head. "A few years ago, I was unemployed when Chet came to Arizona, and if anyone'd told me I would be in charge of anything, I'd have laughed all day. But, boys, things have changed in all our lives, and I'll be the hay expert, funny as it even sounds today in my ears."

Everyone laughed and cheered him on.

"I have never been impressed with the men Mitch hired," Tom said.

"They work cheap enough," Victor said.

"That's it. Who else would have them even at that low a price?" Tom shook his head.

"I need to know if the ranch can hold the number of cattle he's currently running."

"Yes," Hampt said. "We need to look at that hard. That south half of my ranch is still recovering from being overgrazed before we bought it. And if we hadn't shipped two hundred head of mother cows to Lucy's bunch, I'd be out of grass."

"When do you want to start looking?" Chet asked.

"Since we're here," Tom said. "Let's ride over there today and tomorrow. Go home tomorrow night and come back to the party here Saturday. Monday onward, we can spend whatever time we need to wind it up."

Jesus arrived on a fast horse. Chet met him at the door going out. "You and I can talk on the way. We are going to start looking at the Three V's as a possible addition to our operation."

"I'd seen the auction posters and wondered what you'd do about it." Jesus wore a knowing grin.

"I have all these thinkers and doers on my payroll, so we will all look at it and collectively decide if I need it or not and what we need to do to make it better."

Jesus agreed with the plan.

Chet kissed Liz good-bye and rode with the others to the Three V's.

Like lots of ranchers, Mitch never strung barbed wire. He hated it. His ground was enclosed by lodgepole-like fences. It required a lot of expense and time to maintain. For Chet's part, barbed wire was the way to keep cattle out or in whatever you

167

needed to do with them.

The house was large, rambling, and in neglect but nothing that a few good men couldn't fix and paint to bring it back. Alice was a sweet old lady with arthritis-deformed hands. Chet could see she really had aged since Mitch died. They had hot tea and she asked him about his lovely wife. As they were leaving, she thanked him for coming to see her.

After his visit, he and Jesus went and studied the irrigation of some of the alfalfa fields. His first look told him they were late with the application of water. Several small leaves on the plants had already turned brown from lack of water, and he called that a "you don't give a damn" care. He found three of the workers, and made them work the water. Once the water was going down the field, it spooked bugs out of the plants and noisy killdeer were there to gobble them down. The ranch employees went and napped, on the ground in the shade, until a change was needed.

Had they ever heard of doing two things at a time? Obviously not.

Chet and Jesus found more of the small fields down the line needed water, too.

"Isn't it artesian?" Jesus asked riding along.

"I guess so. These irrigated flats are small compared to what we do at Verde. It's like he developed one, then added another and another."

Jesus chuckled. "Like he did one, then another, and said, 'Oh, hell, I need more.'"

Chet twisted in the saddle and looked back. "Exactly."

"Why are there three men irrigating?"

"Good question. I bet the others noticed that, too."

"Where are his corrals?"

"I guess farther back."

"He doesn't have many haystacks. Either old or new."

"Victor would be concerned if he was here." Chet reined up the roan horse.

Jesus did the same. "I know I am. It's midsummer. They don't have enough hay for one snowstorm, let alone more."

"I bet you have more hay at your new farm than this?"

"I sure do. My neighbor has the equipment but his mower was worn out. I bought a new one from your buddy Ben and we do it on the shares. I have lots more hay stacked on my small ranch than this place has."

"I've seen some in passing your place. Nice. Let's go find the corrals. I think the others are looking at the cattle and the stock water."

Half an hour later, they almost laughed when they arrived at the site.

"This is a horseback roundup site?" Chet said, amused. The fallen-down pens would be of little or no value, and that meant they had to hold the stock in place with riders until they could build new.

"This place will need more than three men —" Jesus was laughing hard.

"I've seen enough. Let's go home. The others can size up the rest of the deal."

"Have you decided anything?"

Chet nodded. "It will take a helluva lot of work to repair, but it could be a helluva ranch. I want the cowherd size and the range quality information. I see how this place caved in during Mitch's last years. He was like the man who slapped his son upside the head for taking a new nail to pound down a board when he still had bent ones to straighten and use instead."

Jesus laughed even harder.

"That's the truth. I knew men like that back in Texas."

"You've taken on some deals rougher than this one. What do you think about it?"

"I want the rest of them to tell me what they think."

"So if it don't work you can say you told me to go ahead?"

They both laughed all the way back to the ranch.

Toby, his wife Talley, and Miguel had just ridden in.

Liz was out greeting them. So there was handshaking all the way around.

Talley asked him if he didn't have enough places already.

"Always room for another good one. Getting any hay put up this summer?"

She gave a really smug nod. "At home we had a great crop and we have mowed three of those places that the land man bought for you. I have calluses to prove it."

"Chet, we are going to have plenty of hay, she's telling the truth," Toby said. "Three of those places were fenced and they have tons of hay stacked on them. That went real smoothly."

Chet hugged Talley. "There is a Joseph Chavez at Socorro that I am going to wire to gather cows for you."

"You found the cows for Rustler's Ranch?" Toby asked.

"Yes. We will go get them soon."

"Miguel told me about the ones you got for the Oracle Ranch, and now I am getting some, too. Thank you."

"You two and those helpers of yours have been working hard this summer."

"The boys wanted to keep working after they cleared that entire hay field. Toby asked them if they could put up hay. They said they could. I cooked and we camped at those places while we hayed them. I also mowed a lot while they stacked. Those boys worked their backsides off getting through all that hay. Now Toby has them hauling a lot of it to the home place for feed next winter. I know you're busy, but you should see it now."

"I promise I will come see it."

"Talley and I talked a lot. If we fenced three more of those homesteads that Bo bought for you, we could cut hay on all of them next year and we could run five hundred to seven fifty mother cows."

"Sounds good. If those boys still want to work, then let's fence them."

Toby winked and kissed his wife's cheek. "See, darling, that was no big deal to get him to agree to that."

"On that," she said. "I am going up to the house to talk to your women. I miss doing that."

"You still need us to go look at the ranch?" Miguel asked.

"Yes, I do. But remember, Saturday is fun

day here. Sunday is rest day. Monday go back and make a final survey of the Three V's and Tuesday we all report what we found. Toby, if you hay your place and six homesteads, that will be over a section and half of land to mow."

"I may need more than two mowers, won't I?"

"I'd say so."

Chet put his arm on the shorter man's shoulder. "You've done a great job. Thanks and you, too, Talley."

Talley paused and turned at the foot of the porch steps. "I had to." She chipped in.

"How is that?"

"First, you found me." She began to count on her fingers. "Second, you saved me from a horrible life where I was headed. Third, I needed to show Toby I was tough enough to be his wife. Fourth, I wanted to show the world I was not some dizzy lazy you-know-what."

Chet walked up and hugged her, then spun her back toward the stairs. "You are wonderful, girl. Now, get up there. Those women will talk with any old hay maker."

When she disappeared into the house, Toby said, "She misses that the most. Talking to another woman about anything. Being around those boys who idolize her she

173

speaks Spanish like she was born there. She learned that, too, on purpose, since we took over the ranch. She's my idea of what a wife is supposed to be. Maybe someday we'll have kids. I know you want some, too. One day we will both be blessed. Miguel's back and he wants to show me some things. Guess I am excused?"

"Excused is right. Toby, you are cutting a great trail. Keep up the good work."

"Thanks, I try."

He and Miguel were barely gone when Sarge, Susie, and Irwin arrived.

"Ready for the party, big brother?" she asked.

He swung her off the buckboard and on her feet.

"I damn sure am."

"Toby already here?" She straightened out her dress.

"Yes. And we are having a foreman contest here."

"What for?"

"The foremen are telling me what they think about me buying the Three V's ranch. Sarge can get into it tomorrow."

"Well" — she looked at him with a small smile — "wrestling me out of the wagon, could you tell anything?"

He laughed. "Lucy asked me two months

174

ago if you were keeping up with her."

Sarge laughed. "She is now."

"Wonderful. Get inside and talk. Talley is there, too. She's been putting up hay and wants to talk about it."

"That bunch really have been busy," Sarge said. "We put up some but they have hayed several of those homestead places. Those two are hustlers and have lots of hay. He says he will get cows this fall."

"Yes. He will. How is the Navajo deal going?"

"Super. I know Susie wrote and told you but the agent confirmed that the ring is not getting our beef contract."

"I knew that. They threatened me hard when I was in Washington D.C."

"You weren't able to do any good at all about the Navajo selling coal then?"

Chet shook his head. "Could have done more here than I did up there."

"They said you really tried and told me to tell you thanks for all you did do."

"Well, it was not much. I think the Tucson Ring had an under-the-table deal made before I got there. How is Tom's son-in-law working out for you?"

"Cody Day is really a smart young man. The men listen to him and he gets it all done. I hope I am not going to lose him?"

"Don't worry, but we need to increase his pay and get him some more time off to come back here and visit with his folks."

Sarge winced. "I've tried to get Cody to take more time off but he just shakes his head."

"Well, he needs to take some time off."

"I'll handle it. He is taking this month's cattle to New Mexico. Which gives me a breather."

"Sarge, we have come a long ways since you joined me down on the Verde."

"I have never regretted one single day doing that, Chet Byrnes."

Both men hugged and then nodded.

"I bet there is some cool tea inside."

"I'm ready."

They went into the living room.

The others rode in shortly after that.

Tom found Chet and shook his head. "Needs lots of improvement. I did some day work for him back when I was unemployed. I thought then he was letting the place fall in bad and no one was doing anything about it. I was glad to get the day work at the time and he even hinted he wanted to talk to me about a permanent job. He never did. You hired me shortly after that and I forgot about him."

"Did you think he would hire you?"

"He never really had a foreman. Oh, they called themselves that but they weren't."

"Well, I am glad he never hired you."

"Me, too. When Fred came for me last night, I talked to Millie about what you might have found."

"We better talk about that later. Let's get in a party mood. My wife was upset I was breaking up plans for the big ranch party to celebrate our victory at the trials in Tucson with our success."

Tom laughed. "Well, let's enjoy ourselves."

"Thanks."

Chet mixed and talked to the wives, listened to them, and talked to Lisa privately in the kitchen, where a half dozen ranch wives were helping her prepare the evening meal.

"You are doing great," he assured Lisa.

She rolled her eyes like she was dizzy. "I have good help. The food will be served on time. Liz says things are going fine, but it is my first test and I want it perfect."

Suppressing his laughter, he shook his head and mumbled that would be impossible.

She heard and punched his arm. "Damn you. I want it to be one hundred percent."

He patted her shoulder, and she, shaking her head, told him thanks and broke out in

177

a grin of pride.

Boy, she had made a real person out of herself.

Back in the crowded living room, Liz caught his arm. "Susie tell you?"

"As I put her down."

"I knew you were close —"

"Do not worry, my dear. We try and I am pleased to have you."

"I try not to. I know we have lots to be grateful for. How is the ranch doing?"

"The V's?"

"Of course."

Chet shook his head. "The jury is not in yet."

"Can it be saved?"

"Oh, any ranch can be revived. It is the cost that it will require to do it that worries me."

"One more thing. You recall the Talley you brought home?"

"Yes."

"She acted like marrying Toby was the last resort for her?"

"Sarge said that they have really stacked tons of hay on those fenced homesteads that Bo bought for us."

"She and Toby want a real ranch like Lucy and Shawn have. They already asked me to talk to you about it."

"Well, they damn sure might get it."

"Toby always was serious. But *Miss I really don't care* woke up out there," Liz said, laughing.

Supper was served. It was damn near perfect. The wonderful prime rib proved delightful. Lisa's roasted potatoes were done. The green beans were fresh from the garden. The yeast rolls floated on his plate. Yet another tough-cursing female he had brought back and turned wife, she was seated with her husband, who wore a snowy white starched shirt at the table, and everyone was bragging on her meal. Liz announced besides her great cooking Lisa had eleven Hispanic children enrolled in the Cherry School in grades from one to seven because of her tutoring.

When they stood and applauded her, she blushed.

After the meal and her pecan pie dessert, the women helped do the dishes while the men went out on the porch in the cooling evening.

"Tomorrow we can rest and prepare for the party. That will be another great event."

"Tell us about the trials," Hampt asked him.

"It was a white slavery ring. Men had been

selling kidnapped girls for large sums. Two were prominent Tucson businessmen, and we rounded up every one of them. It all started with the kidnapping of two farm girls from Thatcher's community. We arrested them red-handed and hauled them to the Pima County Jail until the trial. A judge listened to what we had to say, and would not bond them. We finally got one of their own to testify against them. They will be serving long prison terms. Jesus and Fred caught one of their cohorts, a slave dealer from below the border, on the U.S. side, and arrested him and brought him back for trial, too. How many innocent children they sold I can't tell, but it was more than a handful. Unfortunately this job isn't over. There are more evil men out there with no morals that must be stopped. But those two girls are safe at home tonight, thanks to my associates."

All the men nodded.

"Who among us is looking at the Three V's for our opinion about the outfit?" Hampt asked.

"Everyone on the porch. JD and Shawn are too far away to come. Monday we look again, and Tuesday I want everyone here with all your opinions."

Hampt shook his head. "It is a damn sight

better place than the Quarter Circle Z was when you bought it."

"Hampt, that ranch had a river running through it."

"I still say Mitch's place is a better buy than that was." Hampt was laughing by then.

"Boy, did I buy a wildcat by the tail?"

"And got half of us, too."

Hampt went up and hugged him. "Sarge, Tom, Cole, Jesus, and I have ridden through lots of hell to make Arizona a damn sight better place and we are still winning that war. I will be there Tuesday and proud to be invited."

"Most of you don't know Cole. He rode with Jesus and me after I was told I had to have two guards to bring me home alive. In the only battle I had with warlike Apaches I was taking our first herd to the Navajos. A war party of boys attacked us. Cole shot one. I captured one and left him to bring him in while I went to make sure we had enough cattle to feed the Navajos. When Cole caught up to us, he had no prisoner. I asked him why. He said the Apache drew a knife and he had to shoot him. Then he asked if he was fired."

Everyone laughed.

"That boy expected to lose his job. He

really was worried I would fire him. He was the one that ran the stage line and telegraph wire for me and my partners."

"Now, everyone has beds. Tomorrow is party day. Horseshoe pitching. Rifle range shooting and anyone who thinks he can ride broncs, we have some that need gentling."

They shook hands and broke up the gathering.

Liz joined him as he walked through the living room and hooked onto his arm. "How is the ranch examination going?"

"I am not asking them. Monday we go out again and reexamine it and Tuesday we gather and talk about it in the living room."

"Well, thank you. That means our party will not be interrupted by the Three V's purchase."

"Or nonpurchase."

"I doubt that." She poked him.

"We will see."

"Your friends will be here tomorrow. I invited them all."

"Cole and Val invited?" Cole Emerson was a former ranch hand, now one of Chet's guardsmen. Valerie was his wife.

"Of course, and Rocky. Rhea is bringing Adam. Victor went back to get her, him, and Millie from the Verde Ranch." Adam was Chet's son from a previous relationship.

Rhea and her husband, Victor, often took care of the boy when Chet was working.

"You do good work."

She poked him as they went up the stairs. They laughed. How nice to be back home with this lovely woman. *Thank you, Lord.*

CHAPTER 10

Morning slipped in with doves calling and quail whit wooing around the house in the cool morning air. Chet was sipping steaming coffee on the front porch as the golden sun shone slantwise across the polished floor.

"You are up early," Miguel's tall wife Lisa said while standing in the doorway with her own coffee.

"I always rise early. I have to think about what trouble I need to avoid for the day."

She chuckled. "Monica warned me, 'he will be up before you in the morning, but he knows where I keep the coffee. His will be too strong for the rest, so let him make his, and you make it for the others.' "

Chet rose and went to the edge of the porch. "There's a bald eagle up there circling this morning. I think Ben Franklin wanted the turkey to be the American bird, but they chose the eagle. He was the stronger one when it came to a fight."

He went back toward the bench and his coffee. Standing to sip it, he said, "Did you ever regret coming here?"

"Never. I came and your wife said, 'Lisa, no one here knows your past. What you do here will be what they know about you.' When Miguel first spoke to me, I froze and wondered if he knew about me. We started to talk, and I let things progress to see if he really wanted me.

"I asked Liz if I should go ride with him. She said, 'If your heart tells you to ride with him, but only if your heart tells you to.' I had to think about what she said. She told me of her first day with you. I was not in a rush. If he was really in love with me, he, too, had time to wait. I felt that when I was strong enough to tell him the truth about my past and he accepted it and me — I would know. I did."

"That is a great story. Almost as good as the one about Liz and my meeting down at Tubac."

"Don't you ever think I was ungrateful for you bringing me here. I never thought anything horrible riding down here with you. I thought I was tough and mean enough to make it on my own. I quickly saw I wasn't that person and I am happy. Liz told me that the longer Miguel rides with you the smarter he will be. I see that happening and he also learned to read — that from me. I am so proud of him."

"He will learn it all. I know you love Liz, but why did you take Monica's job?"

"Oh, I have so much I want to learn about being a real woman. Doing this job I am learning something new every day. Never worry about me. If I was not here, I could never do any of this and expand my mind."

"Thanks. I will remember that. We are glad you chose to do it. You are doing great."

"I hope so. You ready to eat breakfast?"

"Yes. Where is Miguel?"

"He and Raphael are checking cows. He is teaching Miguel how to tell if a cow has a calf in her."

Chet narrowed his eyes at her. "Seriously? Do they punch her?"

"No they simply ride by her."

Chet was amused but curious about the method as he followed her into the kitchen.

She looked over her shoulder. "Miguel says Raphael can see if a cow is carrying a calf by the dark greasy hair on the cow from the tail forward."

"That sounds simple enough."

"Miguel wants to use it riding through the Three V's herd. He says some of the bulls are old and he fears there are not enough of them to breed all the cows."

"You two make a great pair."

"He asked me one morning where else could we learn so much working for people we like. I told him nowhere."

"I won't let him know you told me this."

"Thanks. I really care about you and thank you for all you do." She soon had a meal of scrambled eggs, ham, and biscuits on a plate in front of him.

After his meal he went by the ranchmen busy setting up tables under the huge tent he had bought from a circus stranded in Prescott several years earlier. One of the wives was making sure they were spaced just so, two more washed them and were critical of any with a problem. Everyone was cheery and happy.

Hispanic people knew how to celebrate. They could have less than anyone and still celebrate. It was in their blood. His wife, too, had the same blood flow in her when it came time for the excitement of a party. He loved it.

His gringo friends would all attend, sharing the fun of eating with him, his crew, and their families. It was tradition.

All his operations ran so smoothly that when he had time to stop and breathe, he felt guilty about not doing something.

People began to arrive and the hands parked their buggies and rigs. Others came on horseback, and were tied up at hitch lines. Stallions were put up into pens to save a war starting. There was cold beer in kegs. Cold tea, sweet or without, lemonade, and even some good whiskey at the bar.

The mesquite smoke of the cooker joined with the sizzling aroma of cooking beef and pork filled the air. Baked potatoes, boiling frijoles, garden veggies steaming, and hot bread and tortillas. For dessert, fruit or pecan pies and a towering cake.

The musicians in the background were playing guitars, accordions, drums, and fiddles. The sun hadn't set yet, but the Chinese lanterns were ready to light the night. The guests were hungry.

Bo Evans, Chet's real estate broker, who'd always done good work for Chet, arrived with his very pregnant wife, Shelly, and their young son, Lawrence. The boy ran to Chet like he really knew him. The three of them laughed.

"Seems like you have lost your son," Chet teased.

"Oh? Then I will just need to make another."

His wife shook her head. "Two is enough."

It was all in fun and when Liz joined them she just had to say hello to the little boy.

"He is sure growing. He will be a big boy sooner than you can imagine."

Chet motioned Bo aside. "You know those five homesteads we now own between Rustler's Ranch and Sarge's? Toby and his crew have already put up all the hay on those fenced-in ones and they are now ready for cows."

"Holy cow. That's lots of acres to mow and stack." Bo looked astonished at the news.

"They said next year all of those places will be fenced and hayed."

Bo shook his head.

"Toby and his wife are damn hard workers and are determined to have the best ranch in our whole bunch."

"I'll find him and congratulate him."

"His wife, too. They are tough kids. Oh, and I met a man, John Slaughter, over near Tucson, who is gathering cows for the Oracle Ranch. He also told me about another man who will supply me cows for Toby and his Rustler's Ranch."

"That is really getting things done. I understand you are looking at the Three V's Ranch."

"My foremen are. I am asking their opinions on Tuesday."

"I understand there are several out-of-state people with deep pockets looking at it. But we both know it will take a real superintendent to make a ranch out of it like yours, and it needs to be someone who knows all about our Arizona seasons."

"Why, buddy, any old boy could do that," Chet said, smiling.

Bo shook his head. "You may know one, but I bet they don't and it won't work. When Mitch's health failed that ranch began to go downhill and it's been on a snow slide to hell ever since."

"I have entrusted consideration of this purchase to my foremen, and they will tell me what I must do to make it work. They know. They have been running all my ranches."

"I think it may sell too high."

"If I go for it, I will set a limit. If it goes over, they can have it."

"Good. And good luck." Bo shook his head and told his wife, "Go get a plate of food. I will hold him."

"Good to see you, Chet, as always." Shelly went off for the food and talked to two other women.

"Bo, you have a nice wife."

"She was married for ten years to her first husband and never had a baby."

They both smiled.

Chet left shaking his head. Bo was Bo, but he was sober and stayed that way.

Chet spoke to Ben and his wife, Kathrin, telling him they might have a record amount of hay cut with the new machinery.

"Well, you sure have several of them."

"I know how hard you worked to get them out here."

"You have a babysitter tonight?" Chet asked.

"We do." She laughed. "Chet Byrnes, I still owe you for freeing me."

"Your debt is paid."

"No. I met Liz's new in-charge of the house lady, Lisa. We shared some similar tales about coming to Prescott. She is another person who also owes you her life. And she seems special."

"Liz has a friend and partner in her. We miss Monica, but Lisa is great and she works hard doing most all of it herself. You two get busy eating and enjoying our party."

"We heard part of the story about the trials. Those two girls are at home now?" Kathrin asked.

"Yes. Safe and I am sure they will be able

to overcome anything in their lives, after living through that. Those criminals will serve long terms in prison."

"God bless you and thank you for having us as part of your family."

"Thanks."

Lisa brought him a plate of food and told him to join his wife, like a schoolteacher would a sixth grader.

He was still smiling as he sat down at the table beside Liz on the platform.

"What is so funny?"

He shook his head. "My boss, Lisa, told me I must get up here and eat with you."

"Good for her. She doesn't want you wasting away."

"That won't happen for a long while."

"It could. I know you like to meet and greet but you also have a position to hold."

"But I am very simply Chet Byrnes. A marshal and a rancher."

"Maybe you view yourself as that person, but you bear the burden of this whole empire on your shoulders. You don't have to act like a king, but you are their leader."

"I like to meet my friends when they come to my house."

"I know. You did and now I felt you needed to be here."

"Ain't worth arguing over. This is a lovely party. They did a great job with this beef."

Her hand squeezed his arm. "They always do."

She was right. His outfit knew how to make good meals and have fun fandangos.

Tuesday morning rolled around fast for the final vote on the Three V's. After an especially nice breakfast, everyone moved into the living room, where two ranch girls kept checking on them, keeping them in coffee and anything they needed. Chet felt that it was good for the men to mix like this once in a while, and he was confident that his men would come up with the answers on the ranch.

Lisa set Spencer up with a thin board to go across the Morris chair arms as a desk. Everyone was seated, and Tom began the conversation.

"Several of us knew Mitch and he had lots of good ideas that built that ranch, but he should have retired and let someone else lead when age and his aches and pains took over his body. We all found lots of steers that should have been marketed. He sold some to me for Sarge's project. He sold some to butchers down in the gold camps in the Bradshaws, but there are lots more that needed to be off his range and turned into cash.

"Many old cows should have been culled. His watering holes need repairing. There are tanks that have holes so a lot leaks out into the sand. Corrals are beyond using. I'll yield to Hampt, who is next."

Hampt cleared his throat. Hunched forward on the couch, he shook his bare head and shoved back a curled lock. "That's exactly what I saw. There are three guys there to irrigate and all they do is open a gate. The fields of hay are too small and unyielding. The alfalfa needs to be reseeded. Here it is midsummer and every one of us have our winter hay stacked. Just by a wild ass guess I'd say they have half enough feed as they need if we have a snowy winter. They need more hay land and I think it could be done. They have artesian wells. There is large sagebrush flat that needs to be cleared, sown, and a new well drilled to water it. Those small plots are fine for a small operation, but that place needs to be expanded. Can I add more later?"

"Sure. Victor?"

"I will say that Hampt saw the same thing I did. That place needs more farmland opened up. Those few-acre patches are not the answer for us to get up enough hay."

"Anything else?"

"Chet, I'll let the others keep going, and maybe on the end I can add some things."

"Thanks, Victor. Jesus?"

"Their horses are all old. Most of his help is old, too. Mitch was old. One thing I would bet on is that not one horse in their *remuda* would buck."

"So we need a new string of saddle stock."

"My legs would get tired keeping them walking."

"Anything else?"

"What count does the auctioneer give on the cattle they have?"

"Approximately three hundred and fifty plus."

"And a hundred need culled."

"That's one out of three?"

"There are at least that many old ones I saw."

Nods around the room told him they all agreed.

"Sarge, I won't leave you out."

"I am learning a lot here. I take the good cattle you guys send me to the Navajos. That bunch I saw down there are a mess. I agree the hay business is not good. I didn't see the new hay land when I rode the place because I am not a farmer. But to cut those small patches and even irrigate them is for a small farmer not a ranch operation."

"Spencer?"

"Whoever buys it needs new help. Everything has fallen down, and nothing is being fixed. I woke up Sunday morning, here, to hammering. Raphael noticed the barn needed some repairs, so he was already out there fixing it, like it was that important. No one noticed or did anything on that place in years. His bulls looked like a ragged Mexican army. They are every breed and form of cattle known to man."

Everyone laughed.

"Anything else?"

"Yes, from a contractor's standpoint. The new foreman will probably have to work every Sunday for a year to get things straightened out."

"Toby?" Chet asked.

"Get the cull cows off it. Sell the marketable cattle. Replace the sorry bulls and let the range recover with the numbers left. Each year save half the heifers and grow it back into a working ranch. It will take three years and rain to make a difference."

"Thanks, Toby. Many of you know Toby has a two-year hay supply on hand for his new herd. His wife Talley was a big part of that job."

"Miguel?"

"My father and I rode though the cows. I know Raphael is not my real father, but I feel he is. This man has an eye for things. He can ride though a herd of cows and tell you the ones that will calf and won't. I suspect the sorry bull situation up there is the culprit, but according to his looking at many of them he's saying only half will breed back. That means next year's calf crop will be around a hundred and twenty. That number will not cover the labor costs alone."

"Do you have a solution?"

"The bull situation needs to be fixed now. Try to get them all bred as soon as possible. Even later calves would be better than none. If we could get that many more bred, it would help next year. There are lots of cows that did not calf this year but they will next year."

"Miguel, we all need a class in how to tell if a cow will breed," Hampt said. The others agreed.

"It isn't hard. I think he taught me that in one day."

"So we all heard this ranch is in decay. Can we make it work? Show me hands.

"Spencer, may I ask why you don't think so?"

"We are stocking two ranches now. The Slaughter cattle were a good buy for the

197

Oracle Ranch. Then we have a cattle drive from Socorro to Toby and the Rustler's Ranch up on the General Crook Road. Personally I wouldn't touch the Three V's Ranch with a long pole."

"Spencer, look at my place. The Verde Ranch was more rundown than the V's place. We ran off the foreman and made it work," Tom said.

"Yes, but you had the Verde River, too."

"That place isn't badly watered though there are portions that need to be worked on. But for an Arizona ranch it isn't a dust bowl."

"Before we clear that sagebrush, I'd damn sure want a strong artesian well up and working."

Tom agreed and sat back.

Toby struggled up to his feet. "We have Rustler's Ranch ready for cattle. Chet gave me all the means to clear land, build corrals, and fix the house. Bo bought us homesteads fenced that made perfect hay patches. We mowed and stacked them with hand laborers who work hard. Next year we will have two more fenced for hay. We get this herd settled we can build to eight hundred head of mother cows on that place. I say buy it." He sat down.

Miguel stood and nodded. "We can handle it."

Sarge stood next. "More work on your shoulders, Chet, but you are great at these takeovers. I vote buy it."

Jesus rose and nodded. "We have not failed at anything we have done. And I want to vote for Shawn, Cole, Robert, and may as well vote for JD, your nephew, as well. Buy it right and we can make it a great spread."

"Spencer, they change your mind?"

"I say yes."

"I am not going through the roof on the price. Bo and I will set a goal price and if it exceeds that we will quit bidding. I thank all of you for coming. I'll let you know what happens."

They all shook his hand and left but Toby, who hung back.

"You have something on your mind?"

"I do, and I want your permission. Talley and I never had a real honeymoon. I'd like to have a real one in Prescott at a hotel, eat out, get her some nice new dresses so she can wear them when she comes to town with me to get supplies."

"The whole deal is on me. Get a suit to wear for yourself. You've done well, and I am proud of the two of you."

"I have money set aside —"

"My treat. Charge it to me. And have a good time doing it."

"Thanks a lot."

"You two take a buckboard to town and really enjoy yourselves."

They shook hands and Chet went to find Fred.

He had a young horse in the round pen making him gallop. Horses running in a round pen think they can escape. Chet took a place to watch. When Fred stopped him, the horse looked confused. Fred never raised his voice but insisted the horse come to him.

Twice the horse started forward and twice he tossed his head like he had enough and wished to be free, but Fred continued to talk to him. At last the pony came to him and they walked away together.

"Nice horse."

"He will make one. Your nephew found him for me. I paid for him myself. I hope you don't mind feeding him?"

"No problem. I didn't hear your ideas on the ranch."

"Personally it would scare me to death to be responsible for that mess. But I am not you and have no experience on fixing up such a down-at-the-heels place."

"You'd be afraid of the job?"

"Chet, I hate to fail at anything. Especially since you gave me a chance to work here for you. I consider my being here my last chance to make it good in the world and to not have to sleep in the alleys of Prescott. I never owned anything worth ten cents that belonged to me. Now I have a saddle, a horse, and a job and, oh yes, a bank account."

"It all sounds good. What about the Three V's?"

"There was so much wrong I couldn't start to fix. You see where someone shot up that rooster wind vane on the house?"

"No, I missed it."

"Those featherless chickens running around that place — Jesus told me that was because they had poor diets. I have no idea what to feed chickens to make them grow feathers. The rosebushes all died because no one watered them and they never pulled the bare plants out. I bet when they bloomed they were beautiful. The peeling paint on the house, broken windows boarded over rather than replaced. That porch needs new boards. It's a death trap. Only one hitch rack. The other two need a top rail. I could go on and on."

"No one else saw that. How would you

have seen that place before you came out here?"

"A poor place to ask for work. They could not afford to fix it and they probably could not pay me."

"You are getting an education."

"Oh, big classes of things. But I'd have voted with Spencer's first vote. Forget it."

"There is something else that bugs you."

He chewed on his lower lip. "Yes, but I didn't want to say anything. Now you've asked, I had a girlfriend when we lived in the alleys, who meant a lot to me and who I still worry about. I know we are kids, but we were more than that. I was so damn glad to escape that life I forgot about her. No, not forgot, but my thoughts about her were set aside. She may hate me to death by now, but is there a place for her here, if she will come with me?"

"I am sure we can find a place, if that is what she wants."

"Lisa told me about you bringing her back from Colorado. Talley told me the same story and there have been others."

"Yes."

"Ben's wife at the store told me you saved her life, too."

"You want to go into town and try to find her?"

"Yes. I want to clean up, go into town, and try to find her and convince her to come out here. I will tell her not for me but for her safety and if we get together, fine, but if not she will have a way of escaping the way she is living now. I've got enough money I'd give her to escape if she won't come."

"Do it."

"Thanks. Oh and I have been thinking I could fix that house up like new."

"Get going."

"Yes sir, soon as I get Stormy put up."

"He's a grand horse."

"I thought so, too."

An hour later, cleaned up, Fred took the number two buckboard to town. Chet had told him Talley and Toby had the number one reserved for them for their honeymoon. Fred laughed and agreed they needed one, hard as they worked.

After lunch it was cool enough to sit on the front porch and explain to Liz about the next arrival that might come to the ranch.

"Did you even catch her name?"

Chet shook his head. "Fred wasn't even sure she'd come out here. But he felt guilty in his own flight not to have brought her out of there."

"Were they having an affair?"

"I suspect they may have been living together under those unrespected conditions."

"He never said?"

"Fred was very closemouthed. He did say Lisa and Talley told him about their journeys here and Ben's wife did, too."

"If she'll comes back with him, I will request she sees a doctor and be certain she's healthy."

"That is up to you. I have no idea about her except she is what they call part of the street people."

"Was Val the first one you helped?"

"Yes, Cole's wife, Valerie, wanted out. She hated the role and immediately went to being a waitress and she guided us to Jenn's daughter, Bonnie, who would not leave that life at the time."

"But in the end you got her back from the kidnappers by paying a powerful man in Mexico with golden horses."

"Yes. Had I not done that you and I may have never met."

"How true. I thought about my checking on this big rancher at his office — a rough ranch place, but there he was hat in hand. The most gorgeous man I had ever seen and he took me wading. God wanted us together. That is the only answer."

Chet smiled at the memory, then frowned. "I think you had better warn Lisa that sometime in the next twenty-four hours Fred will probably be bringing back another lost girl. I have no doubts about that."

"He's grown up a lot in the few months he has been here. I am anxious to see his woman. We will welcome her, but she may not want to stay here."

"He knows that. He never spoke at the foremen's meeting, but I went and found him working a new horse. He noticed the wind vane on the house was all shot up. I never saw that. He also noticed that all the roses had died from not being watered. He even asked Jesus why the chickens had no feathers. Jesus told him they had the wrong diet. That was his picture of the place."

"He was observant."

"I could tell he's been worrying about it for a while. No use talking more about this until we see what happens."

"Okay. Will you buy the ranch?"

"I will only bid so much."

"I understand. There was lots of talk at the party, and some big buyers are supposedly coming in for the sale. I think your other young foreman, Toby, has certainly learned a lesson or two. This honeymoon trip they are taking is very nice for them, but I still remember Talley not at all certain she should marry him. I think she thought she had no other prospects and didn't want to be an old maid. She's curbed lots of her mouthy ways and found this man she married was a real worker and he matched her better than she even dreamed he could. I am just pleased they have not killed one another and are really taking a honeymoon."

"They have done a miracle job amid Indian attacks and all. Those were simple boys he took up there to clear his meadow, yet they put up an enormous amount of feed. We will get him the cows he needs. That will be a great ranch when all is said and done. We are damn lucky."

"No. You can pick people who lead and want the same goals you want. You have money set aside to pay more than all your bills and debts. You make my head spin at times, but I am so pleased to be your wife and see this empire expand. You are an amazing man."

Fred didn't return that night, and while eating breakfast, Chet worried if his man was all right. He and Lisa had the kitchen to themselves while he ate and she sipped coffee.

"Do we know her name?" Chet asked, breaking from his eating to drink some of his own coffee.

"Josey. I think. He never talked much about her, but it was eating him up how he escaped and left her behind."

"He's talked some about living like that. But yesterday was the first time he mentioned he left a girl behind."

"We talked pretty frankly about my life. I told him my past was soiled and I came here and started anew. No one has shunned me, and Miguel knows all about it and accepts me. Val, too. Bonnie with JD. And even Talley. I am so happy those two are really going to make it, and that they went to have a honeymoon to make up for the one they didn't have."

"Happy times are here again."

"I hope so for Fred and Josey, if that is her name, too."

Chet went about his bookwork. The day passed quickly and close to suppertime someone was ringing the yard bell. Liz came in the office. "Is there a fire?"

They both rushed out on the porch and there stood Fred holding a girl in a deep blue dress in his arms. She was laughing, kicking her feet and legs while he waltzed her around in circles.

"This is Josey. My wife," he said to a vaquero's wife who was standing the closest.

"Welcome to the Prescott Valley ranch, Mrs. Taylor," Chet said as he and Liz reached them.

"You must be Chet Byrnes, his boss."

"And you are his wife, I hear."

"And you are even prettier than he described," Josey said, turning to Liz. "Put me down. I won't run away, Fred, I promise."

"I ain't so sure. You tried to, a few times."

"You crazy guy. Put me down."

He did and laughed — she did, too, and hugged Liz.

"When were you married?" Liz asked.

"We woke up a preacher about midnight to marry us." She began to cry. "He found me yesterday. I thought he would never come back, and here he came all dolled up." She wiped her eyes with Liz's handkerchief. "When I shook my head at his request he got real demanding — how he had a good job with you and we could live on the ranch — I still was shaking my head — he did not understand. I told him I was with child. He asked whose. I told him his. He said good, good I was going to have a baby, and then he said we needed to get married. I demanded to know why he was even back

208

here, that he'd left me. He told me he was back and was going to marry me and bring me back here. A nice preacher married us, we slept in the same hotel as Toby and Talley, and today he bought me two new dresses. I am so glad to meet you and that you have not yet ran us off the place."

"Nobody is going to run you off. Are they, Chet?"

"No one will do that. Welcome to the Byrnes Ranch family."

She hugged him. "It is pretty serious being in a family way without anything but your wits. God answered my prayers. He really did."

Liz shooed the crowd away. "You all will meet Fred's wife Josey in time. Now we need to feed her and find her a room in the house to rest. She has had an exciting time coming here."

After the newlyweds went off to their bedroom, Chet and Liz were in the living room visiting about her.

"She doesn't talk tough, does she?"

"I don't believe she is tough."

"She sounds religious."

"I think she has a story that she may tell when she knows us better."

"I agree."

"Well, matchmaker and boss man, should

209

we go to bed?"

"Yes, I am glad the suspense is over."

"Yes."

They went upstairs to bed.

Chet lay there for a long time thinking about how every couple got together. Finally he slipped off.

CHAPTER 11

They fixed Josey's hair. The doctor found no signs of disease, and she was healthy, as was the baby. She fit into the house as Lisa's shadow and looked and acted like a very happily married young woman.

Two men came by to meet Chet. His business partner, Hannagen, had sent the men, who wanted his opinion on what the Three V's needed if they bought it. Ruben Coleman and Arthur Regis were from St. Louis and both told him they wanted to be in on the western expansion with a large ranch operation.

"Before I tell you what I think," Chet began. "I have been running a ranch since I was sixteen. Here and earlier in Texas. For now, there is no railroad to export cattle from up here. That shortens the market. From Texas we drove cattle to Abilene. There was grass and water all the way there. We drive cattle from near here to Gallup using water the Navajos allow us to use. At times we must freight hay just to get them there. There aren't any nearby packing plants who slaughter cattle."

Coleman leaned in close to Chet. "Mr. Hannagen says you are a doer. He doubts there would ever have been a stage line or telegraph if you hadn't gotten it done."

"My men do good work," Chet said.

"Obviously they do. This place looks like a storybook deal."

"I have a ranch I am setting up fifty miles from a new railroad track coming to Tucson," Chet answered. "It will have a good set of cattle on it shortly. A new quality headquarters that will be finished and a real ranch superintendent who knows how to run a ranch and will stay."

"What do you want for it?" Regis asked

"Finished. Three hundred fifty thousand."

"When will it be ready?" Regis asked.

"It will all be done by the first of the year."

"Why sell it?"

"I can part with it for a profit."

"How many acres?"

"Forty sections deeded land."

"It is ready to go?" Coleman asked.

"In my opinion, yes."

Regis chuckled. "You sell us a ranch and we won't bid against you here."

"No, you can still buy another."

Regis shook his head. "When can we see it?"

"I will check with my men and have an answer in the morning."

"Is it this cool down there?"

"It is. It's on Mount Lemon."

When they left for the day he told Liz he might have sold Oracle Ranch.

"For how much?"

"Three hundred fifty thousand dollars."

She blinked her lashes. "Really."

"I priced it. We can show it."

"Do they want Mitch's place, too?"

"I told them selling cattle without a railroad here would be tough."

"That was the truth."

He hugged her and laughed. "If I can sell the Oracle place, it will be a nice cushion for the rest of our businesses."

Spencer and Jesus took the two men, by stage, to Tucson and then by buckboard to examine the property. In four days Regis wired that they wanted the ranch. For Chet to hold it for them while they arranged the money.

He and Liz danced around the room.

Josey came in and looked bug-eyed at them.

"We are celebrating," Liz said. "We sold

our first ranch."

"Did it sell good?"

"Yes," Liz said. "It sold very well."

"Lisa called from the kitchen. Lunch is ready."

"We are coming," he said, herding the women into the dining room.

After lunch a boy on horseback brought a telegram from Spencer and Jesus asking if they should remain down there and move the cattle to the ranch.

He replied.

HIRE ENOUGH DAY HELP TO GET THEM THERE. TAKE YOUR TIME. THANKS FOR YOUR TAKING CHARGE. THEY WANT THE RANCH. CHET BYRNES

Fred and Josey were living in the house. Both were quiet but very much honeymooners. Lisa and Miguel had been residents for almost a year and they, too, were nearly invisible. Chet informed them he wanted to go up to Flagstaff to talk to Cole about a letter he received from Hannagen in Gallup.

Dear Chet,

I want to warn you but this is secret.

The railroad officials have approached me regarding them purchasing the telegraph company. They want nothing said about it and are offering a very top price for it.

I am inquiring as to your opinion since you are part owner and a very good friend of mine. We have done considerable work and we hold the keys to controlling it. They can't get a competing line built with government money as we did so their costs will be very high. Keep this in mind. I won't do anything unless we talk face-to-face. But understand if we want top price we need to move on it.

Your Partner

Chet sent him a wire that told him to make them buy the stagecoach line as well. It would close when they completed the track across the territory, so let them own it until then if they want the telegraph bad enough.

He was convinced that if the railroad wanted the wire they'd pay for the stagecoach line as well. Better than them having to have a closing sale and dealing with it all. That was why he wanted to go see Cole, to see what he wanted to do if it all took place.

He could understand Cole leaving him if he was offered a job to stay. But that was to be his decision.

Chet left with Miguel and Fred plus two packhorses, bedrolls, and camping gear and some food for along the way to Flagstaff. The horses were calm and they jogged off. This was Fred's first turn at being an actual guard for Chet.

Chet had to reassure Liz he would be safe with those two. Both men were extremely loyal and while they were new at the task, the trip to Flagstaff would not have much exposure to ambush. They rode off the mountain for the Verde ranch. That would give Chet an hour with his son Adam at the big house with Rhea and Victor before they pushed on toward the rim.

Tom came over as he played with Adam and they visited.

"You decided about the ranch?" Tom asked.

"No but I sold the Oracle place to two men who came to look at the Three V's."

"You sold a ranch?"

"I priced it for three hundred fifty thousand dollars and they took it."

"Wow. That is a good price."

"I thought so, but we have to finish the place. Jesus and Spencer are settling the

Slaughter cows up there while they are there. If the sale backs out, we will still be all right."

"I wondered about that."

"No problem. How are the Herefords?"

"Good calf crop on the ground. Ninety-seven percent. I have some good hands and they make sure the cows have milk and everything else when the calf hits the ground. They baby some who may be born early but it works. We have two hundred purebred cows now."

"Sounds good."

"You be careful. I can send a hand or two if you need extra."

"I will be fine. Thanks."

Chet waved good-bye to his son and they forded the shallow Verde and began to cross the valley and, in the sundown, climbed the steep Military Road. They made camp and had some jerky and coffee that had boiled on their fire before turning in. The morning was cool and they hustled to get repacked and on the road. Chet liked the two men's eagerness. He had no qualms about his others, but these two were really on the ball. Loaded and mounted, they rode north. In the early afternoon they checked in with Betty, Robert's wife. She came out to greet them with her baby girl Caroline in her arms.

"Robert will be sorry he missed you."

"Tell him not to worry. He does great work. We may catch him going home."

They waved and rode on.

They were almost there. They stopped at the Pine Flats store/bar, and Chet started toward the door ready to buy some hard candy for the kids in the stagecoach compound.

There were several people coming and going through the entrance. He read anger in a man's face and eyes when he saw Chet, and he went for his gun. A woman screamed and everyone tried to get out of the way, which impeded him from drawing his own gun. Jammed back to the wall by a big man rushing to escape, Chet finally had the gun in his hand.

The man had his gun up at arm's length aiming, when Chet shot him in the chest. He went over backward and his bullet went in the ceiling. The store boiled with gun smoke and coming through that veil, guns drawn, were both his men.

"Who is he?" Chet asked the room.

People going by to escape the burning fumes shook their heads about his identity and hurried out with their purchases.

Both of his men stood there with their guns drawn.

"Who is he?" Miguel asked as he knelt down beside his boss.

"He's dead." Chet holstered his gun. "You ever see him before?"

"Not that I recall, but he recognized me and went for his gun. Folks stampeded over us though I still managed to get off the first shot."

"I want to know why he wanted to kill you," Fred said, angry as all hell.

A man in an apron came from behind the counter. "He don't live around here. I never seen him before. You guys going to haul him outside?"

"Damn right." Miguel handed the letters he removed from the dead man's vest to Chet, then he and Fred carried him out the door and laid him on the ground. The curious crowded around to see the corpse while Chet read the name on the envelope. Phillip Jordan. Meant nothing to him.

Why in the hell would he want him dead? The address was general delivery Camp Verde, Arizona Territory.

Had he been waiting around there to ambush him? He read the letters' content.

Phil,

Be very careful he has many employees in that area who will defend him. The thousand-dollar reward for his death is only if he is dead. I know you are capable, but he is a very deadly man with handguns. He will be traveling through there at different times. He has several guardsmen who ride with him. Kill them, too.

Frank

This guy was a hired killer? Who in the hell was Frank? It was mailed from Tombstone. Who wanted him dead? Damn, this incident was one more unexplained attempt like the street shoot-out.

Letter two:

Phil,

The money is enclosed to cover your expenses to get to Prescott. His ranch is about five miles east. I would not suggest you approach that area. It is well guarded. He also goes often to this place they now call Flagstaff where he has a stage line and telegraph wire. I cannot tell you often enough but haste is needed. You know your business. Get him buried.

"What do we do with him?"

"Pay someone to bury him."

"Damn, don't ever go in anywhere we have not checked first," Miguel said as Chet paid a man two dollars to bury the gunman.

"I won't. Fred, go buy two dollars' worth of hard candy for the kids. That was all I was going in there for."

"I'll get it."

"Gather the horses. I want to get to the headquarters. That was crazy." He stepped into the saddle and took the reins of Fred's mount. When he came out, he put the large sack in Chet's saddlebags, took his reins, and they left.

"Is there an organization down there after you?"

"I am going to have to figure it out. I think he was shocked to see me. And in the wild rush I was lucky to shoot him before he shot me. I'd thought an assassin would be more discreet than that. He was like those three that came out of the alley and tried to gun us down."

"We need to go down there and dig them out. I can go back in rags and find them."

"We may need to do that before this is over."

"Well, they are not too smart sending only one guy to kill you."

"Crooks are not known for being smart, Fred."

They rode into the stage line headquarters a few hours later. Val shouted to them and, with little Rocky beside her, they came to greet them.

"How are you, big man?" Chet stepped down and hauled him in the air. The boy really was getting big.

"I am so glad you came," Rocky said. "I have my pony. He is real good, too."

"Chief Manuelito sent him to Rocky," Val said. "He is a dandy."

"I'll see you ride him, Rocky. Where is Cole?"

"Anything wrong?" Val asked.

"Things are going on underfoot. I need to talk them over with Cole."

"He's in the main office."

"I can find him. Love you." He kissed her forehead. That made her smile.

"How is Liz?" she asked.

"She sends her love." He headed for the office building.

In the door way, his tall buddy shook his

hand. "What's up?"

"It is private. We need to talk."

"My office has no ears." He showed Chet into his office. They sat.

"This is highly secret. The railroad wants to buy the telegraph line so they don't have to build one of their own, I guess. Hannagen wrote they are willing to pay lots for it."

"What does he want to do?"

"If we get enough money, sell it of course. I came up here to tell you if they offer you a big job to take it."

"I don't know if I want a job with someone looking over my shoulder like I expect they'd have for me."

"If I sell my share you are entitled to a portion of it."

"Chet, I don't need a desk. I'd come back and ride with you or look after a ranch."

"You might rise to vice president working for them."

"I have enjoyed this job once we got it settled down, but I'd take a horse under me any day. Money is not all of it. What about the stage line?"

"The stage line dies when the train tracks go through. I suggested we sell it to them as well. If we keep it we will have to have an auction so if we can make the railroad take it, we will get back our full investment of the stage line."

"Whew. I knew that would come someday. It has lots of my sweat and blood in it."

"We can get that out of the stage line, too."

"Hey, the inevitable was coming. They are crossing western New Mexico now with tracks."

Chet stood up and stretched. "We can talk more after I hear from Hannagen."

The pine trees around the headquarters made for a nice picture from the window. Chet turned back. "Oh, and I have sold the Oracle Ranch to some investors."

"Get a good price?" Cole frowned as if taken aback by the news.

"Three hundred fifty thousand dollars."

"Whew. Do you even have a hundred thousand in it?"

"No. There are lots of things we still need to fix for the sale, but it is a good price."

"Everyone is talking about the Three V's auction. They say it may bring half a million dollars."

"No telling. My bunch appraised it. Spencer said not to buy it, then changed his mind. It needs lots of things. Miguel and Raphael rode through and say as of now half the cows are not bred back. The others all had comments on the land and buildings."

"That would hurt, about the cows."

"I had two investors Hannagen sent to me about the Three V's that are now taking the Oracle Ranch. With the Three V's, the railroad will be over three years getting here. Where could they sell their cattle?"

"Chet Byrnes, I have to say you have gotten some big things done since that first drive we made to Gallup."

"On the way here, an assassin tried to shoot me down on Pine Flats today. I never saw him before. We were in a crowd at the store entrance."

"What did you do?"

"I gave a guy two bucks to bury him. The gunman was connected to a guy named Frank in Tombstone."

"Never heard of him."

"I bet no one else has, either. But I have his handwriting which may be worth something."

"Hey, let's go eat supper. Val and Rocky will be there. Who came with you?"

"Fred and Miguel. Spencer and Jesus are waiting for the cattle I bought for the Oracle Ranch, and the cattle go with the deal. They are great cross cows with calves that I bought to make money. The men that bought the ranch will make money and, if they have a good manager running their

225

outfit, they will have real headquarters to come visit in the winter."

Cole locked the office, and they went to the building where they fed the workers.

Rocky came to meet them and hung on to both of their hands to take them to the table. "Here she is."

"You get all your business done?" Val asked.

"Most of it," Cole said and waved Chet's men to come over and sit with them.

"Good. Now tell me more about Liz."

"Doing well. She and Lisa have a dozen ranch kids in the Cherry School. They coach them when they come home so they understand better."

"Lisa is doing Monica's job?"

"Don't worry about her, Val," Miguel said. "My wife loves it all. She has lots of energy. And you can bet she learns lots of things every day."

"Wish my husband thought that about me."

Cole shook his head at her. They all laughed.

Chet said, "Lisa is a real force at the house."

"Fred, how about you?"

"My wife's name is Josey. She supports Lisa."

"Oh. New?"

Fred agreed. "Pretty new. A week, huh?"

Chet nodded. "Yes. Fred and Josey were reunited and married last week."

"Welcome to the ranch," Val said. "Chet saved my life and this tall cowboy married me. Then Chet and Liz lent me Rocky to raise. I am the luckiest woman on this earth."

"I was on my own for two years in the alleys of Prescott. I am even luckier being here and Josey is with me now."

She reached over and squeezed his hand. "God bless you and Josey, too."

"Thank you, ma'am. I have a lot to learn, and I am learning. Miguel and I watch for Chet the best we can. We had an incident today. A man tried to shoot Chet. Chet had him buried."

"I am glad you two ride with him. Cole did it for years and he learned how to run a business doing it."

"I know about that. I hope I can follow in his footsteps."

"You will. You will. I am anxious to meet your wife."

"You will."

Chet sent a telegram to Hannagen that he was in Flagstaff, checking on things if he needed him.

When he awoke there was one waiting for him at the desk.

CHET. I AGREE ABOUT THE STAGE BUSINESS. IT IS IN THE DEAL. THEY ARE GETTING MORE SERIOUS. YOU MAY NEED TO AGREE BY WIRE. HAN-NAGEN.

"Hannagen says they are serious, which means he may think they are at the peak price. The stage business is in there, too."

"How much would that be?" Cole asked outside the tent.

"He has the cost there. I hope he doubles it."

Cole grabbed him. "So do I."

They went in to join the rest.

"Hey Rock, I want to see that horse when you get through eating."

"Yes, sir. He's good."

Chet smiled. What a shame. He might have done different had he known Kathrin carried him when he left Texas. But he had to get his family out of there. If he stayed, it would only be a short time until he'd bury more kinfolk or they murdered him. Was that assassin at Pine Flats hired by the Reynolds family? Had they brought the feud to Arizona? He'd been convinced over the years that he was far enough away in Arizona to be beyond their grasp. Who else wanted him dead? Under the shingle roof of the building he felt a chill go up his spine. Goose bumps ran up the back of his arms.

"You all right, Chet?" Cole asked him.

"Yes, but I am concerned. I may know my enemy."

"Your eggs will get cold."

"I know. But I believe that the same family I left in Texas has come out here to destroy me."

He began eating. "They have a killer in Tombstone. I need to find that sidewinder."

"That the Reynolds family?" Cole asked.

"Yes. I really believe they have a guy hiring these killers. And I will find him and end his existence."

"How can I help?"

"Hold the telegraph and stage together until it is settled. I will find a way to ferret him out."

Cole nodded. "What will you do next?"

"Tell all my people to be on alert. They may not know there is any danger, but I do. They are ruthless."

"Can I help you write the letters?" Val asked.

"I would appreciate that."

"What can we do?" Fred asked.

"We will need to find this killer that is hiring these slayers. I think he's hiding in Tombstone."

"I can find him if he's there," Fred said.

"I believe you can. Let us get some things settled here, then we will move on down there and find him."

Everyone agreed. He and Val sent letters warning everyone to be on guard. That he and his men were looking for the source but two attempts on Chet's life made him concerned that it was a planned program and they could be in harm's way. The letters told them to double their defenses and report any act against any of them. Chet promised to find the killers and stop them, but reminded them to be prepared and alert. Chet signed all the letters and thanked Val for helping him.

A wire from Hannagen came that evening.

I HAVE SOLD THE TELEGRAPH AND THE STAGE LINE FOR THREE POINT FIVE MILLION DOLLARS. ONE POINT FIVE IS YOURS. YOU BUILT IT AND IT NEVER WOULD HAVE BEEN POSSIBLE IF YOU AND YOUR COWBOYS HADN'T MET ME AT YOUR SISTER'S HOUSE. TELL HER HELLO AND THANKS. YOU DID THE IMPOSSIBLE EVEN WITH MY

OWN MEN WORKING AGAINST YOU. IF
YOU EVER NEED HELP CALL ON ME.
HANNAGEN.

"What next?" Cole said.
Liz had sent him a telegram.

I HOPE YOU GOT HANNAGEN'S WIRE.
A MARVELOUS THING. I KNOW WHY
YOU RAN UP THERE AND YOU HUG
THEM FOR ME. TELL THEM LISA AND
JOSEY ARE EXCITED FOR US, TOO.

He sent her one back.

GET TWO MEN TO BRING YOU UP TO
THE RIM. WE WILL MEET YOU AND GO
TO GALLUP AND CELEBRATE WITH
HIM. WIRE ME BEFORE YOU LEAVE.

In no time she wired a response:

I WILL BE ON THE RIM TOMORROW
AFTERNOON.

He answered that he would be there waiting.

Fred drove a company buckboard and
they took the horses and gear, planning to
meet her and camp overnight on the rim.

231

All the way, Chet watched the forest for any sign of ambush. The Pine Flat incident had him more cautious than usual. He hated having to be that way, but that single assassin, no matter how clumsy he had been, had shattered his peace for his everyday safety and concern for his men as well. The next guy those people hired might be a really clever killer. Damn. He needed to find the source and this trip to Gallup would just be another chance for them to strike except, he hoped, they might not be able to trace that he was going there.

Here he was with more money than he dreamed about ever having and someone wanted him dead. That was life. He could recall, perfectly, when those three Reynoldses had him pinned down and he was on his belly under those pungent cedar grove boughs with his sweaty hands on his Winchester stock figuring out how to kill them. That happened after he went back to close out the Texas deal. A cold wind blew off the Arctic that day. He still had a ranch deal out there he would need to sort out, and here he was pinned down by three crazy killers bent on killing him. But in the end, one by one, he killed them, found his horse, and rode on home. He had come way too close to death for him to be able to forget that cold day. His nose filled with the smell of cedar sap.

He sure didn't need to get into any traps like that again. They reached the campsite on the edge of the Mongollon Rim and set up camp.

"Can I ask what Cole will do next?" Fred said when they sat down on a log to wait.

"Oh, you still have a job. Cole will get an opportunity to work for them or work for us."

"He say what he'd do?"

"No. But he knows I have work for him if he doesn't like the railroad's offer. That's up to him."

"I wasn't being nosy."

"Ask away. That's how you learn things."

"I guess being last man hired, you might not need me if he came back."

"Not to worry. You are part of us like Miguel, Jesus, and Spencer. It takes all of us to handle things and keep me out of jams."

Miguel laughed. "I know how Fred feels. When I was last man hired, I always worried that you would send me back to be a vaquero."

"Well, where I came from nothing is permanent. You live hour by hour and under a threat of another bully wanting whatever you have."

"Did you have any trouble bringing Josey to the ranch?"

"No. But I wore my gun. I sure didn't want to use it but I figured I might have to in order to get her out of there."

"I bet you did."

"Guys, she hoped, but really didn't believe I'd come back. She could've found a protector." He shook his head. "She didn't, but she'd about given up, knowing she and our baby would need help. At first I had to convince her I came as quick as I could, that I found a place for us. That's when she told me she was having a baby, asked me if I wanted out? It was touch and go. I hated I didn't come back sooner but I was too insecure to ask to leave and find her. She wouldn't go into the Palace to eat with me that first day. We ate that meal in the alley, then we woke up a preacher and told him we had to get married. He married us and we got a room in the hotel. She'd never slept in a hotel in her life. Well, we didn't sleep much anyhow."

Chet and Miguel shared a nod and smiled over his honesty.

"I bought her some dresses and brought her out to the ranch. She couldn't believe I had a bank account, a saddle, and horse of my own. She never wanted to go into the big house that first day. Now Liz and Lisa have tuned her up to living there."

"Tuned her up?" Miguel asked.

"Aw, that's what you do to a guitar to get it to play."

Both men laughed.

"Fred, we are proud of you and Josey. Now maybe you can have a real life of your own like Miguel and I have."

"Oh Chet, we know we will, and that is why I asked about Cole's next move."

"Cole Emerson, if he returns, will run a ranch or a business. He was a great saddle partner, but an even greater supervisor."

Liz and three ranch hands arrived at sundown. They were heavily armed and were glad to be there. He helped her down off the buckboard and kissed her.

"Have any trouble?" he asked her.

"With my army that Raphael sent along — no."

"Good. We have a nice roast of elk meat. Let's eat."

Handshaking went around, then hands were washed in a pail, then dried on a towel Fred provided.

Liz stopped them. "Chet, say a blessing for the safe trip and this food you three have prepared for us to share."

"Our Heavenly Father, bless this fine food

Miguel and Fred cooked up for us. Thank you for delivering my wife Elizabeth here safely through the hands of these grand vaqueros who join us. Be in our lives tomorrow as they ride home and we continue our journey to Gallup. Guide and protect all our family on the scattered ranches and keep us in the palm of your hand as we go through life. Amen."

They made the sign of a cross and nodded approval of his prayer.

"All fine at home?" Chet asked.

"Oh yes. Lisa and Josey sent their best to you all as did your foreman before we left. Everyone is wondering what comes next in their lives," Liz answered.

"Ranching as usual," Fred said. "The Three V's will be on sale when we get back. Who knows who will buy it? I may bid some on it, but it is rundown and needs much attention. Someone inexperienced may bid more, then let them have it."

They all laughed. Damn, it was great to have Liz here and everyone laughing again. He needed to restore that atmosphere. He had been far too somber. They had plenty of space to enjoy all this good fortune that has fallen on them.

"Cattle are being moved to the Oracle Ranch. They have hay wagons and water wagons hired. Spencer says unless you need him, he wants to go over to the headquarters before coming back home. He wants to be certain everything is being done right and will be completed on time for the new owners. The plans are to scatter the cattle in groups. Spencer and Jesus bought the bulls that Slaughter had with the herd and hoped that was the thing to do. I wired yes in your absence," Liz said.

"How was the Oracle Ranch foreman down there?" Chet asked.

"The word was excited, Spencer said," Fred said.

"One down and one to go," Chet said.

"How is that?" Liz asked.

"I came up here on a secret deal to talk to Cole because Hannagen told me the railroad wanted the telegraph line and Hannagen was about to move on it. I also convinced Hannagen to sell the stage line with it, since it would end when the tracks got here. He did that, too. Then I told Cole to do what he wanted, but I would have a job for him if he didn't get a good offer from the railroad."

"I had wondered about that deal."

"They wanted that four hundred miles of line and the stage deal wasn't that big to hold them back. They took it."

"What happens next?" Liz asked.

"We'll see if they offer Cole something or not. I bet those stuffed shirts want their own person in charge of it, but we will see."

"You will get your money back on the headquarters?"

"It is in the deal but, heavens, we can buy and build hundreds of headquarters for what we made off it."

"I told those buyers on the Oracle place you would be in contact with them in plenty of time for the closing — before the first of the year."

"Good. You have been working hard." He was chewing on more sweet elk meat. Things were working like good watch gears did.

The next day Chet and Liz drove on to Flagstaff in the company buckboard and then to the headquarters. He took Liz off the buckboard while hostlers took charge of the horses.

Val and Rocky came running.

"Momma Liz, you are here."

She swept him up. "How are you, Rocky?"

"I have a great pony. I can ride him, and I bet you could, too."

"I will have to see him. I bet he is great."

Val took him. "He's getting big, isn't he?

But come, supper's ready."

"Yes, he's darling. I know how much you enjoy him and he is so bright."

"He is growing up too fast."

"That happens with them." The two women hugged each other.

Chet showed her to a place and plates of food soon appeared before them.

Cole asked for silence. Then he asked Chet to stand. "We need you to ask a blessing for the food and our activities."

With a nod Chet began raising his voice. "Let us pray." He asked for the Lord's blessing on the food, healing the sick and injured, and protecting them all. "Amen."

Everyone applauded and sat down to eat. This might be the last time for him to eat here and know these men and their families. The company they formed to start the move to rails across the entire territory. A company born to die when the iron rails took the stage line's place. But more jobs would open in the wake of the trains. Already people wanted ranches along this route. And with trains they'd have markets they never had before which had led to all those empty homesteads Bo had bought as a bargain.

The steam engine chugging across ruts left by wagon wheels would stir up new blood along the entire route of this land.

Damn. Time and progress marched on. By coincidence he came to Arizona to escape persecution of a feud in Texas and found bargains were all around if he had the way to make them work, and he had. From the sacred Navajo Mountains that surrounded Flagstaff to the Mexican border he and his ranches moved on. And ranches like Rustler's were blossoming in plenty of time to succeed.

"You've shocked some people selling the Oracle Ranch."

"Liz," he said between bites, "there is time to pick fruit when it is ripe. It may be twenty more years before that place exceeds its value today."

"Things are beginning to sell."

"They will with a train coming. I told you I saw it as the light we needed to open this land. But it still borders on a drought every season. I love it, but it is not the Garden of Eden for everyone or even us at times, though we are more prepared to live through them."

"I know and it has worked well."

"No one was haying cattle before we started. The free range is not virgin anymore, and winter does not have the carry-over of graze it once had."

"I wondered about the Oracle place not

having hay ground?"

"It may have pushed my decision."

She smiled. "I never doubt your thinking. I just need to understand and be filled in from time to time."

"I know I have been closemouthed. I will try to share more in the future."

"When do we go over there?"

"We take the stage Friday."

"I have two days here then?"

"Right."

Cole and Chet strolled through the cool morning checking out goings-on. Coach horses were being reshod in the blacksmith shop, the air saturated with sharp coal smoke from the forge that heated the shoes to shape them. Hammering on the anvils rung in his ears as he met the individuals manning the hammers.

The harness shop where the leather goods were washed in saddle soap and then dried and oiled came next. The aroma was saddle oil and they repaired any cracks that might break in service. Collars were all checked for wear and then soaped. Stitching machines repaired parts.

They went to where they were rebuilding a broken coach. It was quickly being reconstructed like new.

"You have an amazing amount of crafts-men here."

Cole nodded. "It's what you did on the ranches. I found the fix-it workers. I know this will all be in the past someday, but we have safe vehicles and they run smoothly."

Chet wondered what the buyers would do with this operation. Why should he care? It was sold. Trains were on the move. Step aside horses and wagons.

They walked through the pens of horses eating hay at the feeders and fussing around like strangers deciding who is boss with their sharp teeth or a fast kick. Then it settled for them and they went to eating grass and rolling in the dirt to salve itchy backs or to suck up cool spring water at the clean troughs.

What luxury for the fine stock that hauled the coaches and mail buckboards across the high desert trip after trip. They earned their oats every trip. But he was sobering up to the fact that horses were being replaced by iron ones. And the whole scene was chang-ing right before his eyes.

Meanwhile, Fred and Miguel had been listening around the village and in the saloons. None knew or had heard of the dead man and they learned no scuttlebutt about anyone wanting him dead.

So when they climbed on the eastbound stage, Chet felt more secure than he had than when Liz came to him from the rim. Spencer and Jesus were working on getting the Oracle headquarters finished before the buyers came back. The auction of the Three V's was only ten days away and he needed to be there for it.

In a day and a half they were in Gallup and riding in a surrey out to Hannagen's place. Liz had hoped for a hotel room to get straightened up, but Hannagen's man insisted that they all would stay at the house. Rocky was home riding his horse with his nanny, but Cole and Val, Liz, Chet and his guards, all fit in the surrey.

Val said his rambling house was a castle. Liz was grateful hers was smaller and easier to care for.

They were greeted by Hannagen's wife and shown to their rooms. Baths were drawn and laundry service provided. Fred and Miguel said they could sleep in the bunkhouse, but their offer was declined. Chet wore a suit Liz brought for him. Someone polished his boots. They all looked very nice seated at the dining table. Hannagen's people and their wives were also there. Photoflashes recorded the event from all angles.

Hannagen stood and introduced Chet and his people, saying how successful the association with the Byrnes Family had been for them all. "It never would have been done without them."

Chet appreciated the words.

Cole met his new bosses the next day. They told him they were cutting his wages in half immediately and he had a job only until the track was laid three-quarters of the way across Arizona, then they would close down the operation.

At his meeting with Chet that afternoon Cole told Chet, "When they told me my wages were to be cut in half immediately, I made up my mind I was going back to work for real people. I stood up and told them to not even continue, that, as of now that moment the stage line was theirs, and that I quit and they could all go to hell.

"This big guy got up red-faced and shook his finger at me. 'You will never work for anyone again.' I said, 'Oh, yes, I have work with a great company right now running a ranch and he won't cut my pay or backstab me.' And I warned them that they all better get out there. There will be wagon wrecks, robberies, and drivers quitting from here on."

"So we go back and get our things, leave,

and they have charge?" Chet asked.

"That is the way it will be," Cole replied.

"I am going to tell Hannagen. He knows them. They will regret letting you go before the track is laid."

Chet knocked on the door to the office and heard a "come in" call.

"The tycoons cut Cole's salary in half immediately. He quit and dumped it in their laps."

"Those stupid bastards. They have no one to run that operation. I told them not to do that when I signed the papers. But they know it all. Well, they'll learn the hard way. It will take four or five supervisors to do the job Cole did to keep things going."

"Yes, it will."

"You have a job for him?"

"I am going home and make one."

"Then it's their loss and they may lose more at this rate. They are such chiselers."

"I will remember that if I do business with them again."

"Thanks. You running off?"

"I need to."

"You sold Regis and his buddy a good ranch?"

"Yes. It is already set up to make money. They have a good supervisor, brand-new headquarters, and some great cattle. It has a lot of deeded land, and they can own it for twenty years and make a huge profit."

"They said you made them a square deal. Do you have any more like it?"

"Not today."

"Okay. Should I transfer your share of the sale to your banker Tennant in Prescott?"

"Yes, though he may have a heart attack. I will warn him."

"Tell Cole thanks for all he's done and that I don't blame him for quitting."

Chet waved good-bye and left. They headed back to Flagstaff.

Val asked, "Where do we live now that we are penniless and out of a job?"

"Our house. We only have Fred and Josey. Lisa and Miguel are also there now, so what's three more?"

"Four counting his nanny. And his painted horse makes five more."

"I would kiss that Navajo chief for giving that sweet horse to a boy who will ride him," Liz said.

"I bet he'd take it, too." They'd be home in a few days.

Cole and Val had two large wagons loaded with their things and some draft mules to move them. Chet commandeered a buckboard and a team for forty dollars —

stamped as unneeded on the paper work they were leaving in the office. Liz and Chet were driving south. Miguel and Fred brought the ranch horses with packs and saddles right on their tail.

Cole and a hired driver brought their two wagons while Val, with Rocky and his nanny, drove another unneeded buckboard and team behind them.

It made quite a parade or wagon train and Chet wished he had a U.S. flag to hang at the front of the train. He'd gotten Fred to ride out in front as the color guard and painted Prescott or Bust on the wagons. When he told Liz his plans, she laughed for half a mile and shoved him around to be ornery.

He finally gave her the reins and made her drive for a few miles.

They reached the rim edge and camped for the night. The women cooked some beef and rice and they ate as it grew dark.

Seated in folding chairs around the fire, they talked about the day and how a coyote got all upset trying to cross through the wagon train and jumping back each time until he finally flew between the wagons and buckboards, getting clipped by a wheel and then kicked by a mule until he reached the other side of the road.

"He had a bad day," Fred said, amused.

"He couldn't go around. He had to blunder through." They all laughed.

Afternoon the next day they stopped at the Verde Ranch, so Rocky and Adam could meet up and visit. Rocky showed Adam his paint horse. Adam said he had two sheep, broke to ride, but they had no time to ride them. They would be late getting up the mountain to the Valley Ranch.

"Does Adam really have two sheep to ride?" Liz asked as they headed up the steep mountain in their buckboard.

"Oh yes. He's rode those sheep a lot."

"One son on a painted pony and the other riding sheep Roman style."

More laughter rang out as they wound up the deep canyon.

When the caravan came into the yard, the sun was almost down. The schoolhouse bell went to pealing out.

Lisa and Josey had a footrace from the house to greet them.

Folks came from everywhere to shake a hand or hug someone.

Chet stood in the buckboard. "Look who I brought back with me. Val, Cole, and Rocky are back here with us."

They had music to celebrate the homecoming. Miguel and Lisa disappeared first, then Josey and Fred left, too. Chet and Liz thanked everyone and went hand in hand upstairs to bed.

While undressing, she asked him, "Will this let you go higher on the price for the Three V's?"

He went over and hugged her. "A few bucks more."

"I don't care. You make these deals like the stage line and telegraph and you sell them high as the sky. You made over two hundred thousand on the Oracle Ranch that the bankers couldn't even sell. Did the new headquarters sell that place?"

"Hell yes. I told the banker how it would, but he had all that money he wanted in it and sold it to me at a discount."

"Can you do that with the Three V's?"

"If I buy it right. Next week we will know."

"All this money in one bank?"

"I know banks fail. I am putting a large sum of our money in lockboxes. They can't get it. The rest I will share in the loans with the bank. I have plans."

"May I come along Tuesday?"

"Certainly."

"Val would like to, too."

"I may not buy that ranch."

"We know, but we'd like to be along."

"Plan on it."

"Thanks. You really do surprise me at times. But so far it has worked."

"I have been thinking — I never thought that Rustler's Ranch would have that much potential. Those crazy kids ran away with it. I have to get them more mowers, rakes, and stackers for next year. They will rival Tom's operation in just a few years."

"What did those homesteads cost?"

"Four to seven hundred dollars each. Most are one-sixty acres. Some double that."

"Those two kids sure are explosive together. How much they've grown. Everything was beneath Talley the whole time she was here. She finally agreed to marry Toby and then bitched he was all she could find. Like she was so much better than the rest of us. I never thought she'd go over there and even stay or work that hard. She sure is such a different girl."

"He may be more horse than she thought she was marrying."

She frowned at him. "He is a worker, and I think she caught the fever he has to get things done and likes seeing the results."

"Let's get some sleep. Be a big day tomorrow."

"Why?"

"Hell, I don't know. I am still tired from

all the running around."

Tuesday came. The auction was a big event. Folks came from near and far on wagons, buggies, horses, mules, and even bicycles. Chet and Liz in one buckboard. Val and Cole with Rocky drove a surrey over. Josey and Lisa came in another buckboard and two of Chet's guards rode horseback just in case. They brought folding chairs, blankets, water and tea, plus sandwiches for an army, along with several bags of fresh peaches from Betty Lou and Leroy Simpson's Oak Creek operation.

Set up in the shade of a gnarled cotton-wood, before the sale, Chet talked to Tanner about separating the money. It was done and they struck a fifty-fifty split in loaning a portion for land-backed mortgages at twelve percent interest. If he loaned the whole portion out, and folks paid their interest, Chet stood to earn thirty thousand a year. It would be nice, but nothing was perfect, and Chet took that into consideration.

The auctioneers announced, at the start, that they would sell the land and buildings last. First were the household items and the women clamored, buying Alice's personal items. Doilies, vases, the gold-edged dishes, chairs, tables, stuffed sofas, a grandfather clock that didn't work, blankets, towels, and men's long johns. They broke for lunch and two dogs got in such a hair-tearing fight that men took to slapping them with ax handles to make them quit. Finally the two were parted. Most of Lisa's sandwiches were eaten by freeloaders too cheap to pay the Baptist Church ladies fifty cents for a hot lunch. The auctioneers were back and started selling cows five pair, or five open cows, to the lot.

Miguel had the breed cows marked on his sheet.

The auctioneer sold two pens that Chet never bid on. He asked Chet if he needed any.

"Yes. I'll give a hundred on the next pen." He bought them for one-fifty.

"How about these?"

"Seventy-five."

They brought a hundred but there was an unbred cow in that pen. Chet was still in his budget.

The next pen of five cows and calves sold for over two hundred and fifty.

His top bid on big calves and cows was fifty bucks for a pair and all bred back.

Ernie Howard, whittling on a cottonwood branch, trailed along. "I been watching but I haven't got the handle on how you are buying."

"Oh I just buy what I like and what suits me."

"No." He half laughed. "You got a plan here, like always, and while I ain't figured it out, you're working on something more than that.

"Chet, you bidding on this lot?"

He shook his head.

The auctioneers' help kept bringing five cows at a time plus their calves if they had one. It was a sharp way to sell and these auctioneers were good at it. He bought another pen with calves all bred under his price range.

Miguel had done a good job. If the theory worked he was doing fine. They were down to cull cows, and Chet didn't want them. He bought some large lots of yearling heifers. Most were three-quarter British breeds for twenty-two dollars a head. And he bought three hundred yearling steers to older, for twenty dollars a head. In a year they'd be worth sixty at Gallup.

Everyone got a drink of water and they went up into the yard fanning themselves from the heat with fans marked PRESCOTT UNDERTAKERS.

Now it was the land's turn. It consisted of

ten sections with all the mineral rights intact.

The auctioneer wiped his face dry with a Turkish towel. "Do I hear five hundred thousand dollars?"

"No," someone said and he didn't.

"Four hundred thousand dollars?"

"Three hundred thousand dollars?"

"Two hundred thousand?"

"One hundred thousand?"

"What is your pleasure?"

"Forty thousand dollars."

"Aw, hell you are going to kill me starting that low." The auctioneer drew in a deep breath. "Forty thousand, who will give fifty?"

"Forty-one."

"Forty-one who will give forty-two?"

A hot breath of air swirled the dust up.

"Forty-two."

"Anyone give forty-three?"

Chet got up off his haunches.

"Mr. Byrnes, are you through?" the auctioneer asked.

"I'll give you forty-five. And then I'm going home and do my chores."

The crowd needed a laugh and they took it. Silence reigned.

"Anyone here give forty-six?" No answer.

"Mr. Byrnes, did you recently sell a ranch

like this at Oracle for over a third of a million dollars?"

"Colonel, I sold a forty-section ranch with brand-new fancy headquarters, stocked with three hundred fifty cow calf pairs under four years old. This old place needs a new headquarters, has no cows on it, and it is one-fourth that size. I am actually paying too much, but it is closer to my house than that one."

"Sold."

They gave him a round of applause.

Cole came over and stood by him and stretched. "You higher or lower than you thought?"

"Close to it. That guy was about through. It would take too much more to fix it. We did all right."

"Where do we start?"

"House. Spencer will be back. That is his business. This place is yours, so Val can have what she wants when they fix the house. We need Victor up here to look at a large patch of sagebrush. It might make a hay meadow with two artesian wells to water it."

"I figured you looked at this place before. What comes after that?"

"If it is feasible to make a large hay field, we'll try drilling water first."

"If that doesn't work?"

"We find some hay land to support this place."

"A different challenge, huh?" Cole grinned.

"I'll go write them a check."

The four women were coming from the house.

"Val. When Spencer comes home you and Cole can come and meet with him here. He did wonderful with nothing to start down at Oracle. I am sure it was good enough to convince those guys to buy it. It will take some months, but it will be something you want."

She smiled. "I understand. I had a real nice place up there, but I'll have a better one here."

"It will be good. Besides, Lisa and Liz love company."

"We do," Liz said.

"I could live in it now," Josey said.

The women laughed. "Your turn will come."

"Josey, when I married Cole we lived in a rental log cabin in town for three years."

"I slept in alleys that long."

Chet hugged her. "In time we will find you a place."

She grasped his hand. "Oh, I am plenty happy where I am. So is Fred. Don't think we forgot where you found us. I just had to say I'd live here."

"This is to be Val's house. She, Cole, and my son Rocky will be here."

"Oh, Chet, I never had folks do as much as you do. I just longed for a house of my own."

"It will come, Josey. Trust me."

"I do. Thanks."

Chet nodded to them and went to settle with the auctioneers. He walked into the living room and papers were flying.

"Come in," Sullivan said. "Like so many other sales, you have been fair to me. I really thought the history of the ranch would make it bring more. But you saw the needs and figured out how you can bring it back to its peak."

"I say it showed too much wear. Rich men don't understand how to rebuild. They will pay for the best, but they have no idea how to fix things. And when they do it costs them too much."

"Obviously you know how. I understand you sold the railroad the telegraph wire and the stage line that they will eat when the tracks are strung. Only a genius figured that out."

"I have some great business partners. North Arizona needed that wire and transportation while waiting for the railroad. We speeded up the train coming."

"We will have the deed and a clear title. Can we meet at your bank in two days?"

"Fine. Bring the bill for the cattle I bought with you so we can do it all at the bank."

"That is fine. Thursday at ten a.m.?"

"I will be there."

"I hope you have enough left to pay us?" Sullivan laughed.

"We will. Somehow." Chet shook his hand and thanked the auction bunch before he left.

When he joined Liz and the others he said, "They would not take my check."

"Huh?" they asked.

"No. We settle it at our bank ten a.m. Thursday. Let's go home. Miguel, tomorrow bring some vaqueros and scatter the cattle we bought. We can get them back and sort them later when we get the corral repaired and some cross fencing done. I didn't buy any bulls, but we will deal with that next."

"Lisa, can we celebrate this coming Saturday night?"

"You bet, boss man. We can have a big party."

"Let's go home."

They applauded him and loaded up for

home. Liz leaned on his shoulder. "You pleased?"

"I think so. I didn't expect the telegraph-stage sale to happen so quickly, so that was a blessing. I could see us with stagecoaches no one needed. Oh, the loss wouldn't have been gigantic. Now we don't even have to think about them."

"Is that a weight off your shoulders?"

"Definitely. I am just now realizing how big it was."

"So I guess coming home and being a rancher full time isn't in your future?"

"There are individuals we have helped that had no help coming. I can't turn others down."

"No and I understand. That is the man who stole my heart, his heart as big as a lion."

"Just another Texas rancher who went west."

"No, you are an Arizona empire builder. I heard you say you got here at the right time."

"I really did. And now I have a very lovely wife I ride with, on down the trail laid before me."

He checked the team going downhill on the narrow road hedged in by cedar boughs. Something had upset the horses. He had no idea why, and was wondering if someone would try something on this shortcut back road he'd taken.

His men on horseback were behind them shouting, "Let us by. Let us by."

Chet could see that the road opened ahead. He stood sawing on the horses to slow them down, with them prancing and dancing. Liz was holding on to his belt so he didn't fall off. They emerged into an open meadow.

Cutting across open space in full run was the source of their trouble — a black sow bear and two cubs.

Chet was laughing hard when he pulled off the road and was joined by the surrey and the laughing girls in it.

"Just a bear," he said to the arriving riders who laughed, too.

Fred and Miguel took the lead home from there.

That evening he and Cole planned how to meet the new ranch's people the next day. Since they didn't know them, they'd have to find the leader first and then the workers.

"Early breakfast?" Lisa asked them.

"Yes, please."

"No problem. Hey, that place will be completely different in a year."

Cole smiled at her. "Tell you what is nice for me."

"What is that?"

"No one turned over a buckboard or had a horse go lame today."

She laughed. "I bet that is so."

At Miguel's elbow she went off to their room.

"How do you find them?" Cole asked.

"She and Toby's wife Talley came from us rounding up the bunch that tried to stop the stage line."

"Lisa is not Monica, but she holds down this house and does things Monica couldn't do."

"And very well. She and Liz have a dozen ranch children excelling at the Cherry School house. Those kids learned enough English to attend school and they are making their grades."

"Rocky will start there this fall, I guess?"

"More than likely."

"Everything going on around here is new to me. Can you catch me up?"

"When Talley came back from Colorado with us, you couldn't please her. She acted like we had trapped her. Toby was more of a kid when he proposed to her. She finally accepted. But it was only so she wouldn't be an old maid. None of us expected it to last. They went up there and with some teenage Mexican boys who needed work, cleared up acres of pasture to mow for hay ground, rebuilt the place to get ready for cattle, and took the mowing machines to the fenced-off homesteads and mowed and stacked them. They want seven hundred cows by next year. She worked shoulder to shoulder with Toby. They both can really work. They make a great pair."

"Shawn is with Lucy?"

"Yes. They are expecting their first child together. The little girl loves him. Spud and his wife Shirley really help them. They are still catching maverick cattle. JD and Bonnie will have their first citrus crop this year. It won't be large, but that place is moving, too. They are also selling lots of beef."

"I am going to have lots to live up to on the Three V's."

"Hey, you and I put in lots of saddle time. That railroad bunch was damn stupid cutting your pay, but I bet they will have five guys running it in the next two months just to keep it going."

"That would serve them right. Val and I belong here. I am anxious to get rolling. You have some great foremen. I am proud to be joining Hampt and Tom along with the others who built this operation. How are Susie and Sarge doing?"

"Expecting number two. Tom's son-in-law Cody Day is taking the herd up to Gallup every other month to give Sarge some time off."

"I better go to bed or I won't make tomorrow morning. It had been so long since I rode a horse I'm a little stiff. Jesus coming back?"

"Yes. He and Spencer will be here tomorrow night."

They went their separate ways to bed. It felt good to have Cole back. That dumb railroad bunch would regret his quitting them.

Chet lay in bed a while beside his sleeping wife and thought about finding his enemies. They'd do that.

CHAPTER 12

Lisa served breakfast to Chet, Cole, Fred, and Miguel with Josey helping her. They had already arranged for their horses to be saddled and ready.

"No damn bears today," Fred said between bites. "Miguel and I plan to be at the head of the column instead of boxed in behind."

"You guys did great. She didn't hurt anyone."

"Next time we will be in the right place," Miguel said, with a sharp nod from Fred.

Holding his cup of hot coffee, Cole said, "Get Jesus talking when he gets here. We were the first ones to ride with Chet as guards, and he can tell you stories about that."

"What was the toughest one?" Fred asked.

"Taking him, wounded, in a buckboard to Tombstone while he was shouting orders about how to contain the outlaws. Hell, we had that done and were scared he'd bleed to death before we got him to a doctor."

"Brother, that was touch and go for me and Jesus and the others from the Force."

"That wound ever bother you?" Miguel asked.

"Some, when I get real tired. Not too bad. Lisa, we will try to be back by supper time."

"No worries. It will hold until you do. Josey, give Fred the saddle bags full of burritos and fruit."

"Thank you," Chet said. "You gals are terrific."

Daylight was peeking over the eastern horizon when they mounted up. Cole's horse made three crow hops and he rode him off while laughing among the cheers, "Welcome back."

The man in charge at the Three V's was Santos Carrizo. He met them at the corrals. He was a dried-up old man with few teeth but he was no doubt the boss. He spoke fair English.

Chet asked him how long he had worked on the ranch.

"I was a boy in Texas on his father's ranch. The señor, he came to me and said I could go to a better place to ranch. Did I want to go? I said, 'I am a boy. My mother is here. I hate to leave her.'

"Señor Mitch asked if I wanted to be a peon all my life. Then told me to get my things, that he will make me his major-domo." A smile crossed his broken mouth, and he nodded with a wink. "And he did."

"You have a wife?"

"No. I had three, but they are all dead. I would like to go back to Texas and die there and be buried next to *mi mamacita.*"

"This is not your home?"

"I only came here to be his majordomo. I have done that."

Chet agreed he had done that. "I will buy your ticket home. Who could I hire to take your place from out of your men?"

"Farrell would do that."

"I will hire him. You do not have to leave here, but if you find Texas too different you can come back and live out your time with us."

Santos smiled. "They told me you'd throw me off the ranch when you came. You are a *mucho bueño hombre.*"

"We don't throw anyone away."

"Do you have a list of the workers?" Cole asked him.

"Reuben has one. He has kept the books. I have them in my head. He is at the house."

"Fred, go find him and ask him to join us

with a list of the workers."

"Señor Byrnes, when I came with him here this was sagebrush and pines. But he and I got old. I know you will restore it. Ranching is for young men."

"Thanks. We would like you to tell my man Cole about all things so he can run it. Then when you want to leave we will deliver you there."

"Gracias."

By then it was lunchtime. Chet and Cole were pleased with the ground they'd covered with the old foreman.

The accountant, Reuben Clark, a man in his twenties, showed up; he was limping badly. He wore thick glasses and his Adam's apple jerked like a fish bobber in his throat.

"Mr. Byrnes, I have kept the books for Mr. Van Roy for five years. He never complained. I went to accountant school and everything."

"How much did he pay you?"

"Fifteen dollars a month and my food and lodging. You look funny. Is that too much?"

"Cole, if this young man can do that I think we better double his pay."

Cole finished eating, rose, brushed off his seat, and shook his hand. "Reuben, how about a raise to thirty dollars a month?"

Chet worried Reuben's Adam's apple

might choke him to death.

"*Oh. Oh.* That would be wonderful. Would it be all right for me to get married?"

"Why, certainly. Who is it?"

"Emilia, who works in the kitchen. We didn't have enough money before."

"Go get her and tell her. We can wait."

He handed his pad to Chet, thanked Cole, and limped off to the house. Fred had noticed this kind of handicap before.

"What is wrong?" Cole asked.

"He was too proud to use his crutches to come out and talk to you. He worried you might think him too much of a sissy. He had a disease they call polo as a boy."

Chet knew something about it. "I think they call it polio. Bad disease for kids. Many die from it. One of you boys take him his crutches so we won't worry about them."

Emilia came — she was cross-eyed and looked at them with her head turned, crying. "I am sorry I cry but we have waited so long — I thought we would never get married. I won't lose my job?"

"No, you will have a job. Tomorrow we are busy banking. Friday a cowboy will come get you early and you will go with my wife to see an eye doctor who can fit your eyes to glasses so you don't see double. Then she will have a wedding dress made for you so you two can get married at my ranch."

"Oh. Now I am crying more. Reuben, you tell him I am not a crybaby, but this is more than I can stand. Bless you. Bless you." Reuben was hugging her, holding her tightly.

"We understand. Who else has a problem?" Chet asked of all the gathered workers from the house and the fields.

A take-charge woman stepped for ward. "We are not used to people doing things for us."

"That has changed. There is a new owner here. Everyone willing to work has a job. If you work hard, we can pay you more. We will fix things that are broken. If you don't like us, you are free to go. But we don't put up with lazy people or thieves. No fighting on the ranch. No bullies. No knife or gunfights.

"It will be a new ranch. This tall cowboy, Cole Emerson, will run it. He will be the boss. His wife is Val, and with my oldest son Rocky they will live here with you."

Some applauded at that. He turned to Reuben. "Cole will be back tomorrow and go over this list with you. It is up to him who stays but he is fair."

"I appreciate your generosity. Emilia will be dressed and ready to go with your wife when she comes."

"We are happy to have you all stay, if that is what you want." Watching their faces, Chet decided they were accepting him and Cole.

Cole asked, "Can Miguel come back with me? My Spanish will get better the more I am around here but for now, he would be helpful."

"Jesus is supposed to be back."

"Hell, yes, three is better than one."

"Miguel?"

"I heard him. Fred speaks it good, too. We can all come, learn about this place, and help Cole get started."

Fred was there with their horses and heard. "I'll help."

"Good. That poor girl hasn't seen right all her life and no one knew what to do. Liz will help her and buy her a wedding dress."

"That poor guy got pretty high about his raise," Fred said.

"You guys may find out better, but I fear Mitch was pretty cheap. How many jobs could that cripple boy get? I bet he's a good accountant-bookkeeper."

"That's my thought," Cole said stepping into the saddle. "It was a great day. We have lots to do but we understand a lot now."

They got back in mid-afternoon. Chet

found the girls in the kitchen. He told them about Emilia and her problem.

"That's horrible. To see two all your life is criminal. How old is she?"

"Between sixteen and twenty. I told her you would help her get glasses to straighten her eyes and a dress to marry Reuben in. He has thick glasses himself but didn't know how to help her. He had a crippling disease as a child and he was afraid we wouldn't want him on crutches so he limped out to meet us."

"What did Cole say?" Lisa asked.

"I think he wanted his stagecoaches back."

Val pulled on his sleeve and shook her head. "He missed riding with you every single day he was there. He needs challenges and he wants to work with you. He handled that job, it but he considers running a ranch for you the best job for him."

"You?"

"I can tell you he did well at it, but here, on the ranch, I will have my husband back and I love that. He made great wages, but we had no time for ourselves. I can enjoy having him back here with me and Rocky."

"Good, with you happy, we next need to know if Emilia and Reuben can get married a week from Saturday." Lisa went to snapping her fingers and backing up dancing.

"We will give them a real fandango."

Things went smoothly at the bank the next day. Spencer and Jesus came back from Oracle saying things were well there. After a long day at the Three V's, Cole and the rest came home saying they were making progress ironing things out there.

Chet stayed home the following day and worked on the books. Things were going smoothly there, too. After lunch he wound up the accounting, and went into the living room and asked his wife if she had anything that needed doing.

"No. All is well here. Your men, who came back, will be here with their wives for supper."

"Good. I'm taking a nap."

Liz waved him on his way. "We can handle it."

He had lots of things on his mind. Straightening the new place and getting Cole and Val settled were two of them. His last letter from Chavez promised he would have three hundred and fifty young cross cows at the right price for Rustler's Ranch. But they still had to be driven a good distance over the mountains to the ranch.

Toby told Chet he could leave two armed men to watch their ranch while they went for the cattle. Four of his men were good enough cowboys to be drovers. They'd need a wagon or two and those boys would need saddles and a *remuda.* That was another need he hadn't been thinking about — horses. If Tom sent some hands, Raphael lent him some, and the four men of Toby's plus themselves — why, they'd have an army to drive those cows.

That made him sit up and laugh. He mopped his face in his hands. No nap today.

Then Cole would need cows and bulls. He'd never bid on any bulls that were on that place. He wanted British bulls, not crosses on cows he bought. There were some unbred cows among them. It would not be too late if they were bred in the next six weeks. The calves would be worthwhile. Born after that time frame they'd be hard to fit into the system. They should wait and breed them next year. That might have to be the case.

Good thing he had sold some things. He had the money, and that fact amused him. He needed bulls for Toby. Sixteen to seventeen. Maybe Tom had enough coming on from the Hereford herd. Then Cole might have two hundred cows to start and that meant ten more. He gave up napping to go write it all down.

Liz teased him about the nap when she found him there. "Raphael is here."

"Show him in here. I'll have this written by then."

"I will."

Raphael took off his hat. "I didn't mean to bother you. Could I help you over there at the new place?"

"Have a seat. I am about done. The guys have it going. I will need, in a week, to start a crew to go to Socorro and bring three hundred and fifty cattle back to Toby's."

"How many men?"

"I think three from you is enough. We may have cowboys falling over each other, but I want this to work. Hard as Toby and Talley worked they deserve this."

A twinkle appeared in his brown eyes when Raphael spoke again. "Did you ever believe she'd ever do that?"

"Not the snooty girl we brought back here."

His foreman shook his head amused. "None of the help did, either."

"I think she realized the deal would work and she wanted to be a part of it."

"I think Toby won her, too. They look very dedicated. But I am not familiar with Socorro?"

"It is about due east of us in western New

274

Mexico. We can come up through the White Mountains and get onto the Crook Road at Fort Apache and drive them to the ranch. We are trying to get permission from the Apache Agency. Sarge asked for help from the Navajos and he thinks we will get that passage. Otherwise we must go northwest and take the Marcy Road and then back down to Rustler's Ranch. That is what the stage line uses."

"I have the picture. How many horses?"

"Several. We will need some for Toby to herd later but on the trip we will need each man to have four or five horses. Tom can furnish some."

"When you get close to going, tell me your needs, we will have it all ready."

"Thanks. I knew you'd help me."

"You sure have a house full of women."

"And they are all good looking," Chet teased.

"Oh yes." Raphael laughed as he left the room.

Liz stuck her head in. "Supper draws near."

"Coming."

Lisa went by him with a steaming bowl of corn on the cob for the table. "Cole's outfit is not back yet. Jesus and Spencer and their wives are here. We will eat now. They can eat later. No doubt they had lots to do down there."

"Thanks, Monica."

"That is flattery, because I am doing her job."

They both laughed.

Seated at the table, they ate. Spencer reported the main house at Oracle would be done shortly and in budget. Jesus said the cows were there and settled. Bulls were being bought for next year and seventy-five older cows had been culled.

"The ranch will be in top shape to make them money," Jesus said.

"Yes," Spencer said. "We have it set up for them. They really got a bargain if you compare it to most ranches."

"Not like our new place?" Chet said.

"You bought that right," Liz said. "Besides, you have the crew to run it. And the ladies like that it is closer than the other place."

"I am not complaining. You have it all arranged that Reuben and Emilia will get married here next Saturday?"

Liz nodded. "It will be a big deal for those two. She will have her glasses by then and see only one groom."

Several laughed.

"That gal is a hard worker. How she lived

cross-eyed for this long I can't imagine," Val said, having gone along with Liz on the glasses and dress trip. "Oh, and Cole told me to tell you Reuben's books are neat and very carefully done."

"We have another winner. Party Saturday and we leave Monday for Socorro. Jesus, you are the supply man. Tomorrow we will figure out food needs. And pick a cook."

"Josey and I want to cook. She asked me if she could go along. She has never been on a drive nor seen that country," Liz said.

"It will be a tough trip," Chet told her.

"Oh, Chet, they all are. The two of us will handle it, won't we, Josey?"

The girl clapped. "Yes, we will. Thank all of you. I asked Fred and he said it was not likely to happen, but you, Liz, said you'll get us going. Thank you, boss lady."

"Better get three supply wagons. No, no, I am only teasing." He laughed at the situation.

The Three V's ranch group arrived after sundown. Lisa, standing on the porch, told them she had food and to come up.

"How did it go?" Chet asked Cole as he was drying his hands.

"Good. Miguel has the open cows in a fenced hay field. Hampt came by and he promised us two bulls to be delivered next

Monday. There are forty some open cows and when we get them bred they can go out with the rest. He thinks that hay meadow plan will work if we can find the artesian wells. Situated at the mountain base, Hampt said the water should be there."

"Sounds good."

"He has enough hay to help us this year if we need it," Cole said.

"I knew both ranches up here have the hay if we need it. He's some farmer, isn't he?"

"It has been years since I saw his place, but he really is knowledgeable about it all. He did have Miguel show him how to tell the bred cows before he left. I told him I'd be by for more lessons."

"We head east Monday for Socorro. Saturday arrange so everyone from there that wants to can come to the wedding."

Later that night in bed, he and Liz talked.

"Josey works hard every day since she has been here, so this trip coming is a big treat for her. Her mother died, and her father found another woman who lied about her until they turned her out. That is so sad. At sixteen she lived in the alleys and slept anywhere she could. She had some very bad things happen to her. Fred sheltered her a lot but he had nothing himself. The group

278

they belonged to protected each other. When he came back for her, she said she was so skeptical that he was serious that he had a place that she kept telling him no. Then she was afraid we'd shun her. We have her past all of that now, and she is really excited about coming on the drive."

"Thanks. You do great with the women. I know he surprised us all bringing her back as a bride. But he has big ideas for the future, and that was part of it."

"Like you brought a Hispanic widow back here to your family?"

"That was expected from me."

"No, it was not. But I love all of them."

"Now we are adding Reuben and Emilia."

"They will fit in well. Someday you may consider letting him do all the books."

"Someday I may agree."

"What did your man Chavez in Socorro say in the telegram?"

"That he works on a commission and can get me five hundred head if I want them."

"And?"

"Considering it I told him to get them."

"Oh, Talley will be pleased."

"They and some field hands turned cowboys will make it."

She rolled over and kissed him. "So will we."

He agreed, snuggled her, and fell asleep.

Sunday after church, his men were in the house for dinner.

"Thank all of you for the fine wedding we had for Reuben and Emilia. You did them proud. A great job well done. Now Cole and Spencer will stay here and run things. Jesus and Liz are the suppliers of food and our other needs on the trip. Fred, Miguel, and Josey are going with us. We will start east in the morning. Four hands have been picked from this ranch, we pick up four riders at the Verde Ranch, and Tuesday night we join Toby and Talley at their ranch. We have saddles and horses enough for everyone. That is lots of hands, but I upped the buy to five hundred head. It is because Rustler's Ranch made such a big hay harvest that they can support that many."

Everyone applauded.

"This gives us another top ranch in the territory. Spencer and Val are starting house plans for Cole's new ranch house. Cole is setting up everything else on the new ranch. We have well drillers coming to find artesian wells to water some larger acreage for hay production. The team feels with that we could build that ranch up to at least four hundred head of mother cows. Thanks to all of you for your help."

"Boss man, be careful. We wish you success," Cole said.

"I will and you do the same."

Morning rolled around and the place was buzzing. Chet, Liz, and Jesus led the group. Fred was in charge of the two supply wagons loaded with everything they'd need. He and Josey were on the lead wagon seat. Miguel and two wranglers had the saddle horses. They ate an early lunch at the Verde Ranch without one horse bucking anyone off. The four hands from there climbed into their saddles and they took the Crook Highway east to make camp on the rim.

No tents were struck. The mild weather and no sign of rain made that possible. They were up at dawn. The campfire smoke hung low, but Liz, Josey, Jesus, and Fred made fast work of serving breakfast, then they were loaded and headed east. Mid-afternoon they rode into Rustler's Ranch and were welcomed by Talley. All her menfolk were gone fencing one of Bo's purchases and they would be back by dark. They usually camped up there while building fence and didn't come in every evening so they could complete it faster, but they knew Chet and the crew were coming, so they planned to be back that night.

She told everyone to unload.

She hugged Chet. "I am so excited we are going after those cows."

"I can see that and so am I. We have a promise we can cross the Apache Reservation. So that will shorten our journey with the cattle and for all these folks that came to help us get them here."

Talley was crying. "I will be fine. We are proud to be with all of you. It has been a big year for us. Toby said we could not fail. That you sent us out here to see what we could do with this place. Toby wanted to do more than what you outlined for us. You can see what we did here. Looks better?"

"It looks wonderful," Liz said. "I can't believe it is the same place. I was here when we tried to arrest those rustlers. I never thought you and the men could have made it this nice a looking ranch."

They hugged.

Chet told her, "We know how hard you work. Once we have the cows here, you can chase them, too."

She shouted. "Wonderful."

Things settled down and the women set to feeding everyone.

Chet, Jesus, and Fred inspected the new barn stacked full of fresh hay. It was all well done. And out back, well fenced, was even more neatly stacked hay.

Jesus said, "These corrals, built by your contractor, would make Cole drool."

"With all those cows we are bringing back, he may need more," Chet said.

"I bet he makes it all work," Fred said.

"Knowing those two, I bet they do." Chet laughed as he head back to the house.

"Chet?" Jesus asked as they walked together across the mowed yard, "When you had Bo buy this ranch, did you ever dream it would look this good?"

"Not in my wildest dream. Even the hitch racks are neat."

Sometimes he hired good men and they turned out to be super. He chose Toby, young, a little short on education and experience but with an ethic full of hard work that the job would require on the isolated area of this ranch. He and Talley damn sure turned it around. And he'd thought, when they first came here, that in a couple of months she'd stomp out and leave him.

Toby and his crew arrived about sundown in a farm wagon. He shook hands all around, and then excused himself to go take a shower under the sheepherder in back. Chet watched him come back out in what he called cowboy clothes. Not the overalls and brogans he usually wore to work. More of the Talley touch — starched white shirt, vest, and boots. Amused, he saw her influence. The new Toby who talked seriously to everyone, about their families, how the trip went, how he only lacked a few more days of fencing, and how he was thankful for all the help in going to get the cows.

The beef was good. Potatoes and corn they had just picked. The biscuits were excellent and the blackberry jam very fresh. Then cherry cobbler and good coffee to finish the meal.

Full, Chet sat back on the bench and said, "Delightful food. Thank you, Talley. I feel I am paid back for feeding you."

She rose and shook her head. "I won't ever get that bill paid. I came back to Prescott with you as a spoiled child. I couldn't wait to escape you and your house. But I had some time to reflect on things. I had a damn great man who had lots of patience with me. I came to a crossroad and had a rude awakening. I was wife to a hardworking man who took me even though I was a nobody, though I acted like the queen I thought I was. We talked and I decided I'd be a part of his life. Chet, you won't ever get paid back for doing that for me."

"I am proud. Thank you. Tomorrow we head east. Your men are selecting saddles and horses for the ride. We will head on and get those cattle to populate this grand ranch you and your team prepared for them."

At dawn, they left on the rough road chiseled out by an army team to be able to reach Fort Apache across country but still a long ways from being a real road. The day passed as they went through Fort Apache and on east to drop off the mountains into Socorro. Leaving the mountains they soon approached the village, and Chet decided to hold up, park the wagons at a campground still in enough altitude to be cooler with stock water and wells for humans.

Chet, Jesus, Toby, and Fred rode into town. Someone directed them to their cattle buyer's office.

He came outside to shake their hands when they rode up. He told an employee to go get a horse and show them the biggest of the herds of their cows. Those cattle were down in the bottoms watered by the Rio Grande that ran south to El Paso. Riding through them, Chet was impressed. He asked the man, Art, how they compared to the other groups.

"Oh, the others look this good."

Most were purebred-looking Herefords.

Some still showed longhorn blood, but it was faint. A purebred bull would solve that. He was almost jealous. They were large boned and wide-hipped cows. Twenty thousand dollars' worth, but they'd earn their keep on Toby's ranch. All he needed. He'd be back next year for more for Cole's place if it all went well. They saw two more herds and rode back to town, where Joseph ordered them all beers.

"Got some plain juice?" Chet asked.

"Grape. It ain't wine," the barkeep said.

"I'll take some." He winked at Miguel and gave him his beer.

"All those cattle look great. When can we take them?"

"Any time you want."

"Tomorrow. We don't want to rest here too long."

Miguel lifted his mug of beer. "I am just glad no one tried to stop us coming here. I am not afraid but I hate this business of outlaws set on killing you."

"We should make it home all right. There are enough of us," Chet said.

"Better than that, most I saw are bred back."

Chet shook his head. "Thirty some years old and no one ever showed me that before. You are building a lot of information, ready to run a ranch. There will be one or the Valley one when Raphael decides to retire."

"I understand. Lisa and I can wait. She loves running the house. If I have to go away to run something else, she may not want to go."

Chet shook his head. "I doubt that."

Things were set to bring the cattle all in one herd past Socorro. Chavez made arrangements to graze them on a place west of Socorro the next afternoon. They arranged to meet east of town and then drive the groups to a point to meet at that place. Miguel took the Valley vaqueros for one bunch, Tom's men rode with Jesus for another bunch, and Toby and his men the other bunch. They were to meet the other two herds, combine them, and swing north and around the village.

Chet and the girls in the two wagons went to the overnight stop, found the well with water, and set up camp with one helper while he and Fred rode west to find the next stop. It was ten miles west but it had water. As they hurried back into camp they could hear the cattle bawling from way off.

He hoped they had no problems. It was dry around Socorro. And lots of dust rose into the sky. A few clouds had gathered, but he saw no signs that they'd get a monsoon rain. Several had wet them riding over, and one could expect them about every day at the top of the White Mountains, above their stop, at that time of the year. It could be a quick pass-by shower, or a flood from a towering column of clouds that dumped a load of water.

He dreaded it, but hail sometimes fell, too. That was hard to escape, and a tough job, especially while trying to keep control of upset, hurting cows. They had that ahead of them to watch out for.

Nothing out of the ordinary happened on their trip west. Chet gave some sore-footed cows to small Apache camps along the way and the people were grateful for the food. With all the hands it was easy to slip through the timber finding open meadows and water to camp at each day. The forage was strong, and the cows were gaining weight and licking circles in places on their hides. Two weeks later they drew near their new home, and everyone relaxed in the saddle.

"Stop here. There is something wrong. Don't go closer," Toby told the girls and the drivers in their wagons.

Chet, who had been at the rear, galloped up. "What's wrong?"

"The two men I left to guard are not coming out of the house." Toby stood in the saddle looking the situation over. "Something is wrong. You stay here."

"Hell no," Chet said and drew his gun. "Let's go find out."

Toby nodded and with his gun out they raced for the house.

"The front door is open. And there are no dogs," Toby said.

"Go right and I'll go left. Be ready for an ambush."

Toby nodded and they charged around the house; they stopped in back of the house, and Toby pointed at the barn. "Look Chet. My men. Some son of a bitch hung them."

Two limp bodies, hands tied behind them, had been lynched on ropes hung on rafters of the new barn; their bodies gently twisted in the breeze.

Chet holstered his gun and stepped down.

"Go back to the women. Keep them away from here while I cut them down."

Tears ran down Toby's tanned cheeks. "I left them here, but not to be hung."

"You can't do a thing. Go be with the women. I promise you we will find their killers." He had trouble not vomiting himself. They'd hung there for some time. Five days to a week. There was a note pinned on one of the men's shirts. It read, *Burns we will get you next.*

They'd been jerk hung and strangled, then the rope tied off. Chet sliced it and the first man fell to the ground. He did the same to the second one, looking carefully around for any evidence.

The two crying women came around the house.

"Why did they hang them?" Liz asked, hugging the sobbing Talley.

"They said on a note they wanted me. I was next."

"Oh, Chet, when will it ever stop?"

He hugged both of them. Toby went off for help. In a short while Jesus, Miguel, and Fred were all there. Josey stayed with the wagons, and the other men with the cows.

"We have no idea who did it. They did it five days to a week ago, far as I can tell. Before anyone else comes we will search the area and house for clues. Look for anything that will point to a clue. Anything. When enough help comes we will bury the two boys."

"They hung them?" Jesus asked looking sick over the situation.

"They jerk hung them so they strangled at the end of the rope. The note pinned on one of them said 'Burns, we will get you next.' "

"Son of a bitch. Who were they?"

"We have to find that out, Jesus. That's all I can tell you."

"I'll get some blankets and wrap their bodies," Fred said.

"Rollo and Christopher were such good guys," Talley said. "Toby and I thought they could keep this place from harm. They were good shots with a rifle. We bought new Winchester rifles for the men. They all have serial numbers on them. Their killers must be very mean men."

"I have those serial numbers in my files. Can that help?" Toby asked.

"Oh, yes. That will help a lot."

"How would you do that?" Liz asked

"We'll start jerking out rifles, checking the guns and see if the numbers match, looking for the two no doubt stolen from here."

"What if they didn't steal them?"

"I know they wouldn't leave brand-new rifles here."

Talley wiped her eyes. "I will go get those numbers."

"Good. That's our first break. There will be more. I am so sorry. I can hear the cattle coming. I hate it more than anything that these boys aren't here to welcome them."

Jesus found a letter lying on the ground. It was sent to Rodney Harris from Fort Worth.

Dear Rodney,
Your paw got the bad arthuritis and can't work anymore. We are living on neighbor's gardens but we not got any money. This winter we fixing to starve, Any money you got pleases send us some.

Maw

Chet read the smudged address. Tucson, Az T. The box number was not clear, but a postal worker in the post office would know and could tell what it was. Then they could watch the box if it was still in use.

Fred rode up. "There is a dead horse out behind the barn. He was shot in the forehead. The buzzards have been eating him. He has a Circle T brand."

"What color was he?"

"Red roan."

"The state brand inspectors have a list of brand owners."

"He damn sure isn't one of ours," Toby said. "My men are digging the graves. You will do the services?"

Chet nodded.

"Thanks. I want to ride down and speak to my neighbors and see if they saw anyone."

"Do that, Toby. Anything they saw or heard might help us."

Chet went into the house and hung his hat on a peg. Talley brought him some steaming coffee. "Sit in the big chair."

He thanked her and picked up the cup to blow on it. Then he remembered that neither victim had boots on. Why? Did the killers steal their boots, too?

"Talley?"

She came back in the room. "Did those two have shoes?"

"No, they had new boots. All the men went to Prescott with Toby, two at a trip, and bought them with money they'd earned. They were proud of them. Why?"

"Those murderers are wearing them. I'd bet money on it."

"You think of everything, and I bet you find those devils. See, I even cleaned up my mouth."

Chet laughed. "You sure did, Talley. I am, and will be, searching for them hard, and we will find them. I suspect they only stayed here a short while. They didn't take anything else, like the coffee, for example, so I say they hit and run. They possibly knew the number of men we had with the herd and didn't want to face them."

"If I find them, they won't have a thing to worry about but the fires of hell."

"I know. But you need to go back to being a great ranch wife and hay mower. I can handle the bad men deal."

"I know. Those two were special. That's why we left them. They were our leaders, and we had such grand plans. I know the others are as shaken and mad as I am."

Toby's neighbors Chrystal and Cecil knew nothing about the raid or the raiders, which left them up a blind alley.

Chet did a solemn service, closing with, "Lord, hold these two great young men in the palm of your hand. Amen."

Four young sad men finished covering the bodies, then everyone went to bed.

Chet wondered who the killers were but knew he'd track them down somehow.

CHAPTER 13

Back at the ranch, that evening, Chet met with Cole and Spencer. They talked around the kitchen table.

"Two of Tom's men drove five service-age Hereford bulls up to the ranch. Beautiful bulls. They are now out with my cows."

"That settles that, doesn't it?" Chet smiled at Cole.

"Sure helps. How are the cows you moved?"

"I wish I had five hundred more like them for you. We gave about a dozen to the Apaches for food, but the rest are at Rustler's Ranch."

"This attack on Toby's men was bad?"

"Yes, very much so, but we will find them. I have a ranch-branded horse that they had to shoot because, we think, he broke his leg. He wore a Circle T brand. I have a wire into the Brand Inspection Office asking them to look up the brand ownership, and I wrote a letter to the postmaster in Tucson about a letter I found in one of the raiders' pockets. And we have the serial numbers on the two Winchesters Toby bought for their defense. New 44/40s. I am making copies of the numbers so we have the numbers with us, and might find a gun, or both somewhere, someday."

"No one saw them go in or out?"

Chet shook his head.

Chet's men and other U.S. Marshals began searching for the stolen guns. Every saloon with horses hitched outside, they stopped and checked the rifles in the scabbards on the saddled mounts. Chet called it looking for a needle in a haystack, but his men were persistent in their search. Someone, or two someones, had those two rifles.

The letter had been forwarded to Tombstone general delivery. No help, and no information from the letter he found, but Chet did write Virgil Earp to keep an eye out for a Rodney Harris, the only name he had for one of the killers.

Raphael sent Toby two more good boys to replace the two he lost.

Talley wrote him a letter thanking him for getting them through their loss and that the new boys were great. The cattle were settling, and Toby had ordered two more hay outfits for the next year. Would they need to go take delivery of the bulls they'd need next spring?

Chet talked about it at their weekly meeting. He took Miguel and Fred down to the Verde Ranch and Rocky went with them riding his horse. Val hoped he wouldn't ride off the side, and they assured him they'd watch him carefully. When they arrived and Adam saw Rocky's horse, he told Chet that he needed a paint horse, too. Then they raced out to the sheep.

Chet knew his nephew, Tye, would find one. He was the horse dealer in the family, gathering a *remuda* for Toby's ranch boys.

Tom said he'd find more than two dozen bulls for Toby by Christmas. He might have to add some shorthorn bulls to the mix, because Herefords were still preciously scarce. Shawn, at the top ranch on the rim, needed ten more, too. Tom said he already had that listed.

While at Camp Verde they checked several rifles in scabbards hitched outside the saloons. No match found.

Spencer and Fred went down to Oracle to supervise the final work on the headquarters. Chet told them to check guns coming and going, as they rode down there. The settling of the Oracle sale wasn't until

November. The bulls for that place had been bought from Slaughter, and the man in place there, Foster, said they and the cows were doing wonderfully. His wife wrote the letter for him, but added that it really looked like the old ranch they all knew, now with great livestock and the headquarters near done, was going to be a great place and asked that they were wished luck pleasing the new owners.

An official letter came for Chet from the state headquarters of the U.S. Marshals in Tucson:

Have you heard anything about a banker who ran away with the Mesa, AZ, bank's money? Giles Jacobs is the man's name. Forty-two, blond hair, blue eyes, and six feet tall. He left behind a wife and three children and is thought to be in the company of a gambling dove named Sadie Rose, which is, it is known, a name she took to hide her past. Jacobs's take is estimated at forty-two thousand dollars. The banking systems examiners are still sorting out the mess left behind, trying to uncover not only the theft of the money, but the many illegal deals he pulled.

Would you have the time to go look

into finding him — local authorities have given up trying to locate them both. If you are too busy, please send me word back. I will try to find another marshal to investigate. Really, Chet, you have the best record on finding these crooks of all the marshals we have in the territory.

Randy Carter,
Acting Chief Marshal, Arizona
Territory.

They damn sure seem to have trouble keeping a Chief Marshal in Tucson.

He wired Spencer and Fred that they needed to meet him in Mesa in two or three days.

Miguel and Jesus were with Cole so he'd get them word that evening. They would be the ones riding with him down to Mesa. No telling where they ran to but every day they roamed free the less money they could recover for the investors of the bank.

"What next?" his wife asked from the office door.

"Someone ran off with a Mesa bank's money. They can't find him."

She snickered. "I knew they'd have a problem that they'd come to you to solve."

"I wired Spencer and Fred to meet me in Mesa. Miguel, Cole, and Jesus can ride with me down there and then we can spread out."

"You five should be able to find him."

"I have written each sheriff in the territory about him. Maybe we will hear something. While we are out, we will try and find that Rodney Harris. He is someone we need to interview about Toby's boys' double murder. I also included the serial numbers of those two rifles that were stolen at that time. I will mail the letters on my way out."

"Who is the one robbed the bank in Mesa?"

"Let me look. His name is Giles Jacobs. He left a wife and three children and ran away with a dove named Sadie Rose."

"He go to Mexico?"

"The officials have no leads, according to the head marshal."

"How many like these have you found for them?"

He smiled. "Several. But I always had help. I am hoping some folks will step for ward and tell me where they are or if they have seen them."

"I will stay here. It will be still very hot down there, and I like the cool of here."

"I don't blame you."

"Your cattle business settled?"

"The Three V's will need more cattle, but Cole needs to expand his hay ground or we need to buy some land he can grow hay on, first."

"And?"

"Two well drillers are moving over there to bore for artesian sources."

She stepped over kissed his forehead. "Be careful. I don't want to lose you."

"That goes both ways."

"School will be starting soon and Rocky will need to attend. Here or over there? Val and I have discussed it. Their house is nowhere near fixed."

"He's growing up fast, isn't he?"

"You hardly know he's around here. He rides his horse so much. I never saw a boy that age so interested in riding."

"His mother was horsey. But maybe he is simply going to be a darn good cowboy."

"Were you that horsey?"

"I can't recall. I wasn't interested in going to school back then and something turned inside of me. My father had lost his mind looking for our kidnapped kids, and there was no one else to run our ranch and keep it going except me."

"You were a teen by then?"

"Yes. Fourteen or fifteen. I was older later when it was my decision to send cattle north in the first herds that went up there to be sold. Many said it would never work. We ended up with thousands of dollars for our cattle that were worth nothing back at home. That was our recovery from the war."

"Then the feud came?"

"Yes. Arizona was sleeping when we got here. Places are five times higher now than when I first came out here."

"And now. I can't believe you have sold two ranches."

"Oh, those two ranches never deeply appealed to me. Letting the Boyd family have the one on the border was good for him and his family to have. It was too far from Prescott. The Oracle Ranch made lots of money selling it. I knew I bought it low enough to make a real profit when the time came. I even told the banker what he needed to do. He had no interest except to get rid of it. I never expected the windfall from the sale of the stage line and telegraph wire."

"Kinda unreal, isn't it?"

"No, the real unbelievable thing that happened was when the railroad management told Cole they were cutting his salary in half right then. I bet they will spend four times that managing it."

"Yes. You said at the time they had no sense whatsoever, when they did that. But enough of that, Lisa is close to having lunch ready, and Lisa is having a cookout for the ranch. I expect Tom and Victor's bunch to join us"

"Great. And as to the sales — it's nice not to have any of that business to worry about."

"Val says she's glad Cole's back to ranching."

"I heard. I am glad he's back with me, too."

He stood, put with his arm around her, and they went to eat.

"No one is here yet? Jesus is home today so I'll send word that I need him for a trip, and I am counting on him to select what we need to take along."

"He and Anita are coming to supper. Tell Miguel, he's helping down at the cooking."

"Yes, ma'am."

She gave him a poke. "That way, if he misses anything I will personally deliver it to you."

Rocky came and hugged Liz. "I helped them bring in a calf who lost his momma."

"I bet that was exciting."

"He didn't want to come here."

"Sounds like the work of cowboys."

Rocky smiled at his father's words. "I thought so, too."

They took seats and Chet blessed the food. Lisa had brown beans, fire-grilled beef strips, and green beans with biscuits for lunch. A peach cobbler was ready for dessert.

Lisa took a seat with them. "This meal was not done by me today. I was busy helping the crew. In the yard, getting ready for tonight. Josey helped Val. They did everything here."

The group thanked them both and Val put all the praise onto Josey. She blushed. "I am so grateful for my marriage to Fred and getting to live with you all. I wake up every morning and thank God I am here in a place where people take me as their own and not take something away from me."

"Did you know Chet had taken Fred in?"

"Yes. I saw him drive Liz to town and ride with Chet, but I figured he was just a stable boy and had no room for me. The first thing he told me when he came for me was he felt so afraid to do anything that might get him fired that he didn't dare do anything at all except what he was told to do."

"I am sorry. He must have been busting to go get you. He should have said something sooner. Of course we would have allowed it."

"I know. It was even scarier when I realized what we did, getting married and coming here. But I am most grateful our firstborn will not be delivered in an alley."

Val reached over and dabbed the tears on her cheeks. Then she hugged her. "Josey, you are safe and so is the baby. This is the greatest family anyone will ever know and you are one of us. All of us are survivors."

"Amen."

CHAPTER 14

Miguel smiled, when, after lunch, Chet told him to get the horses and pack saddles along with needs for five of them for ten days. They were going to Mesa with Jesus to meet Fred and Spencer to try to find a banker who ran off with a great deal of money.

"I bet they have no idea where he went," Miguel said.

"Why else ask us to find him?" Chet replied, amused.

"Well, I'll have everything ready. Does Jesus know about it?"

"No, but he and Anita are coming for supper. He will learn then. Everything else going good?"

"Yes. Raphael and I decided to put the tent up for the ranch meal tonight. We've had some afternoon showers this week. You never know about them."

"Good plan."

"I'll have everything ready to go."

The ranch folks began arriving. Ranch hands from the Verde. There were three farm wagons of Victor's field hands and their families. Cole's people came in wagons and a surrey. Hampt had a wagon and the hands rode horses. His farmers, Betty Lou and Leroy Simpson from Oak Creek, brought two wagonloads of peaches, blackberries, and garden vegetables. Chet knew that they would be the big hit because of the food they brought. Toby and Talley arrived with a camp wagon and four riders.

The Hereford crew who looked after the purebred herd at Perkins came alone, but the ranch women, young and old, would dance with them.

Talley and Toby found Chet.

Before Chet had a chance to ask, Talley said, "The cows are doing great. They are licking their hides in circles."

"Please tell Mr. Chavez he found us some great cattle. I bet they were the best ones for sale this fall."

"I met John Slaughter down there. He's a sharp cattle trader and he told me Chavez was the man. He saved us two weeks or more work, finding that many good ones."

"Chet, having cattle makes that place a real ranch. Thank you."

"On the bad side, have you learned anything?" Toby asked.

"No, but I wrote letters to all the county sheriffs asking about finding that Harris and those two rifles."

"I guess that is all we can do. We still don't know much about who they are. Maybe your letters will get us some leads."

"I am going to Mesa tomorrow. Some banker ran off with the bank's money and they don't know where he went. I will be checking there, too. We won't quit trying to find them. I promise."

Talley hugged him. "We know. We know. If they hadn't murdered those two boys it would have been the highlight of our lives, getting those cows."

"It still is good. You two are building a great ranch."

They agreed and shook his hand.

"Cole's back. He went to shower. A driller was there today and is going to set up next week."

"Is that Davis?"

"Yes."

"Sounds good. That test will decide our next move."

Jesus arrived and must have talked to Miguel before he met up with Chet.

"How is your wife feeling?"

"Good, she says. We leaving at dawn?"

"Yes. You have help to watch the place? If not, she can stay here."

"Yes. And they can help her, too, but I'll ask her. She will probably want to stay at our house."

"The deal is the U.S. Marshals want us to try and find a banker who left Mesa with a load of money. I sent a wire for Fred and Spencer to join us."

Jesus smiled. "He left no trail?"

Chet shook his head. "You knew that or they'd have arrested him."

"If it had been easy, they'd never asked for us." Jesus was chuckling.

"Hey, you three need me?" Cole asked, fresh from his shower and in clean clothes.

"I was thinking about it, but you have enough to do here. Spencer and Fred will join Miguel, Jesus, and me down there."

Cole grinned. "Sounded like fun."

"Did Davis think we have a shot at hitting water?"

"He wants a water witcher to check it."

"Liz can do that. I don't know if she would do it, but she can witch a well with a peach tree fork."

Cole chuckled. "I'll try to get her to do it."

Chet shrugged. "Good luck."

The new people met the hands from the other operations. The cowboys politely danced with the ranch wives and they all had a good time. Everyone ate until they were full, and Chet didn't know of anyone who didn't have a good time. He thanked them all for coming. Some would sleep over. Others would go home. The women promised breakfast at sunrise.

Jesus said he'd take Anita home and be back before dawn. Chet thanked him and went to the house with his wife to find some shuteye. Miguel said he would have it all ready. Lisa asked if he'd eat with the morning bunch. He told her yes and bragged on the job she did.

There was a letter for Fred from his wife, who'd already gone to bed. She'd left it on the kitchen table for Chet to take to him. He put it in the jumper pocket that he'd wear against the cool morning air.

"Did Cole ask you to witch for a well?"

"I figured you'd told him I did that. What if I can't find any?"

"He may need two opinions."

She broke out laughing "I will go try it while you look for this runaway banker."

"We may not find him, either. His trail will be cold by now."

He lay in bed wondering, before he drifted off to sleep, if they would find him.

CHAPTER 15

The next morning when he awoke he heard distant thunder. There was rain on the bedroom windowpane. How unusual. It seldom rained at night in the monsoon season, but any rain in late summer was always a blessing to ranch folk.

He would have bet all the overnighters were grateful for the big tent. It must have been raining for some time. Liz woke up.

"Is it raining?"

"Yes. You getting up now?"

"Of course. When did it start?"

"I discovered it when I woke up. I'll take it all, but the overnight campers may wake up to a shock."

"I imagine so. The tent is up, so they have cover."

"I'll wait for you."

"I won't be long. I like to see you off, though you may be swimming away today."

They laughed and when she was dressed

they went downstairs, put on their long-tail canvas raincoats, and under old felt hats headed for the tent in the now gentle rain. Lightning flashed and thunder rolled across the sky but they were under cover of the tent when the next, stronger rainfall came.

Lisa came to greet them. "Maybe you should plan trips more often, Chet?"

"I'd do that once a week if it brought rain every time."

"Well, Miguel has the packhorses loaded. He said a little rain won't change his mind."

"Daylight is not far off. One day won't matter if it continues this hard."

"The ladies have breakfast ready. Get a plate and eat."

"Thanks. Tell everyone how much Liz and I appreciate the hard work all of our workers did to put on that great party."

"I will."

A wet Jesus arrived smiling, shedding his slicker. "Whew, it's been raining between my place and here. The creeks and arroyos are full of water."

Chet sat down to eat his pancakes and ham. One of the ladies brought him and Liz cups of coffee.

"Is Anita doing all right?" Liz asked.

"She has some morning sickness. We thought it was early, but the doctor said it hits women at all stages. She is excited. You know how hesitant she is about things, and I think she dreaded it happening at first, but she's over that and happily planning for it."

"Good. Get a plate and join us," Liz told him.

"I'll just have coffee. I had breakfast with her before I left."

"Miguel must have the packhorses loaded to suit him. He just came in to eat."

"He asked me a few things last night," Jesus said. "I told him he was right on."

"I knew he'd be worried about doing it right but he does need to know how."

Jesus agreed.

"I am impressed by him. You know he has learned to read?" Liz asked.

"He won't be left out. Most men don't bother at his age, but he has a good teacher," Jesus said. "When we brought Lisa back I thought she wouldn't ever be anybody worthwhile. But I think you, Liz, converted both Lisa and Talley to become real doers."

"I don't know if it was me or the atmosphere we have here."

"Whichever. It has worked well."

"You guys started with Val and Bonnie. Then you brought Ben Ivor's wife Kathrin back from Utah."

Jesus shook his head. "Then he brought you here and you brought Anita for me."

Thunder rumbled close by.

"You going to postpone leaving for a while?" his wife asked.

"A while."

"Good. Want more to eat?"

"No. I'm full."

Miguel came by with his plate of food. "I have the packhorses in the big barn alleyway with our saddle horses."

"Let's let the rain pass or slow up. I'd hate to be hit by lightning."

Miguel laughed. "Me, too."

Cole came by with his plate full. "Great rain."

"A wonderful one. Liz, did you tell Cole that you would try the witching but you needed a peach tree fork and a real witcher there, too?"

Liz laughed. "No. I didn't have a chance to, and you just told him."

"Oh great. I will get it set up," Cole said.

Liz shook her head, smiling. By then Rocky had climbed onto the bench beside her and asked her to go riding with him when the rain quit.

She agreed.

Chet realized his son had his second

mother tied up in his little fingers, too.

The rain went north and the world around them sparkled in the sunshine by the time they climbed into their saddles and headed south. Chet was on one of his solid roans; Miguel rode a stout big bay and Jesus was on a dun, leaving his own horse behind. The six packhorses jogged along behind.

Miguel must have brought everything. Four packhorses were usually enough. But he needed to learn how to do that and he was serious enough about this job that the next time he would do it. Meantime, Chet would have bet they wouldn't need a single thing except for rounding up the two suspects.

They camped at someone's windmill on top of a mesa late that afternoon. And by sundown the beans were edible. That and some good camp coffee closed the day. The next evening they were on the edge of the desert and Chet expected to be at Mesa the following day.

Spencer and Fred met them at Mueller's Livery on Main Street. Chet's back had begun to complain after that long in the saddle even though they had good horses to ride in the search for the getaway crooks.

Spencer reported that the ranch headquarters would be finished in less than a month.

His foreman was proud of the cattle and the bulls Chet bought from John Slaughter, but his wife stated she wished Chet had not sold the ranch. She worried she would never have the chance to meet Liz.

Since Spence and Fred had gotten to Mesa a day early, they had the police chief's reports on the pair. Photos of both and all the information they had on the crime.

"Chief James said he could not believe how those two made such a fast getaway. And they left no trace. He swore he'd interrogated everyone he could find and no one saw them leaving town."

"I kinda slipped around town today," Fred told them. "To see what I could find out. I never learned a thing."

"Jesus and Miguel can look in the barrio tomorrow. Is the bank open?"

"No. The examiners are still looking at the books. Besides what they stole, the guy I talked to said Jacobs made many large loans before he left. Loans that far exceeded the collateral they took in exchange."

"Whew. Do they think he was paid off?"

"More than likely."

"Maybe those people know where he went. There has to be a tie to this man somewhere. I want to interview his wife."

His men agreed. But she probably knew

nothing. He felt certain the police chief must have talked to her. If Jacobs liked doves well enough to run off with one, there might be more of them that would know something about where he went.

They hashed it out in a restaurant over a good meal.

The man who owned the business came by. "I met these two men," he said pointing to Jesus and Fred. "I am Abe Carter. This is my place, and I am one of the people that lost money in the bank theft. You marshals, too?"

"Chet Byrnes. They are Jesus Martinez and Miguel Costa. We are here, as they told you, to find the thief."

"I am so glad to meet you, Marshal Byrnes. I have heard that you have a very successful record of finding the likes of Jacobs."

"We try. Do you know anything that would help us?"

"You might ask —" Carter looked around like he wanted to be certain no one could hear him. "Rowell Jennings. He is big rancher east of here. Those two were real close."

"We won't mention you. Thanks."

When Carter left, Spencer asked, "Why didn't he tell us that before?"

"He was scared for his life, I'd say. Let's check him out, too."

Spencer agreed.

They talked about how things were going for Cole and how Toby and Talley were doing.

Chet told them fine.

They went to back to the hotel and promised to meet for breakfast, when the small café down the street opened at six. Chet and Jesus shared a room.

"What will we do about Jennings?"

"Go talk to him."

"What if he won't tell us anything?"

"We'll figure out a way to get him to talk."

"The way Carter acted, he sounds like he might be tough."

"He can't be tougher than others we've dealt with."

"You're right. But somehow when he gave us his name and how he gave it to us made me think he must be a real son of a bitch."

"Most crooks are. They have something to hide and will do anything to protect themselves, at any cost."

"I noticed that there are not many roads leading out of here. Everyone sees the traffic, so how did they get away with no one seeing the two leave?"

"It was well planned."

"Like someone hid them in a wagon?"

"Probably."

"We'll find them, but it's good night now."

"Yes. Good night."

Over breakfast the next morning they decided what they needed to do.

"Jesus, Miguel, and Fred, take on the barrio. Spencer and I will talk to the bank examiners."

When they parted, he and Spencer went to the bank. A policeman guarded the door.

"U.S. Marshals," Spencer said, and showed their badges.

The man nodded. "I know you. This must be Marshal Byrnes?"

Chet shook his hand. "Nice to meet you."

"Sam Holt. My pleasure. I wish you luck, sir."

"We will need it, I fear."

Sam nodded.

Norm Fuller was in charge and greeted them.

They sat down and he showed them the list of borrowers he considered phony.

"David Andrews has a bad credit record. Giles Jacobs renewed a loan this guy never paid on in over two years. The interest owed on the past one was probably paid for from the new loan. He has a zero balance in his bank account and received a five-thousand-dollar new loan. His assets are twenty cows. There is no description of them."

Chet took out his pocketbook and wrote down, "David Andrew — borrowed $5,000 and owes the bank $7,500. Has twenty cows."

Then there was a loan to Andre Michaels for $4,000 secured by his flock of three hundred sheep.

Fuller said he asked the sheriff to look at his county tax forms. He listed twenty sheep as his herd.

"The man either lied to the bank or the sheriff, who collects the state tax, said he only claimed twenty sheep on his tax form."

"Who's next?"

"Maria Cantal who owns a cathouse south of town. She borrowed five thousand dollars to expand her business and he gave her a second mortgage on the property. The first loan is for eight thousand dollars which, I believe, exceeds the value of her house four hundred percent."

"I am looking for ways to track him down. We can confront these borrowers and demand they tell what they gave him out of that money."

Fuller agreed.

By noon he had twenty borrowers listed

as having seriously bad loans.

He and Spencer ate lunch talking about it.

"What about Rowell Jennings?"

"We need to look at him hard. He wasn't on the borrowers list we got."

"Carter said they were close."

"That might tell us a lot, but I figure he won't tell us a damn thing."

Spencer smiled. "What can we arrest him for? A few days in the hoosegow might loosen his tongue."

"Let's work on it. That would be a perfect way to get him to talk."

The others found them in the lobby mid-afternoon. They had the place to themselves and each one had found out something about Jacobs.

Jesus began with his. "I talked to some doves. They said he was a frequent user of ladies of the night. He had a few favorites. I interviewed one of them. She said she didn't know where he went but she missed the money he paid her more than anything else. I named some places he might go and she said he never spoke of them, but she did say he would probably have gone where there were Hispanic whores."

Fred agreed. "The women I spoke to said

he liked them better than white women."

"Did he do this frequently?"

"Oh yeah," Miguel said. "From what I heard he really liked them."

"No clues to where he went though."

They shook their heads.

"Spencer suggested that if we could pin a crime on Jennings and jail him he might talk to us."

"What crime could that be?" Fred asked.

Chet shook his head. "Carefully, tomorrow, two of you get a look at his operation. I'm going to try to talk to Jacobs's wife."

"Fred, Miguel, and I can do that," Spencer said. "We'll get directions to his place while you and Jesus talk to her."

"Handle it." They turned in early and met for breakfast. His other team had a map to Jennings's ranch.

Mosel Jacobs lived in a large two-story house on one of Mesa's broad streets. Mormon founders planned these streets to be wide enough to turn a wagon and team around in the middle of the block. He knocked on the door and a straight-back woman in her thirties, dressed rather upper class, answered the door.

"My name is Chet Byrnes. I am a U.S. Marshal and I need to ask you some questions."

"You want to know more about Mosel?"

"If you would be so kind."

"I guess I owe you that being a federal lawman."

"This is one of my men, Jesus Martinez." She had them sit in the formal living room. They turned down her offer to serve them tea.

"Do you have any idea where he went?"

"No. I was shocked at the news that he robbed the bank. He never indicated anything was wrong to me. He spoke about plans to expand the bank and increase his deposits."

"They say a woman left with him."

"I heard that, too. I never heard of her before they said her name. I understand she was a dove and gambler. I couldn't believe he would do such a thing. We have been happily married for five years."

"You had no idea he frequented several such women for their services?"

"No. He was a good father and husband. I think these are lies people have made up about him."

"He never suggested places where he wanted to go?"

"No."

"Thank you. We have others to question."

"I am sorry I couldn't help you more."

On the way back to the business section he and Jesus reflected on her words.

"She lives sheltered from this world around her," Jesus said. "You couldn't convince her of his wrongs if they were testified to on a stack of bibles."

"I agree, and she couldn't stand the embarrassment that her husband did that."

"Does she have her own wealth to live on like she does now?"

"Damned if I know. I hope those guys of ours find out more about Jennings than we did from her."

"Amen." Jesus laughed.

Late that evening, Chet and Jesus waited at the livery for their return. They dropped out of the saddle looking weary.

"How did it go?"

"He keeps some doves around. His men are a lazy lot, and he runs some Mexican cattle that looked half-starved on his desert ranch. His neighbors hate him and say he eats their beef."

"Wait. They say he eats their beef?"

"Yes. They can't catch him rustling, but they are convinced he eats their cattle."

"Does he have a stack of hides?"

"Why?"

"We once proved a rustling case by finding a neighbor's branded hide in a criminal's stack."

Jesus nodded. "People stack them up and cash them in when they need money."

"How do we find that?"

"Get a search warrant, and look for a hide brand he does not own."

"That would get him in jail," Fred said.

"Tomorrow I will find a district judge to issue us a search warrant."

"I'd bet ten dollars there is one in that stack," Spencer said.

"We will see. Let's go eat."

"I thought you'd never remember we need to do that," Fred teased.

Chet clapped him on his shoulder. "I'm hungry, too."

"Guys, we are going to get a chance to learn where this guy ran off to."

"Yes. His wife wouldn't tell us anything. Said people were lying about him running around with such women."

"That must have been fun."

Jesus shook his head. "She doesn't live in the real world."

The next day after a meeting with the prosecuting attorney Pat McClure, they went before Judge Roger Watkins to seek the search warrant.

Chet told him that neighbors had been complaining about him stealing their beef. "With a search warrant, I think we can find evidence to prosecute him and his foreman."

"Marshal Byrnes, I appreciate all the time you spend clearing up crime in this territory. Obviously you expect more than a cowhide to be found there."

"I do, sir."

"I will sign for it."

They went out to eat and Chet felt much better. They had a lead whether Jennings told them what he knew about Jacobs or not. They needed to find some evidence against him. He could only hope it worked.

CHAPTER 16

The quarter moon sat in the east high over Superstition Mountain. In the cooler time of night they rode two by two through the saguaros down the wagon track road. Silent owls and bats swarmed, hunting for prey. They could hear the creak of saddle leathers and the soft plod of hooves on the loose sands, and in spots where the caliche protruded, it sounded louder.

The dark outline of Jennings's ranch huddled in an open patch save for some palo verde trees. They left their mounts in a draw and armed with Winchesters strode forward to circle the sleeping headquarters.

There was lots of starlight and the small moon was still overhead. When Chet felt satisfied he had his men spaced right, he levered a cartridge in his rifle chamber and fired an earsplitting shot in the air.

"I am a U.S. Marshal. Come out with your hands in the air, and get down on your knees. Any move for a gun and you will die. I have ten men out here armed, with their guns cocked ready to end your life."

A few women, scantily dressed, stumbled out the front door screaming, "Don't shoot."

Jesus made them get on their knees.

Someone burst out a side window. Spencer fired his gun and the man screamed, "I'm hit."

"Anyone else want to be shot?"

Men hurried out the door hands high. The last one out was a big man and Chet knew he had to be Jennings. All of them in their underwear were kneeling in dirt and stickers.

Fred began handcuffing the men, by the wrist, to each other. Miguel put leg irons on the grumbling Jennings.

"You ain't got anything on me. You can't do this. I'm innocent."

Spencer laughed. "You don't know what we do have on you."

Jesus brought the wounded man around and made him sit down. "He isn't going to die." Then Jesus went in the house to get something for his wound.

Chet lifted the first woman to her feet. "Can you two women cook us some breakfast?"

"Oatmeal?"

"Make lots of it." He helped the other one up. "No tricks."

"We won't. What are you going to do to us?"

"I know no crime you have done. I will provide you transportation to town and twenty dollars apiece."

"Oh, God bless you."

"Go make oatmeal." He didn't need any gratitude from them.

The wounded prisoner's arm was wrapped. One at a time the prisoners were taken to dress, come back, and re-chained. Their guns were collected and checked. None bore the numbers they sought.

With a candle lamp, Chet and Jesus went through the hide piles and found three hides not wearing his brand. Then Jesus moved a pile of junk and spotted a green box. He clamored over to get to it and really fought to get it out. "This box looks like those Wells Fargo boxes stages carry."

"Does it have a serial number on it?"

"It damn sure does. Chet, I am thinking this is from a stage robbery."

Chet sat back on his haunches. "This may be the best break so far. I think we have found a real prize."

Spencer came into the shed. "Do any good?"

"Jesus found a Wells Fargo strongbox."

"You think it came from a robbery?"

"Yes."

Spencer took off his hat and pounded his leg with it. A smile crossed his face and he shook his head. "By damn, Chet, we are a real fighting force for justice, ain't we?"

He and Jesus began laughing. "We damn sure are."

With three hides and an empty green Wells Fargo strongbox, they loaded the six men in one rickety farm wagon hitched to a team. He hitched a horse with harness scars to a one-seat rig and told the women it was theirs along with the two gold twenty-dollar coins he had taken from Jennings.

There wasn't much else in the place that they wanted or needed. He stepped in the stirrup, swung his leg over, then lifted the roan's head. With a nod to Fred on the wagon seat, he said, "Let's deliver them to Mesa."

"Get up." Fred flicked the lines and the team started out. The iron rims were crushing the ground.

The creosote smell of the desert rode strong in Chet's nose. Tired with some stiffness between his shoulders, he had accomplished one goal, but where in the hell was Jacobs?

CHAPTER 17

The reporters had left the sheriff's sub-office in Mesa. The six prisoners had been booked for rustling and they waited for the verification telegram of the strongbox serial number from the Wells Fargo headquarters in San Francisco. Prosecutor Pat McClure was confident the Fargo report would convict Jennings and his men of a stage robbery and which one.

No wire came. They went to supper and then to bed. The next day the wire came through that the stage robbery happened the year before on the Mesa to Globe run; two passengers, the guard, and the driver were murdered. Wells Fargo would pay Chet's men a two-thousand-dollar reward for settling the case.

Chet walked back in the jail. "Jennings, where's Jacobs at?"

"Damned if I know. The sumbitch owes me money."

"How is that?"

"He promised me a thousand dollars. He never did pay me."

"You got him out of here?"

Jennings had ahold of the bars with both hands and nodded his bearded face. "That was the deal."

"To where?"

"Lordsburg."

"Where did he go from there?"

"How should I know? One minute he and that witch were here, the next they had disappeared."

"It ain't that big a place." Chet shook his head.

"You can have my money when you find him."

"Thanks. I will."

"Hire me a lawyer. You got more ranches than I got fingers. You can afford it."

Jesus smiled as Chet walked by him going out of the jail. "Lordsburg."

"That's where he lost them."

"We have us a trail?"

"Worth going to look."

"All of us need to go?"

Chet shook his head. "No. Jesus, your wife needs you."

"She could."

"Fred, how's yours?"

He shrugged. "I'm sure she's okay."

"Spencer? Lucinda needs you?"

"I could go home or go with you."

"Miguel?"

"She's fine."

"Jesus and Fred, take the horses home. Spencer, Miguel, and I will go to Lordsburg."

They nodded.

"In the morning we will ride over to Hayden's Ferry and catch the stage to Tucson."

"So at noon Jesus and I ride home?" Fred asked.

"To Josey. She'll be as glad to see you as Anita will be to see Jesus. I asked all of you down to Mesa. We found a lead on Jacobs and so now I want you at headquarters while I am away. Both of you are two of my best men. We don't need five of us away just in case something happens. And you might hear leads on the men who killed Toby's two boys."

Fred shrugged. "I want to do my part."

"You both do your parts."

"Fred, our wives will appreciate it. Both are facing having a baby and Chet knows all about pregnancy and wives. I understand, but someone does need to support the ranches. And as he said, we may even find leads on those rifles or the killers," said Jesus.

"Okay. I'm fine with going."

"Good," Chet said. "We have photographs of Jacobs and the woman so if he was around Lordsburg, we may find where he went from there. The end of the tracks should be close to Benson by this time. He may have gone to Silver City, but I bet he went to Mexico at El Paso."

"Safer for a wanted man," Spencer said.

"But Mexico's bad guys prey on gringos who have money."

"Right, and they do it quickly," Jesus said.

"Well, we got this case after he got far away. All we can do is follow his route from there to wherever."

"Let's get some sleep. Breakfast at six a.m., and get going quickly."

That evening he wrote Liz:

I am sending Jesus and Fred home tomorrow. They both have expectant wives. We only need a few of us here. We need to find the killers of Toby's men. Find the stolen rifles. There are lots of things that need to be done. Make sure to share any concerns with the two. My choice was based on the wives who needed them the most. We are off to Texas to find Jacobs before we can return home.

Your loving husband, Chet

They parted at the Ferry. Fred and Jesus, with all the saddle stock plus packhorses, rode north on a two and a half day's ride to home. Chet and the other two took the Tucson stage south. He planned on the eastbound one and was promised a train ride to Lordsburg from east of Benson.

While in Tucson laying over for the stage, one of the superintendents spoke to Chet. "We heard you sold your stage line to the railroad."

"I was a partner in it. They wanted the telegraph to start with and if they continue with the rails we'd have had to sell the stage at an auction and who would need coaches and horses? So we sold it to them."

"The train gets here, they will lay off some of us supervisors. They won't need us. You were lucky to sell it to the destroyers before they got here."

"They'll still need supervisors. I bet they'll need people that can manage their business."

"I never thought like that. I may sign up with them."

"Who else knows the people better? Who around here knows about handling travel?"

"Thanks, Chet."

"I bet you find a place to land."

"You have any ranch hand jobs?"

"I might."

They laughed.

"He worried about losing his job?" Spencer asked.

"Sure. When the train gets here, the stage line is gone. But the Tucson to Hayden Ferry will be here until they build a track up there."

"And the railroad bought yours?" Spencer laughed hard.

"They really wanted the telegraph. Four hundred miles of it from Gallup to Hardee-ville already strung."

"I put in lots of long days on that," Spencer said.

"I bet without a train to work off of they'd never got it built in two years," Chet said.

"They'd have to go to China to find the labor."

"I doubt many Indians would have worked for them."

"You're right. We had over half Navajo laborers. They worked hard stringing it with pride, then they sang and danced at night.

It was a friendly place, and we provided transportation back home for them when it was over."

"But in two years we'd have been be out of the stage business. We had to sell it. We did the right thing. They wanted the telegraph wire and they paid for it all."

"Miguel is going to replace Raphael someday. Jesus has a ranch of his own. Cole has the new one. You figure someday you will buy another one or two?"

Chet laughed. "For you and Fred?"

"Right."

"Spencer, I am all for it, but that place I sold the Boyds was right on the Mexican border. JD's Diablo ranch has had problems and may have more. Mexico has revolutions all the time. Border places are risky business. I'd rather have a place higher up than Oracle. That place was ripe to sell. Obviously the buyers had the money. I will find more ranches down the road. But they may be isolated."

"I don't care about that, but I'd appreciate being considered."

"If I don't have more wire to string."

"We can do that, too."

They climbed on the stage for Benson and the end of the tracks. The trip required an entire day and it was after dark when they found a meal and beds in a hotel.

In the morning, after breakfast, they rode the new tracks to Lordsburg. Once there they split up. Miguel went to the barrio section of town. Spencer took on the saloons and bars. Chet checked the local law, who knew nothing about Jacobs or his lady but would be on the watch.

They met at noon and ate off the lunch bar in the Cactus Saloon.

"No Mexicans I talked to had seen either of them," Miguel said.

"Saloons are all sleepy in the a.m., but no one recognized the pictures of him or her as being through here."

"Deming and then Mesilla and if they are not there, that will lead us to El Paso."

"Jennings told you he lost them in Lordsburg. If Jennings couldn't find him, I bet he'd skipped out of here."

They climbed aboard the eastbound train and it clacked all the way to the next town — Deming. Two days there they found nothing.

Three days later, after some rail delays like a bridge washout from flash flooding, they reached Mesilla. By this time, Chet had begun to suspect the roadbed construction of the Southern Pacific tracks had much to be desired.

Chet noted that they'd pile up powdery dirt with slips and teams to make the roadbed. They never watered and packed it. A two-inch rain dissolved their work and the roadbed was gone. Water was scarce out there, but the roadbed needed to be wet and packed to avoid that happening.

When Chet commented on that, Spencer shook his head. "They want miles of cheap laid tracks but don't want to hire an expensive water hauler and use some sense."

After leaving the train, Miguel had seen and was now talking to a rancher he knew. He came back to where Chet was standing.

"You learn something?" Chet asked him.

Miguel nodded.

"Hank, here, is a rancher who used to have a place in southern Arizona. He won't spill our secret."

"That woman is dealing cards in Eldorado Saloon right now here in Mesilla."

"Good. Let's see what she knows. We will talk again soon, Hank. Sorry, but we've been looking all over for them. I will be at the bar in the saloon. Miguel, you and Spencer make it look like you came in for a beer with me."

"We can do that."

When Chet parted the batwing doors, several customers in the dimly lit saloon

341

looked over to see who came in. Aside from the wagon-wheel lamps set up over the poker table, the place, coming in out the bright light, was like a deep dark cave.

"What'll it be, stranger? My name's Billy."

"A draft of beer."

"You look good for it. Ten cents, please."

"Two of my compadres are coming. Here is a silver dollar." He placed it on the bar. "When we use it up, tell me and I will put another one up."

"Fine. I can count. Your buddies drink beer?"

"I'm not buying them whiskey."

"Okay. No offense." He set the mug of beer before him.

Chet hooked his elbows on the bar and studied the redheaded woman as she dealt cards. She wore a very low-cut dress, the tops of her breasts exposed showing acres of freckles. She was not fat, and the green dress looked to be made of silk. Her bare shoulders and skin showing were distractions she probably used to beat the other players at cards. She had a sizeable stack of money in front of her as she laughed and teased the players who looked more interested in her than their hands.

She lost a hand and grinned big at the winner. "You are a keen player, Hart."

Miguel and Spencer came into the room, nodded at Chet, and joined him.

"That her?" Spencer asked while they lined up for a beer.

"Best I can tell. Any sign of him?"

"Not yet."

"Are we going to wait for him to show up?"

"You hear any word he was here?"

"No, but they knew her. They said, oh yeah, she's in the Eldorado Saloon dealing pasteboards."

"Jacobs may not have stopped here."

Miguel nodded. "I asked several if he was here. They shook their heads."

"Well, I guess we question her next. Here, finish my beer, too."

The next hand was over. Chet stepped out and announced. "This game is over. I am a U.S. Marshal and so are these two men. Ma'am, we are arresting you for bank robbery. Everyone stand up real easy. One wrong move will get you shot. You, too, lady."

Indignantly, she said, "This is outrageous. You can't arrest me."

"Do you have any firearms on you? Miguel, check her legs."

"All right. I have a small gun concealed on my right leg."

Miguel lifted her dress and slip to retrieve it. "Hold still. I need that knife, too."

"Any more —"

Miguel removed a small derringer from her waist.

"Hell, no —"

"Where is Jacobs?"

"I don't know any Jacobs."

"Facing ten years in prison might improve your memory of him."

"I didn't steal a damn thing." She grasped the front of her dress, drew it up a few inches, and wiggled her butt. "You have nothing on me."

"Well, you damn sure don't have many clothes on, but I do have a federal warrant that will ship you back to Arizona for trial and ten years of hard labor."

"I'll have a lawyer fight it."

"You can, but it will do you no good. We have the goods on your involvement with Jacobs in the bank theft, so you will go to trial."

Being angry did not work, so she turned sweet. "It is all a mistake. Let's go to my place and I can entertain the three of you. Men, with my body I can really entertain you."

"Tell us where Jacobs went to?"

"I have no idea who you are talking about."

"Take her to jail. Her memory will improve in that hot hell."

"Keep the change, gentlemen. Excuse us."

They marched the pouty woman to the Mesilla jail and booked her. With a prison matron in a private room, they made her undress and put on a shift. The desk sergeant said she'd be there when they wanted her. Chet could hear her cussing like a sailor while being taken back to a cell. A few days cooking in that oven, and her memory would improve.

"What next?"

"We sit and wait until she answers where he went."

"Let her sit. Let's go to El Paso and see what we can learn down there about him," Spencer said.

"Fine. We will go by the jail, get the deskman to forward anything she says by wire to us at the Brown Hotel. I'll leave him a dollar to telegram us."

They were in El Paso by dark. Before Miguel and Spencer took off, they made him promise to stay in the hotel and not be exposed while they were gone. They woke him up before midnight.

"He's over in Juárez drinking, but the two

345

men I talked to said they could get him back into the states alive for one hundred U.S. dollars."

"That is not a bad price. Let's tear a hundred-dollar bill in two and try it."

His men laughed. Miguel said, "I told Spencer if you'd pay it we'd be on our way to cool Prescott in no time."

"Lying in that bed soaking wet I am ready to go find my wife and the cool mountains."

"We meet them tomorrow at midnight on this side of the border."

"Take another day to get back to Mesilla and get her and then have a U.S. Marshal come to Benson and take charge. You guys did great. Here is the hundred. Tear it in half and we will meet them with the other half and a rig that can take all four of us to Mesilla. We'll get her on the train. I'll wire the Marshal office in Tucson and tell them when to expect us in Benson."

"Whew. I feel cooler already," Miguel teased.

The two went and met the men whose plan was to bring Jacobs across the shallow Rio Grande two blocks away from the bridge near midnight.

Chet hired a man with a surrey for four for twenty-four hours.

Midnight came and went and no sign of

them. At two a.m. Miguel was watching for them while Chet, Spencer, and the driver catnapped slumped in their seats.

Someone, cussing violently while being dragged through the shallow water, was what was first heard. Before Miguel could wake anyone, Chet, woken by the racket, put his hat on, woke the others, and said, "Keep your guns ready until this is over."

Obviously they were bringing Jacobs out of Mexico the hard way and he was resisting all he could.

From the river one of the men shouted, "Señor. Señor. He was hard to catch and he got away once from us, but we have been coming."

Miguel jumped down and helped push him up the steep bank.

"Thanks. We wondered where you were. Hello, Jacobs, you ready for jail?"

"I am not Jacobs."

Chet struck a torpedo match, and when it flared he smiled at his prisoner. "You will do. We're going to Tucson, but first we have to pick up your girlfriend in Mesilla."

"No! No!"

"Oh, shut up, or we'll gag you."

Jacobs fell silent.

Chet gave the two the rest of the hundred-dollar bill and thanked them. Then loaded up and headed for New Mexico, laughing about how they got their prisoner. They put Jacobs in the Mesilla jail and told the jailer they'd get both of them out the next morning to take back to Arizona.

They found her a plainer dress to wear, and she looked ten years older in it than she had when they found her in the card game. Her cursing was no better until Chet said he'd gag her with someone's dirty sock. She sulked the rest of the way back to Benson.

A man and a woman from the U.S. Marshal's office took charge of them at the Benson depot. The guard woman looked tough enough to arrest any man Chet ever knew and the man was a no-nonsense bailiff named Brown who handled criminals in federal court.

Chet hated the thought that the two Mexican men who delivered Jacobs to them probably got what was left of the bank money. But Jacob was going to pay for his theft and maybe she'd be charged as an accessory. Only judges hated sentencing women to prison unless they murdered their husband or castrated him while he slept. Those were territory crimes and ones the law enforced.

They'd probably be tried for bank robbery in the federal court in Tucson, so no one would testify. Chet and his men could simply go home and cool off.

He wired Liz they'd be at Hayden's Ferry that night. When they drove up, under the stars, to the stage office, everyone was yelling and shouting. A couple of ranch hands started playing their fiddles, a guitar joined in, and soon they were having a barn dance in the middle of the street.

Liz came, kissed him, and made him dance the set.

"Whew, you gals are ready to have a real fandango." Then he gave a loud, "Eeha!"

They danced some more. He hugged Lisa, and Josey, then Lucinda and four of the ranch wives.

"It is so good to have you home," Liz whispered in his ear. Then she hugged him. "I am so glad they didn't harm you."

"So am I, Liz," Chet answered.

Lisa came by. "I am so glad you men aren't even scratched."

"I didn't even get wet dragging Jacobs out of Mexico. Miguel did that," Chet said, smiling.

"Did he really drag him out?"

"Someone had to."

"You know he'd go through hell for you."

"He does a great job."

349

"Oh, and no one has found those guns you are looking for."

"Lisa, we have patience. Things lead to things. We know it was a small thing but a man in a café told us about Jennings and his neighbors rustling folks' cattle. When we searched, it did turn out he was eating his neighbors' beef. We also found a Wells Fargo strongbox taken in a murder and robbery. From Jennings, we followed until we found Jacobs. It's the small things. We will find those guns and Toby's boys' killers. They always slip up."

"Thanks. And more ranch news. Miguel is getting good at reading, and your wife is a doll. She teaches me a lot every day."

"I am glad you like all that work."

"Oh, I love it."

"Okay, enough talking. We better get to the ranch before the sun comes up."

Everyone climbed onto a wagon or buckboard and the ranch bunch sang Mexican ballads all the way home. The singing pleased Chet and the seventy-degree night cleared his head of heat.

Riding in the second seat, his arm around his wife, he enjoyed the ride home.

She shook his leg. "I really did miss you."

"No more than I missed you. I made as short work of it as I could."

"I think they knew you'd solve it despite the cold trail. You do those things."

"Boy, it's going to be hard to pry me off this mountain before fall comes."

"Good. But any problem will pry you off by one letter."

He kissed her and they laughed.

His men met at the house for breakfast at eight a.m. The girls went all out to cook steaks, baked potatoes, garden-fresh green beans, and yeast rolls with pecan pie.

Cole joined them. He was laughing about eating supper at dawn. "You guys had a dance in town last night and are having supper this morning."

"Do any good water witching while we were gone?"

"Where Liz said there was water, we got our first artesian well there."

"Really?"

"Cross my heart. It is capped now, but we need more water before we clear the land for farming."

Chet noticed Jesus frowning, and asked what was bothering him.

"I want to know how we are going to find those guns and then the killers," Jesus said. "We have checked hundreds of rifles while you were gone."

"Spread out. I bet this bunch is hiding in some backcountry hideout."

"How can we find them?"

"Maybe go out as work pairs to these places and look for the rifles there."

"Don't ride a ranch horse, wear old clothing, don't shave?" Fred asked.

"All those things. But circle back every week or two. Those rifles are out there."

Spencer nodded. "And we need to find them. I think Miguel goes with me and Fred goes with Jesus. Then each pair has someone who speaks fluent Spanish. Good enough?"

They nodded.

"Take two days off and then go look," Chet told them, agreeing with the plan.

"Who will guard you?"

"Raphael has some good men he can loan me."

"Don't ride out of the yard without two good men," Jesus said.

Chet held up his hands. "I promise. Two good men."

They all laughed.

Chet spent the day working on the books. Cole came by in the late afternoon and they talked about things at Three V's.

"The best thing I have is that bookkeeper. How he moves impresses me and remember he came down there to talk to me without crutches."

"You found the saddle maker McCully. The guy is like him — all heart and hard work. Now, can we make your place a real ranch?"

"That's no problem. It will take a few years and some rain." Cole smiled. "I want to be like Tom and have the lead sailing ship in the fleet."

"Hey, Hampt isn't slouching. Shawn is coming on fast. Toby and Talley have a head start. I knew it wasn't going to be paradise, but we are all together."

"I will be in the race."

"Good. I appreciate you. Val said told me she was glad her husband was back."

"I had a plate full. But she is great, and this is almost fun after that job. I want your son to go be with Tye some. Rocky loves horses, and he can learn a lot from Tye growing up."

"Neither Tye nor Reg are like my brother. Reg is like his mother May with music. My brother was no great horse trainer like Tye. Different. But I agree, if Rocky wants to be with horses that would work."

"Just some visits to start."

"I am glad you saw that."

"I am enjoying a quieter, less demanding life, but you and I could check out some places when we hear something of guns and men."

"I say yes. Let's go riding."

"Be good to ride together again, just don't shoot the prisoner this time."

They both laughed.

He sure felt good to be back with his wife. Liz was a warm, loving woman. The luxury of their life together, sharing, having few arguments, and talking softly and confidently about their life together.

When at last before he fell asleep, he thanked God for her.

CHAPTER 18

Chet and Liz welcomed the morning by checking on the huge garden that fed the ranch. Later in the season the pumpkins were blooming, the deep green vines spread out to produce orange pie stuffing. Potatoes had been dug. Sweet potatoes rested in the large root cellar. Apples turned blush red. Pears would need to picked, wrapped, and eaten during the winter when ripe. Quart mason jars of corn, peas, and beets were in cellars deep enough and insulated to keep them from freezing.

The fruit trees were all the work of their Oak Creek orchardist Leroy Simpson and his wife Betty Lou. He showed Raphael's men how to prune, spray, and treat them. They'd watched, and the young trees in Prescott Valley were now doing what JD was doing with citrus and grapes — producing.

"You and Cole going looking for those killers?"

"We haven't rode side by side in the last few years. A few days in the saddle together and Raphael has a man to ride with us."

"You going to beat the others?"

"I don't know, but we are going to see some country that hasn't been checked. Maybe we'll find something."

Liz hugged his arm. "Be very careful."

"I plan to be."

The other pairs had left the day before. Spencer and Miguel rode north to check out "camps" on the rim. Jesus and Fred rode for the Bradshaws and the mining country. Thursday morning, Chet, Cole, and Ric rode south. They were going down into the desert to see what they could find. Chet rode a solid gray gelding Tye re-broke for him and one he considered the best horse he'd ever ridden, a super horse JD had caught down on Diablo for him who didn't have the buck out of him. Hampt took him to his stepson and the greatest horse Chet ever owned came back well broke.

He and Cole cut across country into Bloody Basin. Sparsely populated, it reminded him of a chase, several years back when he first came to this country, of some horse thieves and murderers who raped ranchers' wives and killed people along their way. The killers had stolen some horses from the Prescott Valley Ranch. In their escape they were being trailed by the ranch foreman and his number two man. They were bushwhacked and murdered. Chet had left Raphael to care for the bodies until the posse trailing them could get there. The deputy in charge of the posse wouldn't allow Raphael to go to Chet's aid. By himself, Chet finally ran them down, far across the Verde, and lynched them in a dry wash. Memories about that chase came to him while camped in the junipers that evening and as he listened to a red male Mexican wolf calling in his pack.

"Bet he hasn't many enemies up here."

"No. He's king of these mountains. They've been cleaned out up around the home place. Stole too many chickens to put up with them."

"Many ranches aren't occupied up here. The first two had been abandoned. They used to have people on them. One was a woman they raped coming through here. Her husband was working in the mines over west at Horse Thief Basin, trying to make money to build a herd. They must have sold out or abandoned it. The other place had an old man who trapped some and panned for gold — he's gone, too. This is a tough country. I thought there might be some drifters in here we could check on."

"Why do they call it Bloody Basin?" Ric asked.

"Ten years ago, before I came out here, the Apaches made some bloody attacks on the scattered ranches. They killed many families."

"We going clear across it?" Cole asked, tossing the stick he'd been whittling on into the fire.

"Yeah, we may find some folks. This is a likely hideout for outlaws."

Cole nodded. "It sure is abandoned country so far."

In the morning they made breakfast, loaded the packhorses, saddled their own mounts, and rode on. In places they found wagon tracks washed out by past heavy rains and were forced to go around the cuts.

"What do I hear?" Ric asked, standing in his stirrups.

"I heard it, too," Chet said.

"Sounds like someone hurt." Cole set his mount down next to them as they tried to hear.

"It must be ahead of us. There's sheep, too."

Chet and Cole hurried ahead while Ric

brought the packhorses. They soon found a camp with a canvas shade and the source of the moaning. A Hispanic man ducked out from the shade. A short man in his forties with a white beard, he looked surprised to see them.

He crossed himself. "Mother of God, you have come to help me," he said in Spanish.

"What is wrong?" Chet asked as they dismounted.

"My wife, she can't have the baby in her. Help me. Oh, please help me."

"We aren't doctors, but we will see what we can do. How long has she been in labor?"

"A day, maybe longer." He turned up his hands.

Chet ducked through the flapping canvas and let his eyes adjust to the shady light. A swollen-bodied naked teen with sweat running down her pain-filled face sat up, crying, "He won't come out. Help me."

Then she lay back, moaned in pain, and squeezed her bulging belly. "Oh, come out of me. Please."

Chet and Cole squatted on each side of her. Both men looked warily at one another. Neither one had any idea what to do. Chet could tell by Cole's expression, which probably mirrored his own.

"Well, boss, what now?"

"How close is it?"

"You've got me."

Chet got on his knees and had her raise hers. Very carefully he inserted his finger and then drew it back. "The baby, I think, is right there. Girl, grip our hands with yours and push hard. He may come."

They each took one of her hands and she squeezed. Gritting her teeth, she pushed as hard as she could. Chet saw a black spot coming. "Harder."

By then she was screaming so loud it hurt his ears, but he could tell by her grip she was doing all she could. He nodded at Cole.

"Mother of God, his head is coming," the sheep man shouted.

"Wash your hands and catch him," Chet told the man. "Push harder, he is coming. Harder, girl. You are winning."

"There, that's one shoulder. Now the other. He's getting here. Harder. Push harder." Chet knew she was giving her all as the baby finally fell out. Cole spilled backward on his back and the baby cried.

"Now hang him by his heels and clap him on the back to clear his lungs."

Chet was the first to laugh, then Cole and Ric. The sheepherder and the new mother joined them in laughter. Her tears and pride were glowing as the father handed her the slimy boy to snuggle to her small, swollen breasts. Then she shouted, "God bless you all. Oh, baby, you are so pretty."

Chet agreed, climbing to his feet and still shaken by the event and how well they had delivered a baby.

On his feet, they met the father, Hidalgo Fernando. Chet introduced Cole and Ric.

"How will I repay you? I have little money and you have little use for sheep, no?"

"We came up here looking for some men who killed two of my ranch hands. We have no descriptions — only the serial numbers of the rifles they stole."

"There are some mean men up here. Twice they came and held me at gunpoint and raped my wife. I had no money and they would have taken her but she was pregnant."

"How many are there?"

"Five."

"Their names. Do you know them?"

"Callahan, I know, is the leader. Big man, dark wavy hair. Sam is redheaded and has freckles. Lewis is the one who limps." He looked back at this wife and she nodded. "The kid is pimple-faced, and Brewer has a bad scar across his — left cheek."

"What do they do?"

Hidalgo shrugged. *"Malos hombres."*

"What is her name?" Cole asked of the new mother.

"Felicia."

"How old is she?"

"Fourteen."

"Kinda young to be married."

"She had no one. My wife died. I had no one. So we were married two years ago in the church."

Cole nodded.

Chet knew what he was thinking. Cole'd been married several years and Val never had a child. Elizabeth, either, and here this orphan at fourteen just had a boy under the worst conditions that anyone could imagine and the boy had lived.

"Hidalgo, where do these bad men live?"

"Near the Verde. This is why I am so far west. To avoid them doing it again to her."

"If we can find them, they won't ever bother you or her again."

"*Gracias.* That would answer my prayers, señor."

"Ric, fix us a meal, so we can celebrate this baby and his being so healthy."

Cole went along to help him. The coffee came first, as both of them had not had any real coffee in a long time. They had frijoles, dutch-oven biscuits, and peach cobbler.

Chet knew that people who tried hard

could make it anywhere. With the man's sheep, a small pack train of burros, and camping gear those two would somehow survive. Or get sick and die out there. Survival was the only thing they had and now the baby. Chet hoped they would make it. Felicia wanted to get up and help them, but Chet told her to rest.

The next morning she hugged and kissed them. Told the Virgin Mary to protect them. Raul, the baby, appeared to be fine, and she had milk. Hidalgo said if she ran out he could milk some ewes.

Later on, in the saddle, Cole mentioned it, "You ever milk an ewe, Chet?"

"No and I don't aim to start."

Ric really laughed. "I never did, either."

"Well, we never helped deliver a baby before," Cole said and shook his head. "That was a horrific deal."

"I am not applying for that job again, either."

They pushed on and Chet figured they'd be at a ranch where he caught another bad bunch years before, but they found that ranch abandoned, too. No sign anyone had been there in a long time.

When they had not run into the outlaws by late in the day, he decided they'd search for them on foot. They could get lined up and make a morning raid if they found their camp. Horses put up in a lot, Chet and Ric went one way, Cole the other.

Wood smoke led Chet and Ric to overlook a log house and half a dozen hobbled horses grazing down by the river. Chet decided they probably had a spare horse so maybe everyone would be in camp. He and Ric climbed back to where they left their horses. Cole wasn't back but he came in an hour later saying he had seen three of them fishing so they had to have a camp close by.

Chet nodded and told Cole about the log house.

"Tomorrow before dawn we take them. Remember, outlaws, many times, won't go to jail, preferring to die fighting. They will fight to the death, so don't worry about ending their lives. Even if they didn't kill Toby's men, we know they did rape that young woman. Twice. So they deserve to die, if they won't come peaceably."

"Pretty sorry hombres. If they want war we can give it to them."

"That's how Cole and I think. Just be careful. Most are not good shots, but you can get shot with bullets flying around. They got me one time when I charged a door that I had no business charging."

Ric nodded he understood.

"Even if some run, we will get them later."

They checked their pistols and rifles to be certain they were loaded, not building a fire in case the outlaws might smell it. Eating crackers and jerky for supper and a very early breakfast, they were up before dawn, riding horses under the waning starlight through the juniper. They stopped there and tied the horses so they wouldn't run off, then they crept up to the house.

The sun was about to crack the towering range to the east. Cole took the left side facing the cabin's single door and to watch the one small window in the south wall. No windows were on the north or back wall. There were two small bottle windows on either side of the front door. Ric was on his knees to Chet's right, rifle ready.

A cool wind swept down the valley when Chet shot out the bottle window on the right side of the door. "U.S. Marshal. Hands in the air, come out and lie facedown. Any man armed will be shot and the man on either side of him as well. Now move."

He fired another shot into bottles in the wall, which shut the cussing up. "Come out or we will burn you up in there. I have the kerosene. Boys out back, toss the coal oil on that wall."

A big man came out fanning his pistol and

cursing them. Cole took him down with his rifle. Another, shooting away, met his fate beside the big man.

"Time's up. Two of your men are dead. You can be next burning up in there. Men, strike the matches."

Three came running out in their underwear, hands high and screaming they were giving up.

"Facedown. No tricks. Handcuff them."

The sun had appeared at his back as Cole went inside to check it out. He came out with a new rifle in his hands. "I've got one of the rifles taken during the Rustler's Ranch murders."

Chet nodded and turned to the three. "Who has the other rifle you stole from my ranch on the Crook Road?"

No answer.

"Ric, take your boots off, then take that kid out in the Verde, and drown him, if you have to, but I want to know who has that other rifle. We have two more to drown if he won't talk."

"I don't know," the kid cried out.

"Water will improve your memory. Take him out there."

As Ric was dragging him through the sand, the kid shouted, "I'll tell you — Mac Arnold has it."

"Bring him back. Who is he?"

"The guy hired us to scare them Mexicans off that place."

"Why didn't you burn it?"

"He told us not to. He wanted it all there so he could use it himself when they left."

"How much did he pay you?"

"I don't know — Callahan took the money. We got a free trip to the cathouse, food, whiskey, and packhorses before we rode down here to wait on his word."

"Where does Mac Arnold live?"

"He's got a cow outfit up north of the Marcy Road."

"Why did you hang those two boys?"

"That was his orders. He told Callahan to hang the owner and his wife, too, but they was gone."

Chet glared at the sloppily dressed punk. "He say you should rape her, too?"

"Oh, Mac didn't care as long as she was dead. I'd seen her a time or two. She'd been all right to do."

"How did you get down here?"

"We been using this cabin a long time. Callahan found it a long time ago, he said."

"His bunch murdered the family who was up there on the mountain?"

"Might have. I wasn't with them then."

The guy named Brewer with the scar on

his face said, "Yeah. He cut the kids' throats, shot the guy who owned it, and used her. He got mad one day and killed her over something. I was there then and had to dig her grave since I was lowest guy there."

"No one missed them?"

"I guess not. Callahan sold the cows, calves, and bulls to a guy down at Cave something after they altered the brands."

"Where you wanted at?"

"Missouri. I robbed a bank."

"What else?"

"Raped the banker's daughter and wife."

"Brewer is your name, right?"

"Anson Brewer."

"Kid, what's your name?"

"Jamie Rigby."

"What did you do before coming here?"

"I raped a few women. Robbed a rich guy's house in Silver City. And had to get out of there fast."

"You, Lewis. What crime did you do?"

"Nothing."

"Nothing? The lady in the sheep camp said you raped her. Twice."

"I ain't telling you nothing."

"Your tongue better get real busy if you don't want to drown in that river."

Ric had him by the collar.

He protested. "I'll tell you everything. I

raped some girls in Texas. They found out and I had to leave. I robbed a few travelers to get out here. Callahan hired me in Gallup."

"So you saw the murder of that family on the mountain, along with Brewer?"

"I never had no hand in that. Callahan did that."

"You watch him do it?"

"I was there. That's all."

"But you raped the sheepherder's wife?"

"We all did."

"For that you three will hang and for hanging my workers, too."

"We got to have a trial."

"You had it. I am judge and jury. You three ain't worth hauling back to town, and I don't want you warning Mac Arnold that we are on to him."

"I swear, mister —"

"It won't change a thing. Make your peace with your maker. Ric, find a hanging tree."

"You can't —"

Chet turned and took Cole aside.

"Anything on Callahan?"

"There is a letter from this Mac Arnold. He wrote to him in Benson — no date — told him to get a gang and to meet him at place south of Joseph City. He had work and lots of money for him."

"I wonder how much money."

"Callahan has a money belt on him. He's breathed his last. I'll search their clothes inside."

"If he has some money I want the sheep-herder and his wife to get some to live on. I will try to find who the dead folks' next of kin were. And you and Ric can split the rest."

"Thanks. I never expected to ever find those guns and the men that did it, let alone find out the guy that planned it."

"Thieves are always stupid enough to screw up in time."

"Tomorrow we head home?" Cole asked.

"Yes. I miss sleeping with my wife."

"When will we go after Mac Arnold?"

"Next week."

"How did he figure he'd get that ranch from those kids? You have the deed to it."

"He aimed to spread fear. City-dwelling investors will run in the face of it. Arizona is still a tough, widespread territory."

"I'll search for the money. Ric will be back and we can get this over with."

"I don't intend to bury them. We will put them in the log cabin and burn it. You two can take the horses back and hold them as found strays and sell them."

"Like we always did. Thanks."

They hanged the three outlaws, packed the shot men into the cabin, cut down the executed ones, and tossed their bodies inside. Then they built fires around the cabin walls. The horses rounded up, Chet was ready to close the books on those outlaws.

Callahan's money belt held fifteen hundred dollars, though the rest had less than sixty dollars between them.

The next day, with six new horses in tow, they stopped and met the sheepherder. "Those men that raped Felicia, they won't ever bother you again. There was not much money on them, but we want you to have your share. Here is four hundred dollars."

"Why, that is a fortune. You don't have to pay us anything. You guys saved our baby."

"I know who needs money and who doesn't." He handed Hidalgo the money and shook his hand. The he kissed Felicia on the forehead and they mounted up and left.

On the ridge Cole rode in beside him. "You notice that baby?"

"Yes, why?"

"I guess sheep milk really is good."

All three laughed as they rode down the trail.

■ ■ ■ ■

Everyone was home by Sunday. They had an early morning meeting. Jesus, who went to early mass, missed it, but Chet promised to come by and tell him everything.

Monday morning they would ride north to find and arrest Mac Arnold. It would probably require three or four days' hard riding to confront him, but they would be set up to arrest him and anyone else who resisted Chet arresting him.

After everyone left, a boy saddled up a horse for Chet and he rode over and met with Jesus on the porch. Anita, whose pregnancy was now showing, served them coffee and Danish.

"I missed Liz at mass this morning," she said.

"I think she is under the weather. Lisa offered to take her, but she said no."

"Anything wrong?"

"She went to the doctor last week and he found nothing. Just a bug maybe."

"I'll go visit her while you all are gone next week."

"She likes your company. Of course she is very pleased you are expecting."

"I know it would thrill her to have a child.

Maybe someday." She left them alone.

After hearing the story, Jesus asked, "You found the heirs to the Bloody Basin Ranch?"

"No, but I expect to."

"Strange no one reported anything about them disappearing."

"Big shame, too. They were very nice the two times I was there."

"I recall the place on our second trip there."

"We are leaving tomorrow. It may take three or four days to get to Mac Arnold. Then we arrest him."

Jesus thought about the trip time and agreed on the number of days it would take.

"What made you to think about going over into Bloody Basin to look?"

"You two had checked every scabbard in this country while we were gone and didn't find it. So I decided go look in the lost land."

"You said you found that everyone that used to be over there was gone."

"They'd abandoned the few places we passed. It is real lonesome country."

"Cole said you weren't impressed that it could be great ranch country, either."

"That juniper growth just saps the ground, and that cheats the grass from growing."

"Yes, I recall it was real brushy. Who is

this Mac Arnold?"

"Tanner at the bank found out that he came from around Fort Worth. Left Texas owing some folks large sums of money seems he forgot to pay. He's been in the area two years. Bought a place north of the Marcy Road that consists of four sections. He runs lots of longhorn cattle under two brands. One is the K Bar and the other Wagon Wheel."

"I thought everyone was getting away from longhorns?"

"They are. They're cheap. But that doesn't make them meaty enough."

"So for numbers, you think that is why he runs them."

"They're tough, too. They can survive in rougher vegetation than British stock."

"He's one of those root-or-die folks. You have fewer expenses and with his drawn-out ways I figure he aims to be large. Scare folks off and take over a place that has good enough range for his cattle."

"So you don't think he's not going to hay the cattle when the snow strikes?"

"We get a bad winter, he'll have lots of losses. But that won't be his worry. He will be rotting in jail after we arrest him next week. You can stay home."

"No, I'm going. I have this ranch because

I ride with you. Anita knows that. She has help. I have two hands to run this place. I didn't get this to quit riding. Anita will be fine."

"Good. This is a neat place and you have done a great job. We simply need that second rifle and hopefully Arnold has it to prove he was in on the deal."

Jesus agreed.

"I'll go home now."

"I'll be at the house tomorrow morning. I have a ranch horse I'll ride. Cole told me he really enjoyed that trip, except for the baby deal. That got to him. I told him if he was home when she goes in labor, I'd call for him. He went to backing off, waving his hands."

"And he ain't milking a sheep, either."

"I'd heard that in Mexico, people do that."

"The sheepherder was older than I am, and his wife was fourteen."

"Cole told me. They have a rough existence. But I bet someday he'll be a big sheep man."

"Maybe."

Chet left and went home. Lisa said Liz was napping. He read some back *Miner* newspapers and she joined him.

"Hey, you sick?"

"No. I just have no strength. The doctor

said he found nothing wrong." She came and sat on his lap. "I get exhausted doing nothing. I doubt I could ride a horse to the Verde Ranch. I am fine and suddenly I am worn out. I would love to go with you, but right now I know I couldn't make it. It will go away, eventually."

They kissed and she lay across his lap, in his arms. She really was done in. He sure hoped she'd improve.

After supper she went back to bed.

Josey asked him what he thought was wrong.

He shrugged. "If she's not better, I'll take her to some specialist when I get back."

"I am simply concerned. They said she used to ride all the time."

"She did that. I hope she gets better."

"Oh, I do, too. See you in the morning."

He had a week to ten days set aside to arrest Arnold. Then he would be back and get serious about finding a better doctor. He went to bed early, and she was so sound asleep she didn't wake, like usual, to make love with him. That was serious. He lay awake for a while wondering what was the matter.

He awoke early and went downstairs after he dressed. She was still sleeping. "She didn't get up?" Lisa asked when he came in the kitchen.

"She was in a deep sleep. I decided she needed that."

"I will go check on her after I get the three of you fed. That isn't like her at all."

"I know. But the doc found nothing." He knew the tall woman was seriously concerned about his wife.

"Still. She isn't herself."

"If she gets worse, send me word. I'll come back. We are going to Susie and Sarge's place today. Then they can tell anyone how to find me from there."

"I won't unless it becomes real serious."

"Fine." He turned and spoke to Miguel and Fred, who were discussing the pack-horses. "We ready to go?"

"Just in case, we asked Ric to come along, too. Raphael said he could spare him, and we don't know how tough this guy is. One extra hand won't hurt," Miguel said.

"Fine. Six of us should be enough. Jesus and Spencer are both coming."

"We wanted to be certain you weren't going to be in danger. That is our job. Since Spencer wasn't here yesterday morning —"

"He and Lucinda were at Oak Creek. I never thought about it. She had someone to watch the children and he wanted to treat her to some private time. He will be here."

"That is a beautiful place and has the world's greatest orchards."

"Nice place to hide. I need to take Liz up there."

They finished breakfast. Lisa came downstairs. "She wants to kiss you good-bye."

"Go ahead. I'll be along." He went through the dining room and met her at the bottom of the stairs, sweeping her up in his arms.

"I would have woken you —"

"Oh, Chet, I promise to be stronger before you get back." They kissed and kissed. She finally told him she would be fine and to go.

He caught his jumper going out. Might be cool somewhere up there. They looked like an army all mounted up and with six pack-horses.

"She all right?" Jesus asked.

"She said she would be."

He looked back at the house twice and questioned himself about leaving her. She'd told him to go, so he rode with Jesus at the head of the column. Spencer rode behind, thanked him for the time off, and said all was well with him.

The sun wasn't up until they cleared the steep road and were down in the Verde Valley. They didn't stop to see his son, Adam, Tom, or Victor, just headed for the rim and Sarge and Susie's house. It would be past dark getting there.

The day went uneventfully and the sun had set when they finally reached Windmill Ranch. He'd purchased the ranch several years back when they had the first Navajo contract. It was one-third of the way to Gallup, and the man who owned it was a windmill maker. He moved to Prescott and had a good business going until a heart attack took him. Tom's blacksmith shop began making their own windmills and they still made many, especially for the homesteads that Bo bought for him where they had wells.

Susie was up and welcomed them. Sarge was in Gallup delivering beef, but her hands helped his unload and put up the horses.

She told them all to come into the house and she would have food for them.

"Where now, big brother?" she asked Chet as she started to prepare food for them.

"To arrest a rancher who hired the gang that hit Toby's ranch and hung two of his young men while we were coming from Socorro with Toby's cattle."

"We heard about that — how is Liz? She's not along?"

"She wasn't feeling good. The doctor couldn't find anything and thought she'd get better. Told me to go get this guy."

"She's not pregnant, is she?" she whispered.

"No, or she'd have celebrated."

"I imagine she would. I am getting along so much better this time than before. There's a lot less pressure, and Sarge has made such a wonderful husband. I really am happy with him. And now only making every other trip is really great. Leave it to my bro to find such a great guy as Cody Day to help him."

Two Mexican girls were really moving around to get the food on the table while being teased by the crew.

They soon had coffee and the breakfast meal was coming fast.

Chet played with Susie's son, who was a neat kid.

"Shame he isn't closer. Rocky starts school at Cherry soon."

"I worry I may have to be the teacher for him."

"Nothing close?"

"Nothing. Who is this guy you are going to arrest?"

"His name is Mac Arnold. He has two brands. One is a Wagon Wheel and the other the K Bar."

"Oh yes. We have fought with his longhorn cows. He must have hundreds of them. Sarge told him to keep them north of us or he'd drive them to Gallup. Then he came by and wanted to sell us a few hundred steers. You know Sarge can buy steers, but the man made him so mad he wouldn't have bought his cattle short of having none."

"He plans to expand. According to the outlaws we caught, he wanted Toby and Talley both killed so he could take the ranch. Luckily they and the rest of his crew, four men, were over at Socorro with us getting his herd. I don't know how tough Toby could have been but the men he'd left behind to guard the place paid the price. The outlaws took the two new guns from those boys they killed. Everyone had looked for them — men and guns and the fact that we had the serial numbers of the guns was our only lead."

"And they had them?"

"One. They told us Arnold had the other one."

"You amaze me. You did in Texas, and I enjoyed even those troubled days. Then we came out here and you continue to amaze me."

"And you have a life now."

"Absolutely. I may be like May and have lots of kids, but, yes, we are having a wonderful time here."

He went to bed. Everyone rose early, him with Liz on his mind. The two girls, his sister plus the four men who held down the fort when Sarge and the rest of crew were gone, all had fun at breakfast.

He told them about the gang, their attack, and the man he was after.

"Yeah," Susie told Chet's men, who had now joined them. "After we drove his cows home twice and Sarge told him keep them east, he came back and wanted Sarge to buy a bunch of his longhorn steers. Sarge said he couldn't buy them. Boy, Arnold was still mad when he left."

"A wonder you weren't on his list to be killed," Spencer said. "They were told not to burn Toby's place because he was going to take it over."

"How?"

Spencer put his empty hands up.

"Oh, this guy Arnold is overbearing," Susie said, shaking her head.

"He won't be for long," Spencer said, forking three more big pancakes off the platter the girl brought by the second time.

After breakfast Chet thanked them and kissed his sister good-bye. They rode north after getting directions from Susie's men.

They crossed a grassland of meadowlarks, killdeer, circling red-tailed hawks, cottontails, and jackrabbits. Antelopes watched them from afar. Prairie dogs whistled warning sounds and in late afternoon they camped by a moon lake. They were close to the Marcy Road, on the top of the world, where from any high point every direction was downhill.

Before dark a hard-driving rider came thundering from the south. Chet heard and wondered what he wanted. When he came hopping downhill Chet recognized a young man from the ranch. Del was his name.

"Señor! Señor!" He fell out of the saddle into Chet's arms. "They have taken your wife to the doctor in town in a wagon. Señora Costa said you must come home. She sent me to get you to come now."

"We're two days away from there. You sleep a few hours and we will return."

His men gathered around him.

"Does he know what is wrong with her?"

He shook his head. "He doesn't know, either, except they took her in a wagon to Prescott. That is not good. Something is seriously wrong. I'll sleep some if I can, and get fresh horses at the Windmill and again at the Verde. Jesus?"

"Yes?

"You're in charge. Take no chances. Arrest Arnold, but we need that rifle with the serial number. He won't be some dumb outlaw. I think he may be the toughest one we ever tried to get."

"The five of us can handle it. Should one of us ride with you?" Spencer asked.

"No. Del and I can handle it."

"Let's pray for you and her," Jesus said.

They all locked arms in a circle and Spencer led the Lord's Prayer. "Our father in heaven, hallowed be thy name," and the prayer went on. There was not one dry eye in the lot of them when they finished.

Chet and Del slept a few hours and then took their horses and rode through to the Windmill. Susie fed them and they slept four hours and rode into the night for the Verde Ranch.

They woke the bunkhouse for fresh horses. Someone found them food while others saddled fresh horses. Tom came and told him that Millie was with her at the doctor's in Prescott. He would ride with them if they wouldn't sleep.

Tom rode up the mountain beside the two of them. They stopped at the ranch. Josey was at the house with Rocky. Red-eyed, she hugged him.

"Lisa and Val are with her at the doctor's office. Millie is there and some other town ladies. I don't know them all. I am so sorry, Chet. We did all we could for her." Then Josey went to bawling.

"Take care of Rocky. I must go see her." He rocked her in his arms.

"Tell her I love her like a mother."

"I will, Josey. I will."

Raphael made him ride in a buckboard and they raced to town. He was close to dizzy from lack of sleep. Bo jumped off the porch of the doctor's office, and helped him down off the buckboard.

"Damn. I wish I could give her strength. It isn't fair. You've done so much for all of us. Damn it, Chet. I am beyond myself for you over this."

"Bo, if God needs her there isn't one thing we can do about it but cry."

Lisa had his arm at the door. "You must have caught an eagle to get back here so fast."

"Del and I rode hard. Tom's out there. So is Raphael."

"I am so sorry, Chet, but she is slipping away. I did all I could —"

"She knows that."

The outer room was crowded with every

woman he knew and some he didn't. Lisa led him into the room and, as pale as the sheets she lay on, his wife forced a smile.

He dropped to his knees, hands clamped together at her bedside. "I smell like a horse. How are you?"

"I can't smell and I know you came a long ways. I am so sorry I can't go wading today. You have been such a special husband. Give the hacienda in Mexico to my brother. He can carry on the family tradition."

She wet her lips. "And promise me you will look for another wife. You are still young and no need not to do that. I am so grateful you chose me —"

He blinked his eyes at her. Nothing happened. He closed his eyes so tightly they hurt.

"God! God! Don't do this to me. I need her. I need her badly. She is too young to die."

He turned around and sat on the floor, his back against the bed, as tears rolled down his cheeks. *How long did she fight to stay alive to tell him all that?* The door opened the door, and Lisa stood in the door way. Seeing Chet, she broke into tears.

"She's gone, isn't she?"

"Yes."

He struggled up. Then he hugged her.

"She was such a star in my life. I should never have left her."

"No." She pushed him back a little. "She knew how many important things you do for all of us. She never wanted or expected you to stay behind. When I told her I was sending for you, she told me not to bother you, that you had things to do and your men needed you. But I couldn't stand for her to die without her talking to you —"

She burst into bawling. Chet pulled her to him, her tears soaking his shirt. "I sent for you anyway."

"You did the right thing. She told me what I must do with my life."

"I have it on paper, too. She was afraid she'd slip away before you came."

The doctor came in and took her pulse. "I am sorry, Chet. I can't tell you what took her. Could we do an autopsy and maybe have an answer? I know that is cruel sounding but it might tell us more."

"She would want that for other women."

The doctor covered her up. "Will you tell all the ladies or should I?"

"I will."

"They will appreciate that."

He nodded at the tearful Lisa, and she opened the door.

He raised his arms. "Let us pray."

He got on his knees with all of them. "Join hands for strength. We need each other's strength this afternoon."

"Our father in heaven, we thank you for my lovely wife's strength. Our time together was way too short, but it made for many brilliant days sharing our lives together. From her wading in the Santa Cruz River, to driving the herd of cattle to Ogallala that summer with the lost black cowboys we found. Lord, we shared miles of stage lines, telegraph wires strung, and ranches built. Even Washington, D.C. Today we are sending you this magnificent woman for you to hold in your palm and protect. Thank you, God, for the job she did convincing other women to find better lives. They did, and they, too, have lost a good friend. But we have fine memories that will carry us forward as she would want us to do. Bless her, sir, for all of us — Amen."

He rose to his feet and began hugging and thanking each wet-eyed woman for their support of Liz.

He told Lisa and Val, after people had left, that the funeral would be in two days, because the doctor wanted an autopsy, which might tell them why she died. They agreed.

He thanked them. And then he rode back

with Lisa and Val to the ranch.

The house was silent save for Josey's tears when she learned the sad news. Chet dragged himself aimlessly around until he finally went to bed only to toss, turn, and wake up many times. Elizabeth was dead.

Lisa woke him before dawn and she was crying again.

She collapsed on the bed and he had to hold the telegram up to the faint light to read it.

MIGUEL IS DEAD. SHOT BY ARNOLD'S MEN. ARNOLD ESCAPED. WE DON'T KNOW WHERE. WE SHOT AND CAP-TURED ALL HIS MEN. FOUND THE RI-FLE. SPENCER AND I AND THE OTH-ERS DID ALL WE COULD. WE ARE BRINGING HIS BODY BACK. I HOPE YOU DID BETTER. JESUS

"Lisa — I am so sorry. He was such a brave man. I will personally find this Arnold and have him hung."

"Chet, he was doing what he loved. Riding with you. Making plans for the future and this ranch. He could read and under-stood so many things after riding with you. That was his life. That was what he wanted to do."

"But it does not make it any easier. Girl, we both lost a good part of our lives. I want Liz buried in the Catholic cemetery. Wouldn't Miguel want to buried there, too?"

"No. Where will they bury you someday?"

"I haven't thought much about that. Why?"

"I know him well. He'd want to be buried near you. He came up here from Mexico, and you made him important. Rose up from being a peon in his homeland to being a U.S. Marshal. Put him near your final resting place."

"I can do that."

"Please, can you hold me? I remember coming here with you, and your wife told me she couldn't think of a better place for me, and what a better person I would be if I listened to and learned from her. I did that, thanks to her. She gave me the strength to trust Miguel. I had started my life over. She told me how I should act with him. When I said that I was soiled, she told me that I didn't smell soiled. We laughed at that. Then she told me that that would be a new day in my life. That things might not work with this man, but that I should act like a real woman, not a hand-me-down or someone who has to accept just anyone. She told me that if he was worth anything he would have to respect me and if he did I would have a real good man. He did that.

"We have no children. Your wife wasn't the only one. Maybe God planned it that way?"

"You had some good pages in your life. We will find more. I hope you stay and care for my house like you did before. But if you find it is too hard I will understand and you may leave."

"I fear I am much like he was. Even as your housekeeper, I want to be around you."

"Lisa, I thank you."

"Chet, you've lost a wife a few years ago, how did you recover?"

"Not easily. Being busy helps. I went off and buried myself in the border problems. That's when Liz came along."

"I heard her story. She wanted a gold horse and came by to see a U.S. Marshal camped at a ranch."

"And we had the last supper on Santa Cruz River. It was pretty. I gave her a bath. She and I made love in a hay pile — so every time I smelled hay —"

"I'm sorry — but it was a pretty story."

"I have the memories. My first wife paid my expenses all over town until I made her take the money back. Besides I was engaged to Rocky's mom back in Texas, but I came back and wanted to go look at some new country. She came camping with me. Susie said that she wouldn't do that, but she did. I married her to save her reputation. Liz wanted to meet me at the border. I was going to send Jesus to get her. Maria, the woman at the ranch, told me if it were her, she'd go back home if someone else came to get her. So I went. I nearly messed up both times."

Lisa smiled. "You have some good pages in your book, too."

"Yes."

"Tell me about the lost herd sometime. Your bath will be ready in ten minutes. Breakfast in thirty."

Josey ate breakfast with him. Raphael came to talk after he finished.

"I am sorry I was not there. Miguel was far too good a boy to lose," Chet said.

"He had been your shield. You'd have felt worse. That young man was right where he wanted to be, and he would've made a helluva good foreman. They will be back to tell what happened. Lisa said he would like to be buried by me."

"That would be great."

"I am having Liz buried in the Catholic cemetery."

"Yes, and Miguel would be honored to be

with you."

"We will decide where when we need to."

"You are going to be all right?"

"I guess I have to be. Now, four women have died in my thirty-five years."

"That is bad odds."

"Yes. And now we have to look for the man you want to replace him." They shook hands.

Damn, he hated that Miguel was dead. He liked him like another brother, this man from Mexico who made himself strong — from a simple worker, who walked many hot miles to rise above his birth, to becoming a lawman.

He finally slept, only to wake for no reason at all in a panic. And there was no wife in his bed to hug or love. He felt empty.

The next day he found Lisa crying.

"Anything I can do to help?"

She raised her head. "No, I am just feeling sorry for myself."

"You are entitled to that, but it only makes it worse. Trust me."

"Maybe I will take up knitting. They say it can help." She blew her nose in a handkerchief.

He pulled her up to her feet. "Go take a hot bath. That helps some."

"I can try that. When will they be back —"

"Maybe today."

She nodded and patted his arm. "I will get better."

They came back like a badly defeated army. Raphael immediately took Miguel's body to the funeral home.

Jesus's wife was there, and they hugged in the yard. Fred and Josey cried together.

Lucinda and Spencer held each other and shook their heads. Val was there, with Rocky, to support Chet.

Jesus came over.

Chet asked him, "What happened?"

"We ran into a wall of fire. They were waiting for us."

"How could they have been warned we were coming?" Chet asked

"I don't know. We didn't even get inside the yard before they went to shooting at us. Miguel was shot three times. No one else was hit on our side and we got all of them, finally. But Arnold had fled. When we searched the house, we found the rifle we have been looking for. I didn't expect a trap."

"I wouldn't have, either. He is the first one we have lost. Arnold didn't leave any addresses or papers saying where he might have gone."

"No."

"I hate this for Lisa."

"Everyone — we all hate for her and you. Tomorrow is the funeral."

"I got back in time for her to hold on long enough to tell me to live my life. Lisa wrote down things she selected for me to do if I didn't get back in time."

"They know why she died?"

"They are doing an autopsy today. Maybe they'll find something. I don't know."

"I am taking Anita home. We will be at the funeral and Miguel's will be the next day?"

"Yes. And, Jesus, know that I don't blame you for anything. It could have been either one of us shot there, too. All I know is that I want Arnold caught."

Jesus nodded.

He went back to the empty house and sat down in a chair. When Josey woke him, he found that he had actually slept through the night.

"You need to get dressed, so we can leave for the funeral."

He nodded and went upstairs to get ready.

Chet rode in the buckboard with Val and Cole. His son Rocky sat with him in the second seat.

"Dad, I know Liz can't ride with me anymore. Could you find me another riding partner?"

"Rocky, don't ask your dad questions today," Val said to him.

"He's fine, Val. I'll find another rider to ride with you, son. I promise."

"Liz was pretty nice to do that."

"She was wonderful, and she loved us both."

He bobbed his head in agreement.

Chet knew she'd rode with Rocky around the orchards, but he had no idea how often. More than he'd imagined, he now thought. He would find another to share his son's passion for riding. Who could it be?

At the church, many people waited to tell him how sorry they were. Hampt took it harder than May. Tom and Millie were distraught over it. The priest did a good job.

Somehow he managed to get through the service but it wrenched him inside out — Liz was dead, and he would not be able to share his life with her anymore. Why had he not noticed her weakening? Perhaps he had been gone too much? Was that it? Was it neglect? Hell, he didn't know. He had no answers.

For the first time in years, he wanted a

bottle of whiskey to numb himself. His brain danced around like a dust devil blowing around the open plains. He now had to face the raw world without her. His mind traveled back to when his first wife fell off her mount. The fall had broken her neck. And there were others. Tomorrow Miguel, a good man, would be another to bury. Damn. When would the sad things stop piling on top of him? It was all so bad.

He went to bed early but tossed and turned. With sleep not coming, he sat up in the dark and tried to plan his future without Liz. That did no good. In exhaustion he finally fell asleep.

Josey made breakfast and told him that Lisa was all right. She and Fred were taking her to the funeral.

Fred, Spencer, who had just arrived, and Chet ate breakfast together and told Chet, again, what happened when they went to arrest Arnold.

"It was like Jesus said. We rode into the yard in the predawn, and as we spread out they opened fire. There were five of them waiting for us. We had a running gunfight and Miguel went down. We tried to get to him but there was too much shooting. Our shots began to take a toll, and when there was no more shooting, we ran to him, but

397

he was dead when we got there," Spencer said.

"How could they have been warned?" Chet asked.

"We never found out. They fought to their deaths. We found the rifle in the house. Arnold didn't know we had the serial numbers or I'd bet he'd never left it. But he was gone. He may have even been gone before we arrived. We stacked them in the house and burned them all, so we had no way of knowing who they were or if they were wanted or not.

"We all took it hard — Miguel's death and the fact Arnold escaped."

"I had no doubt that you all did everything right. When things get settled, some of us will go find him. Arnold will leave this world. What did you think of what was left of the ranch?"

"You interested in it?" Spencer asked.

"It is in our region. Heaven knows how many cattle he has. I'll sic Bo onto finding out what he can if he already doesn't know anything."

"The main house has been leveled."

"We've built houses from the bottom up."

Spencer nodded. "I just want you to know Jesus did a good job and so did all of us.

Miguel simply got caught in their line of fire."

"I have so much on my mind. I sat up last night trying to think of what I can and will do. Nothing came to mind. I thought my life was set with her. I didn't see it coming. Perhaps I didn't want to. Oh, I'll live, and I know I have to get over it. She held death off long enough to tell me to go on."

"You will.

"Lucinda is staying home with the kids, so I will be by to get you before lunchtime," Spencer told Chet.

"Is eleven all right?"

"Fine. The funeral is at two."

After breakfast, and after Spencer had left, he went and took a bath and shaved. Then, dressed, he read the *Miner* newspaper. Lisa came by to check on him. On his feet, he hugged her lightly. "I hope I can give you strength for today."

"You will, and you already do. I hope you aren't mad about me deciding to have Miguel placed in your cemetery."

"No. Not mad. I really liked him. He was a third arm to me. I completely agree he should be there."

"Thank you. This will be the longest day in my life. Second only to the day you started back to here with me in tow. I thought I'd lose my mind being dragged off to Arizona. But it was the start of my new real life and one I cherish."

"Good. You know we can talk, anytime?"

"I know that. You had it bad yesterday, and I simply don't want to drag you down even more, today."

"I promise I won't let it happen."

The funeral was as sad as the day before. All the ranch help came in their white clothing. The Catholic church was full of families. Babies cried and there were many wet eyes. All stayed for the graveside services.

The priest knew how much the Byrnes family did for their people, and if he had problems, Chet, or someone from one of the ranches close by, quietly fixed it for him, so he, himself, had no problem with where Miguel would rest.

The father told them this was Miguel's place — to someday be near his boss. Lots of heads bobbed in approval. No one complained.

Chet went there with Spencer, but decided to ride home with Cole. They talked about the cattle. The young bulls were busy catching the open cows. Calving in late May wouldn't hurt anything. He liked April and early May but those dates could be backed up in years to come.

They would always remember that Miguel had shown them how to tell if a cow was bred or not.

They had a quiet meal at the house.

Lisa came to Chet, hugged him, and thanked him for all he had done, then said, "I want to keep my job."

"I had no other plans but that."

"That is good."

"Don't let yourself become insecure. The ranches are here. This house is here. I need you here."

"Fine. I know I will be better in time."

"Life is for the living. Remember that. We can't bring them back and we have the hard part — rebuilding without them. Rocky asked me yesterday to find him a new riding partner. I guess she rode with him often?"

"When you were gone, even as she grew weaker, Liz went with him almost every day."

"Well, we will find someone to ride with him."

"He is so grown up. I can't believe he starts school in a few weeks. The ranch children will look after him. They already include him in a lot of the things they do."

"Good, and I will also pay him more attention."

Lisa excused herself as the day finally pressed down too hard on her and she found herself crying. He hoped that she didn't revert to her old ways over the loss of her husband. She had been doing so well.

When Lisa left, Chet made sure everyone at the house had rides home, keeping Bo and his banker aside. He then told Bo to look up Arnold's ranch, see what he could find out, and if it was available. Then he asked his banker, Tennant, if there was anything that the banker knew about Mac Arnold and the ranch.

Tennant said, "With him gone, I bet there are bankers that would like a portion of their money back, so you might be able to get it. Why would you want it?"

"Good. I want to know because where it's at, that place will almost touch the train tracks, and with the train coming sometime, it will make the price of it soar. If we can beat anyone to it, we can make some money on it."

Bo promised, "I will have info on it in ten days. My wife sent her blessings to you. She could not come with me yesterday or today. She is very close to having our baby."

"I understand."

His banker Tennant said the same about his wife. And asked if he needed anything else.

Chet told him no. The poor man still acted pleased with his wife. He hoped Kathrin wouldn't cut his heart out, like she did JD's. But who knew anything about people's lives? It was not his problem. Thank the Good Lord.

Things needed to settle more inside of himself, then he would set out to find Mac Arnold.

In the next weeks, he and Cole talked about clearing the first forty or so acres of sage and a few junipers and then leveling it so it could be irrigated. He bought a used surveyor scope and tripod. They trained a young man on the crew how to use it.

Hampt joined them one day and he told them about his land leveling. "I only had a string and a level to do mine. I have the large plane I use to float it out but it takes six teams to pull it. It only works when you get the sage plowed up and the stumps of the junipers dug up."

Cole shook his head. "I never thought about that. You really used a level and a string?"

"I couldn't have asked Chet for more

money back then. He didn't have it."

All three laughed.

Cole already had three artesian wells drilled and capped. Everyone was excited. The final decision was to level it for six hundred feet, then have another system to flood it three feet lower than the first field that length. The drop in the land was too great to make it a quarter of a mile long.

"Let's do this first part and see how we like it," Chet said.

Cole agreed.

In the meantime Chet sent out letters to other marshals about finding Arnold. Fred, Spencer, and Jesus went to solve a rustler problem Shawn was having at his ranch. Ric rode with Chet.

A letter in flowery handwriting came to him.

Dear Chet,

I am so sorry to hear about your loss and wanted to tell you that while you might not recall me, I had known your lovely late wife Elizabeth for years. I also am a great admirer of all your hard work as a U.S. Marshal. I lost my husband Clarence Mullins a year ago, and if you ever plan to come to Tucson, please drop me a line. I have a large house and plenty of room for you and your associates, and would enjoy having your company.

Sincerely yours,
Andria Mullins

"Who was it from?" Lisa asked, wielding a feather duster to the bookcase.

"A widow I don't know who knew Liz and wants me to stay with her when I am in Tucson next." He handed her the letter to read.

"She may be very rich. You smell the perfume. Very expensive."

He wiggled his nose. "I didn't like it."

She stopped and stared at him. "I'd like to find some hay smelling kind. Do they make that?"

"No it comes only in stacks — you, my lady, are a terrible tease."

"At the very least I do have you laughing."

"I will write her a thank-you for the offer, but I am occupied for the moment — well, for some time."

"Good. I am glad you are not desperate — yet."

"I have an appointment with Bo about the Arnold ranch at two p.m. Get ready and you can do some shopping while I talk to him."

"What do I need?"

"How about a new blue dress with ruffles at the bottom to dance in?"

"We going dancing?"

"I'd be honored to take you. We both have been pinned down for weeks in this house and it is time to see the world."

"Chet, I am flattered and would love to do that. But how would it look for your sake, you dating your housekeeper?"

"I don't give a damn what folks think. We have been friends for years. I will buy the dress. Get it made. Would that embarrass you?"

"Hell, no," she whispered. "I would love it."

"Sometimes you slip very beautifully."

She held her finger to her mouth to silence him before calling out, "Josey, would you comb my hair? I have to go to town this afternoon."

"Why, lands, yes. Who's taking you?"

"Chet."

"Oh."

He winked at her. "This might be fun. I need some fun for a change."

"Oh, I'll be ready. I am coming, Josey."

Ric rode guard in the second seat. Lisa,

with her hair in a scarf, sat straight up beside him. Chet drove the buckskin team and they rolled right into Prescott, down the steep hill, stopping at the dress shop. He went around and helped her down.

"A blue dress with ruffles at the hem?"

"Get a second one that you like."

She frowned. "They won't be cheap dresses."

"Money is no issue today."

"I simply wanted to warn you."

"Get two dresses."

"Then you will take me to a dance?"

"Don't you trust me?"

She chewed on her lip. Then she nodded. "I will get them. You sound very serious about attending a dance."

Ric leaned forward as Chet came back around. "If you won't, I will volunteer to take your place."

"I'll remember that." He climbed onto the seat laughing. So was Ric.

Bo met him at the door and invited Ric in. He said no, so the two went inside.

"No baby yet?"

"Any day now. Your man Arnold is very delinquent on his payments. The Gallup, New Mexico, banker who loaned him a great deal of money said he would settle for fifty cents on the dollar. There are three hundred cows supposed to be under each of his brands. He has a mortgage on all the yearlings and bulls and his horse stock of ninety head. There are four sections up there where he lived north of the tracks to be, and one other section down closer to Toby's homestead. The banker never saw any of it, but Arnold told him he had wells and irrigation. I don't know about that."

"I doubt it, too. What is the price?"

"Forty thousand."

"No kidding. I bet there are not that many cows, but at that price, we better buy it. Word gets out the train track is coming and a hundred thousand won't buy it. I want the two brands transferred to me by him before closing on Arnold. That will save lots of labor rebranding. I am sending Spencer and Fred up there to examine things and a half dozen vaqueros to start counting. Tell this banker we will be counting cows and we will let him know what we can pay for it. If the count is close, we will pay him that. If the count is a lot less, we will pay him less."

"Seems like you have bought you a ranch. What else are you doing these days?"

"Sending letters out to try to find the murderer of a deputy U.S. Marshal and who also killed two of my ranch hands and stole a rifle from them."

"That is Arnold, huh?"

"Right. He will show up."

"I will wire the banker right away."

"Make me a property map for Spencer."

"I will have it ready for you. I don't know your guard. Why is he seated in the back?"

"I drove, bringing Lisa Costa, my housekeeper, and left her at the dress shop to buy two new dresses."

"Oh."

"We intend to attend the dance and pot-luck meal at Camp Verde on Saturday night."

"Very nice lady."

"We both need to get out of the house. Tell your wife she is in our prayers and the baby, too."

"She had no problem last time, so I can hope this goes that well."

"I am certain it will."

He stopped at the dress store. He had tied off the team and gone around to get Lisa, when she came out looking hard-eyed about something.

What in the hell went wrong in there? He caught her arm. "Did someone insult you?"

"Never mind."

"No. I want to know. Someone made you mad."

"It was not a clerk or store help. It was some rich bitch who told me I was only house help and a man like Chet Byrnes would only go out with me to have his way and I needed to get back at the barn where I belonged."

"Who was it?"

"Her name is Caroline Hayes."

Chet tried to see the agitator through the glare on the glass door. "I'll go in there and shake the hell out of her if it would help."

Ric scooted up in the seat. "Let me go do it."

"No." Lisa started to smile. "I can fight my own battles. My feelings get hurt too easily. That is something I will work on to change. I have the dresses ordered. The first one you wanted will be ready Friday."

"We can come get it and go on to the Verde dance, all right?"

On the seat beside him she clapped him on the leg. "You are damn right."

And they left Prescott.

Back at the ranch, he told one of the ranch boys to go find Spencer and ask him to come see him, when he had the time. The barefoot boy ran off as fast as he could.

He helped Lisa down and thanked Ric,

who responded with an "anytime."

Inside the back porch door, out of any ranch eyes, he hugged her. "I don't give a damn what anyone says. I asked you to attend that dance. I want you to have the nicest dress there, and it doesn't matter what that bitch said. It is no one's business, but they may make it theirs. We will ignore it all."

She hugged him and kissed his cheek. "I am honored. We are supportive friends. I will curb my temper. If we don't have anything more than a fun evening, I will be pleased. That blue material does look good. What do I need to bring down there to eat Saturday night?"

"Get Raphael to roast you a half-grown fat pig. He has a big cooker to carry it down there in, and we will need a couple of men to serve it."

"Is that showing off a little?"

"Yes. And let her hear you fed the whole party there."

"Thanks, you always save me. Aside from her, this has been a lifesaving day raising me up since the funeral."

"It has been for me, too."

"We can stay at the big house and come home Sunday?"

"Yes. That is why we have it. You can see

Adam's sheep."

"Oh, good."

"Rhea can read English now and she is teaching Adam."

"She and Victor have no children, either, do they? Well, Miguel and I never made one, either. I have warned you about that. I am not a good prospect to deliver you children."

"Makes no damn difference."

"You are so agreeable today. I really must plan to upset your cart."

"I hear Spencer coming."

"You are excused. Thanks so much for the dresses. Will you have time Friday to take me in to get the one?"

"I will. I promise."

She blew him a kiss and disappeared.

Spencer put his felt hat on the rack and then his gun and holster, buckled, on the next wooden pin. "How did it go?"

"The banker is going to foreclose. He wants out so bad he will take forty thousand dollars for it. There are four sections north of the tracks and another section down toward Rustler's Ranch. Arnold told the banker that one was irrigated. Which, we think, is a lie, but it is near Toby."

"Shame we burned the main house. It can be rebuilt for eight thousand. But we needed to clear up things and it was the way to handle it, right?"

"Exactly. I would have done the same thing. Now would you like to be in charge of sorting it all out? I need a count of the two herds because if that number is too low I will lower the price I pay him."

"When can I go?"

"You and Fred get Raphael to find you four vaqueros, take a pack train and a horse wrangler with a *remuda,* and run up there to get me a head count on the cows. You get a close number, then you wire me your count. There are supposed to be three hundred cows in each herd. Then check out all the land. Bo will have a map for you."

"You doubt the number?"

"Most borrowers raise the number they have, and bankers seldom go out to count."

"How low will you allow?"

"Two hundred is the very bottom for each herd. But he may not have branded the calves and yearlings."

"I savvy that. I think we can get a count in a week. Soon as I'm certain I will wire you what we think is close."

"I want you to include Fred to teach him how to organize things, and be careful."

"We will. We have been hearing you bought Lisa some dresses today."

"She and I are going to the dance down

at Camp Verde this Saturday night."

"Good. She is a great lady, and you two should have some fun."

"Some rich hussy insulted her in town today. She said I wanted her for her body and not anything more serious because she was not good enough. Lisa came out fighting mad. I told her to consider the source. Why would that woman do that to her?"

"Maybe she was jealous. Maybe she wanted you for herself. Anyway, I am glad you are paying her attention. She has no kinfolk to help her and she does so many things for the ranch and our people. Most folks work people. Your people are family. Lucinda said JD and his wife are that good, too. Her husband was killed at roundup, and JD made her draw his wages until she married me. Who else does that?"

"I was embarrassed for her. Lisa was my wife's best personal friend."

"We all knew that."

"Fred and I will do it."

They prepared to leave. Three of the team were ranch men and three were ones Raphael sent to help him. Spencer was stopping in town to get the map from Bo.

Chet felt satisfied he would soon have the answers about the Arnold ranch. He told

Lisa that they would eat lunch at the Palace Saloon on Friday and then pick up her dress. She agreed demurely, and Ric brought the buckboard around before eleven o'clock. She and Josey had pinned her hair up and then put it under a scarf to save it from the wind. Chet loaded her in the backseat, sat down next to her, and Ric drove them to town.

They drew some attention when the buckskin team stopped at the Palace front doors and she got off and was escorted on his elbow into the high-ceilinged saloon.

A waitress showed them to a table and took their food order. Lisa wet her lips three times and he reached over and squeezed her hand. "Understand one thing — every one of these people pull their pants on one leg at a time. Some are cowboys who earn twenty-five dollars a month, some are lawyers paid over a hundred dollars an hour. Folks in here own mines down in the Bradshaws that produce tons, not ounces, of gold. You are just as good as any of them."

She smiled. "Thanks. I will stop my heart racing, somehow."

"If I have to bring you here every day I'll do it to make you feel at ease. Tomorrow night you need to let down and be yourself like you are at home. This is your world.

Enjoy it."

"Chet, I want, so much, for you to proud of me. I don't care about that rich — bitch — and I won't ever let anyone like her ever get my back up. But it is hard. Real hard." Then she narrowed her eyelids. "But I will win in the end."

"I agree. Good girl."

"Can I ask you one thing?"

"What is it?"

"I want to know what you expect out of me?"

"Me? Want from you?"

"Yes."

The waitress brought them the coffee they ordered.

Lisa waited until she left. "Do I please you?"

"Yes."

"I am not Elizabeth, but I am not dumb."

"I never doubted your intelligence. You were a model wife to Miguel. Liz considered you the sister she never had. She trusted you with her final words for me. I need a partner, not a goddess. You suit me."

She nodded and their lunch arrived.

After the waitress left, she reached out and touched his hand. "I would enjoy being your partner."

"I am glad to hear that. I just don't want

to force you. And I don't want you to be disappointed. I am a lot older than you are."

"No. You are a young thirty-five and I am an old twenty-four."

He sipped some coffee. "That was nice."

"I will go anywhere you want or need me. I can get accustomed to this treatment." She cut up the small steak on her plate.

"Now we are getting somewhere."

Pleased, she winked at him. "Yes, and I like it."

Later he sat in a chair, in the dress shop, while she tried on the dress. In minutes she emerged wearing it. The dress looked just as good as he thought it would. She even looked taller in it. She made the ruffles whirl and smiled.

"You like it?"

"Oh, it is great."

"Mr. Byrnes, we told Mrs. Costa we were so embarrassed by that lady's words to her last time. She should never have said anything."

"That is that lady's loss. My entire ranch idolizes this lady. She teaches Spanish children so they can attend school. She helps make clothes for them and the wives that can't afford any."

"I wanted you to hear and understand our thoughts and concerns."

"Not to worry. We will be back for more clothing for her."

They applauded him as Lisa went to change into her other clothes, ready to go home.

They left for home, and she held his arm going back. "Is that too fancy to wear at Camp Verde?"

"No they won't notice you when they see your roast pig."

She laughed. "All right. Ric is going to help deliver it, and he and some of the men from Tom's will set it up at the dance hall. Jesus and Anita are going to the dance, too, and will ride with us. They will also stay with us at Rhea's in her big house afterward."

"Fine. You and I are going wading Sunday in the Verde."

She squealed. "That would be wonderful. Oh, Chet, I am so excited."

"So am I, darling. So am I."

She rose and whispered in his ear. "Is there a haystack down there?"

He looked at the clear blue sky for help. This situation was beginning to be funny.

Anita and Jesus came for lunch the next day. Josey and the two house helpers made Lisa sit with him and they served the meal at the dining table. She played the game and she hugged them for their treatment afterward.

Chet drove the team taking the foursome to the Verde, being cheered on by the ranch workers as they left. There was no doubt that Lisa was their candidate for becoming first lady of the ranch. He winked at her and she shook her head. "You're spoiling me."

Anita pushed on her back. "Enjoy it."

"I am trying. I really am."

At the big house, Rhea hugged her and then Anita. Adam broke in and took her fingers. "Come, Lisa, come see my sheep."

"How many sheep?"

"I had two sheep. Then two babies came. One minute there was one. Then two. Now there are four sheep."

Chet was laughing. "Those things happen, Adam."

"Adam can sure count. The next day he asked that ewe if she had any more lambs in her for him," Rhea told them proudly.

Ric arrived, with two of Tom's hands on horseback behind his light wagon. Chet sent them over to Camp Verde and the dance hall. He said there would be someone over there to direct them where to put the pig.

"See you at the dance, boss man," one of the riders said and saluted him.

He returned the high sign. "I have so many employees I don't know all of them anymore."

Jesus chuckled. "Neither do I."

"His name is Jeff Ross," Rhea said. "He's been here about three months."

"Thanks." Chet hugged her. "Rocky has ridden with Lisa twice. The boys are growing up fast."

"They are both smart boys. They will make good men like you." Then Rhea stood on her toes and whispered. "You two don't sleep together yet?"

"No."

She nodded. "I have two rooms ready for you and her. Victor and I are going to the dance. I have a nice girl watching Adam. It's only a few miles away, but with Victor working on the farm all the time, we have not been to a dance there in a long time."

"I will talk to him. I know he is doing his best, but he needs to sit back and enjoy life."

"God bless you, and you have very good taste in taking Lisa out."

"Thank you, Rhea."

"Sarge and Susie are coming. Tom's daughter and Cody are coming, too. I think Robert and Betty will be down as well."

"That's great."

"Yes. I will have a house full tonight, but

that is why I have this big house. It is the ranch's hotel."

He went to find Lisa. She was in the kitchen helping serve cool tea to all the new arrivals. Betty caught him and moved him aside.

"We are so sorry. We did not get word soon enough to be there. I loved Liz and know it has not been easy for you."

"I know that. She knew that. She spoke about you two often and what a great marriage you have. Elizabeth left us way too early. The doctor found that she may have had cancer. Nothing they had would have helped."

"You are in my prayers."

"The girl?"

"My sister is up there with her."

"Thanks."

Susie and Sarge drove up with Cody and his wife Sandy. Lisa moved to Chet's side and they met her with tears in her eyes. His sister hugged him. "Oh, Chet, I am so sorry —"

"I knew you were hung up. I talked to her before she left us. It wasn't a long talk, but she said to tell everyone she loved them and to not to let her leaving stop anyone's lives, most of all not block their lives."

"Lisa," Susie began. "I hope you two are

holding each other up?"

"We are. Chet told me I needed a new dress for tonight. Not a black one."

"Good for him. I have felt so bad we weren't able to attend."

"Have no regrets. We managed. Life goes on."

Sarge turned to Chet. "Spencer and Fred came by. We talked about the Arnold cow count. Four of my men are helping them."

"Thank you. He has a section of land between you and Toby somewhere south of the Marcy Road."

"I know it. He fenced it and tried to grow some corn in the bottomland along a wash. A big rain swelled the dry bed into a flood and washed most of it away. He left it after that."

"He told the banker it was irrigated."

Sarge laughed. "It could be a good native grass hay place."

"It is in the deal."

"Spencer said they had to burn the house."

"That's not a problem. Do you know if he has any British bulls with those cows?"

"Some crosses."

"Oh hell. Things are tough enough in today's ranching. It's damn fools like that that make it worse."

Sarge lowered his voice. "You and Lisa?"

"We are getting acquainted."

"Good. Life must go on."

"Liz told me to do that, too."

Sarge nodded. It was time to go to the supper and dance. Lisa came dressed in her blue dress and everyone bragged on it.

"It is all his fault." She laughed and pointed at Chet.

"Lisa, that dress is darling. Chet, Lisa said the ranch fixed a pig for tonight so that the ones coming a distance and have no dish are covered?" Susie asked.

"Yes. There'll be plenty of meat. Raphael and the ranch women cooked some briskets, too. No one will go home hungry."

"Thanks."

They loaded up and knew from all the parked rigs when they got there, there would be a crowd. Toby and Talley, all dressed up, came to greet them.

They both blinked at Lisa and him together, then rushed to hug them. After their sympathies were expressed, Talley proudly told Chet, "You would not know those cows you brought us. They are fat."

"And next spring we're having a baby," Toby said.

That brought a cheer from everyone. Lisa and the girls went to check on things inside and Chet told Toby about the Arnold situation. Sarge told him about the section and Toby added, "He damn sure fenced it. I like that place. I really never knew who owned it. He got away?"

"Yes. The men said they thought he was warned that my posse was coming."

"Who would have done that?"

"No telling. We had a shoot-out with the gang that hung your men. He got away from there, too."

Toby shook his head. "How will you ever get him?"

"He will slip up. When he does, I'll get him."

Chet and Lisa in the blue dress were well received. Many gave them their condolences and regret that they could not be there because of the distance and short notice of the funerals. Others bragged on the meat and the vaquero in the apron yielding the sharp knife to cut the meat. They wanted him to work for them.

Chet and Lisa danced the night away. Finally, in private, she whispered. "Am I asking too much to wade in the river tomorrow?"

"No."

"I know this sounds brazen, but can we wait until we get back home to do the rest?"

"Anything you wish."

She wet her lips. "Liz said she had such fun talking about the river and wading. I always thought about it as part of a test leading up to a climax. But that will be in the big bed at our — house where. . . ." Tears began to spill down her cheeks. "Oh, I — I wish I could tell you how proud I am. I never yearned for you. I had Miguel. But these last weeks you have turned me around, and her words are ringing in my head, for us to continue our lives. Damn it, Chet Byrnes, you have taken my heart and mind." She put her hand on his chest. "I look back and you saved me, but now I can pay back all you have done for me."

He kissed her forehead and realized how tall she was. *My dear wife, thank you for telling me to continue. The two of us will carry on the tradition.*

CHAPTER 19

Lisa waded in the Verde, held her regular dress up, and kicked the water.

"Can you swim?" he asked.

"I did as a teenager." She shaded her eyes with her hand from the sun. "I was a big tomboy growing up."

He was seated on his butt watching her. "We better not today. People might come by and think we're crazy."

She agreed. "But we need to do that, too, someday."

"The Verde is a little muddy. I know a tank up on the Valley place that is better to do that in."

"You ever take Liz there?"

"No."

"Your first wife or anyone else?"

"No. We can go and it will be our place."

"Yes. Then that will be our place."

"Yes."

"I am ready to go home." She waded out

with the skirt hem held up to her knees. He had her sit on an old peeled cottonwood log and dried her feet.

"Thank you so much for pleasing a silly girl. I love the red rock mesas around here." They kissed hard and he held her tightly for a long time, then, loaded up in the buckboard, they drove back to the big house. Jesus and Anita had left earlier, catching a ride with someone else. After playing with Adam for a while, they thanked Rhea and Victor for all their work putting people to bed and feeding them breakfast.

While the women said good-bye, he told Victor, "This ranch will always be here. You have done lots for it. Now you tend to Rhea. Picnics, dances, whatever she likes because you never know how long the Good Lord gives us to be together. You can't make that up when she is gone."

"I understand. I can do that."

"Play the guitar more, too. I love your music."

They shook hands.

After all the good-byes, they climbed on the spring seat to go home.

"I really didn't know Adam before, and I have learned lots about Rocky since they moved down. They both are amazing boys."

"Rocky acts more like my nephew Tye.

He loves horses. As for Adam, who knows? They are going to be educated and what paths they choose will be theirs."

"Are you sure you don't mind about my inability to have children? If you wish to find a more fertile woman, please tell me."

"Let's not worry. I have two sons. If God gives us one, fine, but don't ever fret or worry about that for me."

"It has left me a more than a little upset. All these ranch women having children. Now Talley."

"I have no problem with it. Stop your concern. I won't ever love you less because of that."

"My past —"

"Is your past. All that is over. Buried. No need to even be concerned about it. Today we start a new life. You are a delightful, generous pretty woman. Continue to be that as we share our lives."

She hugged and kissed him as he drove the mountain road. "I will do that. I promise I will do that. I thought, when Liz began to really fail, I would not know what would happen to my life. Then when I lost Miguel I wanted to commit suicide and not face the world one more minute. But you told me we would support each other, we would have each other to lean on. That made me feel like I could go on."

"And to be a husband and wife —"

"I guess that's your purpose though I never heard you propose?"

"When we get on top of this dang mountain, I will officially ask you to marry me."

"Oh, that will be the best place. Looking over all that country."

He clucked to the horses. "You can have that private memory, too." He parked the horses and they walked to the edge of the sheer cliff. "Lisa, will you marry me?"

"Chet Byrnes, I certainly will. To love and keep you forever."

"Amen." They hugged and kissed.

At the ranch it was quiet. A boy came and took the team.

He swept her up and carried her, protesting, all the way into the house.

She called out for Josey. No answer.

Still in his arms, she frowned. "Put me down. I don't want you lamed by doing this. I wonder where everyone is."

He put her down. "There's a note on the table."

"It says, *the house is all yours. We know you two need to be left alone. Tonight you have the whole house to yourselves. Love Josey and the crew.*"

"That is real nice. You reckon they know

what we planned?" he asked.

"It may be pretty obvious. You can't carry me upstairs. We might fall. I bet your bed is fresh made."

"I can't wait to find out."

He swung her around and kissed her hard. "I can't wait to see it."

She poked him. "It won't be that grand."

"I say it will be."

They rushed up and found the bed freshly made. They laughed.

He went over to the door and closed and locked it. Then he turned and winked at her. "Just in case."

CHAPTER 20

Monday morning they slept in. When they finally went downstairs, the strong aroma of coffee filled the house. In the kitchen, holding a pancake flipper, Josey turned, "I see you two came down to have breakfast."

"Yes. Thanks for the notes and the fresh sheets."

"Well, when's the date?"

Lisa spoke up. "Saturday. Two weeks. Here. We've got lots to do."

"The wedding dress?"

"The blue one."

"Oh yes. I like that."

"Some men just rode up into the yard," the house girl Soli said.

Chet went to see. It was Tom and his son-in-law Cody. They both sat their horses as they talked to him.

"Chet, yesterday Cody and I rode up into Falcon Canyon and caught two men butchering a yearling. I plan to have them charged

431

with rustling."

"Aw hell, why? Do you think they thought a big rancher like you wouldn't miss one big calf," Chet mocked at him.

"If they needed food, they could have come and asked. Stealing is serious. When I asked, they told me they have wives."

"Do they have kids?"

"They said no, but now I am I worried the women might starve because their husbands are in jail."

"No need for the wives to suffer while the men do prison time. Find them, set them up so they can eat and live while the men learn their lesson that rustling doesn't pay."

"I'll get that done or have Millie do that for them."

"Good. You guys did the right thing. Now do the two of you have any plans past that?"

Both shook their heads.

Lisa had come out and stood at the top of the porch steps. Chet pulled her down to him and hugged her. "Be here at the ranch on Saturday in two weeks."

The two men turned their horses around and Tom said over his shoulder. "Count on Millie and me to be there."

"I'll be heading back to Gallup, but Sarge and Susie and my wife will attend."

"Hey, we will have fun."

■ ■ ■ ■

Spencer's wire came on the cow count.

WE FOUND AROUND FIFTY COWS.
THERE MAY BE MORE. HE HADN'T
SOLD ANYTHING. THERE'S LOTS OF
YEARLINGS AND TWO-YEAR-OLDS.
MAYBE OVER A HUNDRED FUTURE
COWS, TOO. SPENCER AND FRED.

Chet and Lisa drove into town, where he told Bo to set up buying the Arnold ranch since the cattle numbers were there. Then he told Bo that he and Lisa were getting married in two weeks and if he and his wife could come, they were invited. Then they were taking a honeymoon for a week, so if the ranch stuff could be done before he left that would be good.

No baby at Bo's house yet.

Chet took Lisa to lunch at the Palace, and several people who knew him came by to meet her. Chet told them the plans and he knew they'd have more people there for the food and music than they could shake a stick at.

He was really charmed by his wife-to-be, and the ranch settled back down to normal. Their intimacy only grew stronger with each

433

passing day, and he started to wonder if they were perhaps better suited for each other than his other relationships. Not dismissing his past but they simply felt like one, rather than a couple.

Lisa set to filing things in a more orderly fashion and could find a paid receipt or invoice he wanted in a flash. She always re-added things before she filed them. If something didn't suit her as right, he checked it and would find the mistake. She did most of the recording and that saved him time.

She discussed expenses, and had good ideas on ways to save. She made a list of all the farm machinery. If a mower was reported broken, they needed to explain if it could be fixed, when and where, and the cost. But not to spend more money on ones that needed frequent repairs.

One day Lisa mentioned that Sarge's men were all cowboys. She suggested he needed some farm hands. Cowboys were good with cattle but not mowing machines. Mowers were not made for running over wooden fence posts or barbwire tangles left in the field, and the use of bronc horses as mowing teams needed to be abandoned for the cowboys' safety as well as the horses'.

As for their loving — he never had to ask

her. His blowing in her ear was enough to arouse her. A familiar squeeze, a rollover, and his arm thrown over her was enough to ready her to be engaged. She slept in her own skin, which he found very natural and alluring — all a man could want.

They packed a picnic lunch and rode up to the spring-fed tank and they swam. She got a little sunburned without a bathing suit. She agreed the clear water up there beat the Verde's dingy-colored flow.

Any wedding at the ranch required lots of work, and for the boss's they went all out. More tables and benches were required. Then the area to park needed mowing and hitch ropes strung. Things like kegs of beer needed to be ordered and were barely ordered in time.

In the middle of getting ready, Lisa got word Bo's wife, Shelly, was in labor, so she and Josey took a fast buckboard to town to help. Word was out later that Lisa finally ran everyone out of the room so she and Josey, without a midwife and the doctor off in the hinterlands helping another woman, got the delivery moving and they delivered a bouncing baby girl into her arms.

Later, snuggling in bed, Lisa told Chet, "I bet she makes love to him with her clothes on. We were working our backsides off to get her going. Us the only two in the room and she kept saying, "Cover me up. I can't stand to be naked."

"Heavens to Betsy, who cared?"

"I sure wouldn't have at that point."

"And I love it."

He'd have sworn she blushed and he didn't care. He liked her this way.

Cole had decided to clear only the first section of land to be leveled for flood irrigation and Chet agreed. The first places for the water needed more leveling. It was tilled again and, under Hampt's direction, planted with alfalfa, then irrigated.

They planned to level the other eighth of a mile over the winter and in the end have eighty acres of hay ground.

Cole was so pleased he bought Hampt a gold pocket watch for his help on the project. Hampt sure checked it a lot.

The New Mexico banker, Monty Rubio, who came from Gallup to close the deal on the Arnold ranch, stayed at the house. Fred showed him the area topside and the entire Verde Valley spread out. He was impressed with the new hay meadow.

The papers were signed. Tanner was to ship the money to Gallup so Rubio didn't have to carry it home. Rubio told Chet if he ever needed money he had it to loan.

The big night came and they all flooded in that Friday. JD and Bonnie came and brought lots of grapes. She was very pregnant but told Chet she was not going to miss this event. She and Lisa hit it off and were laughing all the time. Susie and Sarge came with their son this time. Lucy, Shawn, their girl, the baby, and Lucy's sister came to help as well. The Oak Creek couple brought apples for all. Robert and Betty with Caroline made it. Talley and Toby and their neighboring ranchers came.

Spencer and a vaquero he borrowed rode in late Friday night. He told Chet they were making progress collecting all the big steers to sell and help clear up the range pressure there.

"How many head do you expect you have to move?"

"Six hundred head. They haven't been worked. Some aren't even branded. Some are bulls."

"You know six hundred head sold over at Gallup would almost pay for that place?"

Spencer grinned and agreed. "That's what I want to do. And, I know they don't grow on trees, but I am going to need twenty-five or more British bulls next year. Between cows and heifers I am going to have six hundred head to breed back."

"Aren't there any there now?"

"There's some sorry crosses and we'll cut them and when they heal ship them."

"Talk to Tom. He does our buying and selling. What will we do if we get a snowy winter?"

"I am looking at hay sources. There are some farmers on the Little Colorado that have hay. I may buy all I can before we have any winter. If we wait, it would be too late. Buying now might cost us, but I'd like to have some supplies on hand."

"Get it bought. Fred going back with you?"

"Yes. We looked at two homesteads they say are for sale. Both have houses our wives would live in but I'd want some men to be around any headquarters over there. It is isolated, and you never know who's going to ride by."

Chet nodded that he understood.

Then Spencer asked, "Any word in the mail about Arnold's whereabouts?"

"Nothing so far. We will hear someday and go get him."

Spencer shook his head, then smiled. "You and Lisa have really hit it off, haven't you? I can see it. I never knew your first wife, but you and Liz had a good marriage going. But there is something about you two fitting like a glove. I'm sure happy for the both of you."

"I thought it was way too soon, but the last thing Liz told me was find another woman as soon as possible and get on with my life."

"You hear any answers from the doctor?"

"Some. He said it was cancer related."

Josey came and brought his jacket. "Time for you to get up there. Raphael is bringing the bride."

She helped him get the coat on. Gave it a jerk or two and was finally satisfied with how it looked. "You know, I lived on my own for almost four years. I never saw you once except at a distance. I heard them talk about you, but never saw you in person till Fred married me. I thought we'd be right back scrounging for things to exist. He kept telling that wouldn't happen because you made him a marshal." She hugged him, tears spilling down her cheeks. "I want to thank you. This child in me and Fred and I will hold our heads high being a part of your family. Don't ever forget how glad and proud we are."

He kissed her forehead and headed for the altar. A Methodist minister was to marry them. His bride stood straight and tall beside him; they repeated their vows and then kissed.

Hampt shouted in his big voice, "God bless both Chet and Lisa. Thanks for the food, and now let's eat!"

Lisa kissed him on the cheek. "You did well."

Chet and Lisa stood at the beginning of where the food was served. Everybody came past, shook their hands, and divided into two lines, one on each side of the food tables. Chet thought there was no end to them, but after a while they were able to follow the stragglers down the line for food.

"Did it suit you, Mrs. Byrnes?"

"Being number three?"

He frowned.

"Quit worrying. I'll be here to nag you when you're old and gray."

"May not be far off."

"No. I'll keep you perked up — too."

He didn't doubt that one bit. Though he never knew exactly why, she did keep him spiked up since their courtship began. They spent five days of wedded bliss in Oak Creek. She waded in the cold trout stream and he even caught some fish to eat.

They drove home Friday and stopped at the Verde place. Played with Adam, visited Tom and Millie, and Victor played his guitar for them. He told them his corn was going to yield heavy on the new farm east of the village. Rhea made popcorn that evening and they went to bed early.

They wore slickers going home in the morning and he drove the team up the steep canyon hemmed in by thunder and lots of rain. Nothing changed the pleasure they found in each other's company. At the ranch a boy in a rubber coat came out and told them to get into the house because he'd unhitch the team. Their things would come later.

Josey had lunch for them, and there were several letters waiting for him. Most said they were sorry there was no word on Arnold. One came from a retired lawman.

Dear Marshal Byrnes:
That no good shypoke Mac Arnold has been causing trouble since he was 16. He broke in Green Door Saloon one night in Brown Hill, Colorado. Drank so much whiskey he passed out on the floor and the owner discovered him the next morning. As the town marshal I locked him in the city jail for thirty days and made him repair the boardwalks and clean the horse watering troughs. You had to force him to do anything and I

thrashed his ass I bet a dozen times in that month.

His mother Viola Hawks worked in a house of ill repute and she could do nothing to make him behave. When his jail sentence ended I kicked his behind out of town and told him not to come back.

Next he got arrested for stealing hawgs in the next county and they ran him off. He robbed two men who were drunk in Casket, Colorado. They had a warrant for his arrest outstanding. If I hear word on where he might be, I will wire you.

Sam Router, retired Colorado Sheriff

He'd read the letter to her and she nodded. "Now you wait to hear from him. At least they are looking." With that she bent over and kissed him. "I am going upstairs, take a hot bath, get all clean, and change my clothes."

"Save the bath water and holler when you get out."

She bent over and whispered, "Better yet, you come scrub my back. I will scrub yours and we can take a short nap afterward."

"Something like that, anyway."

She gave him a small push, smiling at his answer. "Josey, we are —"

"I heard all right. Taking a nap after that."

He rose up, stacking the letters. "I can do them later."

Josey came in the room with a dust mop. "I think you two take the prize for the best married couple. You two are always having the most fun. Lisa laughs all the time and so do you, Chet. You are like a pretzel all wrapped up in and around each other. I am so happy to have Fred, but boy, you two beat us all."

"Josey, you are the best person while carrying a kid around. Most women have so many aches and pains and have to sit down all the time. You are the model mother-to-be."

"Listen. Back when I was on the streets and found out I was expecting I got afraid. What would I do? Fred was gone. No way he knew of my problem. I prayed. I prayed every day and one day I saw him. He got off his horse, came down that alley, and said, 'I've come for you, Josey.' Well, I didn't believe him. He bought me two dresses. I thought I was in a dream. He got a hotel room and I took my first real hot water bath in forever. Then I told him he didn't want me — I was pregnant.

" 'Well, that's nice,' he said. I said he is yours. I haven't slept with anyone but you.

Not anyone else. He said we have to get married. I thought he is crazy. We have no way to live. He told me we did. That we had a real nice place at your ranch. I didn't believe him, but I married him, and he brought me here. I kept thinking that these real rich people will hate a pregnant nobody girl. He was not lying. He didn't need to come back for me. He had escaped our situation, so why risk losing it? But you all made me family. I have no pains, no hunger, no fear, except I know he has a dangerous job. I have fun when he comes home and love it. I thank God for all of you. Go have fun."

"Fred's shared things with me about his past. I am glad he went back for you. It shows the character he's made of. You two are lucky."

"Josey," Lisa said, "he brought me back kicking and cussing. His wife right off told me I needed to eat some lye soap to remind myself I am a woman not a hellcat. It took a while for it to sink in but I realized I was in a different world here. No one was slapping me around, being abusive to me for no reason. I had three meals a day here, not just eating whenever I found a dead animal."

"That is different, isn't it? Sitting down and eating three good meals every day. All you want. Not having to beg or steal it. Or cook for some filthy old men and get to eat their scraps. I could not believe that first night in camp. Chet said, 'Women eat first. Fill your plate.' Was he crazy or going to kick me for trying? All his men stood back. I grabbed whatever and went way off to the side, kind of hiding, like a dog with a bone, so I didn't lose it."

"Josey, we are glad to have you, and I know Fred is, too."

"It has been a dream. And Fred has really grown so much, at times I feel I am not good enough for him."

"You are not the little street girl he brought, you are his lady. Josey, you really are. Hold your head up. We have accepted you because you are that lady and a part of us."

"I hope so."

"We all have a past. They found Val in Tombstone. She and Bonnie went there to work in the houses of ill repute. She hated it. Chet sent her up here to work for Jenn. Bonnie didn't come, but slavers kidnapped her and Chet traded some horses for her return. Toby's wife was rescued from more no-accounts. Those stories go on and on."

"Thanks. I will try harder."

"At what?" Lisa asked. "You do everything here well. Be yourself."

Chet and Lisa went upstairs, scrubbed each other's backs, and napped some, too.

CHAPTER 21

Spencer telegraphed that he needed five thousand dollars. He had found a great place for sale close by and they wouldn't need to rebuild the Arnold house. But the deal was now. Chet trusted him. It may be the bargain of the century, and he could handle it. No mortgages on the property, and it was worth every penny they were asking. He'd get the whole thing in his name and they'd be surprised.

Chet had Tanner sent the money to Spencer at Holbrook.

In three days Spencer wired back:

DEAL IS MADE. I WANT YOU TO SEE IT WHEN YOU GET TIME. ALL IS WELL.

Spencer and Fred came home. They were bushed from riding so hard and for so long in the saddle.

"The vaqueros are getting the branding

done at the Arnold place." Shoulders stooped, Spencer had his hat in his hand and was beating his dusty pants.

Why, two fingers would have pushed him over, Chet thought. "I am sending someone to get Lucinda and some clothing. Go inside and the girls will run you a bath. Fall asleep in a bed upstairs. You hungry?"

"Too damn tired to do anything but sleep."

"Me too," Fred said.

"Both of you take baths. Here comes Josey."

He called to a youth. "Go tell Lucinda her man is back. To bring him clothes, too."

"Sí, señor." He took off, feet flying.

"Josey, get Fred into a bath and then put him to bed. Lucinda will be here for her man by then to do the same."

"How is it going?" he asked Spencer while they waited for Lucinda to come.

"Smoothly. We wanted to come home. The men have a week's work and plenty of food. They work hard as any men we know. They like it. Our cattle numbers keep growing. Why didn't he sell some of them?"

"Where could he sell them?"

Spencer nodded. "I bought one helluva place. I can't tell you a thing about what I found. You have to come and see it. Can you wait on the surprise? The women will love it."

"I trust you. You ready to move in?"

"Damn right. You are going to be shocked. We will have to do Arnold's like we did at the Verde years ago. Start over. New bulls and a new calf crop the next year, then we start replacing those longhorn cows year by year."

"I understand. But I think, when we are through, from what you say, we may have a thousand steers to sell."

"That would pay for it all."

Lucinda came running into the room. She tackled Spencer and he swung her around.

"You have someone to watch the children?" he asked her.

"*Sí*. How are you? You look so tired."

"Fred and I had a few days, so we thought we'd come and get you, but it was lots farther than we thought. We found us a great place to run the ranch from."

They hugged and kissed each other.

Chet herded them toward the stairs. Lisa winked at him from the top. "You coming up, too?"

He checked the sun time. Must be nap time for them.

In the next two days, they loaded two farm

wagons with needed supplies for the Arnold ranch. Some medical items, painkillers, bandages and iodine, needles and catgut to sew up people and livestock. Coffee, flour, frijoles, lard, sugar, baking powder, canned vegetables, canned fruit and tomatoes. Salt for the cattle and horses. Extra blankets, slickers, towels, soap, britches, and shirts in case they lost their own. And a few cheap hats. Then came more things — girths and latigos, a roll of hemp rope for lariats. Smaller rope for tents and to tie up canvas shades, two rolls of canvas to make shades and ground cloths.

They selected two teams of draft horses from Victor's bunch, big Canadian Percherons, and two of his men to drive them over there. A *remuda* of sixty saddle horses and two wranglers to herd them, a chuck wagon they used for roundup at Tom's, and a pair of mules to haul it. Spencer had the family's things in it. Josey added enough to get by and to share the house with Lucinda.

"You have to promise to come back here six weeks before the baby comes, Josey," Lisa insisted.

"Okay."

"There will be no one to help you but Lucinda up there. Now promise me."

Fred spoke up. "I promise she will be back

here by then."

Spencer chuckled. "Yeah, me and Chet ain't good midwives."

Hell no.

Lisa said she would ride along with him. Jesus said he, Raphael, and the vaqueros could hold down the ranch. They started out on a nice mid-September morning. Chet told them bring jackets and blankets as it might frost up by Flagstaff. They didn't stop, but Tom and Victor joined them, and they rode north for several miles, talking about their plans. Victor planned to use the same big wagons to haul corn. He would harvest soon.

"You have any buyers for the corn?"

"Several feed stores in Prescott want to buy some, and I have had some hog farmers want to finish their hogs on it."

"Sounds good."

"I want some to grow bulls faster. I need them working sooner," Tom said.

"That sounds good, too. We have so much going on sometimes I wonder how it works out."

Tom laughed. "I have been doing that for years as one of your foremen."

"How many windmills have you made this year?"

"Eighteen. I am waiting on some bearings

now to finish six more."

"Are we getting them spread around?"

"Shawn got several. Sarge got seven to put on his homesteads that have wells already. Cole wants some for his new place, and Toby hasn't had cows long enough. But he has several homesteads that I bet have wells and that will need the windmills."

Tom and Victor parted at lunch. In the afternoon Chet decided they'd go up the steep road to the rim in the morning. His men agreed. They camped at the base and ate a meal, rubbed down the draft horses, and slept in bedrolls, while the women slept in the wagon.

Day two they made the sawmill and had a reunion with Robert, Betty, and the baby.

"Tell Cole that from what I hear the stage line is not running on schedule. They've fired two men running it since he left. And several drivers quit when their pay was cut."

"I could've told them not to cut Cole's pay, but they'd never have listened. He walked out the door and he should have. Those stuffed-shirt executives have no idea what makes a business like that run."

"I think half the telegraphers quit over their pay cuts."

"They are not easy to find. And living out on the frontier where they do on that line is not an easy life."

Later in their bedroll he asked his wife how sore she really was.

"Sore, but happy. I knew I would be. I have not ridden much lately, but I am not too sore for any attention."

"Good. This has been a fun day."

"I think so, too."

Dawn came and they re-harnessed while the women made breakfast. Oatmeal and bacon with coffee was served and then they got under way. They didn't stop in Flagstaff but camped ten miles east at a watering place on the Marcy Road. Chet and Lisa had stopped at the various stations and they all said they wished he was back. The railroad made for a sorry partner.

The third day on the road, crossing the open rolling grassland, they turned north onto wagon tracks in the prairie. The forage was belly deep on the saddle horses. This land had never held buffalo like the eastern plains had. Spencer shot two fat antelopes; they had brought along enough wood to cook them.

The women complained that there weren't even dry cow pies out there to use for fuel.

When they came over the last rise they saw, spread out, the place Spencer bought.

It was a huge log house set by two moon lakes. Everyone stopped their horses to admire the panorama of the storybook look of the sprawling headquarters. There was a profusion of good, large corrals, well-constructed barns, and even hay in the mows. Two dug wells that Spencer said held sweet water and a windmill filled a house reservoir. Then they all moved down to the house and dismounted.

"What was the story about this place?" Chet asked. "You bought this for five thousand dollars?"

"That was the price. A rich man in Kansas City sent a man out here. His boss said he wanted two lakes close by, a great view, and plenty of country to build a large hunting lodge. Then barns and corrals for a great ranch. He wanted the mows filled with hay and a cowherd of Hereford cattle. The man couldn't find any cows. The owner got mad and brought two surreys out here to buy them himself. He found nothing and went home disgusted. Never came back. A real estate man in Joseph City said I could buy it for ten thousand dollars. I offered five and he sold it to me. There are two sections of land here, and it is five miles from Arnold's location."

Chet stood on the porch holding the post

and shook his head.

"It's gorgeous, boss man," Lucinda said, so very excited she hugged him.

Her action impressed him. Oh, hell, she'd finally become family.

Josey came out of the house and stopped. "I can't believe this place, but Lisa is right. I will come back to Prescott to have my baby."

"Where did the big pile of firewood come from?" Chet asked.

"Two Navajo boys who have strung wire for me wanted work. I'll have a huge stack before fall. That's ten dollars' worth. They are going to plant some trees later."

"Good. We can afford the boys."

"There are two Navajo widows who need work and a place to live that are coming, and there are several small houses scattered around for help to live in. They won't be alone here."

"Five thousand dollars? I can't believe it."

"Chet, what do you think it cost to build?"

"Those logs came from Flagstaff and the lumber, the mill, and the labor had to be imported. I would say two hundred fifty thousand dollars."

"The man said with the land and all, it was four hundred thousand dollars."

He nodded. "But no one could afford to

own it. Even if they gave it to someone there was no way to make a living here. Like the horse rustlers' place we cleared up. It is now a cow ranch but we drove cattle over a reservation of wild Indians to stock it. Most fools wouldn't have done that. You and Fred did one hell of a wonderful job here." He hugged Lisa, who bumped his hip with hers.

"Time to eat supper, you land barons. Neat nice place but I like Prescott Valley." Spencer added, "We have lots of dust to clean up, but it is gracious and I told Lucinda very fancy. There are even crystal glasses in the cabinets and you will eat off English dishes and honest-to-God silverware. There are eight bedrooms. They have been shut up, but dust has crept in."

Spencer continued, "It has a water heater like my house and water in the faucets, two large fireplaces, one in the dining room and the other in the front room. There are also fireplaces in each of the bedrooms. It should be toasty in the winter."

"And you won't hear the trains going by."

"It is like finding a perfect ship floating at sea all equipped and it only needs a crew."

"He must have had the hardwood flooring shipped out here from Missouri," Chet told them.

The antelope was perfect. The canned

green beans were good and the frijoles were well cooked.

In bed with his bride in one of the large eight bedrooms with its own fireplace, he said, "That idiot could imagine his rich buddies coming out here, hunting game and having a high time on his ranch, but, until the train comes, it would be a helluva long ride."

"It was an unbelievable dream for them, just like you were to me six weeks back. You tired of loving me yet?"

He laughed. "Not yet. You sore?"

"Not that sore."

The next day Chet and Fred covered lots of country on horseback. Water development and windmills would make it a great ranch. Riding through the meadowlarks and the killdeer was entertaining. Screaming red-tailed hawks protested their presence.

"Hey, thanks, Chet," Fred said. "You and Lisa did wonders talking to my wife. She told me what you said, and she took it to heart. We are not going back to those alleys. But when it's been your life for so long you think you can never escape that hold."

"She will be fine. We simply reminded her."

"You look like you are having a great time

with Lisa?"

"It is always different. A new relationship. We've both been burned by deep losses and then we became, cautiously, involved. I tried hard and know she did, too. We are doing what Elizabeth wanted us to do. She gave Lisa a list of things she wanted me to do if I didn't get back in time."

"You have done some different things. I was curious about that. Selling the Oracle Ranch?"

"I made a profit with it and was able to buy this bargain and Arnold's ranch. I sold the stagecoach line so I wouldn't have to sell it at auction when the train came. They wanted the telegraph line so badly they bought the stage line, too."

"What about today?"

"I have nothing for sale. Will you and Josey stay here and help Spencer build this ranch?"

"I'll do anything you need for me to do. I like riding with you, but I understand Spencer can use my help. I can learn a lot from him."

"No one will ever believe this happened. Bo will die when he hears. I might have given the full price, so Spencer did a wonderful job getting him down."

They laughed about it and rode on. They

saw that they needed a well driller, and Tom needed to make more windmills so cows could better graze this place, but it was going to be a great grassy ranch.

The girls got the men to fire up the water heater, and Chet took a bath and changed clothes.

He and Lisa talked about his day and the things needed there.

"They need two sheepherder showers for the men to use," she said.

"We need mattresses for the bunkhouse. The bunks are built. They have woodstoves in there, and the doors can be open on the hot days so they have a breeze. More brooms, mops, a sickle cutter to mow some weeds and grass. Those trees Spencer has coming will make it great if they're watered. There is a kitchen for the help, but until they get to be large numbers, Lucinda and Josey will feed them at the house. The two Navajo women are coming today. The men brought another big wagonload of wood and unloaded it. He said Spencer already paid him. We will also need a well driller and lots of windmills with tanks."

"Tomorrow you ride to where they are working cattle?" Lisa asked.

"We'll stay overnight and come back the next day."

"Fine. I can't believe how he did it. Can you?"

"It was the buy of the century. If there had been tracks laid south of here, it might have brought half a million dollars. We are getting set for that next rush of people, and a market as well with what the trains will bring in and ship out."

"Will you build pens at the tracks to ship cattle in and out on?" Lisa asked.

"If they realize this is Arizona and not KC or Saint Louis. We own land beside the tracks at Flagstaff. We can have them built when the tracks arrive, but we need a shipping rate we can afford. All they have done so far is cut the pay and raised the costs. Stagecoach ticket prices have tripled since they bought it."

"Being married to you is sure exciting," she said.

"A lot different for you?"

"I taught kids English. I took women to the doctor who were afraid to go. I planned parties. My late husband, bless his heart, came home and told me all you had been doing. I listened but it was not part of my life. Now I am riding with you and it is. And you talk to me. Like my list of needs is important."

"Let's go to bed. I need to be up early.

Spencer wants to show me a lot tomorrow."

"I'll get up, too. Like you say, this is our outfit, and I feel a part of it because of how you take the time to tell me all the things that are going on," Lisa smiled at him.

Thanks, Lord, for sending her to me.

CHAPTER 22

There were enough men at the ranch for them to leave it for a day. Chet, Spencer, and Fred rode for the herd before the sun began to peek over the horizon. They trotted their horses southward in the cool air. They crossed the Marcy Road, a glimpse of pink on the horizon to their left, and flushed quail in their path. They spooked two large antlered mule deer bucks who bounded off on stiff legs as they rode on.

Two hours later, as they came over the last rise, Chet heard cattle bawling. Branding iron fire smoke filled his nose as they reined up. There were lots of cattle assembled and men were working them from horseback. This bunch was serious. They'd already been at it a while that day.

A man under a sombrero rode out to greet them. His name was Dobe Quantrill. His mustache was trimmed and his smile genuine. "*El patrón,* at last you come to the cow camp. So nice to meet you."

"I'm Chet. You have a grand bunch working here. How much more is left to do?"

"I want it over in four days. Those are my plans."

"Have you seen the new headquarters?"

Dobe smiled. "*Sí.* I never thought such a place existed. I have been working on ranches up here three years. I heard about the big lodge, but I never thought no more. I was busy working for the Bar 99 and they came from south Texas. They didn't like it up here, so they sold out to Arnold. I didn't like Arnold, so I quit him and went to work for the Three T's. They are farther east.

"I met Spencer in St. Joseph and he asked if I wanted work. I told him I won't work for Arnold and he said he worked for you and you'd bought Arnold out. I brought three good men with me. Some of the men here work for you at your home place, some work for the man drives the cattle to the Navajos for you. Two work on the Verde Ranch. There are others, and we all work hard. The men from your ranches want to go home, and I know more vaqueros that would love to work here. So when we get them all branded they can go home, and if you approve, I will have others here."

"Pay everyone a month's wages as a

bonus. If you need help, send word to my ranches and they will come to your aid."

The man looked stunned. Then nodded. "You know these men well, don't you?"

"Is there a house for you over there at headquarters?"

"He never said but I think one would do."

"How many kids do you have?"

"Five and one more coming."

"Spencer can build you a casa. I'll tell him."

"He said you were a generous man." He stuck out his tough, callused hand to shake with Chet.

Dobe rode off and Spencer came by. "He is a young Raphael."

"I agree. He will need a bigger house. Build him one."

"He has five and soon six kids. Maybe one more. His wife's sister lives with them. I never asked him any questions but I think she is his second wife."

"Build him a bigger house." Chet chuckled.

"Yes. All these hands work hard."

"I told him to pay the men an extra month's wages and if he ever needs help, our other ranches will come. There's some riders coming," Chet said. "Wonder what they want?"

"Beats the hell out of me. Maybe just to talk?"

Fred slid his pony in beside them. "Who are they?"

"We're asking ourselves the same question."

The dozen riders reined up in a line. Dobe joined Chet and the others. "That is Fred Holcomb. He owns the Tepee Ranch."

Chet nodded and stepped for ward. "I'm Chet Byrnes. What can I do for you?"

The man wearing the clean white shirt spat tobacco sideways then poked his stud horse for ward. "I'm Frank Holcomb. How many of my cattle you got held up here?"

"Dobe, tell the man."

"Not one. We are branding Wagon Wheel and K Bar ones."

"By God, I want my men to ride through them and check. There are too damn many cattle here not to have some of mine."

"You can leave a couple of men to check what we brand. But we are holding these cattle and a bunch riding through would spook them and we could lose some. We worked too damn hard getting them up."

"By damn, my men will ride through them or I'm starting in to shooting your asses off."

By then, a large number of Dobe's own hands came to back him. Chet said, "When

465

that shooting starts, you will be the first to die. Get your hand off your gun butt, leave two men, and we will feed them and let them check, but you damn sure ain't busting through those cattle and ruining all our hard work."

"Get off that damn horse. I'll whip your ass and wipe up the blood with you."

"Stay right there, boss man, this one is mine." Spencer, off his horse, tossed his hat aside, unbuckled his gun belt, and handed it to Chet.

Holcomb jumped out of the saddle with his fists raised high and made a run at Spencer. But he met the fastest array of punches Chet ever saw, and Holcomb was soon on his back with Spencer telling him to get up. Six Winchesters were cocked and ready on his ranch hand's side.

"The fight's over." Chet booted his horse in close. "If you doubt me, I told you to leave two men. We won't hurt them. But don't ever come threaten my men or my outfit again, because more than likely you won't go home alive."

"I ain't leaving shit here. I'm going to find the law and have you arrested for rustling."

"You do that. We have nothing to hide. But don't come back to bully us around."

Holcomb mounted his stud that one his

men had been holding and rode off. They followed.

"Well," Spencer said, "We just met our neighbor. Real nice guy. When he's sitting on his ass. Where's the damn cactus? I want him to sit on some of that next time."

If that was a sign of the other ranchers, it would probably happen again. Chet hated the vision.

CHAPTER 23

Things were settled. The wagon folk were ready to go home. They decided the wagon wheel would be the brand they'd use in the future. It would be the hardest for a rustler to work over. Spencer planned to scatter the cattle after the branding was complete, but he planned to use line riders to keep the cattle on the range around him and other cattle off it. He intended to use tents, a corral, and hay if they got snowed in.

With over a thousand market steers, they'd start shipping them with Sarge. Some were three years old and larger so they'd be accepted at Gallup. Spencer and Fred got busy contracting hay. They would have fifteen hundred mother cows and springing heifers when they made the count final.

Back home, Chet shook his head. Wagon Wheel would be the largest operation they had. And the first-year cattle sales would pay for the entire deal.

Tom planned to double his blacksmith shop output of windmills. Spencer found a broke well driller family and hired them. They rebuilt his equipment and had him poking holes. His name was Hugo Smith, his wife Alania, two teen boys, Ruff and Tumble, and a daughter, Claudia. They lived in a sheepherder's wagon when out with the rig and draft horses hauled the tower around on wheels. They pounded the ground nearly every day and found lots of water. Two were artesian, and Spencer hired Navajo rock masons to make some large tanks for them.

Tom bought eighteen young Hereford bulls in Kansas and had them shipped to the end of the railroad tracks over in New Mexico. Spencer hired two Navajo families to drive them carefully from there to the Wagon Wheel headquarters. They had a hay wagon and a water wagon. They made it there with sixteen. The man in charge said two broke their legs in prairie dog holes and had to be shot and eaten. Expensive food was Spencer's reply.

Fred bought ten young shorthorn bulls from a Mormon farmer who had brought them hay and the man had a brother south of there who had ten more. They were even larger but cost the same price, $100 apiece. Spencer and Fred felt that that should cover the Wagon Wheel's bull needs. It snowed over two feet deep on most of the Wagon Wheel range, the third week in November.

They only got a dusting at Prescott. Chet was pacing the living room floor and Lisa stopped him. "Whatever is wrong?"

"I have not gotten one new lead on Arnold, that man who plotted Miguel's murder. I thought by now someone would have located him unless he died of snakebite, off by himself, in the desert somewhere."

"Start over. You always get leads on those criminals."

"You're probably right. Spencer said in his wire they were going to be all right. Toby and Talley I have to trust to have their matters in hand. Shawn and Lucy know —"

She slipped in and hugged him. "I think they all will make it fine. Let yourself relax. Go upstairs and we'll make love."

"I guess you are right."

"Oh, Chet, I know I am right. I know you will solve it."

He, Tom, and Jesus planned to go elk hunting. Anita had a spell and Jesus stayed home. Cole went with him and they picked up Tom. A cowboy named Hank Moore drove a supply wagon with tents, camp gear, and a way to get the racks, meat, and hides home. They made camp up on the rim and the bull elk were bugling.

Cole got a big six-by-six the first day. Chet missed getting a shot through the junipers at two different ones. Tom put a four-by-five bull down the next day. The third day it snowed lightly, and Chet met his trophy bull head-on and dropped him with his first shot. He cut his throat, then rode back to camp to get help. Hank and Tom came back with him and dragged him, with the help of their horses, to a large pine and pulled him up to gut him. Cole came down to help them. They were busy dressing him when a great roar made them turn. When Chet whirled around, forty feet away a giant silver-tip grizzly was growling at them. The horses broke their hitched reins and fled.

Hank with his bloody dripping hands tossed Chet the 44/40. He caught the gun, levered a cartridge in the chamber as the bear, in a rage, was charging them to claim the carcass. One shot, two shots, and three, and the bear went facedown less than six feet from the muzzle of the Winchester. Chet sighed.

Cole on his knees on the ground had his six-gun in his hand. Tom had an ax in his.

Hank hurriedly went off and pissed.

"Where in the hell did he come from?" Chet asked still shaken.

"Downwind. He must have smelled the kill."

"Boys, that was just too close." Chet felt his weak legs still might fold. "I am still shaken. Best thing happened here is that damn bear is dead."

Tom said, "You've got a great bear rug. You are going to mount him?"

"Hell, yes, and get the elk skins tanned to make Lisa a long coat."

"There's three."

"Yeah, Cole. Millie, Val, and Lisa can all have one."

"You're right, Chet. The coat idea is bound to make them happy."

"Won't they love that?" Tom asked.

"We better butcher that bear, too. Raphael loves bear meat."

Tom put his ax aside. "It is going to be a damn big job."

"I think we had a great hunt and I am grateful I got to go along," Cole said.

They had plenty of meat and the next day went home.

They rang the bell and ranch folks came out to see. It took two men to hold up the hide and show everyone at the ranch the grizzly. They couldn't believe the meat. Chet had brought home the hides, the racks, the bear carcass, and the elk hindquarters.

Lisa, wrapped in a long, black coat, shook her head at the bearskin. Raphael's men took charge. They, like Chet, figured his foreman really was excited about the bear meat.

Cole shook his hand and took his saddle horse hitched on the back of the wagon and drove up the mountain.

"Who shot the bear?" Lisa asked.

"Hank was the closest to the nearest rifle leaning against a tree, but his hands were all bloody, so he tossed the gun to me. I levered in a shell as the bear was coming right at us. I pumped three bullets in him and the third one stopped him six feet from my boot toes."

She hugged him. "Oh, my Lord."

"He's going to be a rug on the floor. I am tanning the elk hides and you, Val, and Millie are getting long coats."

"Oh, I have seen coats like that. Do they know?"

"No. It's a secret."

"I can keep it that way. But the bear was that close?"

"That close. Now, let's you and I go get closer."

"I thought you'd never ask."

Anita turned out to be all right and Jesus said he wasn't sure he wanted to have been charged by an 800-pound grizzly. It still didn't stop him from eating his share of elk meat at the next feed Lisa put on.

Chet received another letter from another ex-sheriff in Colorado. Maybe he'd have to go to Colorado and see these men.

Dear Marshal Byrnes,
My name is Harold Shell. I am a retired county sheriff but during my early terms of office I arrested a Mac Arnold once for stage robbery. He got off by producing some false witnesses to testify he was with them at the time of the robbery. I recently attended a funeral of a fellow lawman in Raton, New Mexico. I am certain I saw Arnold. He must have seen me because he went the other way. He's much older now, but I am good at remembering and recognizing faces.

Harry Gould is a former sheriff, too. He lives there and he has had some dealings with Arnold himself, so he'd know him and could tell you if he was in the area. I wish you lots of luck finding that no-good scoundrel and putting him away.

Harold Shell

Chet wrote a letter to the postmaster, with a second letter addressed to Harry Gould, saying the man was an ex-lawman and he was a U.S. Marshal and the enclosed letter needed to reach him.

Two weeks later Gould wrote him saying his letter made it to his house.

Yes, I know Harold Shell well. Mac Arnold doesn't live in Raton but he visits the area off and on. I didn't know Arnold was wanted or had any outstanding warrants or I'd have reported him. I think he knows people around here and may come to sponge off them since he is not dressed as fancy as he was in his heydays. I will check and try to learn who he sees when he visits here.

Harry Gould

Chet now had a lead in southern Colorado or New Mexico. But Arnold didn't live either of those places — only visits. Something might break soon.

"Well, what did we learn?" Lisa asked.

"He visits there is all."

"Well, if he does that you will get him. Now, I need to talk to you about Christmas. I know Liz gave every man on the ranch a pocketknife last year. What do we do this year?"

"Suspenders?"

"Sounds right and they can use them. Dress material for the ladies? They won't hardly buy it for themselves."

"Good idea."

"Liz had marked down what she gave each year at Christmas so she didn't repeat too close. I am going to continue that."

"Nice. What else?"

"The foremen and their wives."

"The coats will be ready. The elk skin ones."

"I almost forgot them."

"Give the other foremen's wives a letter to go get a coat for themselves. And the men can use a Boss of the Plains Stetson hat. Shawn, Cole, Toby, Fred, Spencer, Raphael, Sarge, Cody, JD, Ortega, Tom, Victor, and Jesus."

"I forgot how expensive it gets." She looked around with a smile. "Everyone is gone today."

"Fine, we can solve this later. Let's go hide."

She laughed and hugged and kissed him.

476

"You are habit forming."

Two days later in the mail was a letter from San Antonio.

Dear Chet,

I hope this letter finds you in good health. My name is Niles Craig. I am a Texas Ranger and ran across some interesting things while investigating a case about some killers for hire. They were involved in a job to murder a rancher. That man lives around Kerrville. We stopped them but they had papers on them about killing you. $2,000. Chet Byrnes rancher Prescott, Arizona Territory. The person for them to contact was N. M. Reynolds. We could not locate any NM so we had to let it go. I thought you should know. I understand you are a U.S. Marshal too.

Niles

"What's wrong?" Lisa asked.

"My old enemies in Texas tried to hire some killers to murder me for two thousand dollars."

"I'd pay more money than that for them not to." She dried her hands on a tea towel.

He shook his head at her answer. She had a sense of humor and he loved it, but some folks still might not give her a chance.

"Why are they still mad at you? You've been out here almost five years, haven't you?"

"Yes. But some folks never forget."

They prepared for two big parties. They would have a ranch party on Christmas Eve, then on Christmas day everyone they knew was invited to come eat. There would be music to dance to. Lots of food and beer, but no gifts. It would be too much.

Lisa sent out invitations to all on the list.

"Aren't there teenage ranch girls in school?"

"Yes. Why?"

"Hire them to do these kinds of mailings next time. They will be thrilled and take some of the work off you. Josey did lots of work. Hire two girls to do what she did. They need the work and you don't need to do it all."

"*Sí, patrón.*"

"Lisa?"

"I miss Josey, but I don't need or want a bunch of help now your guests are gone."

"You are the boss not the worker."

"I can handle it."

"I appreciate you to death. But I don't need you to be worn out to save a few dollars that those people could use. Now who is the leader for this Christmas event? She needs to report to you. You don't report to her."

"Reba. She is one of the best women to organize everyone and not make anyone mad."

"Great. Add in a few more women so you have a council."

"I hadn't thought about doing that."

"Start having lunches for them when you get your help picked. They will be proud to eat with you in this house and that will get you more workers."

"Can we go to the Verde Dance this Saturday?"

"Sure. Tell Raphael to cook something and we can go down and play with Adam, and sleep overnight in the big house again."

She bent over and kissed him. "I'm so glad to have you. These are the nicest days of my life."

"You have earned all of them."

On Friday of that week, the cold rain started. Above freezing but steady rain that shifted in and out. No doubt, up on the rim, at Flagstaff, it was snowing. Moisture was so critical to ranching and the territory Chet seldom complained. The men were getting ready to cook half a steer and he'd put on his canvas coat and old hat to check on them.

Four vaqueros in rubber raincoats stood in the barn alleyway.

"It's a heck of day to have to cook, isn't it?" he asked.

Ric shook his head. "No, we could be back in Mexico wondering what we would feed our families tonight."

The others nodded in agreement.

A man in his thirties, Ramon said, "We have warm dry houses here. Our children go to school, and we always eat three meals a day. Plus we are paid cowboy wages where most people pay their workers much less than that."

Again, they all nodded.

Ric smiled. "It is never a bad day, rain or shine or snow, working for you and your wife."

"Thanks. If it doesn't drop colder and snow we will go, otherwise we will stay home."

The weather stayed the same. Lisa, bundled in rain gear, went to the Verde with Chet and a vaquero named Juan. Raphael promised they would have the meat set up that afternoon.

The rain came in shifts, the overcast keeping the sun away. They arrived at the big house mid-morning. Rhea shouted from the door for them to come inside.

"After you put the horses up, come around to the kitchen. We will feed you."

"Gracias, señora."

"This your first trip down here?"

"Sí."

"You will have fun. We won't go to the dance until later in the afternoon. You can stay in the house until then."

"I will do that."

Chet and Lisa went inside. Adam had something to show Lisa. Victor marked a place in his book, closed it, and rose to shake Chet's hand.

"What are you reading?"

He showed him the spine. *How to Farm Agricultural Crops.* "Hampt loaned it to me. He said he could have read it himself but he enjoyed May reading it to him when the kids were asleep. There's lots of information. One thing I learned from it was how to check how good my seed was."

Chet took a chair at the table. "How does that work?"

"You take burlap sacks, wet them, and put the seeds in a layer. Keep them moist and in a week or so they germ something and hatch like babies."

"I think that word is germinate."

"Have you read this book?"

"No, but I have heard that word spoken. So that is Hampt's bible on farming."

"Yes and we seek him for help. Shawn planted his alfalfa from a letter May wrote with his instructions. He told me he had a perfect stand. And he showed me how, too. Hampt and May are a wonderful couple."

"Her parents had disowned her for marrying my brother and then he was killed. May originally didn't want to come out here with the family, but she had little choice. She came. Hampt asked me if he could ask her to a dance. I never noticed, but they became serious and, one day, they asked if they could get married. It was a match in heaven. We never knew she could sing or play the piano. My sister and May were close as could be and Susie didn't know, either. Hampt brought that out of her."

"I remember him courting her in the early days. He is the man to ask about things in farming."

"And if you ever get in a fight he's the man to back you. He took a handful of black cowboys on that drive to Ogallala and taught them how to shoot rifles. They turned back several war parties on that drive."

"Chet? Rhea has a question. Adam will be

five next year. They will let him start school. Do you want him to go to school here or at the Cherry School?"

"Rhea, what do you want?"

She looked close to tears. "I want what is best for him."

He stood up and hugged her. "Then he stays here with you. That was the plan from the start. You have done all I asked. He accepts and listens to you. He belongs here."

"See, what did I tell you?" Lisa said.

Rhea hugged him. "I don't know what Victor and I'd do without him. Thanks so much."

"Rhea says the word is out. The Byrnes Ranch is cooking again and there will be a crowd at the dance even with the rain."

"Good. We enjoy it. And we know many people can't afford to do it. We can."

"How are Spencer and Fred doing?"

"That last snow worried them, but they fed most of the cattle. No losses. Said in their letter they learned a lot. They say the best answer is to buy a ranch on the Little Colorado to raise hay. So they are looking for one. They have fifteen hundred cows and heifers plus yearlings. That makes them the largest ranch I own. They have bought hay since they took it over and are still buying more. With the size of that herd they eat lots when the snow covers the grass."

"Arnold didn't ever feed hay?"

"I guess not. There is no irrigation. He has one section, might make farmland, south of the Marcy Road. He planted several acres of corn there a year back, then a midsummer storm came and washed it away, so he fenced it and left it. Spencer and Fred haven't decided what we should do with it."

"Dry land corn is iffy around here. We raise some but it has to be irrigated."

"He only planted sixty acres."

"That cost money."

"And it did not work."

"Lunch is ready," Lisa said. "You two joining us?"

"We will, my dear. I see it is raining again."

"I hope folks from up north across the river are already here. I bet that river rises today."

"I never thought about that. It can get big."

Victor agreed. "Floodwater never got up to the houses here, but it got within a hundred yards once and it was two miles wide."

They damn sure didn't need that. Millie and Tom joined them and rain was the topic.

CHAPTER 24

After lunch the men talked about future plans. Tom suggested they increase the purebred herd at Perkins, rather than the range cows under the operation they now grazed in the irrigated field. They could fence lots of deeded land and let the Herefords out to graze it and have more hay land.

"How large?"

"We have enough free range down here to move those other cattle down here. We cleared up these ranges last year when we drove the free-grazer cattle down in the Verde wilderness."

"Tom, let me pencil in the cost of fencing it. You have, what, three line riders up there?"

"It takes four now."

Chet nodded. "Finding that many purebred cows might be a chore."

"If we can find them, I'd rather have heifers. Those first Kansas cows we bought are pasture cows but the heifers born up there do real well on the range. I think heifers would learn what to eat and do better."

"Good observation. It will take miles of fence and won't make us popular even if we now keep their cattle out with our line riders."

"It is your deeded land."

"Yes. Let me think on it for a few days. It is a good plan."

Victor agreed. "There is more land that can be opened and irrigated."

The rain let up and they drove to the dance.

On the way, Chet talked about his first coming to the area and the kids all adjusting to being in Arizona.

"When we came here, those boys of May's were in their early teens. They fished every day and brought them home to Susie to clean and cook. Most were catfish but one day they caught a huge carp. Must have weighed ten pounds. Of course carp are bony, and Susie, rather than mess with it, fed it to the cats. That made those boys so mad we nearly had a revolution at the ranch."

"Tye and his brother?" Victor asked.

"Yes. Once or twice I had to lecture them

when they treed poor May, which they used to do even when they were small."

"They grew up to be good men."

"I think that was May's doing, though Sarge had a later hand in it."

"It was their brother that got murdered while here with you?"

"Heck was such a rebel with May I brought him out here with me, and he became so grown up. That's when I bought Verde ranch. We were traveling home, when stage robbers took him hostage, murdered him, and threw him in a canyon. In my anger, I shot them all and then went to find his body. I carried him in my arms, for I don't know how long. Worst day of my life. Why, as a boy he'd ridden clear back from Kansas to our ranch in Texas to tell me they'd murdered his father."

"Your first wife came to your aid."

"She saved my life."

Tom joined in. "Me, I get a little mad at times when I hear how rich guys walk in from Texas and go to buying up ranches. You've had hell but continue to save lots of people like me. I am thankful."

The ranch gang had the meat set up. The aroma of the mesquite barbeque filled the damp air in the hall. They had a stove going to drive out the cold in the building and the tables were full of food dishes.

Rufus Ramsey of the Box 8 came by and shook his hand. "I hate we ain't got boats to ferry them folks across the river to here."

"Are there many up there?"

"Mary and I drove up there earlier and waved at some of them on the other side."

"It is a good rain."

"Damn right. So, if they can't get across, they can come next week in the dust."

Despite the flooding there was a hall full of folks. A preacher offered grace and everyone moved through the line choosing food to sample. Chet and Lisa were eating on a bench with Tom and Millie when Talley and Toby came in drenched.

"How did they get across?" Millie asked.

"Probably swam their horses across," Tom said.

"Did you swim over?" Lisa asked when they joined them.

"He found us a place when there weren't any trees floating down and we swam our horses across."

"No big deal," Toby said. "We wanted to come see you all and dance. It's a long way back not to get to join you all after we'd made the trip to the river."

"Was it a powerful current?"

"I knew it would sweep us some downstream, so I went in judging where, around the bend, there was no bank and we could get out."

"Good thinking."

Lisa found Talley a towel to dry her face and hair. They were the center of attention and got several good-natured laughs.

"Those two are doers. I guess the baby she carries had no problems, either?"

"It may be half fish. I know she is pregnant and you aren't, and if we could do something we'd have done it."

"I know how badly she wanted a child. I try not to bring this up with you, but each time a ranch wife is pregnant we talk about it. Know that, yes, I would like to have our own child, but that is in the hands of God."

"Amen. Lisa, I love you and we have a — What in the devil's going on? Someone is having a fight."

Then he heard a familiar roar and over the crowd he heard Hampt shout, "You two dummies want to fight, get outside." He had two men by their shirt collars and was parting the crowd headed for the door. And out they went.

Chet hurried over, drew the .45 out of the holster on the wall peg, and held it against his leg. He excused himself through the crowd on his way out. The two were still at it — wrestling and hitting each other in a fury.

He fired the pistol in the air. The blast caused heads to swivel.

"Stop your damn fighting. This is a community family-attended dance. We don't allow fighting even out here. What kind of an example does that make for the children here? Fights solve nothing. Now get up and separate. Fight any more here, and I'll send you both to hell to solve it with the devil. Do you understand?"

"Yes sir," they both repeated.

"Now everyone civilized get back inside. It's raining again."

He turned on his heel and went back indoors. Men, going by, were thanking him as he reloaded his gun.

"Boy, when you get mad you really get mad," Lisa said standing close. "I bet they heard you all the way down at Hayden's Ferry."

"There ain't no mistaking Chet Byrnes when he gets his collar up," Hampt said. "And he saved me kicking the tails off them."

Cole and Val were standing there when Chet and Lisa went back to their chairs.

"We just got here," Val said. "I talked to

that crazy Talley. They swam it flood and all."

Chet kissed her forehead. "You can't stop any of the Byrnes family because of a flood."

"And we damn sure know how to stop a fight," Hampt said.

May ducked through and hugged Chet. "You stopped people from fighting at dances in Texas, too."

"How are you, sister?"

"Great. Save me a slow dance."

"You got it."

The gun put up, he and Lisa danced off across the floor. Things were back to friendly.

When the fiddle music started he went over and got May for the slower one.

She laughed as they waltzed. "She is not as tall as number one but close. You know I loved Liz, but afterward I wondered if you would even notice Lisa. Some men never see the woman standing right in front of them. I am so glad you two got together. You act like you have been together for years."

"We have. Not actually, but we do things in step and life with her is super."

"I have told you often enough that you have done so much for me. My Hampt is so dedicated to me. We have had such a great life together, children all through it, and if it hadn't been for you neither of us would have had this great a life."

"And I had to order you to come to Arizona."

She laughed. "Thank God you did that."

Rhea had a house full but there were rooms enough for all. Chet, Victor, Toby, and Cole talked about Tom's plan to expand the Hereford business. They liked the idea.

Before they went to bed Chet told Toby not to swim the flood to get home. They could stay there all week. It didn't matter. They were too important to his operation to risk losing.

"We won't. I promise."

"Thanks. Sleep tight."

"You told him not to swim to get back?" Lisa whispered to him in bed.

"Yes and he agreed not to."

"You have to give those two credit. They do get things done."

"They do. But I never expected her to do all she does. I knew Toby would give his all, but her, well, she acted like a perfect snob about everything when she first came to us. It worked out wonderfully. Just don't get in their way or they'll run you over."

He went to tickling her and she caught his hands. "I really enjoyed myself again. I don't have a real good reason, but my life is like floating on a cloud. It was great before and now it is super great all the time."

They slept in each other's arms like honeymooners.

The rain moved on and it turned colder. But no snow came to Prescott.

Talley and Toby came up to the ranch. Tom said he'd send them word when the river was down.

The four of them talked about their men and Christmas. The decision was reached to have it early and the two of them to come if the snow wasn't too deep or the river flooding.

Toby told Chet, "Someday, one or two may want to go back to Mexico to see how things are going. Others will want to stay and get married. I'd like to keep them. If they want to marry, can we build them houses?" Talley nodded that she agreed with what Toby said.

"I see no reason why not. The plan has worked well here," Chet told them.

"They live pretty far from anywhere. Toby and I want to, from our own money, buy them extra from what you are giving them."

"What is that?"

"Two pair of pants and two shirts. A canvas jumper, gloves, a suit of under wear, and a stocking cap for cold weather."

"Put it on our bill."

"Are you sure? I have the sizes they wear. Those guys work hard every day. The place shows it."

Toby said, "It really does and they are making great cowboys. They have all those horses you sent us well broke."

"Tomorrow, if it isn't snowing, take a wagon into town to get what you need. On our account."

Talley came over and kissed him on the cheek.

"And you go by the dress shop, order yourself a full-length coat. Don't say a word. It's a Christmas surprise for all the foremen's wives this year. You are one of those. Now, not a word and don't get it until Christmas," said Chet.

"Well, that is sure nice."

"We want to be sure they know we appreciate them, too. We have so many good ranches because we have such great workers."

"Amen," Toby said.

The Verde River went down Wednesday and Toby drove the loaded wagon and horses while Talley led his pony.

"Didn't the doctor make Talley stop riding after two months?" she asked watching them leave.

"I doubt anyone told her or if she'd listen." She hugged him. "Probably not."

Things grew busier. The spirit was there. A tree in the living room was decorated with strings of popcorn strung by all the ranch schoolchildren who ate about half the amount they strung and really brightened up that Saturday. Lisa and the new girls made candy and cake for them, with hot tea in small cups she'd found in town. They sang Spanish and English carols.

The ranch women gave them a statue of the Virgin Mary praying. And Lisa thanked them, saying she knew it was a gift from their hearts and she would cherish it.

Christmas Eve was the ranch event with hands and family. That afternoon the children came to the house with lighted candles and sang carols at the foot of the stairs and then came in for hot cocoa. Lisa and the foremen's wives treated them to cookies as well.

Then they all went to the large tent kept warm with heaters since the weather had a nip. The priest had communion. It was the first time it was held at the ranch but met the workers' approval. The superintendent wives thought it was very good, and even Hampt said it set the stage for the occasion.

Everyone ate supper and then gifts for all were presented. Children were first and suitable things were given. A small girl, a doll. A teen girl in school, a sweater and skirt. Wives received dress material, and men suspenders and tough jeans with rivets, the ranch foremen's wives received long winter coats — four got elk skin ones. Lisa added one for Anita since Jesus was supposed to have gone hunting with the men. She swooned. The foremen there got their Boss of the Plains Stetsons.

At the end, Lisa and Tom called Chet to come onto the stage and gave him a box.

He thanked them all for coming and hugged his wife. "This is all her and all these wives' hard work." They stood up and applauded.

"Open the box," she insisted.

"Oh the box, yes."

He raised the lid and couldn't believe his eyes. There was a gold-plated .45 single-action Colt with an ivory handle and a longhorn steer's head carved into it.

Tom took the box. "Every family put what they could afford into the fund to buy it. Every family."

"My Lord. What a beautiful gift. I love you, family. All of you."

CHAPTER 25

Christmas morning came with a lively discussion at the breakfast table.

"Reckon Fred and Spencer had a great Christmas?" Jesus asked.

"They planned one like JD and Bonnie planned theirs. Lucy and Shawn were holding one last night, and Spud and Shirley were all excited about what they were going to do."

"Robert and Betty didn't come?"

"They gave their crew a party and nice gifts. Their baby Caroline is very young and the weather threatened. Lisa has her measurements and is ordering her a coat. Betty Lou and her husband had some activities in their church they wanted to attend. We of course said we understand. We are so big now it is getting hard to get us all together in one place."

"I want to shoot some tin cans," Val teased. "Can I use your new peashooter?"

"If you promise not to scratch it."

"I think that left you speechless."

"It did."

"Good. You deserve it."

Lisa went to the back door and came back. "It's a telegram for you."

MAC ARNOLD IS IN TOMBSTONE. I DON'T KNOW FOR HOW LONG. VIRGIL EARP.

"Tell that boy to wait. I need to send an answer."

"He's right here."

Chet ran to the office and wrote a reply.

HOLD ARNOLD FOR THE U.S. MARSHAL ON CHARGES OF MURDER. I WILL BE IN TOMBSTONE IN TWO DAYS. U.S. MARSHAL CHET BYRNES

"Send that to him." He paid the boy two dollars.

"Jesus, Arnold is in Tombstone. I asked the law to hold him on murder charges."

"We need to go down there?"

"Yes. Raphael can pick us a man."

"The ranch can run. I want to go along," Cole said.

"We'd love to have you."

"Damn right. It's time you did some real work," Jesus teased.

"Taking the midnight stage?"

"Yes."

"Val, I am going home to get ready. You can stay and visit."

"No, I'll help you. Thanks, everyone."

Anita was up and Jesus had her coat.

"Anita, you need any help, send for me," Lisa said.

She smiled. "Thanks, Lisa. I promise I will if I need anything."

They followed the Emersons out of the house.

"The party is definitely over," Lisa said to the two new girls.

They smiled. Tina, the oldest, asked her, "Does this happen often?"

"Just a normal part of our life. It will happen many times. You girls will get used to it. Do the dishes, mop the floors in here, and the back porch. Then take a siesta. I will make plans for who will be here for supper."

"*Señora?* Mona and I really like our jobs here."

"Good. And I thank you for coming to work with me. Now, Chet, let's go pack you a bag."

"Yes. Girls, you make her take breaks

while I am gone."

"Oh, *sí, señor.*"

Lisa shook her head at him as they headed upstairs.

Midnight, the three Marshals kissed their wives good-bye and climbed on the Black Canyon Stage Coach for Hayden's Ferry.

"It's been a long time since the three of us did this together," Chet said.

"Too long." Cole stretched out his long legs. "What's our plan?"

"Mac Arnold, I hope, is now in or will be, shortly, in the Tombstone Marshal's city jail."

"He's the one behind those two boys' deaths up at Rustler's Ranch while you brought the cattle over?"

"He hired the men who did it. We found them down in Bloody Basin and they chose to fight us. Two-bit wanted men that he told to hang the boys but not to burn the ranch. He wanted it when they were cleared out."

"This the ranch Spencer and Fred operate?"

"Spencer, Fred, and Miguel and others went to catch them all at Arnold's place. From what they all told me, somehow they knew we were coming and poured out a deadly wave of gunfire. In that gunfire, they caught Miguel. He just lay there. None of them could get to him. I guess anger made them able to start taking them out. In a short time they were dead, or wounded. They cross-examined the living and they said that Arnold knew they were coming and if they killed me he'd pay them a thousand dollars. The men did try to get to Miguel, but it was too late.

"They recovered a rifle stolen from the Rustler's Ranch when they murdered those men guarding the ranch. They killed the rest of them, and burned them in the house. Arnold gave the orders, which makes him a murderer."

"I should have been there."

"Miguel was a great lawman and a great guy. When we made those trips to Colorado to finally get those guys stopping your stage lines he was the best man I ever saw on the job," Jesus said.

"He never asked for anything but for a house to marry Lisa and live in."

"I bought the ranch and cattle when the bank was going to foreclose on it."

The stagecoach rocked and jolted them around as it headed for the valley. Chet slept some only to be awakened by a bump and tossed around. Through the coach opening, a slip of a moon timed out the old year. Stars spread silver light across the towering mountains that hemmed the stage road in. The arms of the saguaros were held up to the sky. The night air grew warmer by the mile. Trying to sleep was difficult.

They stopped at Bumble Bee to exchange horses, giving them a chance to vent their bladders and stretch stiff muscles.

"Every stop has our history in it, doesn't it?" Cole asked.

"Most do. No one's tried to make this a run a railroad track yet."

"Do you miss running the stage line?" Jesus asked Cole.

"The telegraph saved me lots of false runs, but there were no ends to problems in those four hundred miles of road."

"What did you think when they told you they were cutting your pay in half?"

"Let's go, guys," the driver called to them.

"I said to hell with you. I am through."

Jesus laughed, taking his seat. "You shock them?"

"No. But they sure didn't know one horse apple about running a stage line."

Chet laughed. "I heard they are on their third manager."

"They run railroads and no one dares to tell them they are doing it wrong."

"We are not getting much sleep. Our next stage leaves for Tucson at two p.m. So we may be in Tombstone by eight tomorrow night. If Arnold was still in Tombstone when my wire got there, Virgil Earp has him in the city jail for us."

"I hope he knows where he went if he doesn't have him," Jesus said.

"Everyone leaves tracks. We are running this guy down, no matter what it takes. I vowed I'd bring those killers to trial. Arnold's men, under his orders, shot down Miguel Costa on duty as a U.S. Marshal. Arnold needs to pay for that. Wherever he tries to hide, we will find him."

"He is a con man to start with, right?" Cole asked. "He conned that banker to loan him the money to buy the ranch and cattle. Then when he couldn't sell the cattle, he decided he better do something else. How was he going to stock that ranch he planned to use of yours?" Cole asked.

"Con another banker," Chet said. "I think he discovered it and thought Toby and Talley owned it. Those men raided it to kill the owner and the help. Maybe make it like Indians did the raid and with all dead he could hide out down there next."

"It damn sure is isolated," Cole said. "I still can't believe that Talley is Toby's wife and is the same girl you saved in Colorado. She was so stuck up and now, pregnant, she

504

swam her horse across the Verde flood to get to the dance."

"They are a great hardworking couple."

"I hate to ask, but like Jesus, I loved Elizabeth and want to know if the doctor found out what killed her?"

"The doctor who did an autopsy said cancer had spread through her body. There was nothing that could have been done. And I didn't even know. No one knew.

"I made it home in time to talk to her. She told me to go right on living. She gave Lisa a list for me to do if I didn't get back in time. We didn't have much time but she squeezed my hand good-bye. I didn't know then that Miguel had died. Lisa had a rough time losing both."

"Hey, Chet, we know you'd have done anything. You should know, Val and I have talked and we feel that you did right. You and Lisa make a good couple. She isn't like any of the past ones, but she laughs, she's sincere, and she works hard on things for the ranch."

They were at Papago Wells by then. The creosote smell of the desert was strong on the warm night winds. There were people in the bar, horses stood hipshot at the racks. Cole took off to the bar to grab a drink.

An Indian prostitute came by, pulled on

his arm, and then, under in the light from the saloon and stage office, opened the blanket to show her naked body.

"You want me?"

"No."

Her face darkened in anger. "Why not? You have no woman."

He pressed a silver dollar in her hand. "God bless you."

She looked at it in her palm in the light. "Plenty good cowboy."

Then she closed the blanket tight and walked away her head held high.

"You're generous tonight," Jesus said under his breath.

"I guess I listened to Fred too long, thought about Josey. How tough life is for these people. They have no family, no bed at night, no meals like we have. And I just felt generous. She may drink the money away or get killed, if that is what is around the corner. It's a damn tough spot in life to be in."

Cole came back from the bar.

"Was the beer cold?" Jesus asked.

"No and it wasn't that good tasting."

"Ten cents?"

"No, twenty-five cents. That is an uptown saloon, in price anyway."

"Any pretty women to look at in there?"

"No. They don't have pretty women in saloons way the hell out here."

They all three laughed as they climbed back on board the stage.

A great *eeha* and they went south to the Pichaco Pass, the next stage stop. Chet, by then, realized they'd miss the last stage of the night to Tombstone and would have to catch the morning one.

In broad daylight, still bleary-eyed from lack of sleep, the three U.S. Marshals shared a stage with a woman in her twenties. She sat beside Chet and reset her skirt ten times before they got out of Tucson. Chet asked if she had relatives in the boomtown.

"No. I am a widow. My husband died. They told me back in Texas that Tombstone was the wildest town in the West and ladies of the night made hundreds of dollars there."

Chet frowned and his face hardened.

She sat up straighter. "Did I say something to offend you?"

"They lied to you, Mrs. . . . . ?"

"You ever do that trade before?" Cole asked her.

"Why no. Am I that ugly? My name is Florence Malloy."

"No, you are not ugly, but it takes a tough woman to work in those places."

"I can handle myself."

Cole shook his head. "You won't like it. Those men have no respect for women."

"Well, I am flat broke and I have no money. I guess I will have to suffer."

"No. I own a large ranch north of here at Prescott. I will buy your stage tickets, and my wife will meet you when you get to Prescott. I have a friend who owns a café. She will pay you a living wage with tips and you can live safely and for a long time."

"Why would you do that for me?"

"We have saved lots of ladies this way. You don't like it, you can go to work in the same town. They have houses there, too."

"I bet the ticket will cost you twenty dollars."

"Trust us. Take the tickets and go up there. I will wire my wife and tell her to meet you."

"Why did the man who bought my tickets back there in Texas tell me it was so good?"

"Did you pay him for the trip?"

She bowed her head. "I didn't have the fare or food money."

"So you had to demonstrate to him you could work that way?"

She hung her head lower.

Chet raised her chin up so she could look at him. "We are happily married men. Go.

508

Meet my wife and she will steer you right with no services needed."

"How will I repay you?"

"Find a good life."

At Tombstone his men took her to breakfast, bought her tickets for Prescott, and gave her money for meals.

Chet ran off to find Virgil Earp. He was not at the jail nor was there a prisoner in either of the two cells. His heart sunk as he hurried to the Alhambra Saloon. When he shoved in the divided batwing doors he saw Virgil bust a seven ball in the right side pocket.

"Where did he go?"

"He left the day before your telegram came," Virgil said straightening and looking for his next shot. "He may be down on the border at Los Olivios."

"Think he's there?"

"I think he has a woman there." Virgil put the eight ball in the side pocket and held out his hand for the money some guy owed him.

There was no time to get horses from Tubac. He'd have to buy or rent them. The stables were high priced. He asked Virgil.

"I can get you how many horses and saddles?"

"Three. Are they good?"

"Better than the O.K. Corral has and only cost five bucks a day with good saddles."

"Fine. When can we get them?"

"Thirty minutes out front."

"What is the deposit?"

"They will trust you if I say so." He put the pool cue up on the rack. "Oh, Charlie. Come back."

Charlie never stopped or answered him and busted out into the street, nearly knocking down a woman who cussed him out.

"I hate poor losers. I'll get those horses ordered." Virgil went outside and told a barefoot boy he needed three *caballos* and saddles *pronto.* The boy tore off.

Virgil came back in and Chet stuffed a ten-dollar bill in his shirt pocket. "I owe you more, let me know. I have to find my men."

"I'm sorry he'd already left," Virg shouted after him.

He found Florence Malloy eating breakfast at the counter with Jesus and Cole. The waitress saw him and said, "I have yours ready."

"Good."

"Well, is he here?"

Chet shook his head. "Virgil thinks he is at a place on the border called Los Olivios."

"You know where that is?" Jesus asked.

"Yes, I've been there."

Florence had reached over and opened his coat. "I didn't know you three were U.S. Marshals."

He shook his head at her and pulled his coat closed. "We don't want the bad guys we are after to know, either."

"Well, I feel much better. Safer. I have your wife's name written down. I get on the stage in an hour, go back to Tucson, then Hayden's Ferry, and then Prescott, right?"

"Yes. Lisa will meet you."

"I guess you can't go too wrong being advised by a marshal."

"We told you the truth."

They took her back to the stage depot, and told her to use the tickets.

She agreed.

Chet dropped into the telegraph office. He stood in line waiting. When he finally got to the agent, the man had to go help a key man about something. When he came back, Chet handed the agent the sheet. He read the message aloud. "Is that all. Love You?"

"Yes."

"It will be two dollars and I can get it out in ten minutes otherwise it will be —"

"Here's three. Get it off in five minutes."

"I —"

"That's fast enough." He left the office and ran a half block down the boardwalk to find his men who, he hoped, were standing in front of the Alhambra Saloon with the rented horses.

He hurried the two blocks through the crowded boardwalk and could see Virgil and his two men talking in front of the saloon with some horses hitched at the rack. Good. Things were moving. He crossed the street as Cole was lengthening stirrups on the bulldog horses' saddles for himself and Chet. Out of breath from the run, Chet thanked him.

"Hey Virgil, you sure know where to find good horses. These mountain ponies look great."

"They damn sure are tough. If you need dependable horses, they will be there no matter how tough it gets."

"Thanks," Chet said as he stepped onto the saddle and waved good-bye.

They took the road to Bisbee, going southeast through the grassland and hills, then wound up the steep canyon to the pass above the mining town buried deep on the far side of the next canyon. There they ate lunch off a saloon food counter, went back out, climbed onto their tough horses, and rode out into the desert again.

Late afternoon they reined up at the water trough. The huge towering green olive tree looked like a giant weeping willow hanging over the rusty roofed buildings set around its base in the drab desert of the dusty border country.

Chet drank the last of the hot water from his canteen. "Hope."

"Yeah. I want to soak my head under it," Cole said.

They dismounted. Cole got on the pump handle and went to pumping. He laughed as a stream of water finally started. Chet and Jesus congratulated him on getting it running.

Chet took over pumping. "We need to share this pumping. Those horses are thirsty."

"I'd say damn thirsty."

"We can get them full."

"I'm just glad we don't have a whole herd to water."

"Hello, *mis amigos.* Wow, you three are handsome *hombres,*" the woman said, wiggling while walking around them in her low-cut blouse and skirt.

"Hey, is my old pal Mac Arnold here?" Chet asked, looking around like he expected to see him.

"No. He left here two days ago."

"Where did he go?" he asked, sounding concerned.

She looked around as if to check to see if they were alone.

"I think he stays at a ranch in Dixie Canyon in the Muleshoe Mountains."

"Really?"

She nodded.

"What is that brand?"

She poised as if in deep thought. "Engels owns it. Nick Engels."

He gave her three silver dollars and smiled. "Thank you so much."

They mounted up and rode back toward Bisbee.

"You ever been to Dixie Canyon?" Jesus asked.

"Hell, no, but if there is such a place in those Muleshoe Mountains we can find it."

Cole agreed, smiling ear to ear. At a gallop he reached over and slapped Chet's arm. "I think, maybe, we have a real winner going, huh?"

"Damn right. The three of us always had one, and we may be on the best lead yet today."

They stopped at a small crossroad store about five miles short of Bisbee, hitched their horses, and Chet explained to the man behind the counter that they were U.S.

Marshals and needed his help to find a hideout. "It is in Dixie Canyon over in the Muleshoe's."

"That must be Nick Engels?"

"I think so. How do you get there?"

The owner took a piece of butcher paper and the pencil from behind his ear and drew a map of the next road west of there. Made an X at what he said was a wrecked wagon up that road for a marker. "And then you ride straight up the canyon. You can't miss his place." Then with his pencil, he used it to punctuate his words. "Let me warn you. There may be some tough guys up there. I mean tough desperate men. Engels has lots of friends like that."

"Thanks very much. We won't tell them who sent us." He gave him two ten-dollar gold pieces.

"You don't owe me anything."

"Yes, I do. Have a good day."

"You guys do, too. I've got a sawed-off shotgun I keep under the counter and those guys up there know it. I won't miss their business."

Chet smiled. "I guess even storekeepers have to defend themselves."

"Hey, arrest them all."

"We are going in for one, but if they want war, we can hand it out. Thanks."

They left the store and rode west onto the wagon tracks going north. The Muleshoe Mountains rose close by and in a half hour they found the wrecked wagon parts and stared at the opening in the mountains called Dixie Canyon.

There was a wagon track going up beside the dry wash that wound up the canyon. In places a ledge rose fifty feet. Not a well-traveled road. A few miles into the mountains they smelled smoke and that meant people.

Chet drew his Winchester out of his scabbard and checked the load. Satisfied, he snapped the lever shut.

"I am not sure what we will find but be prepared."

They nodded, looking sharp-eyed at everything around them.

The road came off a high perch and Chet could see an area that was dammed up to form a water pool. A few bare-breasted, brown-skinned women who'd been on their knees washing clothes stood up to look at them.

Jesus rode up and told them in Spanish they meant them no harm and asked how far it was to the ranch.

The lead woman pointed west and the way she pointed told Chet that it was only a short distance away.

Jesus thanked them and they rode on. The women went back to washing, smiling at them as they went by. Shortly there were corrals and some canvas shades ahead. There was a rock building that looked like a residence. Some hipshot horses stood at the hitch rail.

How many men were there? He wished he'd asked the storekeeper for an estimate. He spread his men out. Mid-afternoon they might be taking siesta. Then a woman, carrying her skirts, left her cooking and ran for the house, looking back warily at them.

A man with his suspenders down, in a red underwear top, peered at them from the door way then came farther out from the house. He was partially bald and showed no sign of defense.

"Howdy. You lost?"

"Your name Engels?"

"That's me."

"We came here for Mac Arnold. He here?"

"Whatcha need him for?" He hooked his thumbs into his waistband.

"Murder of a U.S. Marshal."

"Mister, are you the law?"

Chet nodded, keeping a look out for any sign of trouble. "Is he here?"

"I don't want no trouble with the law,

understand me. None."

"Then show my men where he is at."

"Okay. He's sleeping in the house. No trouble?"

"As long as everyone stays out of this. But one peep and we will settle it quickly."

The man motioned for someone to come with him.

Jesus was off the horse carrying his rifle. Cole took his bridle rein as Jesus followed Engels up the path. The woman who told Engels they were there stood by chewing on her knuckles.

Chet knew how she felt. He felt that way, too. No one came out and time had stopped.

Two sleepy-looking guys started to come out of another shade. They were not armed, pulling up their gallouses.

"Stay right there," Chet said. "You heard me. Stay there."

"What's going on?"

A man half-dressed came out ahead of Jesus, who followed with his gun in the man's back. His hands were cuffed behind him, and he looked rumpled to Chet, as if rousted from bed.

He booted his horse up to face him. "You Mac Arnold?"

"Who the hell are you?"

"Answer me."

"Sure, but you ain't —"

"Listen to me, Arnold. You are under arrest for murdering my man Marshal Miguel Costa, and arranging the murder of two of my men. I am going to see you hang by the neck until dead. Engels, find him a horse. He got a saddle?"

"He's got both."

"Get them out here."

Engels shouted, "Get his horse and saddle him now!"

The two men standing on the side ran off to obey, Chet hoped. Two more men unarmed came out to see what was happening. Chet told them to stay right there. They obeyed him.

The horse saddling took a little time and the woman brought a shirt and hat for Arnold to wear. Jesus released one handcuff. He put the shirt and hat on and was re-cuffed.

Cole rode in closer. "What do you think?"

"No one here wants to die over him."

"Suits me. Here they come with the horse."

"Load him up," Chet said. "Thank you, sir. Let's go, men."

They rode out of the place. Chet's back itched all the way out of the canyon. They finally had their man and in due time he'd be back with Lisa. Once they were out of this place he'd feel better.

Sleeping in his own bed at home was something to look forward to. He'd wire Lisa from Tombstone.

Sundown found the four riding up the steep Bisbee Canyon.

Cole said, "We always made a good team. I'm glad to be back, guys. No matter how tough it gets you can't beat riding with you two. I'll be close enough now to help you two once in a while, and that beats running a stage line for sure."

"Amen," Jesus said.

"Let's trot these horses. Home's still a long ways away, and it will damn sure be cooler up there."

Chet Byrnes knew one thing. The prisoner on that sorry horse was one less person intent on killing him.

If he had a better idea who else was set on creating his funeral, he'd felt better. He knew who was wanting it. Finding the persons going to try and do it was another mater. Time would tell.

Riding over the pass in the sundown, he looked forward to being home.

AUTHOR'S NOTE

Dear Fans,

We sure thank you for your support of the Chet Byrnes novels. Thanks for the notes I get, and for the questions that you send to me about the books. I try to answer the e-mails as fast as I can, but if you don't hear from me in ten days, it is possible I did not get your note to me.

Writing westerns is a dream come true for me. Since my boyhood days growing up in Arizona, I read both fiction and history. In those days I could read a paperback book in an evening. I wrote my own when I didn't have one to read. They were not that great back then.

When my girls were teens, they found them and read them. A lightbulb went off. "Dad, you need to get your books published."

I scoffed at them, but they insisted and I began my pilgrimage to writing something publishable. I put in an apprenticeship, and worked my way up the ladder to seeing my books published. I get a lot of pleasure when a new book comes out and someone says they like it or they couldn't put it down until they finished it.

As long as I can, I'll keep spinning yarns out of what I have read and dreamed life was like in the second half of the 1800s without cell phones, TV, Internet, cars, or all the gadgets we have today.

Right now I am already starting another adventure to entertain you.

God bless each and every one of you,

Dusty Richards
dustyrichards@cox.net

ABOUT THE AUTHOR

Author of over 85 novels, **Dusty Richards** is the only author to win two Spur awards in one year (2007), one for his novel *The Horse Creek Incident* and another for his short story "Comanche Moon." He is a member of the Professional Rodeo Cowboys Association and the International Professional Rodeo Association, and serves on the local PRCA rodeo board. Dusty is also an inductee in the Arkansas Writers Hall of Fame. He currently resides in northwest Arkansas. He was the winner of the 2010 Will Rogers Medallion Award for Western Fiction, for his novel *Texas Blood Feud,* and was honored by the National Cowboy Hall of Fame in 2009.

www.dustyrichardslegacy.com

The employees of Thorndike Press hope you have enjoyed this Large Print book. All our Thorndike, Wheeler, and Kennebec Large Print titles are designed for easy reading, and all our books are made to last. Other Thorndike Press Large Print books are available at your library, through selected bookstores, or directly from us.

For information about titles, please call:
  (800) 223-1244

or visit our website at:
  gale.com/thorndike

To share your comments, please write:
  Publisher
  Thorndike Press
  10 Water St., Suite 310
  Waterville, ME 04901